Thomas Gibson Bowles

Flotsam and Jetsam

A Yachtsman's Experience at Sea and Ashore

Thomas Gibson Bowles

Flotsam and Jetsam
A Yachtsman's Experience at Sea and Ashore

ISBN/EAN: 9783337405519

Printed in Europe, USA, Canada, Australia, Japan

Cover: Foto ©Andreas Hilbeck / pixelio.de

More available books at **www.hansebooks.com**

FLOTSAM AND JETSAM.

A YACHTSMAN'S EXPERIENCES AT SEA AND ASHORE.

BY

THOMAS GIBSON BOWLES

MASTER MARINER.

"The sea's a rumbustical place."—BILL WIGG.

NEW YORK:

FUNK & WAGNALLS, PUBLISHERS,

10 AND 12 DEY STREET.

PREFACE.

I do not pretend to be a sailor—none but a sailor knows how much that word means—but I love the Sea. From my boyhood (I once ran away to go to sea, but was captured and ignominiously brought back when well on my way to Liverpool) I have sought to learn sea-lore ; and I have now learned how little I know of it. But seafaring has become, and still is, to me, a school, a consolation, and a refuge from the trivialities, the meannesses, and the confusions of land life. The grand, solemn, serious Sea, so exacting yet so loving, so remorseless yet so kindly, always reminds me—sometimes when I have well-nigh forgotten it—that there are real things in the world as well as unreal phrases ; plain duties as well as doubtful opinions ; proved methods as well as shifting speculations, philosophies, and policies.

So it is that these writings arose. I did not set out to make a book. I did think these thoughts, such as they are, and see these things, and simply set them down as they came to me. They are not mere inventions ; they are the expression of what was struck out of me in the conflict between the realities of the Sea and the fancies of the shore. This is my only excuse for them.

T. G. B.

Cleeve Lodge, Hyde Park Gate, London.

FLOTSAM AND JETSAM.

FLOTSAM.

CHAPTER I.

ON BOARD THE BILLY BABY,
Cowes, 8th May, 1874.

A REAL man is always alone in the world. Were he not he would not be a real man, as I understand it—that is to say, a distinct entity, not a copy of all other men, but with the principal and important part of him thoroughly belonging to himself. How shall such a one find a mate who shall really be such to him ? Pieces of looking-glass indeed he may find, which will according to their quality more or less reproduce the outside of him as they will of any other—they have been quicksilvered to that one end ; but a duplicate of himself ; nay, or another at all like himself, he may not hope for in man or woman. For his especial character is that he is what he himself and Providence have made him ; that he has set up in the chaos with infinite labor and good fortune a little platform of his own just broad enough for the sole of his foot. Another cannot stand *there* with him, though many be above and some perhaps below. If he be the real man, that place is his and his alone : he is a separate being and principle, and as such he can have no companion.

This is no part of my story—or of my notes, or whatever

form this writing may take, for I have not yet made its acquaintance—but merely a reflection on John Stuart Mill's autobiography, which I read coming down in the train. *He* thought he had found a mate, and labors touchingly to prove her such ; but to my mind he fails as touchingly. Only I was struck by the fact that he who was a great man, and I who am a little one, have both come very independently to the same conclusion—that for any man, great or little, it is at least impossible to find companionship there where most usually it is sought. "There is," he says, "an inclination natural to thinking" (and he might have added, to unthinking) "persons when the age of boyish vanity is once past for limiting their own society to a very few persons. General society as now carried on in England is so insipid an affair, even to the persons who make it what it is, that it is kept up for any reason rather than the pleasure it affords." To me, who was then on my way to limit my own society to three North Sea fishermen, this was very satisfactory, and I settled once for all that Mill was at any rate a social observer, if not a social philosopher.

"The society of three North Sea fishermen, indeed !" I think I hear some refined one exclaim. Yes, indeed, the society of three North Sea fishermen—of three men who have passed their lives among stern realities, who are ready and brave, true and intelligent, and who have not been demoralized by a daily consumption of platitude and sophistry. Not from Cowes are they, nor like the men of Cowes, who have been demoralized thus and by other means, but fresh from the Dogger, with all their rough honesty upon them. If I were in London I should be in contact with A and B and C, notorious and self-admitted imitations of a dishonest ideal. Are these not much better than they ? Yes, indeed ; and I am mistaken if they do not leave me purer and higher notions of society than any one of my three Londonners, infinitely superior persons though they be as the common scale of comparison goes.

*   *   *   *   *   *

Why on earth will this stove *not* burn ? I need it badly

enough, Heaven knows, for it is as cold to-night as the face of a great lady ; and the mere run hither down from Southampton through the murk of the evening has chilled me to the bone.

And withal somebody must have run down the Spit buoy again, for though I never went close to its proper place, and saw all the other buoys, we none of us made this.

*　*　*　*　*　*

But I remember that I have not yet given an account of myself and of these notes. I came down in the train with three strangers. One of them offered me a light, and said it was a fine day. That was not true, and if it had been true would not have been important. Nor would it have been more true or more important if I had known whither that man was going, and what his portmanteau contained. Yet these are the first questions people seem determined always to ask and to answer any man, instead of the last as they should be.

How can I say who or what in the world I am ? I don't know—do you ? You have no doubt a form of words ready on your lips—" M or N, as the case may be"; but words without ideas are mere *abattis*, trees without root ; of no further consequence until they have been converted into the form of some new idea.

Certainly I am not a hero. Yet I am going, so far as I see, to talk of myself, which is, in fact, what we all always do, whether we know it or not. A very impertinent habit, no doubt, and quite indefensible ; and yet at the end of the account, as the French say, what you and I most want to get at is a notion of me and of you, which is also what we get at, or even near, the least often. Otherwise we should perhaps hate, envy, and despise each other less than we do. Just think of the force of human sympathy. Any man who gets up at Charing Cross, and opens his mouth, will have a crowd of people about him before he has said two sentences !

*　*　*　*　*　*

POOLE, Saturday, 9th May, 1874.

Ah ! it was a lovely sunrise this morning for those of us who
saw it, and the outline of land and sea, of mast and rigging,
pencilled themselves softly on the gray sky as the light stole
after us down the Solent.   And to think that there are people
who live in houses, and lie abed of a morning !

*   *   *   *   *   *

I remember there was once a man who invented the principle
of self-interest as sufficient for all mankind all through life.
Jeremy, thou wast a noodle.   Didst thou not see, dost thou
not now see, that we are all of necessity mere trustees ?   Here
is Ned, for instance, roused up at three this morning, and now
striving all he knows to make out that black buoy.   Yes, I do
pay him a salary, and as between us it may seem at first a mere
affair of self-interest.   But is he not a trustee for his old
mother at Aldeburgh, to whom he is going to send a post-
office order for one-pound-ten this very day, and also for his
young woman, whom he intends some day to endow with the
scanty bliss of a seaman's marital attentions—nay, even for the
fabricator of those sea-boots and the Chinaman grower of that
tea which makes me shudder, but which he gulps down scald-
ing with so much gusto ?   *All* for self ?   What, even his
young woman ?   Then self has no longer a meaning, and we
are stumbling as usual over words.

*   *   *   *   *   *

Was there ever such a rich, bountiful, delightful climate as
this maligned one of ours ?   I know none, and don't believe
there is any with so inexhaustible a play of light, shade, and
atmosphere.   Here, while I have been looking from my deck
at this decayed, sordid town of Poole, have I seen in ten
minutes at least half a dozen different cities in it, each with its
particular tone of beauty, and all various.   They say it is like
Venice, wherein they are wrong, for it is far better and more
beautiful to look at, and with far more, if with other, beauties
than Venice.   Not to live in, though—nor to sit for in Parliament—but just to look at from the deck of a boat.

*   *   *   *   *   *

How strangely the mind of man is constituted! Here is Bill, my equerry-in-waiting, groom of the chambers, and *cordon bleu*, quite unable to see that nothing will save one from losing all the bedclothes in the night except tucking them up. I have explained this to Bill, and shown him how it is connected with the eternal laws of physics that when a man rolls about with an unquiet spirit, clothes must go if they are not tucked in. I suppose he intends it as a hint to lie quiet. I will take it as such.

*   *   *   *   *   *

HAVRE, Wednesday, 13th May.

There are two situations in which a man feels that he is quite alone, and that he can look for help to no human being but himself. The one is on the back of a runaway horse, the other in command of his vessel at sea when he is running for a tidal harbor in a gale of wind, and finds he can't save his tide in and will have a lee shore to deal with. Woe betide him if he dare not then trust his own judgment! Woe betide him indeed if he cannot readily form new plans! On the whole, I think the runaway horse is the better place of the two. I saw a barge deep laden come out of Poole yesterday, and watched him going up Channel—I wonder how he fared in the breeze —and it was at the time a pleasure to think that we had a better craft under us than he. Poor fellow! I dare say he thinks just as much of his skin as I do of mine, little as either of them is worth in the general scheme of creation!

*   *   *   *   *   *

The art of the true use of garlic is the whole secret of tasteful cookery. Rub a crust of bread with garlic and put it in your salad, and the whole thing at once has a savor which nothing else would give it. And so with men. I know one, for example, who would be simply nothing were he not known for the profession of infidelity; but having that, he is supposed to have a flavor of his own and is considered accordingly;

whereas in reality he has only been rubbed over with other men's garlic.

* * * * * *

How hard it is to do the very smallest thing precisely as it should be done ! Just go to the very centre of anchors and cordage and try to get a two-hundred weight Trotman and ninety fathom of seven-inch warp. It will make you respect failures for the rest of your life.

CHAPTER II.

Off Cape d'Antifer, 14th May, 1874.

Some men are born lucky and others have luck thrust upon them. How many of us are there who pass our lives in running away from our own happiness, and are never overtaken by it till both it and we are well-nigh exhausted ! Lucky are they who are brought to book by Fortune, who get a fall early in the race, and who are perforce compelled thenceforth to go limpingly and to give their good angel a chance. A great Grief has often made a great man, a little grief has still more often made a little one completely to fulfil that purpose in his existence which else he would have missed. Solomon was a wise man, yet it took him a long life and seven hundred wives to find out that there is nothing worth doing but to eat, drink, and make love, and enjoy the fruits of one's labor. Some of us unwise ones must indeed have had our luck thrust upon us to find it out while we could still do all these things. A splendid summer day, wooing the very coat off your back and the shoes off your feet, a fair wind, just enough if it lasts to take you to your port, and a dinner composed by the cunningest cook in Havre, with nobody, not even the postman, to stand between you and your wildest fancies, these will compare—nay, they do being now present (for that is the test) compare—with any kind of luck I know in these days ; and certainly none of these would have been mine if I could have had my own way say four months ago.

*   *   *   *   *   *

The curse of labor was a very short-sighted curse to inflict upon man, constituted as he is. Indeed it is no curse at all ; but rather the one only blessing in life, the source of all real content and the great consolation for all sorrows, and even for all worries. Of course one must have work that one *can* do, but that is a mere question of choice in a world where there is so much to do of so many various kinds ; and not a difficult question either, for almost anybody can do almost anything if they will but address themselves to it. The choice once made, what is there to equal or to come near to the delight there is in grappling with the work ; what moments are there like those when, bracing your nerves and setting your teeth, you rejoice as a giant refreshed, to run the race before you and feel the distance disappearing beneath your feet ? Not the triumph of the victory, still less the repose on the other side the goal—for that is but a kind of death between the races in which alone you feel that you really live. I can understand those who work for the sake of the work, I can't understand those who work for the sake of the rest that is to follow. See the man who has " retired from business" of whatever kind— is not his first act to go into business of another kind ? He leaves selling cottons and takes to buying pictures and society. What then ? He has only exchanged a work he could do for one he cannot, and he will certainly gain no more but rather much less profit and glory in the one than in the other.

*   *   *   *   *   *

I am persuaded that this world was organized for an entirely different set of creatures from those who inhabit it. Looking at this infinite multitude of stars above me, many of them certainly, and all of them possibly, inhabited, I can well understand how easily the wrong set of inhabitants may have got into our Planet by mistake, just as in the old stage trick of putting the wrong letter in the envelope. "The only thing that is at all decently done on earth," said a great man once to me, "is the coming of the leaves, which we do at least get when we want shade ; all the rest is wrong ; for instance, the days are long in summer when, the sun being hot and the night pleasant, they ought to be short, while they are short in winter when the sun is so valuable that we want more, and the night so detestable that we want less of it." Look again at winds. If they were sensibly arranged we should have them blowing strongest on shore, where gales are of no great importance, while they would always be moderate at sea, instead of the reverse being the case. Then there are the tides, so arranged that they run strongest when they rise highest, whereas it would be manifestly better if they were to do so when they rise the least, because that would give one so much better a chance of getting into tidal harbors.

The moral order of things is an old subject of complaint. Yet it only needs one reform in order to make them perfectly easy of treatment—that is a means of comparing moral capacity. For then we should have nothing more to do than to say that every man shall have all the enjoyment he is capable of containing, but that he shall not steal from other men's measures that which will not go into his, but only run over and be absolutely wasted. There is enough enjoyment in the world for all, and to spare, but your two-gallon man will get three, four, or five gallons more than can be of any kind of use to him, while your one-gallon man is perhaps empty altogether.

*　　*　　*　　*　　*　　*

DIEPPE, 15th May, 1874.

Why it should always blow half a gale of wind right on the shore whenever you are waiting your tide to get into these French harbors is another thing I should like to know. The only advantage I at present see in it is that it keeps you up all night hove-to off Cape d'Ailly, and furnishes you with the

work and excitement of furling half your sails and double-reef-
ing the rest. Which illustrates what I have already said, for
now we are in I only feel rather tired and bruised with our
knocking about, and have lost all interest in the weather.

*   *   *   *   *   *

I fear the French are now at least beginning really to experience the effects of the war upon their commerce. At Havre it
is impossible to get freight of any kind for any vessels, and this
port of Dieppe has not above five vessels in it where usually
there are two or three hundred. Never did a place look so
utterly deserted. I have just had my hair cut in order to talk
about it, and this was the conversation that took place to a
running accompaniment of scissor-clicking :

" C'est qu'on n'a pas de confiance dans la solidité du Gou-
vernement, et alors les affaires ne marchent pas, comme monsieur voit." *

" On avait cependant confiance dans l'Empire."

" Oh, pour ça, oui."

" Et pourtant il n'était pas bien solide."

" Non, mais enfin on croyait tout de même à sa solidité."

" Croyez donc à la solidité du Septennat."

" Oh ! Monsieur !"

*   *   *   *   *   *

A charming people are these French. The whole of the Hotel
Royal turned out to welcome me when I went to dine there
yesterday, asked me affectionately all round after my health
and my doings, and provided me with a *sauce Hollandaise*,

---

* "When people have no confidence in the strength of the Government, then affairs do not get along, as monsieur sees."

"Yet they had confidence in the Empire."

"As for that, yes."

"And nevertheless it was not very solid."

"No, but upon the whole people did believe in its strength all the
same."

"Well, then, trust in the stability of the Septennat."

"Oh, monsieur !"

which was like eating the kingdom of joy. I remember an old French *gourmet* once said to me, " Jeune homme, quand vous aurez épuisé les délices de l'amour, des affaires, de la politique et de la religion, vous finirez comme moi par vous rabattre sur la cuisine." I begin to fancy I must have already arrived at that stage.

*   *   *   *   *   *

I never saw yet a woman so ugly that her lover could not believe in her beauty ; but I have seen one to-day so ugly that I doubt if she can believe in her own. I have loved many women, but never a beautiful one in all my life, and yet I have for the time always believed each to be the only one of her sex.

CHAPTER III.

ON BOARD THE BILLY BABY,
DIEPPE, May 19th.

WE ought to be very grateful to Providence for having implanted in each one of us that admirable conviction that *I* am the centre of the universe. If we, any of us, really believed that the world went round the sun instead of the sun going round the world, or that we went round the world instead of the world going round us, life would be unendurable. As it is, all men and things are instruments and playthings for each one, even the most mean of us. I am not more intimately convinced that Bill was invented for my service than Bill is convinced that I was invented for his ; and he is right. I can't escape from revolving round Bill, and in all our dealings I am forced to feel his attraction and repulsion just as with all other bodies heavenly and earthly. His notions of making beds and coffee are my masters, and I have at last finally submitted to them ; yet he has adopted my notion of brushing clothes and boots in part, and on the question of table napkins and clean knives and forks we act with about equal force on each other. So that Bill is now so far reduced as it were to the position of a mean sun, which is never quite in its right place, but which must be supposed to be there for practical purposes.

*　　*　　*　　*　　*　　*

SHOREHAM, 21st May, 1874.

I wonder why in pictures of vessels at sea they are almost always represented as under full sail, with a fair breeze. In reality they should be represented close-hauled in a gale of wind, beating up for port against a head sea. It is a fine feeling to be proud of something, and I was proud of the Billy Baby last night when I saw her stripped like an athlete for the struggle, with storm jib, close-reefed mainsail, topmast struck, bowsprit reefed, and all snug, and felt her flying along under me within four points of that cruel north-easter—while my crockery was equally flying about the cabin below. Truly those that go down to the sea in ships, that do business in great waters—these see the works of the Lord and his wonders in the deep. And it was a wonder, indeed, to note the first red streaks of morn away to the north-east, and to see them grow into the blessed light of day. A beautiful and lovable world indeed if people would only come to the right places in it.

*　　*　　*　　*　　*　　*

The Billy Baby lies ignobly on her bilge inside the harbor, a scorn and a rebuke to the inhabitants of Shoreham, and provoking even the reflections of the cheap butcher who has come down to sell his joints by the sound of trumpet, forgetting that he too has a soul to be saved. For even Ned is but human, and turning up this narrow and, to all of us, unknown passage, he ran her ashore at four o'clock this morning. It should be a warning to every one never to go into strange places on a falling tide without a pilot—even when it is impossible to get one. It matters little ; the next tide will take us off, though at present there isn't a teacupful of water in the harbor

—and after all you must be somewhere. I know people who
are in bed at this moment.

*　　*　　*　　*　　*　　*

There are things that would have been too much for the
apostle John. Here is one such. When in Paris on Tuesday,
I provided myself with a bunch of asparagus as big as a five-
inch cable, and brought it down triumphantly to Dieppe for a
Billy Baby dinner. Moreover, I got particular instructions
from my valued friend Henri of the *Café Bignon* how to cook
it. Now yesterday, struggling as we were with half a gale of
wind, I, of course, could not dine at all to make any sense of
it ; but to-day, lying tranquilly at the end of the Shoreham
canal, within two miles of Brighton, I thought of my asparagus, and retailed to Bill all Henri's instructions as to its treatment, the prominent one of which was that it was to be lightly
scraped before cooking. And now will anybody imagine my
dismay to find that Bill, being ignorant of the ways and qualities of " grass," has scraped away all the heads, and cooked
nothing but the white stalks ! I feel as if I had lost a day.

*　　*　　*　　*　　*　　*

The only revelation we have of things unseen must be such
as we can derive through reasoning by analogy from things
that are seen. Let us leave Invention and learn from Experience. Thus doing we shall soon see that Thought at least is
eternal. No idea ever dies. It may be thrown into the air,
but the very winds will take it and plant it, maybe in a far distant soil, to germ and grow into a tree, in the branches of which
the birds of the air shall lodge, and the trunk of which some
day a workman shall take and make one half of it into a god
to fall down and worship, and with the other half shall kindle
a fire. Neither is an idea ever born. Create it you cannot.
You take other ideas, and by their apposition you build up out
of them what you call another and a new one. Alas ! no, it is
not given to you. You will find that same idea in David or
in Solomon, or else it is in the Vedas, in the Koran, in Socra-

tes, or Plato. Nor was it new when they gave it a form. It came to them as the sun comes, first indeed to those who earliest rise, but sooner or later to all. It rose upon them as it has to-day risen upon you, as to-morow it will rise on some other, and so to the end of time—which is the end of eternity.

* * * * * *

PORTSLADE-BY-SEA, 25th May.

There is an idea which has been faced and accepted, adopted and propagated by all writers on civil organization from the greatest to the least, and which I am yet presumptuous enough to think absolutely false. It is this, that man in a state of nature is an animal utterly lawless and utterly solitary, a naked brute without a moral sentiment to clothe his immaterial, or a rag to cover his material nakedness, having no fellow-man in any kind of relation to him. It seems to me that that is, on the contrary, a conception of man in a purely *unnatural* state : for the first impulse of his nature is to clothe himself with a companion—even if it be but a woman—his spirit with an idea ; his body with a covering ; and his actions with a rule. Before he has done this he has not yet followed the imperious dictates of his nature ; when he has done it he no more ceases to be in a state of nature than an oak does because it was once an acorn, or than a swallow when it has built itself a nest, and flies away on its first winter journey to warmer climes. Find me a man placed on the earth, an acorn under it, or a swallow above it, content to remain as they are, and I will admit that the state of nature is a state preceding the effort to follow the dictates of nature. Till then, never.

This then being so, what becomes of all the elaborate theories and systems of polity and economy that have been built on the erroneous notion I have cited ? What becomes of the materialist and the self-interested conceptions (however modified by " enlightenment"), all these being founded on the assertion that all law, all society, all intellectual or moral motions of man are mere human inventions, ingeniously and for a purpose embroidered on to the original man of whom they formed no part ? Why, they disappear, are extinguished, condemned, lost and gone forever. Let us more rationally—yes, more rationally—believe that man in a state of nature would be in a state of perfect sociability, ideality, and Law, and that he falls short of that only because he is so far *not* in a state of nature.

* * * * * *

When you see a man drowning before you, do you hold that you have done your whole duty to him because you have paid your yearly subscription to the Humane Society ? I trow not. And now about the poor. Shall we say when the wretched cries for alms, that we have paid our poor-rates ? Are we to reply that his claim to a living share of the earth's fruits is a claim on the whole of society, and that we have discharged our quota ? Not so. I admit that this man who has done a day's work, and created for me a slight commodity, has a claim on me for his wage. Yet he has a claim only on me, for the commodity is for my own sole use. Shall I then refuse him whose claim is not only upon me but upon all my fellows as well ? If so, I declare society bankrupt along with myself.

* * * * * *

To-day is Whit-Monday, and I see a string of seven omnibuses filled with people vulgar, and probably imperfectly washed, jaunting along the road on an excursion, the while they affront the air with many various songs, having only this in common—that they are all out of tune. Thanks to heaven I do not know them, and I can therefore rejoice that they in their way rejoice. And now if only one of them, through the sight of new objects, shall get an idea into his or her head, if merely that cornet-player shall discern dimly the harmonies of these dark piles planted in the blue water, of these yellow masses of pine awned with soft gray sky, and crowned with fleecy chaplets of cloud—why the day will be a profitable one to him, and maybe through him to all mankind.

* * * * * *

I once loved a woman. I held her for the best, the truest, the purest, and the strongest of God's creatures, and I could not endure to be near her for the doubts that arose every instant whether she really were all this. I love her now no more. I know her for a poor make-believe ordinary person ; and now her society is just as pleasant to me as that of any other human creature—neither more nor less.

*   *   *   *   *   *

This is an ungenerous world. Last night I set my trammel, thinking to catch at least a plate of fish for breakfast. This morning I found that somebody had hauled it in the night, taken out all the fish, and cast the net ashore on the bank. I cannot approve of that. The fish no doubt were as much his as mine, but considering that the net was mine alone, he might have left me half the take.

CHAPTER IV.

On Liberty, June 1.

Bill having given me a week's leave to go and see my mamma and my young woman, I had a good cry over leaving the frigate, and took my departure to be among those incomprehensible people who choose to live ashore when they might have a comfortable ship for half the money, and little more than twice the trouble. What a strange twist this is in men's minds that makes them all seek their pleasure in doing what they can't do well, and leaving what they can so do as a tiresome business, only to be done under dire compulsion ! Whether there is anything beyond the bare sweeping of a crossing that *I* can do I know not, but it is clear to me that at any rate I can never be but a very poor sailor-man, and I am amused with myself to find that playing at sailors is nevertheless my most cherished delectation. I am sure if I only go on long enough I shall fancy myself quite a salt. What curious humbugs we all are !

*   *   *   *   *   *

The art of war consists in knowing when to run away. So does the art of life. For it is always to be remembered that in battle both sides are all the time in a terrible fright, and that the question on which hangs the fate of the day is not which side is most brave, but which is least frightened. Therefore a good general who doubts the relative capacity of his troops to stand fright, will judiciously run before he meets the enemy, and while he can still do so under pretence of making a scientific ulterior combination. I once knew a man who had been disgracefully handled by a woman. He confided in me, used very strong and very proper language as to her baseness, and told me that he had taken steps to meet her under circumstances which would enable him to show all the contempt and disgust he felt for her, and how thoroughly he had been cured of his deception. I advised him on the contrary to run. He would not, and now he is a married and miserable man.

*   *   *   *   *   *

2d June.

I have seen a minster which has made me ask myself once again how people can believe the common fable of the historians that the English were up to two hundred years ago a poor, uncultivated, half-savage people. This cathedral represents an amount of wealth, of labor, of sentiment, of loving art, and of devotion which ten Englands, and the natives of the Continent to boot, could not produce in these days. There are the pulses, the sinews, nay the very heart and life of thousands in those aisles, and the whole soul of a man in every touch of the chisel on those sculptures. Are we really richer, do we really work more effectually, are our aims higher and our feelings stronger and purer than in those so-called barbarous times? Then let us build but one edifice equal to this and I will believe it.

*   *   *   *   *   *

I never knew a single-minded woman. Their ideas are always married to themselves—and sometimes polygamously to somebody else besides. An abstract notion or principle is quite beyond them. The other morning going ashore to buy some eggs for Bill, I asked the woman who sold them if she could assure me that they were fresh-laid. "Bless you, sir," she replied, "I wouldn't sell them for fresh-laid if they wasn't."

*　　*　　*　　*　　*　　*

The necessity of having in all things an immutable, invariable standard that can be appealed to, has always been held to be, and is in fact, manifest. Some people believe in the Bible, some in the Pope, some again mount higher and believe, as it were, *through* the Bible and the Pope, in the Divine truths of which they are the exponents. If we would be exact, allowance must be made, in every case of exposition of higher law, for the deviation of the material instrument. But what if it is believed that there is no deviation at all? What if the vessel is navigated in that belief, and one day it is discovered that the bearings of things are all at sixes and sevens? The other day, to my horror, I found I had got Cape d'Ailly on a bearing by my hitherto unsuspected compass, which would if it were a true bearing have put me a couple of miles up the country on the French land, whereas in fact I was at sea. Which brings me to this : that it is a thousand pities we cannot "swing" the Bible, the Pope, and other great standards, find out, as I am about to do with the "Billy Baby's" compass, what their exact deviation is with their head in any given point, and so make a table of corrections for future reference.

*　　*　　*　　*　　*　　*

3d June.

Never leave the side of a woman you love. In a day she will cease to regret you, in two she will replace you by somebody else, in three she will refuse to believe that you exist. Here have I been away from Billy Baby for a week, and I can eat and drink as though nothing had happened.

*　　*　　*　　*　　*　　*

What strangers we all are to each other on the face of this

earth ! and how certain we all are to get credit precisely for
the qualities we do not possess, and to be reproached with failings from which we are free ! How many men are called su-
percilious because they are timid, ill-mannered because they are
shy, ill-natured because they love their fellows too well not to
seek to benefit them at their own cost ! How many again are
pronounced generous because they are selfish, wise because they
have stolen other men's ideas, and able because they have
placed themselves under other men's conduct ! I find the people at the various ports I put into all call me " captain"
already, and I expect to end as admiral.

*   *   *   *   *   *

4th June.

It is always the leaders of men who play them false. It is
the judge who perpetrates injustice, the priest who invents impiety, the minister who misgoverns his country, the popular as-
sembly which betrays its choosers. This is inevitable when it
is a trade to judge, to pray, to govern, and to talk ; for the
trader looks only to the profit and permanence of his trade, and
cares nothing for the wares he sells or the customer who buys
them. You find men to pass Adulteration Acts to prevent
chicory being mixed with coffee, sand with sugar, and water
with milk, yet the idea has never been so much as conceived
that it is a fraud to mix profit with public duty. Nevertheless
this is at the bottom of all public troubles.

*   *   *   *   *   *

The most delicious, the most fascinating and artistic woman's
dress I ever saw was one of which I caught a glimpse in Paris
lately, made of black glazed calico. It belonged to, or at any
rate it was on, a lady who was stepping out of a brougham into
a shop in the Rue de la Paix. I saw it but for three moments,
but I shall never forget it. And the most beautiful face and
figure, the most finished grace, the most unaffected wit and
frankness, and the best manners I ever knew belong at this moment to a young lady who lives, we will say in Nottingham,

and dresses on £20 a year. If she were mine I would make her into a company, advertise her, and benefit many shareholders besides myself. Being as she is more rare and precious than many mines, I shall carefully say nothing about her but this, that the London drawing-rooms are poor places to look for anything of really superior kind.

CHAPTER V.

Off Beachy Head, Saturday, 6th June.

There is a use in everything no doubt, but I really should like to know the practical use of fogs in this well-regulated world. It is not that I doubt their use, but only that I should like to be able to explain it to the misbelieving advocate of fine clear weather—such as Ned. This same mania for explaining everything, the determination to bring down every mystery of the universe to the level of Pinnock's catechism, is probably at the bottom of a good half of the blunders of mankind. We have applied the universal rule of three to, and made a net result of profit and loss out of, most things. Even religion is captured and set to work to make the best of both worlds. Are we forever to pretend to seek out the Almighty to perfection, and not believe in his works till we can measure them with our foot-rule, or his laws till we have written them in articles thirty-nine or more ? Should we not rather be content to leave some few things in mystery ? I also could invent a use for fogs if I chose. I could repeat what some wiseacre has invented as to their causes in and their influence on the atmosphere. Nobody would be the wiser, though somebody might be the more presumptuous for it. I prefer to rejoice that here is one more of the many things I don't understand. It is contrary to my little interests for the moment, since it hides even Beachy Head light from me. But the first thing we have to learn—and this is one thing the sea teaches—is that we are each of us utterly unimportant atoms in the universe.

* * * * * *

DOVER BAY, Sunday, June 7th.

My man Tom believes that the right way to land on the beach in a broken sea is to pull the boat before it as fast as possible, and as he gave me a ducking by so doing to-day, I have been explaining to him that the right way is to back her against each wave, so as to keep her on the outer or safe side of each. Tom cannot receive this, being accustomed to get ashore at all hazards as fast as he can ; but I have explained to him that the sea will carry him there quite fast enough, and with all the more safety for his pulling gently against it.

Is it not absurd to think that we have had rulers and governors in whom men still believe (Lord Palmerston, the overrated, was one), who opposed the making of the Suez Canal, and spent five times what would have made it in such erections as the Alderney fortifications, the Spithead forts, and the Martello towers ? Nay, have we not still rulers and governors who are allowed to build ironclads, to support volunteer corps, and to maintain the Declaration of Paris ? It is charitable to suppose that we have all gone mad. But it is impossible to read what has been said and written on public affairs by the side of what is now said and written without being struck by this immense difference, that while formerly the speaker or writer used the language of an authoritative guide, he now uses that of an anxious follower. Formerly he laid down principles, and insisted upon them ; now he seeks a humor and flatters it. Then he was a stern, unbending schoolmaster, knowing more than his scholars, and walking among them not unfrequently with the rod; now he is a flycatcher, producing any one of the various catchemaliveos most in vogue. No politician or writer ever now sets himself to expose or to oppose a false principle which has taken a hold, or a delusion which has any considerable number of supporters—for they are not leaders, but mere venders of themselves and their prints ; and being so they will supply forts, ironclads, volunteers, or anything else that may be demanded by two or three strong-lunged lunatics gathered together.

* * * * * *

I have two Queen Anne silver candlesticks on board with me, just to remind me that I was born in a civilized country ; and they are not without their influence even on Bill, who cleans them lovingly in odd anchored moments. He puts them on the table with something of veneration and respect, which I am sure he never felt for the tin and brass of his home, and although, I am convinced, he must know that a candle would give just as good a light from those as from these.

I cannot understand Voltaire's hatred for priests. I saw a country parson to-day, and I did not hate him at all. I said to myself, " There is a most respectable and useful man, if only he lives in his village, if he succors the widow and the fatherless, maintains in himself a local standard of cultivation and refinement, and limits his preaching to an enforcement of the decalogue and the Sermon on the Mount." Joseph de Maistre says there is no religion absolutely false, for that every one contains some grains of eternal truth. So indeed it is. A religion is in fact merely the form under which man has reproduced and represented the Divine law as he best could. To mock at it because it is not in all respects perfect, is as though you should mock at man because he is not divine.

* * * * * *

It were worth while to live at sea were it only to see the sky and the stars. To think that each one of them has perhaps peoples and nations, constitutions and ministers, and that to you and to me they are all together but one mere speck of blue light in the black canopy of the heavens ! Possibly at this very moment some mariner sailing over the seas of the pole-star is taking an observation of this planet of ours figuring in his system of constellations as the hind leg of a donkey ; if, indeed, our existence has yet been discovered there. For there are stars which are not even so much as a speck of blue light to us, all our telescopes notwithstanding, and notwithstanding, too, that they may be the very bodies whose attraction just keeps us in our balanced place.

Some of the men who have the greatest influence upon the history of their country, and the welfare of their race, own names which have never met the eye of the most inveterate newspaper reader. I know two or three such whose existence is only so much as suspected by a select few, who will not be found in any biographical dictionary, and who are yet at this moment moulding the destinies of Europe.

* * * * * *

TUESDAY, 9th June.

Coming into the river from the sea makes one understand how a shy man who has always lived in the country feels when he is one day bundled into London society. Surely we shall never be able to move among all these craft ; surely these craft themselves are not real. Manifestly they are not intended for service of any real kind. Here is a barge heavy-laden with hay down to the water's edge, merely drifting with the tide ; there is another gaudily decked with green bulwarks, a red tiller, and a blue and yellow sprit ; here again is a shoal of small craft all legs and wings, full of men more carefully got up to represent real salts than if they had passed their lives off Cape Horn ; and here is a party on a steamer, packed as close as herrings, and supposed to be having the greatest enjoyment. Surely I have seen all these things before in London society. Here is a gentleman in shirt-sleeves and beaver-hat, leaning over the tiller of a barge. As he passes us he looks with a contemptuous eye at our too fishing-boat-like cut, and asks, " Well, I'm blowed. Where did you pick *her* up ?" This also, I think, I have heard before.

* * * * * *

GREENWICH, Wednesday, 10th June.

I am anchored just opposite a celebrated inn at Greenwich. It is a lovely evening. The windows of the hotel are all open, and I see in them perhaps fifty people who all think they have been dining. Poor wretches! they don't even know the difference between that and eating. Some of them may have heard that there *is* a difference, but they believe it to be solely in the matter of cost, whereas it lies in palate and in trouble. Without these you may eat whitebait devilled in all the colors of the rainbow, whiting pudding, (what a horror!) flounder souchés and broils to the end of time; but you will not dine. With these you may linger over the simple chop fresh-marked with the gridiron, toy with an omelet, a couple of tomatoes, a basket of fresh-gathered strawberries, and end with the only salad in England and the only coffee in Europe—all prepared by one to whom such things were as the Greek particles a month ago.

Yet there are those poor people who think they have dined, and beneath them are three naked little boys diving for coppers which they in the fulness of their generosity—or rather in the generosity of their fulness—throw out. Truly we are a brutal people, we English.

CHAPTER VI.

GREENWICH REACH, 15th June.

To go down the river and back again, just to pass rapidly through as one passes through France or Italy, or other such low-born countries, is what many of us have done, and found that there is nothing in it beyond a number of ships lying in unintelligible places, and doing unintelligible things for unknown purposes, and a large number of dirty people not within the pale of humanity. But to live here, even for a few days, is a very different matter. I begin now to see that the real London, the great throbbing, restless energy which makes the capital, and England too, what they are, is all on this side of London Bridge. The barges working up the river with the young flood, twenty of them in this Reach all one on top of the other, yet never breaking an egg ; the thousand slender wands that have pointed to every zenith in the celestial conclave, lying clothed in their cobweb garment of cords ; the chimneys, the clamor, the high-pressure puffings, the uncouth tide-enslaved lighters ; nay, even the toiler, even on Sunday when the unfrequent blacking is on his monstrous hobnailed pachydermatous boot, and the paper collar and lavender tie are round his neck ; all these seem to represent something far more real, far more satisfactory, and far more representative of the better England than that ostentation of purse-proud servility into which it all passes through the crucible of Temple Bar. Yet most of us know nothing of all this, can see no beauty in it, and would, if we could, sink it in the bottom of the sea, as an uncouth, ungainly, rude spectacle to which the finer sort of mankind are not to be brought at any cost.

How thoroughly the belief—once so strong—has died out, that Englishmen are all men of the same nation, brothers of the same family, bound to stick close together against the world if need be ! We are now, it appears, brothers only of those of our " class." The " gentlemen" are of one race, the middling classes of another, the working classes of yet another, while the women are of no race at all, but only of that of their children, cousins, and husband, or lieutenant male, as the case may be. And then the gentlemen and the other " classes" make themselves up into infinite subdivisions, each of which is as alien to the other as all are to each. So that we are all strangers and enemies to each other in the same land, with no sentimental ties and no recognized obligations to bind us together, and a whole world of interests to separate us. I have heard of a house in that condition.

*   *   *   *   *   *

I love to linger over those old prints of naval battles fought when England could meet and defeat the banded nations of Europe. Here is one of them in a gilt frame, stained and soiled, a wreck probably from some master mariner's household goods, hanging in an old clothes shop—a crowded, highly-wrought engraving, defective in many points of art, but stirring the blood nevertheless. A principal figure in it is that of a sailor nailing his ship's colors to the stump of the mast while he is shot at by a hundred of the enemy's small-arm men.

So even this most magnificent and moving pile of Greenwich has been taken away from the poor sailor, who was to spend his old age in it to all time according to the intent of its founders, and has been made into a college for the richer naval officer. The perpetual old shameful tale of taking from him that hath not and giving to him that hath. Thus did they three hundred years ago with those lands of the Church which had equally been set apart forever to the pious uses of God and the poor. I wonder who has fingered all the rich Greenwich endowments, shares, parts of prize-money, and others. I know we are told that the poor sailor is to have a money-pension given to him in lieu of his palace-home, just as the other poor have had indoor and outdoor relief in lieu of their own property and inheritance. But what is to replace that feeling that every English seaman who sailed up the Thames once had that here was his home, here in this most splendid shape the expression of the great value a great nation set upon his services ?

*   *   *   *   *   *

TUESDAY, 16th June.

" What the gridiron do you mean by running into me ?"

" Ask my mamma, you friend of mankind—you should get out of the way."

Such is the account, so far as words go, of an interview I had this morning with a professor of navigation in charge of a barge laden with hay. He had run into me with all his weight, and the strength of a spring tide, thrown me from one end of my cabin to the other, and startled me out of a peaceful calculation of azimuth on to the deck. Beyond this, and knocking off a piece of copper as large as Mr. Gladstone's intellect, he had done me no harm ; in fact he had rendered me a service, for he gave me an excuse for feeling injured and being angry for five minutes—which is one of the greatest luxuries I know.

Once there was a man—not indeed once only, for the adventure is being daily renewed—who suddenly became aware that his friend was a traitor, and his sweetheart a jilt. He complained bitterly, declared that there never was an injury like his, and swore that he must die without remedy. Yet if you look him over now, but five minutes as it were after the shock, you will find it hard to discover where he has even had a rub of his paint.

*   *   *   *   *   *

THURSDAY, 18th June.

If my eye really were at the surface of the sea my rail would appear far higher than it now does, and the sun lower ; so that this correction for Dip by which I bring my sun a few seconds lower than I observe him from the deck, is in truth a testimony to the fact that he is higher than my rail, as it is also a proof that as one enlarges one's horizon, that which is in itself low appears lower, while that which is really high appears higher.

A graceless Frenchman once said : " Les grands ne nous paraissent grands que parce que nous sommes à genoux—levons nous !" * Whereby he meant not the truly but the apparent great.

Once I knew a bald man, a man in public life, who was too old and too wise for words, very far removed from my time, and for whom I felt the respect one entertains for the generation of fathers and uncles possessed of infinite wisdom and knowledge. I remember I was quite astounded when he married, and thought it hard on his wife. Now that a few years have passed I have become aware that he is not old at all, but of a mere decent and reasonable age, which quite entitles him to give his own name to his children. Moreover I have no

---

* The great appear to us great because we are kneeling—let us rise.

longer the slightest respect—but contrariwise, a great contempt
—for his public self and work.

I knew also, at the same time, a thinker, who seemed to me
superior certainly to most men, but not so very greatly superior. He has now so risen in my estimate that I open the records of his thought with fear and trembling lest I fail to seize it.

*   *   *   *   *   *

Reading a law case of the time of Edward I., I find that before the Conquest one Hugh de Longchamp—" *tient play de la
coronne, e aveit fourges, et prit redempcion de genz a la mort
juges, par reson deu maner*" had pleas of the Crown, and had
gallows, and took ransom of men condemned to death, by reason of his manor.

Is it not strange that men should be found who can amass a
fortune out of the blood and bone of their fellows, and who
yet thoroughly believe that they have no duties to fulfil toward them ? I know a good dozen who, finding themselves
in a strong capitalist castle, have taken from hundreds—nay,
from thousands—that lifetime of toil, which is all the toiler's
wealth, and who will calmly stand by and see the executioner
Hunger step in to make an end of what little life there is left
in them—answering, if they be questioned, that the right of
grace, if anywhere, is in the master of the workhouse.
Surely, this is breaking the bargain.

*   *   *   *   *   *

The Thames Conservancy have a way of punishing an offending master of a barge by taking a cloth out of his mainsail,
which is to that extent a diminution of his sailing-power, and
consequently of his profits, always felt. One passed me to-
day who had scarcely any mainsail left—evidently a hardened
sinner of some kind.

The Jews are the most persuasive race in the world, and I
fancy that when King John pulled their teeth out one after the
other, on their refusal to part with their moneys, it was in order to diminish the seductive flow of their speech. What

now if we should take to that again ? What if we were to
draw a tooth from every minister convicted, in the usual way,
by a majority of the Commons, of having ill-administered his
country's affairs ? That would in some measure replace the
rusty old weapon of impeachment at which everybody laughs
nowadays. For it is no longer held to be a crime in a man to
betray his country for the sake of his " party "—which is the
modern word for himself.

*   *   *   *   *   *

To have the sky for your only philosopher—to be read as
you may be able to read it—the sun, moon, and stars for your
only guides, and the sea for your only companion, is of all
things the most delicious when the sky writes fair weather in
plain characters, when the sun and the moon and the stars tell
you clearly where you are, and when the sea is in an amiable
mood. But when the sky speaks angrily, when the heavenly
bodies refuse to speak at all, and the sea turns into an inveterate and pitiless foe—then I fear them all, and regret bitterly
that I ever left my fast moorings in London. I have known
men who maintained that they had never felt fear. I am not
of those. I confess that whenever I see Death about me I am
horribly afraid of him—and I have seen him in more than one
shape, always with the same effect. But that same sinking of
the heart into the boots, and the raising of it again to exertion
by a mere dead determined pull, that is not without pleasure ;
and the more restless—or in other words the better—kind of
men have always placed their enjoyment in it. It is enough to
make one believe that fear is one of the chief luxuries of life ;
and, in truth, there is nothing in existence equal to the sweetness of sailing within an ace of the greatest possible danger and
yet coming off untouched.

Our great contemporary professors of religion have made a
capital error in suppressing eternal torment out of their system,
as all they do who admit that those of any other way of thinking than their own can escape it. If a religion does not make

you feel that it has enabled you to sail close round destruction and yet to weather it, men will content themselves with natural philosophy.

CHAPTER VII.

"There's a lovely coffin—quite the last thing—the new High Church pattern—*very* stylish—polished ellum, all of it—very fine figure, too—no, not the gentleman, the wood I mean—you see this is one of those jobs that *must* be done, and sharp, this hot weather; that's why I'm rather behind with yours. *Very* stylish, isn't it, sir?" Wherewith the joiner put his head aside, looked at his production through the screwed-up corners of his eyes, and slowly rubbed his hands one in the other as one modestly conscious of having achieved a real work of art, and content to look to posterity for his reward.

I do hope nobody will put me into polished elm when I die. I would much rather somebody even raised an Albert Memorial to me ; that would at least serve as a warning-beacon to show people forever the kind of structure they should not build. I can understand a man wishing to see the immaterial part of him preserved and reproduced—that desire is the better counterpart of the desire to procreate and leave children—but the notion of making much of the material part when it has ceased to be the temple of the spirit is beyond me.

  *   *   *   *   *   *

"A fiddle is as good as ten men on a purchase" is a received axiom on every man-of-war, and yet we are all aware that the force of a fiddle cannot be translated into any known formula of mechanics.

Also there was once a man who lived to threescore years, and was at that age "made a fool of," as people said, by a little girl of seventeen ; but, as should really have been said, had made a fool of himself in living so long and never till then finding out that he had a soul as well as a body.

*   *   *   *   *   *

They say you may tow a frigate with a silken hair if only you once get her started. At any rate there is a little insect of a man perched upon that huge lighter, and looking, as one would say, ridiculously incapable of producing even the smallest effect upon her, yet managing to thread his way without a touch through all this mass of shipping. Of course he has the tide with him, but that any man may have twice a day.

How little can one do, or does one do—how wretched are the efforts one makes in comparison with the great thirst and eagerness within one ! There are moments when a man feels that he could embrace the whole world in his grasp and leave the trace of his fingers all round it. Think what a little it requires after all to move this poor vacillating, nicely-balanced humanity of ours ! What a little ! A mere accident—may be even a trace of disease—in the processes of that brain tissue, a movement of heaven-born sympathy with one of the outside spectra, or even a grosser coupling with it of sordid self-interest—and in due course of time an idea is born that shall change the face of the earth, and even to the least incident of the smallest life of those that dwell therein. What an effect and what a cause ! Also, what a courage should not this give to the most obscure of us who would deal with the mad phenomena we have about us ! And here is such an one, with this chance open to him also, *not* stretching forth toward it, but gone aside into by-paths leading he knows not whither. Who and what is any individual that he should seek himself, or rather lose himself, in such strange ways ?

*   *   *   *   *   *

WEDNESDAY, June 24.

The Thames is the only great river in the world where there are no regulations for traffic, and nobody to enforce them. This morning I saw an elephantine lighter floating up stream without a soul on deck, and as a river policeman was passing me I pointed it out to him, and remarked, feelingly, that that was how accidents happened. "Bless you, sir! they always do it," said he, "and we have no power to interfere, because it is the Thames Conservancy who have the control of the navigation." Why, then, I should like to know, don't they control it? or rather, why should not their business be done by the Waterman's Company, expanded and reorganized to that end? It seems ridiculous, when there are ancient bodies already in existence, to create new ones that will not do their duty.

I was thinking of these things when for the second time a lighter carefully ran into me, though, thanks to my look-out, very tenderly and gently this time, and again provoked me to a free use of river-language.

John Brown, the black man's hero of Harper's Ferry, when he was taken said that he was of more use for hanging than for any other purpose; and so it proved, for it was his hanging that brought about the emancipation of the slaves. All the same, it would have been better for John Brown if it could have been effected at a less cost.

*   *   *   *   *   *

We have all heard yarns of shipwrecked and compassless mariners who have steered a course by a star, and got safely to port; which sounds very well till you know that the stars, like the sun and moon, rise on one side the earth and set on the other, so that a man who steered by them would be varying his course every minute. Even the Pole-star, which is the best of them in these latitudes, varies a little. But, in fact, the stars are of no use at all unless you can correct them by the sun.

We are asked to believe in and to follow our public men, on the ground that they are honest and reliable. Yet does it not appear that they are each and all of them working for their own interest—or that of their party, which is the same thing? When you find a man of commercial spirit willing to pay large sums of money in order that he may be allowed to perform a

public duty, you may be sure it is that he means it not to be a
public duty at all but a private gain of some sort, whether of
dignity or of cash matters not.   The great concern is to know
where each of them is in his career at the given moment, and
which way he is tending.   Then he may be of some use to
those who are capable of applying the corrections—not otherwise.

   *   *   *   *   *   *

A cautious foreign ambassador in London once wrote to his
Court, "Some say that the Prince is dead, some say that he is
not—I agree with neither of them."

Some people say that the hours of drinking are too long,
others that they are too short.   Mr. Cross agrees with both.

   *   *   *   *   *   *

I have been reading some old books which give strange accounts of a people rich and contented, bold and law-abiding,
of "vilcins" who had lands and brought actions (ay, and won
them) against their lords for infringement of their rights, of
mean men well clad and thoroughly fed, and of nobles who
kept open table for the homeless and the hungry.

There was once a little island called England which seemed
destined to fill the world with its name.   It was inhabited
by a sturdy race of men, not easy to govern, but endowed with
certain noble qualities which made all mankind look upon them
with respect.   They owned no masters, temporal or spiritual.
They had humbled France and Spain ; they had broken the
power of the Papacy ; they had dethroned their own kings
many a time, and bound their nobles in chains of iron.   They
fought for ideas—even among themselves—they carried their
heads high, and their envoys walked as men of a greater stature
among the "beggarly" peoples of the Continent.   This was
three hundred years ago—only three hundred years ; only ten
generations ago—and England is now no more.   An aristocracy contrived to invent the fiction of actual possession of the
soil, then repudiated its burdens, and finally contrived to

pawn the nation to a company of adventurers as a bribe to be allowed to retain their hold over it. The "glorious Revolution" was accomplished, "Parliamentary Government" was established, taxation was imposed, and thenceforward Englishmen at large became mere cash-paying and burden-bearing animals, to be used for the common purposes of the new alliance. Between the allies the bargain has been faithfully adhered to, and he who runs may read its results. Materially and morally, England has become a contradiction. Never did her people produce so large a proportion of the fruits of the earth, and yet never did they enjoy them so little. Enormous wealth by the side of, or rather built upon, enormous pauperism, the richest country in the world inhabited by the poorest people of the earth, the disgust of satiety mocking the pangs of hunger—such is the astounding spectacle that we present just now in material matters. Morally things are as bad—they could not, indeed, be much worse. All faith, all generosity is gone. The privileged, secure in their possessions, look with contempt on those noble qualities in which their privilege—or some of it—took its rise. The peer and the pedlar have combined against the proletarian. They will allow him to live, because without him *they* could not live ; but that is all. If he tries to better his condition by strikes according to all the canons of political economy, that is pronounced flat rebellion, and straightway a law is passed to curb his evil desires for food and raiment in sufficiency. If he asks for education (alas ! what education is more pregnant with teaching than that of keeping a wife and family on thirteen shillings a week !), they give him theological minerals and literary stones—just enough to make him fear the parson and honor the squire. If, in despair, he would take his two hands to freer climes, he is told that it is his duty to starve here in case it may be worth the while of the pedlars to turn him into coin. Poor Englishman ! it were well for him had he never been born. Unhappily he is born, and must make up his mind—such of it as is left to him—as to the attitude he means to adopt toward the

men and things of his country.   Can we wonder if that attitude is one of discontent, distrust, and hostility ?

*   *   *   *   *   *

THURSDAY, June 25.

There was an Irishman who said that he thought the moon
infinitely more valuable than the sun, " because," said he,
" you only have the sun in the day, when you don't want it,
whereas you have the moon at night, when you do want it."
Nevertheless, I feel convinced we should be in great difficulties
if that ingenious piece of mechanism, the sun's lower limb,
were to be taken out of the system of the universe, say for one
day.   Nay, even Sirius would leave a void that would be felt,
for he, too, is a necessary part of the system.

Idleness is the root of all newspapers.   On taking them up
again, after an interval of abstention, two things are clear to
me.   First, that I have lost absolutely nothing by losing the
daily papers ; secondly, that the world to which I have come
back for a time is, as represented in them, a world of lunatics.
I find the British Parliament, charged, as we fondly believe,
with the vital interests of the empire, still engaged on liquor
laws and Plimsoll, the Mordaunt case revived, a lady of Manchester eloping with a 12th Lancer, Lord Henry Lennox laying
the foundation stone of new water-works, and giving an answer
about the light on the Victoria tower, the Duke of Edinburgh
going to the regions of the London Docks to talk philanthropy,
Mr. Burges veneering Sir Christopher Wren, and Mr. Knox
sending a man to prison for a month with hard labor because a
policeman does not believe his account of the way in which he
became possessed of a book.   Surely it must be pretty well time
to go to sea again.

CHAPTER VIII.

GREENWICH, Monday, June 29.

THERE is a barge anchored close to me, the man in charge of which must sleep sounder than any creature I ever heard of in ancient or modern history. When in the silence of the night I am quietly doing some of that work, which seems to take time in inverse proportion to its effect, I hear a voice from the shore calling " Charley," by the half-hour together, till I am fain to lay down my pen and my book, and laugh at its patient pertinacity. Charley evidently turns in early, for the serenade often begins at nine o'clock, and he seems to learn nothing from experience, for it is almost a nightly incident.

There is a lullaby in small things, in ripplings of beer, in ecclesiastical sighings, and such gentle sounds, such as seem to have sent all our national watchmen to sleep. And though one stand and shout one's lungs out, they will not hear—no, not though the existence of the city depend upon it.

   *   *   *   *   *   *

THURSDAY, July 2.

You cannot add one cubit to your stature by taking thought ; and yet we do all take thought (those of us who exist at all, and do not vegetate), and bring ourselves into the strangest contradictions. I, for instance, have taken it into my head within the last week to be devoured by the strangest mania for becoming possessed of a " master's certificate ;" wherefore I have passed the last two days at the St. Katherine's docks, engrossed in calculating problems of navigation and nautical astronomy. It will add nothing to my stature, and I know it ; but yet I have already faced two pent-up days of meridian and exmeridian altitudes, azimuths, amplitudes, and Napier's diagrams, and am going to face the Board of Trade knows how many more, merely for a bit of paper, which will be of no use, heavenly or earthly, to me when I get it—if I do get it—and the getting of which stands between me and the enjoyment of much decent weather and favorable wind. Yet I believe that if I don't get it, I shall be about five times as much disap- pointed as I should be if I heard that Saccharissa had run away with another woman's husband.

The great secret of life is that of the relative importance of things. This also is the secret we none of us ever learn. And for various reasons, the chief of which, perhaps, is that we none of us ever find out what we really mean to do, and that we therefore never get a standard by which to compare the rel- ative importance of two given things. If a man or a woman could only settle on a certain line of life—say that of mere physical self-satisfaction for instance—the matter would be easy. But the mischief of it is that the spirit is always pulling one way and the flesh another ; and so we most of us come to mere drifting at last. See what immense results have been achieved by those who have frankly abandoned the flesh and taken up with the spirit. Moses, Socrates, Mohammed, Fra Bartolommeo, Palissy, Newton, Swift, the Jesuits, Comte, have all moved the world in their own direction, and left a trace upon it such as will never be effaced. Why cannot we, or some of us, also make up our minds ?

* * * * * *

If those who are always lauding the triumph of science, and preaching that we have come to the end of all knowledge and all art, could be abashed, they should be by a consideration of the triumphs lying close to our hand, and which have never yet been even attempted. There is the force of the wind, for instance, immense as it is, now put to use only at sea, or if on land at all, merely for a few ridiculous mills. Then there is the irresistible power of the tidal wave—who has ever caught and bridled *that ?*

Also there is the soul of a man, which is the strangest, grandest, and most divine of all forces. Yet the only creatures who make any kind of use of it at this present time are the Pope and the Communards !

*   *   *   *   *   *

I have moved my second anchor out of the bows to abaft the mast. The principal point to regard in the stability of a given ship is not, as poor Plimsoll imagines, the weight of the cargo put into her, but the manner in which it is stowed. If a light cargo be ill-stowed the ship is far more unsafe than with a heavy cargo well stowed. To replace good stowage by empty space is madness.

The insane desire there now is to multiply holidays, is but another symptom of the general madness. It is an utter blunder to suppose that men do their work well in inverse proportion to its amount. The capacity of man for work is almost unlimited ; but then it must be work of a varying kind, each kind holding its proper place. To expect any human creature to work nine hours a day at making pins' heads is one form of insanity—to expect to relieve him by half a Saturday of stagnation, a Sunday of church, and eight hours at the sea-side for half a crown is another.

*   *   *   *   *   *

A gentleman was being examined in seamanship, and was asked—

" You are on a lee shore, what do you do ?"

" Put the ship about, or wear her."

" But your ship will neither wear nor stay. What do you do ?"

" Let go the anchor."

" But there is no anchorage, the ground being rocky. What do you do ?"

" Let her rip."

This gentleman passed. But he might have thrown his yards aback, and on getting sternway have let her come round on her heel—which shows that we should never absolutely give up, but work right through at whatever we are about, until we are really and finally gone without remedy.

CHAPTER IX.

GREENWICH, Saturday, July 4.

TO-DAY a huge, light steamer signalized herself by trying to run down the guard-ship Fisgard, a frigate built seventy years ago, distinguished in the " glorious first of June," and now put to these base uses. Failing in that she tried to come aboard of me, but finding I was one too many for her, she ran stem on into a poor little slip of a cutter-yacht anchored just below me, carried away her mast and bowsprit, ran her ashore, went ashore with her, and then getting off, steamed away rejoicing down the river. Nothing but the greatest carelessness or the greatest unhandiness on the part of the steamer's people could have brought about such an " accident," as I suppose the running-down will be called, and I hope the owner of the little cutter will be able to make her pay. He was not without fault, however, himself, for he had gone ashore and left nobody on board. Had I been in that case I should have been run down as well.

*   *   *   *   *   *

There are moments in life when the sunshine seems to be taken from the world ; when the glorious earth has no beauty left in it ; and when the very Man himself, so noble in truth, so perverted to baseness in appearance, becomes a declared and bitter enemy. Yet it is not they who have changed, but only the eye that regards them. It is clear it must be so. The great structure of many things which make up the universe is surely less likely to get out of order than the one single eye that regards them ; and if they seem to be in chaos, who shall say that it is they and not his vision that is deranged ? We all of us fancy when we meet troubles that they are greater troubles than ever were met before. It is merely because we know our own troubles better than we ever can know those of others. I never read a tragedy without smiling at it. Here is one single atom of this universe, because, forsooth, somebody has trodden

upon him, affecting to fill the whole world with his complaint
—calling the gods down from heaven to bear witness to his
suffering, and the whole world to weep at his misery, as
though, forsooth, he were more suffering than other men.
And there are those who *will* weep with him in lieu of bursting into laughter at his impertinent assurance. *His* misery
indeed !—Leah's or Othello's misery or mine ! Why, if every
atom is to make a cry about his misery, the world will not
hold the clamor.

*   *   *   *   *   *

To-day another half-dozen lighters have gone athwart hawse
of the Fisgard ; and watching them at it I have become aware
that it arises in every case from beginning too late to count
with the tide. When yet a long way off they think they have
plenty of room to pull clear ; but then they go on thinking it
till they find themselves close on top of the frigate, when there
is nothing for it but to stop tugging and let her drive, which
they do with great composure.

*   *   *   *   *   *

Did you ever feel that you were being tempted to do a wrong
thing—I do not mean what the world says is wrong, which is
nothing, but what you are convinced is wrong, which is everything ? Did you ever see the temptation come toward you,
you knowing it for itself all the time, and then feel its persuasion steal softly and caressingly into your soul, and become
suddenly aware that you had lost the battle even before you
fought ? This is very bitter, for after all we do all of us wish
and intend to do what we hold to be right ; and he who knows
distinctly for himself that he has failed to do that on any occasion, carries thenceforth forever with him the ghost of the
wrong he has done—a ghost which will appear to him sometimes when he least expects it.

*   *   *   *   *   *

MONDAY, July 6.

I have become aware, by finding the air filled even more
than usual with river-language, that Greenwich holds to-day

what it is pleased to call a regatta. I presume it may be pleasant enough for those who are on the land, but for those whose house is on the water it merely means that there are three times as many craft running into you, holding on to you, and putting you generally to the accredited uses. Probably the Derby dog, who is annually chivied over the course, is the only creature who does not thoroughly enjoy the race.

*   *   *   *   *   *

It always seems to me that the love for athletic sports is the one surviving remnant of that grand old brutal English spirit which once made us a great nation. But I suppose we shall soon have this also put down by legislation. There will be statistics in plenty to show that over-exertion is a fruitful parent of crime and disease. We shall be told of the may accidents that attend boat-races, polo, cricket, running, duck-hunts, and greasy-poles, when the "lower classes" are permitted to indulge in them without being regulated ; and some Plimsoll will insist that outriggers shall have a freeboard of at least six feet.

*   *   *   *   *   *

Apropos of Plimsoll, why does that amiable enthusiast, who loves the British sailor so much that he would prevent him from going to sea, not take up the case of Greenwich Hospital ? I went over the hospital to-day, and was made so angry that on coming out I felt inclined to knock off the helmet of the policeman who stood at the gate as the representative of Government. Here is a splendid pile, built by private subscription, endowed and given forever to the worn-out sailor, now taken from him, and turned into a cramming-shop for a few young gentlemen, while the sailor is turned adrift on fourteen shillings a week. In 1865 there were nearly three thousand sailors here, men who had spent their lives in the service of their country ; now there are scarcely more than two hundred boys coaching for examinations, who may or may not end in their serving their country. Formerly it was a centre of glorious traditions, there was not a man who had not his tale to tell ; now it is a mere nursery. The three thousand occupants were bribed to give up their home, and then it was pretended that the home was no longer the property of future occupants— which was false—and the Government has laid hands upon all the endowments which of right belong still to those future occupants to all generations, and to none other ; and have seized the building for their own purposes—a piece of spoliation which is enough to make one go and commit an assault on the Chancellor of the Exchequer and the First Lord of the Admiralty. The hospital belongs to the worn-up sailor, and to him it ought to be restored, not only in his own interest but even more in the interests of the country. Mr. Plimsoll really ought to take it up. He would exercise his undoubtedly great power to some good if he would do this. Let him see a few old sailors, and hear what they have to say about it.

* * * * * *

TUESDAY, July 7.

I believe in a Providence moving and acting on defined, certain, invariable, beneficent laws ; which is to say, that I believe in the existence of these laws themselves, and consequently in the existence of any Being, by whatever name called, representing an attempt to personify those laws. But a Providence ready to break and to disregard those laws, in that I do not believe. How then must this Providence smile—if it ever does smile—to find us men always wanting to have the fox's brush cut off and handed to us without trouble, and to get rid of the pleasure of the chase, which is all that we really enjoy. If *I* were Providence, and were by way of conferring a benefit upon mankind, instead of diminishing the difficulties of the chase, as we are always whining to It to do, I should increase them.

* * * * * *

We little coasting yachts, who only pretend to go to sea, and who are never really happy till we are fast tied to the side of a quay, with a big blue or white ensign flying and a party of ladies on board at lunch, are the most arrant impostors perhaps in England. And yet it appears that we are not the only impostors, for I learn that the ignorance shown by the modern sea-going ships' officers when they come up to be examined in seamanship is something quite appalling. The fact is that steam first nearly put an end to seamanship, and that the abolition of the system of apprenticeship finally killed it outright. We live in times when nobody will learn their trade—no, not even the statesman whose trade is the longest and most difficult of all to learn. I see that the whole of the House of Lords indulged in assenting laughter when Lord Chelmsford " ventured to say" yesterday that its members could not do a rule-of-three sum in three hours.

CHAPTER X.

Off MARGATE, Friday, July 10.

No wonder there is a wreck on the Girdler Sand. These entrances to the Thames are like Mr. Gladstone's opinions, confusing on account of their very number—not to say on account of their shallowness—and when you think you are certain to be able to get ovt through one, suddenly you have to alter your course and take another.

*   *   *   *   *   *

Off HASTINGS, July 12.

The refreshing feature of being at sea I believe to be this—that it is an occupation in itself. You can never find yourself in that most dismal of all passes, having nothing to do. Not a moment passes but demands its thought and its action. Constant unflagging attention is imposed upon you by sheer necessity, and the knowledge that you have nobody by whose advice you can ask keeps you perforce to your work. To-day the weather is so far equally fine in fact and in promise ; a grateful breeze is carrying us between five and six knots through the water ; Bill has surpassed himself over my dinner, and all seems prosperous. But who shall say how long it will last? Who can be sure of anything there where every minute seems to bring a change of some kind? That those who have been all their lives at sea do become careless and inattentive to its varying moods we know ; I can only envy them without being able at all to imitate them ; and am always casting about to discover what I shall do when that hurricane comes which I always believe to be pursuing me. Even when taking a few hours' dog-sleep one carries the thing in one's mind, and takes account of the various things done on deck. "Confound that Ned, he's put her about again !—always hanging on to the land, just like a smacksman. There he is now taking in his gaff-topsail. No necessity for that, I should say. If he doesn't go about soon we shall come near that Tower Knoll, and at low water too. Ah, 'bout ship ! All right ! Now for a sleep ! Why, there he goes again, and the wind falling. I must turn out, and get a cast of the lead."

*   *   *   *   *   *

July 13.

To really appreciate the daybreak you must have passed a night-watch waiting for it. What always strikes me is that in our latitudes the day never does break, speaking strictly, but steals upon you like the love of a woman—scarcely felt at first, until you are quite surprised to find yourself head over ears in light. Another remark I always make is that in reality the sun does not rise, but descends upon you. You see the higher sky and the upper sides of the clouds tenderly pencilled with gray, while below all is still black ; and you may watch the light come down till at last it meets the horizon, and, not till it has put out the stars and even the comet, joins hands, after much waiting, with the sun himself, from whom it came. This is very old, though ; and I observe that the comet, being newer and stranger, gains far more attention than any vulgar sunrise can do. All which explains to me our system of Parliamentary Government and the triumph of nebulous talkers over higher laws.

*　　　*　　　*　　　*　　　*　　　*

OFF BEACHY HEAD.

Ned says that the wind " allus fare to goo round ahead of us," and he adds " that allus hev done so ever since he've been a sailorizing," which he holds to be an especial cross invented for him. I am sure he is delighted to have this grievance, just as Bill is, who comes to me quite radiant every morning and reports of the milk " that hev turned all curdled like." I daresay now if Ned and Bill and I were endowed for our misfortune and that of mankind with the faculty of rhetoric we should get a crowd round us and utter the most dismal and piercing complaints of our lot. As it is, we simply go to work to make the best of it—which, indeed, is the only thing to do at sea ; for you can't steal anybody else's wind or milk, and if you could there is nobody to applaud you.

*　　　*　　　*　　　*　　　*　　　*

Nothing seems to me so amazing as the assurance of the people who talk of the " lower classes" being " uneducated." They are thoroughly well educated ; their whole powers, mental and physical, are cultivated and developed by them in the very highest degree for the work they have to do in life ; and it is not too much to say that, as a rule, they know well-nigh everything it is their business to know. Nay, more ; they are the only kind of people of whom so much can be said : the " upper classes" are, as a rule, profoundly ignorant of those things which it is *their* business to know. When Members of Parliament know as much of history and statesmanship as ploughmen do of ploughing ; when ministers can conduct a negotiation as safely as a hansom cab-driver guides his cab, or a bargeman his lighter ; when parsons have brought their light to shine before men as bright and as true under all circumstances as a few common sailors keep the Varne or the Owners in all weathers ; when judges steer as true a course by the law as Ned will by the compass ; and when ladies have learned to wear their dresses as well as their sempstresses stitch them—then I shall listen with more patience to them when they talk of others being uneducated.

*   *   *   *   *   *

There is no more lamentable, no more detestable, spectacle in this world than that of a man or woman who knows the higher law and yet acts on the lower. For those of us who believe in nothing, or in nothing else than the mere material enjoyment which that cynic Solomon recommends—for these there may be forgiveness : but what shall there be for those who know the truth only to deny it by their acts, who recognize the law only to destroy it by their lives ? Surely the curse of mankind is theirs, and the vengeance of the Eternal.

I know a man who might have been a blessing and a saviour to his kind. He chose to become a chapman and the father of a family. He is rich and tranquil—which is the modern translation for happy. But he knows that he might have been poor, unquiet, and powerful for good ; and when I tell him so he winces.

*   *   *   *   *   *

What, then, shall a man do with his life ? First get rid of himself by providing for that self food and raiment ; and then having, as it were, pensioned himself off out of harm's way, go heart and soul, yes, and pension too, into any spiritual work. If only he be honest—which to have done thus much he must be—his work will not be a bad one, whatever it may be. Which of us would not now rather be William Cobbett than "Loanmonger Baring," Molière than President Tartufe ; Chatterton than the Bristol Alderman ; Paul than Festus ; Washington than Lord North ? Yet while each pair was living together in the world, the choice of the vulgar would have been

exactly the reverse.   And yet also, while making the vulgar
choice, we all flatter ourselves that we are *not* of the vulgar.

*   *   *   *   *   *

Carlyle insists very strongly on the duty of hero-worship—
and very unnecessarily, for men are never backward in worshipping the heroes they set up, but rather the reverse.   What
is far more important is that our heroes should be of the right
kind, and in this Carlyle does not as a rule greatly help but
rather hinders us, setting up, as he has done, some very strange
scare-crows.   As for me, I can't accept a hero unless I am convinced that he is honest—a large word, pushing very many out
of the heroic circle—and strong.   Moses is a hero, David is
not.   Socrates, Plato, Mohammed, Leonidas, Numa, and the
Theban Legion are all heroes, but not Romulus, Cæsar or
Alexander.   Lord Balmeno was a hero, but not Hampden ; and
as much as I worship and venerate the true, so much do I despise and detest the false.   Neither are we without heroes in
these times.   I know four such, and I love and venerate them
as greatly as I do any of the noble army known and unknown
who have gone before them.   They are obscure men, whose
names have scarcely been heard, but men of heroic mould, and
doing hero's work.   In times when notoriety is confounded with
heroism, it cannot be expected that the world should recognize
its best men.   But that it should worship some of its worst is
unendurable.

*   *   *   *   *   *

There are times when one is tempted to think the Americans
the most hateful people of the earth.   Their professed creed,
that on which all their humor and satire are based (for this is
really the test), is that all poetry, all sentiment, all religion—
in short, all that has been from all time held in the Old World
to be the better and finer part of our nature, is a miserable
nonsensical make-believe swindle.   But, in fact, they are the
merest impostors when they put on this mask, and are simply
affecting to follow the laws of that God Majority in whom they
affect to believe.   There is no more sentimental, impulsive,

high-flown people under the sun. They it is, and not we English, who remember a birthday, and send a little token of a flower or a scrap of paper costing twopence. They it is, and not we, who still believe in and who do mad heroic acts ; they, and not we, who devote themselves with their lives and fortunes (as Englishmen of the old time would have said) to the right or even to the wrong if they believe in it. I wish Englishmen were in this like unto them.

CHAPTER XI.

ARUNDEL, 15th July.

SURELY it is an admirable thing to find a Duke ready to spend a million on something else than his own material enjoyment or the purchase of words ; therefore I honor the Duke of Norfolk and his cathedral very greatly—all the more because I see so few men left to do what in former times so many did—part with their substance, and, if need were, their lives, for the sake of their belief. I honor Rossel just as much, for he too did this.

*   *   *   *   *   *

OFF SELSEA BILL, 18th July.

I know a lady who makes it a complaint against seafaring in general, and especially against yachting, that " you are always thinking of your crew ; you can't dine after six because the forecastle gets so hot ; if you want to go ashore you have to wait till the men have finished their dinner," etc., etc. ; yet it seems to me not a bad thing that we should become aware that even these inferior animals have wants to supply and souls to save. To learn, even at the price of waiting five minutes for a boat, that consideration and respect—yes, respect—are due to all men, is to learn no small and no common thing. Dogs and horses are, no doubt, the only living creatures out of one's own

set with which one should really occupy oneself—yet I am very
fond of men and women.

*   *   *   *   *   *

OFF FÉCAMP, 20th July.

I have been "carrying on" with a fine strong breeze, in order to make my light and save my tide ; and watching my topmast bend like a reed under the gaff-topsail, I think of the
Spanish proverb which says that, " It is the weakest pull that
breaks the rope at last," and I reflect that like most proverbs
it asserts a falsehood under the guise of truth. We are getting eight knots an hour out of the Billy Baby, not without
risk of something giving, yet it is not the eighth knot that en-
dangers anything ; but really all the eight together, and rather
the preceding seven than the last one. Indeed, one may go
still farther back and say that it is the whole of my particular
life and character which are now engaged in straining at this
stick. Ned doesn't approve of it ; but then I have learned to
hate waiting outside French ports, to cut things fine and to risk
something—even a spar—in order to carry a point to which
for a moment I attach importance. From which the chain of
cause and effect is plain.

I wonder people are not sick of hearing the oft-repeated falsehood as to great events springing from little causes. It was
not the geese who saved the Capitol, but the piety of its de-
fenders, who had refrained even in the pangs of hunger from
eating those sacred birds ; it was not Hampden's twenty shillings of ship-money that brought Charles to the scaffold, but
the long-settled determination of the landed proprietors to shift
the burden of taxation from themselves to the people of England ; it was not the ordinances of July that brought about
Charles X.'s abdication, nor the prohibition of a banquet
which caused the fall of Louis Philippe, but the hatred and distrust France had learned for the whole Bourbon race during centuries of misgovernment. Some day in England we may have
great effects produced, and they will also probably be traced

to some trifling cause, some bill rejected or some measure accepted ; whereas they will be due to causes which are acting now all over the country, and which no man sees.

* * * * * *

"A new nobility," says Bacon, "is the act of Power ; but an ancient nobility is the act of Time." It always seems to me one of the great causes of our present confusion that all the really ancient nobility were killed in the wars of the Roses. Thenceforth we have had mere impostors for our nobles, men without traditions, who have gone as a matter of course into ignoble ways. At present our aristocracy is composed of commercially-souled men, intent, not at all upon maintaining the honor of an order into which they have been smuggled, but on adding to their rents and the places of their cousins. And yet those people have the face to lament the " demoralization" of the inferior classes, who are, after all, the least corrupted of any. Nay, if our orders were suddenly turned upside down, if the mean men were to change place with the noble, I know enough of both to be sure that things would be far more nearly in their natural order. But we believe too thoroughly in words to care for their meaning or to hold that there is any danger in their perversion. There is something almost sacred in a " most high and puissant," a " most noble," or an " honorable" man —but a most high and puissant liar and traitor, a most noble scoundrel, and an honorable swindler, these are creatures who canot really be anything but despised, even by those who most readily give them their false titles.

* * * * * *

21st July.

There was once a man who set himself to sail across the Channel. He was thoroughly versed in navigation, and with his meridianal parts, his radius, his difference of longitude and latitude, he calculated his cause to within half a degree, corrected it for deviation and variation, translated it into sailorizing language, set it to the helmsman, and turned in, confident that if the wind stood he would make his given point an hour before daybreak. The wind did stand, yet at this hour he found himself fourteen miles to the westward of his port. For he had entirely forgotten to allow for a spring tide.

*　　*　　*　　*　　*　　*

The romancers are still effective teachers ; but they have altogether abandoned the notion of ensamples for imitation, and only seek to display deformities for amusement. The teacher writes rather down to the lowest standard than up to the highest ; whereof the cause and effect are that the reader will not endure to hear of aught higher than himself, and rather seeks in the hero an excuse for his own littleness, than endure to be shamed by him into the effort to achieve greatness. Formerly the romancer called upon " all you who love joy, and delight in honor and noble deeds," to admire an impossible hero—now he calls upon meanness and delight in hypocrisy and indolence to amuse and flatter themselves with a very possible vulgarian.

CHAPTER XII.

Dieppe, 24th July.

I do not think that the sun was a worse sun than it is now when men believed that it was moved round the earth, instead of the earth being moved round it, or that the earth's motion is less true because men say it moves and not it *is* moved. Neither do I hold that the uncertainty as to the authorship of parts of the Bible in any way detracts from its authority. It is a divine work whoever wrote it, and that is enough. I have no conception of Homer, none of Shakespeare, and very little of Dante, of Bacon, of Milton, of Sterne, or even of Victor Hugo—how shall one have a complete conception of any man or men when one has so incomplete a conception of one's self ?—but I have a conception of their work and that is

enough. Why should we apply a different rule to the Bible ?
There it is, a grand record of divine things ; the form is nothing, the incident with which it is clothed is nothing, and above
all the language in which it is rendered is nothing ; so that
when, if ever, the compilers of the now to be " authorized version" shall have turned it into newspaper leader English, and
shall have cut out a few strong expressions, they will not have
changed it one atom. For they cannot touch its spirit, however much they may disfigure its form.

" Every idle word that men shall speak, they shall give an
account thereof in the day of judgment." That is not to say
that men are never to speak idle words, but that they will have
to show that the occasion was such as demanded no others.
You and I, and insignificant people in general, may upon insignificant occasions be as idle as we please ; but not so those who
assume to be teachers and leaders of men. What an account
will *our* leaders and teachers have to give !

" By their fruits shall ye know them." I care not what a
man says, though he should speak with tongues of Gladstone
and Disraeli. Show me the work he has done, and I know the
man for what he is. It is only by the effect of that he has
achieved that he is here at all. If he has lived for himself
alone, if he has in fact achieved nothing, then he is *not* here
at all, but is merely a simulacrum or make-believe man.

*   *   *   *   *   *

Fécamp, 26th July.

I went to-day to the one jeweller and silversmith of the town
to buy one of those delightful old copper-colored gold Norman
crosses for a present. The silversmith had not got one,
" Mais," said he, " j'en aurai bientôt." " How ?" I asked.
" Dame, monsieur, le goût est aux antiquités, et quand il n'en
reste plus on est forcé d'en fabriquer." *

---

* "But," said he, "I shall have them soon." "How?" I asked.
"Well, monsieur, the demand is for antiquities, and as there are
none left, it is necessary to manufacture them."

One thing has somewhat surprised me of late in France— though, indeed, whoever knows France ought never to be surprised—it is that I find almost everybody who speaks to me confidentially avowing that he is a Legitimist. They dare not publish their opinions, but that does not detract from their importance ; for in this country, as in most others, those who hold strongly convictions that cannot be published to-day are the masters of to-morrow. Henri V., by his attitude and his manifestoes of rigid consistency, is supposed throughout Europe to have destroyed his chance of ever coming to the throne. In fact, he has enormously increased it, for this is the one people in the world that believes in principles, and will stand to a man who shows that he values his principles more than his interest.

*   *   *   *   *   *

I started yesterday for Havre ; but after knocking about all night, and reefing myself down to three pocket-handkerchiefs, I find myself here, with no other excuse than that I wanted to see the place, didn't care for Havre, and wasn't going to face a strong breeze and dirty weather, for the sake of getting to that rather than to this port. " You must be somewhere," I reflected, and it matters neither to me nor to anybody else where *I* am, therefore I'll go to Fécamp, get a dry suit, and breakfast, and take a fresh departure.

Years ago, when I was a young man, I knew the most charming, ingenuous brown-eyed little girl that ever gladdened the eyes of a boy. She was at a convent at school, and used to send me messages of remembrance through her cousin. I have seen her again—married, and the mother of many children—and it has brought back to me my youth, and drawn me to a review of the things I have done with it. A sad review is this to most of us, but how sad to one who like me is convinced of the power of every man to do that which he really means to do, and who looks forward and sees the port, only to know that he has never been " looking up" seriously for it, and has played with every puff that blew and made a fair wind of every breeze however contrary.

*   *   *   *   *   *

Most of us who have struggled out of the trammels of education and belongings into our own life here, first become aware of it by becoming confronted with this question : what to do with it ? To do something that shall bear fruit is felt all at once to be a necessity without which existence were *not* existence. " Here am I," says the dazed eager neophyte, " with my head and my two hands manifestly not given to me for nothing ; I am full of life and courage. I could move a world. There is a restless, unappeasable longing in me, which will not let me, even were I so minded, shame my Maker and myself by simply cumbering the earth, which drives me to action that will leave a trace here when I shall be gone. Not a trace of my name, perhaps—that is nothing—but some work which shall be, in any degree, however small, a valuable inheritance to my kind. Something I must and will do ; but *what*, in God's name, what ?"

The answer is found as soon as the question is asked. Do anything, so that it is actually you who do, and not another, and so that the thing is done, and not merely sketched or imitated. The world is full of work, of good work, in infinite variety. Conceive but one little idea, and, having placed it on record, you have planted an imperishable seed, and may go down to the grave content. It may not be a great idea, but if it truly is one of your own, and not another man's which you have put on, *you* have done something. The point is that you must begin while the divine enthusiasm is still on you. If not you will fall into the common ruck and do naught. The basis of everything still is labor, and you must affront the labor now; if you delay, it will affright you, and, like the rest, you will run cunning. It is the conscripts who volunteer for forlorn hopes : the old soldier values his skin too highly, and esteems too lightly the prize. Begin on what you will, but begin.

Remember, too, that it is your glory as it is your fate, that you are here for your work alone. Other matters may and will occupy you, but they are all subordinate. Your friend will betray you, the woman you love will deceive you, you will find yourself maybe one day in deadly struggle with poverty, and with what is worse than poverty—contempt. You will suffer—deeply, bitterly, perhaps—but what is that to a man who looks first to his work in life? He does but go into the wilderness to pray, which only means to resolve and to purpose earnestly, and will come back again all the stronger.

*　　*　　*　　*　　*　　*

27th July.

Fécamp is a charming little town, intent just now on the attempt to render itself a disgusting big watering-place. The casino possesses three half-reclaimed fishermen, who appear as *baigneurs* in the morning, and disguise themselves in tail-coats to do duty as waiters in the evening. There is a splendid old church, evidently much frequented, for in it is this notice : "On engage les fidèles à ne pas cracher sur le pavé de l'église, *surtout* dans la chapelle de la Sainte Vierge." * Also, it is the headquarters of the "Liquor Monachorum Benedictinorum," which is no more made by monks than is Bass's beer, but in the most ordinary lay manufactory.

The church is quite a gem, with its lovingly-carved chapels and oak panels, and its perfect and delicately-arched aisles ; and so, too, is the Chapel of Notre Dame de Salut on the top of the cliff full of those rude *ex-voto* models of ships that recall the perils of sailorizing. But the Revolution has left both much ruined ; and once again I find myself regretting the monks, and noting how imperfectly their principal function of succoring the poor, both spiritually and materially, is fulfilled by the State-salaried clergy and poor-reliever, who in modern times have replaced them.

*　　*　　*　　*　　*　　*

---

* "The faithful are requested not to spit on the pavement of the church, above all in the chapel of the Holy Virgin."

Has it ever occurred to English legislators and diplomatists, sitting in the serene heights of church patronage and Brussels congresses, to note this little fact—that the English fishermen are supreme in dredging oysters, and that the French fishermen are superior to them in catching mackerel and herrings? And will they never make thereupon this reflection, that it would be wise to carry into effect the Convention of 1867, which enabled French fishermen to sell their fish in English ports, and English fishermen to sell their fish in France? The result would be that oysters would be considerably cheaper in France, and mackerel and herrings in England. But then mackerel and herrings are the food of the common people, and of course are not worthy the attention of statesmen and diplomatists. If it were a question of turbots or lobsters, the case would be different, as indeed the law has already declared it to be in a notable instance.

Bacon says " the rebellions of the belly are the worst ;" whence it is to be inferred, if we did not otherwise know it for a fact, that the necessities of the belly are the most pressing. Yet, strangely enough, the bitterness of hunger has scarcely ever found a man with the gift of effectual speech to show all the misery and all the pity of it. For every little sentimental suffering there has been a voice, but none for this great material suffering which always exists. Probably it is because the hungry do not buy books. Yet surely here is a great untouched field. If so much can be done with and for the man who is dying of love, and does not die, how much more could be done with and should be done for the man who is dying of hunger—and does die !

*   *   *   *   *   *

Here is here an ordinary-looking man of middle age. He looks like a retired stockbroker ; he is not in any way lovely or admirable ; and he walks in a solitary manner up and down the shore in a large straw-hat and boots like a Thames lighter, swinging a piteous whity-brown umbrella. He is always deep in thought, and, looking at him, I wonder what such a man can be thinking about.   Not of business, or of any present action, or he would not be, as he seems to be, permanently settled down here, doing nothing.   Not of future projects either, for he is past the age for them.   He is recalling his memories manifestly; and the mere listless hanging of his head and his umbrella show that they are not enlivening or satisfactory.   Now I would wager something that he has in his mind at this moment the recollection of that woman who jilted him, and is thinking how hard it was, and how different everything might have been.   As for that other woman, whom he jilted (for at his age these two things have happened to all men), he never thinks of *her*.

Surely it is an admirable feature of our organization that we remember only the wrong we have suffered, and not that we have done.   Were it otherwise we should not be able to endure ourselves ; and what is perhaps worse, our sorrows would be real sorrows instead of being luxuries.   Of all the treasures in life there is none so great as to feel this—upon such an occasion I truly did my whole duty, and yet was wrongfully treated.   And it is his treasure a man counts when he is alone with his hat and boots and umbrella.

    *   *   *   *   *   *

A lady of quality, learning that a too well-known actress wished to sell her diamonds, and, overcoming her scruples in the hope of a bargain, went direct to her to deal for them. The actress demanded for them a large sum of money, upon which the lady professed to be quite astonished and scandalized at its exorbitance.   At last the actress went into a huff, and cried—

" I see what it is—you would like to have them at cost price."

The lady retired abashed and told her husband, who laughed much.

I am always reminded of this story when I hear of men seeking to be Ministers of State, Members of Parliament, and suchlike things ; and when I see one who has succeeded, knowing the ways by which he has passed, the dirt he has had to eat, and the dishonesty he has had to display—then I respect everybody who is nothing.

CHAPTER XIII.

Cowes, 5th August.

It is curious enough that we always remember people by their worst points, and still more curious that we always suppose that we ourselves are remembered by our best. I once knew a hunchback who had a well-shaped hand, and was continually showing it. He never believed that anybody noticed his hump, but lived and died in the conviction that the whole town spoke of him no otherwise than as the man with the beautiful hand, whereas, in fact, they only looked at his hump, and never so much as noticed whether he had a hand at all. This young lady, so pretty and so clever, is simply the girl who had that awkward history with So-and-so ; that man, who has some of the very greatest qualities, is nothing more than the one who behaved so badly on such an occasion. It is a terrible thing to think that we are all always at watch one upon the other, to catch the false step in order that we may have the grateful satisfaction of holding our neighbor for one who cannot walk straight. No regard is paid to the better qualities and acts, however numerous ; all the attention is fixed upon the worst, however slight. If St. Peter were alive he would be known as the man who denied his Master ; St. Paul would be the man who stoned Stephen ; and St. Thomas would never be mentioned in any decent society without allusions to that unfortunate request for further evidence. Probably this may be the reason why we all have so much greater a contempt for and distrust of each other than would be warranted by a correct balance between the good and the evil that are in each.

*   *   *   *   *   *

•I don't think I would give much for the gift of prophecy, for I have never met with a case in which it has achieved anything like a brilliant success.   Europe is not yet either Cossack or Republican, the British farmer has not been ruined, and the gathering of the tribes into the New Jerusalem seems rather farther off than ever, judging from the hold they have taken upon all the Gentile nations.   And if I would give little for the power of predicting the future, I would give scarcely more for the power of rightly appreciating the past.   What we live in is the present, and neither future nor past are of any value, save in so far as they bear upon that.   The cases we have to deal with are all new and special, and all demand instant resolution and action, in which general rules are of the smallest possible avail.   There are but seven notes in the scale, yet with them infinite melodies may be made ; nay it were even impossible for any composer to make of them with his own wit alone any but quite a new melody.   That we are most of us not composers, but mere parrot repeaters of compositions not our own, is only the explanation of the many miserable failures we supply.

      *   *   *   *   *   *

A huge ungainly government lighter was one day towed into Cowes Roads, and the naval officer in charge began to take bearings and to measure angles in order, as it manifestly appeared, to lay down moorings in a given spot.   When all was at the point of readiness a boat came alongside, and a very superior personage in gold lace and buttons said to the officer : " If you put down them moorings here you'll be foul of my vessel."   " Why, who are you ?" asked the officer, taking a horizontal sight at Egypt Point and the Trinity flagstaff.   " I'm the master of the vessel of Commodore the Earl of Wilton."   " Well, now," asked the officer, reading off his angle, and finding that he had at last got the exact spot ; " which do you think is the greatest person, Commodore the Earl of Wilton or Her Majesty the Queen of England ?"   This was a nice question, and while the plenipotentiary was considering it, the officer resumed, " because I am ordered by the Queen of England to put down these moorings here.   All ready there ?—let go," and down they went accordingly.

*   *   *   *   *   *

I have given much attention to the education of the Queen of Sheba (disrespectfully called Sheba), and have made her understand that she is not to sleep on my velvet-pile cabin carpet, but in a comfortable berth provided for her on deck. She is very fond of me, yet when I came on board this after- noon she slunk away and entirely declined any interview.   I have now discovered that the reason was that she had had the misfortune to steal two mutton chops and eat them.

One rarely meets a man who cannot endure to bear good fortune alone, or who at once sets about seeking another to share it with him.   Yet we none of us can rest until we find a friend with whom to share evil fortune.   It is a blessed thing that merely to describe a sorrow and to have it received with sympathy real or affected is to lose one half of it, and often even to make of the other half a valuable piece of property. What is really hard is evil fortune which cannot be told.

*   *   *   *   *   *

Bill is considered in his native Aldeburgh as a very revolu- tionary character.   He has been known to say that " he don't care to live there always, he don't," a length of recklessness which no inhabitant of that favored spot had ever previously reached, so that he is looked upon as a dangerous atheist and freethinker in disguise, the kind of person to lead an insurrec- tion, or found a new religion, or something equally subversive. Yet even Bill confides to me that he would like a berth on board a lightship.   I point out to him, the dignity of being independent, the advantage of passing his life in cooking omelettes for me in that perfection to which he has now pain- fully attained, and of surveying the world on board the Billy Baby from Greenwich to the Lizard—as compared with lead- ing a mere existence, shut up in the Galloper or the Kentish

Knock. It is in vain. Bill says that a lightship is " a regular good berth, that is," and I see in him yet another who is ready to give up the highest aims and aspirations for a mere assured living.

Men will, I believe, do anything rather than face the trouble and anxiety of thought and action of their own. " Give us a despot, a priest, a rule, somebody or something that shall think and act for us, leaving us only the mechanical part of the work —this, we know we can do ; that, we fear to undertake." Hence arise parties, autocracies, religions, moralities, which are valued as nothing more than so many inventions to relieve the laziness of men. There are many who understand that twice one are two, and even a few who understand that twice two are four, but scarce any who understand that twelve times twelve are a hundred and forty-four. They repeat it as a formula ; if you examine them they will appeal to the multiplication table, which is another formula ; but they have no idea of their own on the matter. Thence too it may arise possibly that men have invented and so grimly held on to the idea of there being a fixed eternal order in the world. Everything seems to announce the reverse, but to believe that things are continually changing, continually taking new faces and requiring a new thought and action, would be to believe that men ought to think and act for themselves. And rather than this they will believe anything.

The strangest part of it all is that, although we thus strongly desire a rule, we none of us will ever thoroughly submit to or act under it. If the world were so constructed that it had to be wound up every eight days it would have stopped long ago.

*   *   *   *   *   *

I greatly doubt whether the real knowledge of things has increased in the world, and whether the progress of science—of which we hear so much—amounts to anything more than an invention of new names for the old forms of ignorance. We once held earth, air, fire, and water as terms sufficient to include the whole material universe ; now we have added gas, and perhaps we may soon add the Odic force. But from the essence of things we are as far as ever. When any man of science can show me so much of the vital force as to take and put it into dry bones and make them live, then I shall hold that our progress has got out of the region of names—not before.

* * * * * *

There were two trees in the Garden of Eden, one of Life and the other of Knowledge. Is this not an assurance that knowledge is something more than the accumulation of observations which inevitably and surely come with life? Does it not teach us that every real step in knowledge is reached, not by putting one stone on the top of many others, but as by revelation from that other tree the fruit of which we have not inherited? If it be otherwise—if it be that true knowledge really is nothing more than the superposition of those kind of stones of which we all pick up one or two in the course of time, then there were not two trees, but only one. For suppose Eve had *first* eaten of the tree of Life, then she would on this assumption have certainly acquired the tree of Knowledge by the mere efflux of time.

* * * * * *

"There shall be one weight and one measure," declares Magna Charta, and this indeed is the foundation of everything. Yet to this day no two kind of men—scarcely, indeed, any two men—can be brought to use the same weight and measure for the same admeasurement.

Professor Huxley is held to be a clever man, yet he palpably only cares to deal in words, and has no notion of the responsibility a teacher incurs who gravely tosses them to the world as though they were realities. "In the early part of the last century," he says, "Society was in a state of corruption—bribery was the means of Government, and peculation was its reward. Four fifths of the seats in the House of Commons were notoriously for sale in one shape or another"—and so forth. He then compares the present state of things, which he

declares to be " in many obvious respects far better than that."
Surely a clever man standing up to say something ought to be
able to say something better than this. If Professor Huxley
really thinks that Society is not now corrupt, it can only be
because he does not know it, and because those who do know
it will not speak out in this generation. Bribery is not less
than it was the means of Government ; the only difference is
that the form of the bribery has changed, while the bribe itself
has been made more magnificent, being nothing less than irre-
sponsible power in England. Moreover the chiefs have found
means to keep the whole prize themselves ; and instead of giving their followers money down, they pay them in promises.
The rank and file, no doubt, now get nothing or next to nothing, but if they are not bought, it is only because they are not
worth buying, being so easy to bamboozle. As to the seats in
the House of Commons not being now for sale, if Professor
Huxley will produce any incarnation of supreme wisdom—say
himself—to any constituency, and get him elected without
money, or " influence," or " party"—all which, be it remembered, involve sale " in one shape or another"—then I will
cheerfully and thankfully agree with him.

CHAPTER XIV.

Cowes, 10th August.

" I always speak of people as I find them" strikes me as
being about the most selfish and cowardly excuse that ever
stole the garb of generosity. It amounts to this : that for me
there is to be no such creature as a thief who has not stolen
my property, no traitor who has not betrayed *me*, no perjurer
who has not forsworn himself to *me*, no adulterer who has not
run away with *my* wife, no wickedness in the world at all unless I have suffered by it ; that, in short, I am bound to sell

myself to the Father of Lies, and lie about all men knowingly —about all men, unless they have redeemed me from the necessity of so doing by inflicting upon me some injury which justifies me in avenging myself by telling the truth about them. Rather it seems to me should we beware of people as we find them, for that is usually as they are not. Claude Duval once danced a minuet on Hounslow Heath, yet many would be surprised if he were to be spoken of as an excellent dancer and no highwayman. For he is dead and gone, and it is only of the living that we are expected to tell lies.

And now what terrible retribution will overtake some who are now living in this false atmosphere with the pleasant belief that the truth will never be known of them ! There is certainly at this moment some Duc de St. Simon or some Walpole calmly and secretly taking notes, hereafter to be published, of these men and things that we have about us. How the readers of those notes will despise us ; how they will wonder that no hint of the truth ever escaped while such strange things as they will learn were actually being enacted ; how they will admire the reticence of those who knew them and who yet said no word !

    *   *   *   *   *   *

You can get eight knots an hour out of anything ; I have got that much even out of the Billy Baby. It is when you come to the extra speed that you meet the difficulty. The Alberta will steam thirteen knots with one boiler, but if now her second boiler be brought into play and the power thus exactly doubled, it is as much as she can do to add another two knots to the thirteen.

Anybody will be indifferent honest ; but to be anything beyond demands a power of which few are possessed. I know many a man who would not be mean or ungenerous for money, few who would not for favor ; many women I know who will hate you for yourself, very few who will love you for nothing else. Few of us can be tempted to do that which we hold to be wrong by that which we don't want—those who cannot be

tempted by that which they do want are honest.   He who fears
not death is no hero, he who seeks it is no martyr ; yet there
have been heroes and martyrs—most of them unknown for
such.

*   *   *   *   *   *

11th August.

We have had for the last week " wind enough to blow the
devil's horns off," as Ned says, and there is enough at this
present time to carry off his tail along with them, nor do
things seem likely to get better until they have been worse.
Dresses are either ruined or, what amounts to the same thing,
are kept out of sight ; expeditions round the island are post-
poned, and persons of the highest distinction are gravely in-
convenienced because no means have yet been found of
thoroughly controlling and laughing at winds and waves, and
because rain still continues to wet that which it touches, acting
precisely as wind, waves, and rain may be presumed to have
done in the uncivilized Garden of Eden.

What, then, if we were all poor things after all, and small
specks dusted, as it were, into the great machinery of this universe ?   When I see Royal Standards hoisted at the main of
the Osborne and the winds and the waves taking no notice,
I have a fearful misgiving and suspicion that after all it may
be so.   If there are powers at work in this respect which are
above and beyond us, and which we cannot anyhow reach or
influence, why, there may also be in other respects.   Were it
not then possible to suppose that even these specks obey some
higher rule than that of some other speck equally subject to it
—neither of them perhaps knowing any more whence it comes
or whither it tends than they know of the winds ?   Were it
not possible to imagine that when they make projects of
authority, of submission or what not, they are still and must
be unable to carry them into effect, save as the unknown rule
may allow ?   What if we were all pretending to do that which
we cannot in fact do ?   Would it be true wisdom to allow an
Almighty Power in the winds because they are strong enough

to blow, and to disallow it in the mind and conscience of men because they are strong enough to deceive ?

*   *   *   *   *   *

12th August.

I have been assured many times that the moon has nothing to do with the weather, but I don't think anything will ever make me believe it, and I have made up my mind that to-day's moon is to bring us an improvement on the very dirty state of things we have had for the Cowes week.

There are some things that you may prove to demonstration, and never get them really to be accepted, for we only believe what we can, and what we can believe we believe in spite of all evidence. Indeed, the things that are most thoroughly believed are those that have the most evidence against them. The selfishness of man, the worth of money, the value of power, the place of self in the centre of the universe, the supremacy of Chance, the blindness of the Almighty, are all notions the belief in which can be easily shown to be false and ridiculous ; yet upon them men every day stake their whole life, which is a much better way of showing that they believe a thing than merely saying so.

———   ——

CHAPTER XV.

Cowes, 15th August.

In itself there is nothing so delightful, or even so improving, as communion with one's kind. Merely to look at men and women is a great pleasure in itself—to look at them under the favorable circumstances of evening light, careful dress, and lawful behavior, and withal to converse with some of them, even if it be in mere prattle, is a still greater pleasure. And yet means have been found to render it the greatest trouble and the most tiresome business on earth, so that any decently intelligent creature will readily prefer even solitude to society. We know each other far too little, only just enough to hate each other with difficulty, not enough to love each other with ease ; which we are certain to do on anything over five minutes' acquaintance.

*   *   *   *   *   *

17th August.

The charm of seafaring, even when pursued in my pottering ignoble coasting way, is that for a man who has serious work on hand that he can take with him (and most serious work *can* be taken with one, for it is not a matter of machinery, but of thought) it offers a continual variety of employment. At sea you have your navigation and seamanship to think of, and must think of them to the exclusion of all else under pain of coming to grief ; in port you can settle down again to your serious work with the knowledge that there will be nothing to interrupt or interfere with you till you telegraph for your letters.

The English system of working and resting by extremes seems to me very bad and very unwise. To think that men can work at the very highest pressure all the days of the year, and that they can be refreshed and remade by a few Bank Holidays devoted to eight hours at the seaside, is a delusion. Far better would it be if the holidays were spread over the whole days of the year. The result of working time would be the same, the increase of working power would be enormous. For where you have overdrawn on a man's energy, you cannot balance the account by placing on the credit side a lump sum of idleness. That is as though we should eat exclusively for six months, and drink exclusively for the other six months of the year. What man requires is not an infrequent alternation of work and play, but a frequent alternation of occupations, each of which shall be work in itself and play to the other. The excursion-trains are to me only so many melancholy proofs that the English people at large have not learned to provide themselves with those recreative occupations which are accessible in one shape or another to the meanest and the poor-

est.   If they had, they would not be driven to such a wretched
device for filling their holidays as a whirl from one place to another, and a whirl back.   They learn nothing by it, they enjoy
nothing, and they add nothing to themselves morally or physi-
cally.   As for " fresh air," that is a mere delusion invented by
enterprising directors, for it may be had as fresh in Kensing-
ton Gardens or on Hampstead Heath as anywhere in the world.

*   *   *   *   *   *

August 18.

The Sunday is a shockingly misrepresented day with us.
People seem to imagine that those particular twenty-four
hours which are embraced in that name have a character and
claims different from other hours, as though we had been told
that the Sabbath-day was in itself holy, instead of being told
to " keep" it holy, which is very different and more difficult.
If there were anything holy in the Sabbath itself, it is manifest
that the apostles could not have ventured to change its incidence
as they did from Saturday to Sunday, nor should we have learned
that it was made for man and not man for it.   The real truth
about it is that we are bound in an especial manner to do on
that day the duty which we are also bound to do on other
days, and especially to keep ourselves in a sense of the higher
law, which we should never forget.   The real Sabbath-breaker
is the man who premeditatedly seeks to lower his intelligence
and to brutalize himself by absolute inaction ; the true Sab-
bath-keeper is he who so uses the first day of the week as to fit
himself more truly for the work of the succeeding six.   The
man of sordid occupations should then seek to elevate his ideas
by any means that are at hand, whether by church, by private
devotion, or the improving converse of friends.   For the converse of friends well chosen is perhaps the most elevating
agency in life, which is one reason why we should all be careful so to choose them on week-days that they shall be available
for Sundays.

*   *   *   *   *   *

We were discussing the weather this morning, and wondering whether of the two, the sky which looked threatening, or the barometer which was most encouraging, would prove right. Some of the best weather prophets were of one opinion, some of another, until at last a mere boatman declared with an un-wavering tone of authority, that " it was all for fine weather." Upon which all the prophets at once put to sea.

The wise men make the fools. For whenever a fool comes to look at a wise man, he finds so little difference between that man and himself that it seems barely worth while to seek for wisdom. And when he comes to look at two wise men and finds that all their wisdom only makes them disagree the more, then he feels certain that the only safety lies in absolute folly. But if now he lights upon a wise man either not wise enough or not honest enough to admit that he, too, is fallible, then the fool will stand by him to the death.

*   *   *   *   *   *

I remember to have seen somewhere the remark that since in all honest proceedings the child, the madman, and the absent are always allowed, when their interests are at stake, to be rep-resented by a person required to act not upon their judgment but upon his own, therefore " the people," which is always at once childish, mad, and absent, ought really to be allowed no influence over the acts of their representative. And this is true. And what must, therefore, be equally true is that when the people themselves choose one to represent them, he is not unlikely to be as they are, either childish, mad, or absent, when their interests are at stake. We must be a wonderful nation whose representatives are never either one of those three.

CHAPTER XVI.

St. Peter's, Guernsey, 20th August.

I think I never conceived so great a disgust for any place as, upon my first view, I have for this. I believe I am not difficult to please. I do not hate Ratcliff Highway, I am positively fond of Wapping, and even the region of Belgrave Square has some pleasant memories for me. But this place is merely revolting, and though I have been here barely two hours, I have seen more vulgarity without manliness, more venality without object, more immodesty without passion, than I should have thought existed anywhere—the whole utterly unredeemed by any spark of those higher fires which sometimes sweeten the most ignoble smoulderings. My disgust began before I set foot on the shore. Of course, in a place where the paternal system of compulsory pilotage exists, I knew I should never get a pilot. No one of us on board the Billy Baby had ever been near the Channel Islands before, so to ease my conscience I hoisted my jack, and positively when I had blundered in my own way through the Little Russel and was in the act of dropping my anchor in these roads, a creature had the assurance to board me and to announce that *he* was the pilot. I promptly showed him over the side, and was doubly aggrieved to find that he had not self-respect enough even to fight the question, and that he proposed I should " give him a trifle" and say no more about it. Then I went ashore, and was immediately confronted by the most incredible statue of a gentleman in the short trunks, silk tights, and buff boots of a transpontine villain, inscribed " Albert, Prince Consort," just as though one should write " Blanc-Bec, Esquire"; then I was reduced to dine at an hotel, and I was more hurt than ever to find that the repast was provided for and with creatures who comported themselves precisely in the same way as though they had been fashionable London people feeding themselves through two hours of boredom. I thought as I looked at them how exactly I could match them all out of the superior circles, and in the end I left them just as one linen draper's assistant was beginning, under the influence of bottled stout, to thaw to the other ; only to find, on returning to my ship, that it has already been invaded by touts for the sale of every kind of contraband produce under the sun. I shall not stay here long.

    *   *   *   *   *   *

The Little Russel, if we had no chart of it, is a charming, picturesque channel at high water, but when the tide is out, to see all those terrible jagged rocks appear, and to remember how one came past them with a four-knot tide, suggests to one a notion of the day of judgment in a very lively manner.

If any ten men in London were to tell all they knew, they would blow the roofs off half the houses in Mayfair. Let anybody hold the frightful review of the secrets that have come across him in the course of even a short and ordinary life, and think what would be the result if only one or two of them were known as he knows them, and he will admire the power of absolute forgetfulness shown by people who bear themselves as though there were no secrets in the world. Nor, indeed, are there so long as they remain secrets ; but it is terrible to think how many there are whose whole existence hangs upon the safe custody of a letter or the tongue of a servant.

*   *   *   *   *   *

Ned lay aloft this morning in a strong wind and a nasty sea to lace the topsail to the mast, and Tom and Bill were so unhandy at the halyards that he got into trouble with the sail before he had laced two holes. He shouted to them again and again ; they did less and less what was required, and at last he, with blundering which is the mark of a smart man, dived headlong into a sea of very strong imprecations affecting their eyes and their morality. This moved them and relieved him, and in two minutes more the topsail was laced.

*   *   *   *   *   *

Of all the developments of faith, I think there is none at all comparable to the belief that every man has in his own ship. There never was and never will be such a vessel on the seas as this particular one that he commands or sails in. Its merits are greater merits of a greater kind than ever before were known ; its defects are only so many merits in disguise. She is

not a good sea-boat, but the pace she sails is incredible ; she is
not fast, but she would drown a good many of them in a bad
sea ; she won't hang to wind, but none of them can touch her
running ; she doesn't run very well, but she'll turn to windward in a way that would surprise you—and so forth.   I over-
heard Ned imparting to a Guernsey fisherman, in a careless
way, the information that we generally got eight *or ten* knots
out of the Billy Baby, and that we had never taken a pint of
water on board, though we had been out in every kind of
weather.   I can quite understand the men who went to sea on
a slab of marble.   I am sure they held it for the finest craft
that ever floated.

Beliefs, I take it, are originated never in evidence, nor even
on what are called reasonable grounds, but solely in their apparent profit.   I believe in this woman because I love her, and
I don't believe in any other, because I love no other.   I believe in my ship because I sail in her, and don't like to think
she will go with me to the bottom.   In each and every case the
necessity or the desire for the belief is the foundation of it.
If there were any apparent pleasure or profit to be derived from
believing that the sun went round the earth, we should all believe it most thoroughly.

*   *   *   *   *   *

St. Helier's, Jersey, 22d August.

" Which do you prefer, Jersey or Guernsey ?"

" I have only been to Guernsey, and I prefer Jersey."

Something of this kind must, I imagine, be at the bottom of
the preference entertained by many reasonable men for infinite
as compared with finite existence.   They only know time,
and so they prefer eternity.   Perhaps, if somebody were to come
back from eternity, they would prefer time.

Thus I said yesterday, but now having come to Jersey, I
prefer Guernsey.   On the whole, if it were not for the excitement of picking up unknown rocks from the chart and the
jumps involved in the chance of being contrariwise picked up

by them, it would not be worth while to make the acquaintance of the Channel Islands even without a pilot.   They seem
to be the resort of the British rough, the rendezvous of the un-
relieved excursionist, and the home of the drunkard.   There is
a statue of one of the Georges out of his shirt-sleeves ; there
are the cheapest and nastiest cigars, spirits, and walking-sticks
in Europe ; there are soldier-officers in uniform and jaunting-
cars making perpetual tours round the island.   If Tottenham
Court Road were swept into one basket together with Seven
Dials, the Haymarket, Plymouth Hard, and the Boulevard des
Batignolles, and the whole were emptied on the nearest rock
off the coast of Spain, the result would be Jersey.   It is the
kind of place to which a philosopher might come to drink himself to death at slight expense and without any risk of regretting those he left behind.   As for getting to it, the coast is so
stuck about with rocks and the tides run so strong and so many
ways at once, that nothing but a most thorough contempt for
the works of nature could give anything like confidence among
them.

*   *   *   *   *

CHAPTER XVII.

Anse du Solidor, St. Malo, 25th August, 1874.

As the only available pilot for St. Malo to be had in Jersey
was incapably drunk, and likely to remain so for several days,
I was in any case under the necessity of finding my own way
here.   I had no chart of the port large enough to be of any
use, but I succeeded at last in buying an old one at a Jersey
public-house.   Its one recommendation was that it only cost
sixpence, and that, although fifty-two years old, it was certain
to be good for everything except new marks, since rocks don't
alter like sands.   Armed with this I left St. Helier's at high-
water, came round the Minquiers, which even at that time

showed black heads enough above water to frighten one, and at last found myself outside that insane puzzle of rocks which makes St. Malo so difficult of approach. What with the Couchées, the Plate, the Pierre aux Normands, the Roche aux Anglais, the Crapauds du Bey, and some hundreds of other rocks, all newly marked, and all therefore only to be avoided by compass-bearings and allowance for the set of the tide, we passed rather an excited hour while winding our way through ; but the pleasure of getting through and of letting go the anchor in this charming little corner was but the greater, and the more calculated to make one forswear all pilots and their works for all time to come. On examination I find that five new lights have been lit and some sixty new marks laid down since my chart was printed ; and herein I recognize the constant policy of pilotage authorities in all countries—which is to be continually changing the marks as much as possible, so that none but their own experts shall know them. Their principle is that a stranger who doesn't take one of their pilots deserves to be lost.

* * * * * *

ANSE DU SOLIDOR, 26th August.

St. Malo is, I think, of all the towns I have seen, that which has most completely preserved the character of the Middle Ages. You have but to look at it from the roads to see that it is the work of a hardy race, obstinate, laborious, narrow-minded, believing, and pugnacious. The massive walls and quaint towers which gird the little rock-island on which it stands would make Von Moltke smile, and would even have been despised by Vauban ; but they are the enduring record of men who had more faith in what they did than to look merely to its overthrow, of men who built not in days for years, but in years for centuries. They loved their home too, for they crowded the houses on the narrow rock one above the other—one upon the other, one might almost say—and rather than leave it, piled story upon story, till hands could be shaken across the narrow streets at break-neck height. It is a living bit of Callot. And when you enter the town, you feel as though you had left three centuries behind you. The almost entire absence of wheeled traffic, the blessed want of gas-glare, plate-glass and *articles de Paris*, the deep tortuous streets, the surprising irregular corners and the impossible differences of level, belong so entirely to other times that one expects at every turn to meet a company of partisans, a guild of artisans, or a bevy of richer burghers not ashamed to wear finer clothes than the rabble, and to hear the question discussed whether the Malouins had not best sally forth against the English trader, or whether they should abandon the League for Henri IV. There are few persons of fashion or pretence to be seen, there are no big new hotels, and everybody appears to go to bed at nine o'clock, for by that time the streets are deserted. Add to this that the people are ugly, and it becomes manifest that St. Malo is a very chosen spot.

*   *   *   *   *   *

St. Malo, 26th August.

I find that the great dainty here is our old friend the dreaded pieuvre or octopus. It is known to the Malouins as the " Minard," and at this time of year, when he has grown to a considerable size, it is the great amusement of the boys to hunt him. I saw two caught to-day on the rocks, and was not a little edified to discover that in spite of Victor Hugo the boys were not in the least afraid to handle the ugly monster. They fish him out of the water with a boat-hook, and then—tearing him away from the boat, to which he clings with all his suckers—plunge their hand into the middle of him, and in the twinkling of an eye turn his peculiar membranous bag inside out. The effect of this is to render him instantly powerless, and thenceforth they handle him without fear of his strong bird-like beak, and dash him to death against the rocks. Then having washed him clean of the inky liquid with which he troubles the water when fishing on his own account, they beat him to a jelly, peel off the dark skin, cook him with vinegar, and eat him cold like a lobster, or even pickle him for the winter. He

is esteemed a very great delicacy ; so much so that his market
price is five sous, which is a large sum in these parts. I am
told that he is when alive particularly fond of shell-fish, which
he breaks open and eats with his powerful beak, and that by the
end of the summer he is often found with limbs three or four
feet long. No doubt he leads a fine, lawless, filibustering life ;
and no doubt, too, that he is held for a very gallant, handsome
fellow by the females of his kind, who, if one could but get at
their sentiments, would probably regard men as the most loath-
some creatures of the universe.

In the greater number of cases of love-making between any
two given people it will be found that one of the two has no
kind of reasonable excuse for being in love at all. And it will
commonly also be found, if the history of the affair be examined, that that one has indeed *not* fallen in love, but has merely
become reconciled to the other, sometimes even in mere self-
defence—just as one would become reconciled to the Chimæra
if one had one's attention fixed by it for a certain time. Put
any dull man and woman together in a dull place, and the
duller one of the two will certainly make advances for the mere
occupation ; whereupon the less dull must either fly or else first
notice, then endure, and finally be reconciled, however bad the
bargain may be. There is no other history than this of love-
making of any ordinary type.

*   *   *   *   *   *

DINAN, August 28.

Dinan is even more striking, more picturesque, and more
thoroughly smacking of the Middle Ages than St. Malo. The
monasteries, some ruined and some converted to new uses, the
walls turned into gardens, the tortuous lanes, full of fifteenth-
century houses, shallow-storied, and pushing their massive carved
beams into the street over deep porticos, the beetling tower-
crowned heights plunging down clean into the depth where the
Rance is embroidered like a silver thread on a green bed of
verdure, the homely dress and manners—nay, the very purity

and price of butter and bread—all announce a favored spot not yet deflowered by the railway. It is just the place where a tired man would love to rest, and to plant himself down never to move again.

I learn that the agricultural laborers about here eat meat daily. A common shipwright, who has repaired my boat, tells me that his father paid a hundred pounds to buy him off from the army when he drew a *mauvais numéro*. Now, we know that the laborers of Essex and Suffolk scarcely ever see meat ; and we know, too, that there are no shipwrights in England whose fathers could produce a hundred pounds. Manifestly, therefore, there must be something very wicked and opposed to the designs of Providence in a country capable of producing phenomena so entirely against the order of nature. Probably that is why all England does not come to settle at Dinan.

*   *   *   *   *   *

St. Malo, 29th August.

> A curdled sky and mares' tails
> Make lofty ships carry low sails,

is a saw I much respect, and I was somewhat exercised on going on deck at six this morning to find, although there was then but a moderate breeze blowing, a very thick curdle mantling up from the south-west, and all the overhead clouds torn into fine hair-like wisps drawn away in various directions, as though the firmament had been cross-hatched with delicate brushes. I had intended to start with the first of the ebb ; but seeing this, and seeing, too, that the glass had fallen nearly two tenths, I so far temporized as to go ashore and buy provisions. By seven the wind had considerably increased. I learned, moreover, that a schooner which went out yesterday was forced to put back, and reports very bad weather and much sea outside, added to which we are at the worst of the spring-tides, which having here a rise and fall of forty feet, and a velocity of from four to seven knots in all directions at once, are not to be trifled with. Finally, to decide the matter, it has begun to rain in torrents, which renders everything invisible ; and it is therefore with the most self-approving conviction of being quite right that I resolve to give it another day or two, all the more so that this is the most delightful of anchorages, in which it must be a real pleasure to ride out a good blow.

I can quite understand that continually recurring phenomenon of men going calmly to be hanged, when once it has been decided beyond hope of recall that they *are* to be hanged. The disquieting period in all matters is the period of indecision : but when once you have made up your mind to a given course, no matter how disagreeable that course may be, you are happy. That is probably what makes us all so eager to run into the first decision at hand, rather than face the wear and tear and worry of thinking over all the decisions possible, until we have arrived at the best. And yet philosophers and moralists who preach, nay, and even novelists who describe, all affect to deal with men and to treat of them as though they were reasonable creatures, who thought out everything to the bottom, and acted upon a calm selection of courses.

*   *   *   *   *   *

ST. MALO, 30th August.

I saw to-day a blind man led by a dog passing through the crowd of holiday-makers, and asking in a piteous song for charity. He was a terrible spectacle, miserable beyond expression; and I think nobody could have looked at him without compassion. But nobody would look at him, and he went from one end of the promenade to the other without receiving a glance or a sou. Shortly afterward there arrived another blind man. He was nothing like so pitiable as the first—he had none of the same look of abject wretchedness, none of the same hopeless, dragging gait, but seemed rather one who felt that he had been provided by nature with an honorable and remunerative profession. He was led, not by a dog, but by a pertinacious boy, who haled him about to confront every creature within reach, appealing to all with the same set whine, and reporting to his chief, *sotto voce* and in natural tones, the result of his appeals, thus : " Ayez pitié d'un malheureux aveugle (rien) ;" " ayez pitie d'un malheureux aveugle (trois sous !) ;" " ayez pitiè— (g'n y a pas de monde—à gauche) ;" " ayez pitié," and so forth.* Coppers and even silver pieces fell into his hat from the hands of well-nigh everybody ; whereupon I reflected that, although many of us do our alms without a great desire to be seen of men, still we do like to be seen at least of that man to whom the alms are given ; also, that possibly there may be less reproach conveyed in the look of a dog at the obdurate alms-withholder, than in the look of a pertinacious boy ; and finally, that a dog is more easily avoided than a boy.

From time to time it occurs to the common people of England that they are miserably off, and they come cap in hand humbly enough to their masters, the superior classes in Parliament assembled, and in Ministers incarnate, begging for some alleviation of their misery. Not very long ago, pressed harder even than usual by famine, they prayed for cheap bread, and certain pertinacious boys from the manufacturing districts, perceiving that cheaper bread meant cheaper labor and larger profits, took them in hand, and led them about wailing till they got it. Now, in these latter days, the same people have asked for wages that will enable them to keep body and soul together ; but as higher wages mean dearer labor, less profits, and even lower rents, no pertinacious boy has been found willing to play godfather to such a prayer. And so, while all manufacturers are increasing their profits, the common people are paternally advised to make themselves scarce, and to try whether haply some other hemisphere will afford them beef and beer, now that England is too poor to give them anything beyond bread and tea.

*　　*　　*　　*　　*　　*

* " Have pity with an unhappy blind man (nothing) ;" " have pity with an unhappy blind man (three sous !) ;" " have pity—(there is nobody—to the left) ;" " have pity," etc.

The Municipal authorities of St. Malo are very intelligent. They have discovered that from time to time a celestial body, vulgarly known as the moon, shines during a portion of the night; and having also discovered that the nights of its shining can be foretold beforehand, they have come to the conclusion that it would be a profligate extravagance to light their few gas-lamps on such nights. Accordingly they do not light them.

But what they have not yet discovered is, that there are such objects in nature as clouds, and that they sometimes so come between the earth and the moon as to conceal it even from St. Malo ; so that the inhabitants sometimes walk over the quay, under the impression that they are walking into their houses.

I always hear with impatience this common colloquy between masters and servants, or superiors in general and their subordinates. " Why did you do this ?" they ask.—" Well, I thought so-and-so."—" Think ! *You shouldn't think*, but do as I tell you," etc., etc. Whereas, what is wanted is that they should think not less but more—in fact, they should think sufficiently for the occasion.

*   *   *   *   *   *

CHAPTER XVIII.

OFF LES HÉAUX DE BRÉHAT,

2d September, 1874.

I HAVE just had one of those frights which are so delightful when one looks back at them, and so very much the reverse while they last. I had become tired of waiting for the weather to settle, and this morning came out of St. Malo through the *Décollé* channel, bound to round the Land's End if the wind would hold in the southwest—or elsewhere if it would not. Now in my way lay those two well-known patches of rock, the Roches Douvres and the Barnouic, the nearest road lying inside and the usual and safer outside them. Naturally, I chose the inside road. There was a considerable deal of wind, and so much sea that, some five hours after leaving St. Malo, I put on my boots, and battened down. But I had no doubt as to my course—probably all the less because I had never been in those parts before. I passed the beacon of *Léjon,* and soon after made what I supposed to be the beacon on the *Horaine* rocks, which I meant to leave on my port, or left hand, at a fair distance, so as to go between them and the Barnouic ledge. Imagine now my horror and my indignation, when Ned announced that he saw *another beacon* ahead on the starboard, or right hand, where no beacon should be according to the charts and the sailing directions. The two ghosts were nothing to this. There it was sure enough, and now the question was whether we were not too far in with the land, and whether this outer, or right-hand beacon, was not the *Horaine,* which was to be left on the left hand. The uncertainty of the situation was only increased by the discovery I thought I then made, that the beacon previously supposed to be the Horaine was not a beacon at all, but a lighthouse. There was then half a gale of wind blowing, and a high sea running full in with the whole sweep of the Atlantic. We were going a great pace, and if we *were* wrong it was a question of another life. I was horribly frightened, and thanks to the lively capers of the Billy Baby, not a little uncomfortable. But I reckoned that with such a sea rocks dangerous to us must show themselves, so I sent Ned to the masthead. He reported breakers on both sides, but none ahead, so I jumped to the conclusion that the inexplicable beacon must be a new one recently placed on the Barnouic ledge, and that we were right as we were going. At any rate I kept on, and I have now at last got the beacon—or as I have now decided it must be, the Héaux lighthouse—on such a bearing that, whatever it is, we must be through the dangers. The glass is going steadily down, and the wind

steadily up, but when once I get clear of the land I don't care.
Much against my own private inclinations, and purely out of a
mean desire to keep up my reputation with Bill, I have made
believe to dine. I trust it will be set down to my credit, as a
great action when all accounts are made up.

A wonderful relief, indeed, is it to feel that one has the
blessed open sea before one, after getting clear of land and
rocks laid out in such a Chinese puzzle as these. I think that
not even the delight of getting safe in is equal to that of getting safe out ; and yet there are those who fancy that the
troubles and anxieties of seafaring diminish as the seaman ap-
proaches the coast—as though ships were commonly lost at sea,
and not on the land.

*   *   *   *   *   *

FALMOUTH, 3d September.

We have had a shocking bad day. Everybody and everything on board the Billy Baby is wet through ; the rain has
come down in one sheet since six o'clock this morning, the
wind has been blowing all round the compass, and the sky has
lain upon us in one dull leaden sheet that one could feel on the
top of one's head. When the wind finally got round to north,
I did not see my way at all round the Land's End, and determined to run into this port and to wait for orders. The port is full
of vessels, for it is one of those, dear to the seaman, by which
Nature herself has marked out England for a maritime nation,
even more distinctly than by surrounding her with seas. Easy
of entry, always accessible, and offering secure shelter to any
number of vessels of any size, it has proved a blessed haven to
many a mariner coming in from the ocean, and it is now more
than ever a favorite port of arrival and departure for vessels engaged in long voyages.

It is curious enough that, in those days of old when (as the
hackneyed writers would have us believe) England was a
thoroughly poor and barbarous country, the great man's house
and table were open to all comers, and that all those who held

themselves to be of the superior or lordly classes made it their pride, as they held it to be their duty, to receive every homeless hungry man who came to them. This has all been mended, for we have come to see that the possession of the good things of the earth involves no obligation toward those who do not possess them. We have learned from an ecstatic contemplation of the blessed principle of self-interest that the one sacred principle in which alone there is hope for mankind is that each should acquire all he possibly can, and be approved and defended in its retention against all comers. On the land every inch is taken up from the centre of the earth to the zenith of the heavens, so that the landless man can only stand, walk, breathe, and have the light of the sun, moon, and stars (for they too presumably belong to the landowner in whose zenith for the moment they are) on sufferance. There is therefore this delight in being at sea, that here at least one is not yet a trespasser. But how long will this last? How long will it be before the blessed inventions of civilization and property freed from obligations are extended to the waters also? How long will it be before a nation which has closed its doors against the shelterless and the distressed wayfarer closes its ports against the shelterless and distressed mariner? Is there any difference in the nature of the duties of humanity due to each? I see none. By a few gradations the thing may be done on the water precisely as it has been done on the land. The ports are no man's absolute property now—no more was the land once. Like the land, they may be made absolute property. Then a system of out-of-port relief may be framed for the distressed mariner ; finally, one or two great ports may be created, into which he may be allowed to come on condition of abandoning his ship. And then those of us who are lucky enough to get possession of one of the old ports once open to all, may enjoy our waters in peace, and sail placidly about them, fishing their carefully preserved depths in our yachts, with such friends as we may choose to invite or such indifferent persons as may be able to pay the price we set upon entry.

Meantime, and as some little step in the right direction, the Solent should be cleared of merchantmen just as the Park has been cleared of cabs, and should be maintained strictly for pleasure-craft, with a force of gun-boats to secure the select from the accidents incidental to unskilful navigation.

*　　*　　*　　*　　*　　*

4th September.

It is a melancholy fact that anything is believed to be good enough for sailors. And Falmouth being frequented exclusively by sailors affords a very melancholy example of that belief. So much trash, trumpery, slop, and shoddy were never exposed in shops as are here brought together for presentation to the admiring eye of the advance-noted seaman. Tarpaulin hats, yellow water-proofs, sea mittens, long boots, tinned meats, strings of onions, rings, trinkets, and watches, all made most conscientiously to sell, are paraded from one end of the long street to the other, and from one end to the other offer to the landsman's eye a humiliating array of fifteenth-class wares. Not so does the sailor regard them. Nothing will tear Bill away from a certain collection of cheap finery, and I am certain the reason he was so long after my letters this morning was that he was engaged in some stupendous sacrifice of wages on the shrine of the being he adores.

*　　*　　*　　*　　*　　*

LATITUDE 51° 20′ 19″ N., 5th September.

I left Falmouth yesterday morning at ten, rounded the Long-ships at midnight in company with a whole fleet of steamers and sailing vessels, some with lights and some without, and turned in for a sleep with the comfortable knowledge that we were safe at sea again. On a careful study of the tides I had worked out and set the most scientific series of courses; they have been faithfully sailed; the distances are recorded to a quarter of a mile; and yet now after making up my day's work I find that on a run of seventy-six miles I am put nearly two miles further north by observation than I am made to be by my dead reckoning. And as both are probably in error, and may be in error in contrary ways, I can't rely upon being within at least four miles of a given parallel of latitude. So that if I went on at the same rate for seven thousand miles I might accumulate an uncertainty of four hundred miles. But seamen have a simple way of accounting for differences between the position of a vessel as ascertained by dead reckoning and as ascertained by observation—which is to set it down to " current," and thus they wipe out all mistakes and make themselves right every day at twelve o'clock. A comfortable proceeding, yet which must not be too thoroughly relied upon, as one would think ; and one which I, who am supposed to know and to have allowed for the current, ought not to have to resort to. But in fact you cannot know currents except within certain very narrow limits, and between the Land's End and the Bristol Channel they have a bad habit of setting in various directions at various rates, and in any event we can't go on long without making something and acquiring a certainty, the continual possibility of doing which is after all the sole advantage of coasting. Charts in general are very deficient in information as to the set of the tides. The French charts give no indications whatever of it, and the English, though better, are not at all complete in this respect. Another point which really calls for attention is the ambiguity and amphibology of the official sailing directions. They continually give you as leading marks objects not specified on the charts, which render the marks practically no marks at all. For instance I am told that " Godolphin hill in line with Carndu point leads two thirds of a mile south-east of the Runnel stone," but as neither Godolphin hill nor Carndu point are to be found on the chart, I am no better off than I was before. The directions should be collated with the charts to be intelligible, for on a coast one sees for the first time it is often difficult enough to pick out a given windmill, a given house, or a given clump of trees, even when they *are* laid down on the chart. The directions are

full, too, of the most insane English, and of sentences which
assert precisely the reverse of what they are presumably intended to convey. Here are some which I have come across
quite casually. Writing of the leading marks for the Bristol
Channel, the author says : " Few of those formerly given
can now be recognized, and are otherwise inapplicable from
the alterations along the channels." The second allegation
here is that few of the marks are " inapplicable," whereas the
meaning presumably is that few are applicable. Then in the
directions for the east coast of Ireland I read that certain
landmarks " were erected for the purpose of enabling vessels
to readily distinguish between Tramore Bay and the entrance
to Waterford Harbor, a mistake that has been fatal to a great
many vessels ;" the sense of which is that the mistake of readily distinguishing this difference has been fatal ! These are
mere specimens of the confused and misleading writing that
occurs at nearly every page of books which it is absolutely essential should be plainly and clearly written, and which, indeed, there is no excuse for writing otherwise. I would pray
the Hydrographic Office to have all their works carefully edited
by somebody possessing that rarest of all accomplishments, the
power of writing plain things in plain English, and I am sure
everybody in the trade will agree with me.

*   *   *   *   *   *

WATERFORD, 8th September.

Sailing yesterday up this beautiful river, seeing the smiling
green uplands and the distant purple mountains on each side of
me, and answering the many boatmen who came alongside to
ask if " my anner" wanted a pilot, I thought mournfully of
the system of Government which has reduced people in our
English island to wish that this our Irish one might be un-
loosed from her moorings in the deep and set two thousand
miles farther away in the Atlantic. And the people of
the country, as one comes into contact with them, only
add to the melancholy of that thought ; while the nature of
the rule under which they live shows that it is really enter-

tained. Dirty, laborious, half-clad, half-fed, gay, mirthful, helpful, and servile withal, these poor Irish bear the character of the slave written in plain characters upon them. And on every side is the evidence that the Imperial rule is still one of force—only endured, but never yet accepted. The police walk not singly, but by twos in the streets—consider what that means—they occupy every railway-station, they are armed with sword-bayonets. No English minister—not even now, after Irish Church Bills and Land Bills—would venture to allow the formation of Irish volunteer corps. Surely here, too, is another series of facts calculated to make us suspect that the blessed system of government under which we live is not so perfect nor even so ingenious after all that has been said of it. For it rests not upon its own merits, but solely upon force, here in the only one of the British islands of which the people still require rule of any kind. I met to-day Miles-na-Coppaleen disguised as a car-driver, and as he was driving me about I asked him if there were any Fenians still in Ireland. " Bedad, sir," said he, " they say there's a good many av em—but you niver know who is and who isn't." " Are you a Fenian ?"—" I wouldn't be bowld to be one av I wanted (go an, Kathleen !) ; there's divil a man ye can thrust (go an !), no, nor woman either—ye know that, yer anner."

*　　　*　　　*　　　*　　　*　　　*

CHAPTER XIX.

Off the Hook, 12th September.

There is much of the Neapolitan in these Irish, much of the same impossibly ragged mind and clothing, much of the same caressing tone and language, much too of the same disregard for facts, and withal most of the qualities of an enslaved race. " May the blessing of God follow yer anner ; sure now, you'll give me something just to keep the childer from starvin'—*for*

your welcome to poor ould Ireland." This was said to me up
the country, and who could resist the appeal of a woman who
had taken sufficient notice of one to discover or to guess that
one was here for the first time? For say what we may, we
do all value the attention of our fellow-creatures—even of a
beggar-woman.

There is a blind beggar who stands on the way to the railway station here. As I passed him this morning, he said,
" Dhrop a copper into a poor man's hat." To see the effect,
I dropped a shilling, which on fingering he recognized immediately. " Good luck to your anner," said he, " and may
the blessings," etc., etc. " Sure an' it's the first piece of
silver I've touched for a month."—" Come now," I remonstrated, " say a week."—" No, by the holy Sire, it's mor'n
a month. May the blessings," etc. Now, coming back
from the station, I was met by the same appeal, and this time
I dropped a sixpence into the outstretched hat. " Long life
to your anner, it's the first bit o' silver I've touched for a
week," exclaimed the old sinner in the accents of the purest
truth and the deepest gratitude.—" Why, you humbug, I gave
you a shilling myself this morning." His face underwent a
change, but he instantly answered in a deprecating tone, " Are
you the gintleman that gave me the shilling; *sure now, why
didn't you say so, and I wouldn't have towld the lie?*" This
pleased me much.

In contrast to this was the last Irishman we spoke. He
came alongside in a boat—a fine fellow—with a certain sturdy
look about his face only just tempered by a bright, twinkling,
untrustworthy eye. After the usual marine talk had made us
the friends all men seem to be on the water, " Are you a
Fenian?" said I.—" Begorra, and I am in my heart,"
replied he, " but hwhat's the use?"—" Well," I returned, to
draw him, " if I were an Irishman, I think I should be a Fenian."—" Divil a fear of your being a Faynian, you've got too
much money. God send you a lucky passage anyhow." And
with this he lay down to his sculls and left us.

*   *   *   *   *   *

It is surprising how a solitary vagabond life grows upon one. I left Waterford last night intending to go round the Land's End again, and so away to the eastward, and now, when half-way there, I find myself debating whether I shall not rather run across to Ushant, and work down through the French ports on the Bay to the north of Spain, and thence through the Straits to the Mediterranean. The weather is enough to tempt one to go anywhere from this advantageous position, so well to the westward. The barometer is steadily rising, a fine northerly breeze is blowing, and though exposed here to the whole range of the Atlantic, one is only aware of it through the long gentle swell which always rolls in, and over which the Billy Baby rides like a duck. It is a splendid opportunity to go south, and in all probability the last there will be before the equinoctial gales set in, and I feel much inclined to let everything slide and seize it. But even the least important of us has what he thinks important engagements surrounding him in that network which we all seem bent on contriving to take away our liberties ; and I, too, alas ! have retained more or less of the notion that I ought to be in certain places at certain times. Wherefore I suppose I ought to carry out my original plan, and once more leave aside all tempting projects of distant voyage. Yet in weather like this it is a horror only to think of going back to London and winter when Italy and summer are practically so near, and when one is over the threshold as it were. There is only this consolation, that like all unendurable things and men, even London and its inhabitants have qualities when once one has made up one's mind to frequent them.

*   *   *   *   *   *

At Sea, 13th September.

I don't know that I ever felt more satisfaction with myself than I did to-day after giving Ned his first lesson in navigation, and acquiring the certainty that he really knew what a

zenith distance was. In presenting to him this entirely new
notion of taking the sun, and of doing such things with the
resulting figures as to bring out his latitude, I felt something
of what I fancy must be the missionary spirit, and experienced a real pleasure in watching his mind take the successive
steps from principle to inference, and from inference to calculation ; and what was most pleasing of all was to dog his intelligence as it moved, to see it amble gently along through the
mere acceptance of my propositions, then hesitate when it
came to the jump ; and finally, after many refusals, to have the
satisfaction of coaxing it over, and see it landed on the other
side. Instruction is commonly confounded with bald assertion on the one hand and blind belief on the other, and thus
understood it is a hideous process ; but it is one thing to tell a
child with authority that two and two make four, and another
thing to make a child understand the proposition, and adopt it
for itself. So, also, it is really interesting to find a man who
has no notion what an angle is, and to bring him at last to see
how it is that a sextant will measure an angle, and how he can
find his latitude by believing that there are three hundred and
sixty degrees in a circle, and that the angle of incidence is
equal to the angle of reflection, or by acting and calculating
as though he believed it. For one really must have faith
in mathematics at sea to that extent, contrariwise to faith
ashore, which never extends to acts, and still less to calculations. Yet I am told that somebody has discovered that the
angle of incidence is *not* equal to the angle of reflection, which,
if it be true, upsets all our instruments and all our acquired
facts. Moreover, I saw yesterday in an Irish paper a letter
from a gentleman in Dublin, who declares that he has found
the means of squaring the circle, which he says still further
upsets everything. It is very distressing. Perhaps nothing
at all is true, even in geometry, and perhaps, now that I fancy
I am steering a series of scientific courses which will take me
on a rhumb-line to the Longships, I am going quite another
road ; and, if so, what kind of responsibility have I not in-

curred toward Ned by teaching him my beliefs as articles of faith, and telling him nothing at all of those new discoveries?

*   *   *   *   *   *

OFF THE LONGSHIPS, 14th September.

Since we last passed this spot a Jersey brig was wrecked here in a southerly gale, and all hands lost but one, who was picked up by another vessel. It is certainly a nasty spot in bad weather, and it is not so long since the inhabitants of the coast believed that it had been specially made so by Providence in order to give them good opportunities of wrecking, often incidentally accompanied by the murder of any sailor ill-advised enough to be washed ashore with his cargo. These were very wicked people, affording the only instance on record of any beings not of superhuman rank taking away from him that hath not, even that which he hath.

*   *   *   *   *   *

AT SEA, Tuesday, 15th September.

It has been alleged that there exists a specific disease of the brain-tissue called "genius." And, like all allegations made with audacity, this has been repeated without inquiry until one might fancy there was something in it. Now I do not believe it. I regard it as one of those idle words that men speak, originally invented and subsequently adopted in order to excuse the disposition we all feel not to take any pains about anything in the universe. Let me be understood. I do not say that we are all equal in point of moral and intellectual quality; but I do say that there is none of us so immensely superior as to be able to produce work that thousands of others might not equally produce if they would only take the trouble. It is hardly necessary to say much in support of that proposition, for it seems to me capable of demonstration. As thus: Socrates, Bacon, Homer, Dante, Shakespeare, Michael Angelo, Reynolds, Richelieu, Sully, Cromwell, Goethe, Byron, are all of them men who are credited with this genius; and we of the meaner sort are accustomed to console ourselves for our inferiority by setting it down merely to the want of that divine spark which we call genius. But now how can the excellence of philosophy be recognized save by a philosopher, of poetry but by a poet, of art but by an artist, of statesmanship but by a statesman? Can any take the soundings of the sea who has not line enough to reach to the bottom? Can any appreciate the poet who has not all the poet's qualities, or the artist, or the statesman? I wot not. And so the fact that these poets, artists, and statesmen have been appreciated is sufficient to show that there have been many men endowed with their qualities, and who only have not thought, spoken, painted, carved, or acted. Here, then, lies the sole difference between the so-called man of genius and those who recognize him as such, of themselves and not upon mere hearsay—that the one has set himself to work while the others have been content to look on, having all the time the same qualities which, had they but had the courage, would have produced the like effects. It is no doubt very pleasant and consoling to believe that we have all pulled well up to the collar, and that if we have not stirred this huge machine behind us, it is because God has not given us strength to do it. To say that looks, too, so like modesty. But in fact it is mostly mere cowardice or idleness that prompts the conclusion. All men are not equal, but they are all very much more nearly equal than they affect to believe ; and though neither assertion is quite true, it is yet more nearly true to say that everybody can do everything than to say, as most do, that very few can do anything.

CHAPTER XX.

16th September, 1874.

I HAVE often asked myself which is the most pleasing stage in a successful love-making, whether the going forth to the encounter when as yet one knows not what one's fate will be in it ; the first encouragements, so slight and delicate as to be imperceptible to all but one's own eye ; the open avowal mutually given and received ; or the final admitted lover-state. The common theory is that this last stage is the best because it gives the least trouble and anxiety ; yet I should say that the first stage is by far better, precisely because it gives the most. There is something very delicious in the emotion of watching for the first movements of that particular woman who has taken one's fancy, and who is therefore for the time the one only woman in all the world ; something very absorbing in the eager watch one sets over every gesture, every glance of her eye, every turn of her head, every inflection of her voice, in order to surprise, if it be so, an indication of her feelings. All that disappears when once this stage is passed ; and when that last one of perfect understanding is reached, the whole interest of the matter subsides into, and is centred in, the mere question of fitness of companionship. Here, then, is a grand consolation for the unsuccessful lover, that much as he may, from a sense of decency, lament his failure to arrive at the last stages, he has yet in passing through the first reaped advantages which would have been diminished in exact proportion as he advanced toward success. For this also is true, that the whole delight of that insane passion lies in this—not that that woman loves you, but that you love her. That may stir your vanity, but this moves your very soul. So at least I am informed, and believe.

*   *   *   *   *   *

TROUVILLE, 20th September.

Whether it is better to love before marriage or after, whether it is possible to do both, or whether love is not in its nature a state of ecstatic self-mystification which cannot be lasting, is not dissimilar from that question whether the " provisoire" can be made " définitif," upon which everybody here is engaged. And it is not unimproving to discuss them all in the course of a long drive through a charming country, sitting opposite to two still more charming pairs of bright eyes belonging to as many "Impérialistes enragées." But what I can't comprehend is the admiration which all the hack journalists of Europe pretend to feel for the English system of government, and the readiness with which all readers seem to have adopted the complacent theory that any people that will starve quietly, and be miserable without revolution, is the happiest and best on the earth. And it is especially exasperating to hear that journalistic humbug repeated, and the superior natural prosperity of England cited as a proof of it in the midst of a country where the agricultural laborer eats meat every day. Two points at least the French have of superiority to us—that love of justice which implies hatred of crime, and which makes even my fair friends declared haters of Bazaine, and that spirit of courtesy which is based upon the respect that mankind owes to each other, and which makes this famous Marshal stand, at seventy, hat in hand, talking to them with all the manner of a deferential dancing-master. There is hope for a nation that still believes in justice and politeness (which is but a kind of justice) ; there is none for a nation which habitually excuses great crime from punishment, and makes bad manners an article of faith.

*　　*　　*　　*　　*　　*

TROUVILLE, 23d September.

The sun has crossed the line to-day, and henceforth we go down-hill in the year toward cold, darkness and bad weather. I always fancy that one lives a whole life in each year, and, just as every May I feel young, lusty, and full of purpose, so at this time I feel old, worn-out, and discouraged. It has been found by poets and philosophers, and even by metaphysicians and grammarians, an admirable provision which has supplied us in the objects and movements of the universe with an analogy for everything with which the mind of man can possibly occupy itself. We have assumed, possibly from mere ignorance, to divide ourselves into the two departments

—material and spiritual ; but it is sufficiently remarkable that when we wish to be really intelligible either to ourselves or to others we always find ourselves, in speaking of the spiritual, driven back upon the material for our illustrations, and thus forced to admit that there is a close analogy between the two —an analogy, indeed, so close that it is hard to say whether it be not identity.

*   *   *   *   *   *

I have been to breakfast in one of the many mansions of William the Conqueror, and I have been glad, so far, to make his acquaintance, because I believe him to have been very hardly treated by the historians, and to have been perfectly justified in asserting his right against the perjured and usurping Harold. I was shown a chair (of the time of Louis XIII.!), which belonged to him, and I have come back doubting more than ever whether the condition of mankind has really been improved since the barbarous times we are taught so much to despise. My quarrel with civilization, as it is called, is that it is a failure in material matters ; that it has not made men in general to be better clothed, better fed, and better housed ; that it has not diminished in general by one atom, but rather increased, the burden of labor. Yet, if this be so, civilization has not kept the least of its promises. How it has kept the greater, those may judge who are able to see how thoroughly all sense of law has been lost, and what ready victims men have become to the most egregious and manifest swindles

*   *   *   *   *   *

TROUVILLE, 29th September.

I have been very lucky to-day. I have managed to run a steamer ashore by sturdily refusing to give way to her as I was painfully entering the port ; I have had a most improving conversation with some English oyster dredgers ; and I have seen at least a score of perfectly-dressed women. All this shows that one should take one's own course. The English fishermen start with fewer advantages than the French in the oyster fishery, yet they are far better at it ; French women start with fewer advantages than English in dressing, yet they are far better at that.   One principal reason is that each woman dresses herself, instead of all being dressed to one pattern by the Fashion.   For instance, instead of there being, as in England, one only hat, I have already seen here almost as many hats as women.   There is one especially which fascinates me —a round flat sailor's hat, with roses round it, stuck saucily on the very back of the head.   And, dear me, what a number of pretty people there are here still !

I am exercised to find at Trouville a fine marble pedestal, inscribed, " Au duc de Morny la ville de Deauville."   The statue once presumably surmounting this pedestal has been removed, which makes the inscription comic, and affords yet another proof that emperors, kings, and others who assume the right to give names, are not the fountains of honor, except in a purely declaratory sense.   They may put the whole machinery of the State in motion to tack a title of honor to a man ; they may consecrate it by laws and support it by armies ; but if the quality of honor is not in the man the title means nothing, and will be totally ignored or, what is worse, despised.   It is not in the power of any potentate to take a stockjobbing chapman, a cheating tradesman, or a swindler of any kind, and to make him be received by the world as a *dux* or leader of men. When a Sovereign takes such an one and declares solemnly, " This is a master-man, an earl, a count, a duke, by so much superior to all you others, and by so much the more entitled to your respect," it is not well either for the selected one or for the Sovereign that the others should be able to answer with one accord, " You tell a lie."   Nay, it is far better to be the leader without being called so, than to be' called so without being it.

CHAPTER XXI.

Trouville, 25th September.

There are few books which teach less or suggest more than that one of Erasmus which he called the *Eucomium Moriæ*. Wherefore there are few books more valuable or delightful to read. In the course of the Praise of Folly, to which he devotes the work, he gives a delightful sketch of the truly wise man as he has always been understood—one who is ill-favored, poor, dirty, badly-dressed, repulsive, occupied solely with matters in which nobody takes any interest, a stranger to all passions and to all human emotions, wanting nothing, thankful for nothing, owning no ties and no gratitude, passing his time in ecstatic admiration of himself, believing himself to be the only successful man, the only powerful, the only truly rich, of the world, and despising the whole of the human race besides himself and some two or three others like him. "Who," asks Erasmus, "would choose such an one for a friend or an acquaintance, much less for a father or a husband?" Who, indeed. How thankful then should we not all feel that we are the fools we know ourselves to be.

*　　*　　*　　*　　*　　*

26th September.

It is strange that men reflect so little upon the meaning of the verbal and material ornaments which they are all so eager to obtain as setting them outside the vulgar. Take the meanest title, that of Esquire, which signifies that he who bears it is the faithful servant and follower of those who have devoted themselves to the highest and noblest deeds, and that he is in a probationary state, from which he will rise to be himself a knight only by the entertainment of high aims and the pursuit of a pure and spotless life. How many are there who hold that the mere acceptance of this title implies any such obligation? And how much more truly may the same be said of

such superior titles as duke, prince, and king ! Look, now, at
the material ornaments. A crown or a coronet signifies that
its wearer possesses all the virtues (symbolized by the jewels
with which it is studded) united in one ; the robe signifies the
majesty with which its wearer should be clothed in all his acts
and words, just as the ermine of the judge signifies purity that
can endure no spot, and as the wedding garment of the bride
signifies the purity of mind and body which she brings to the
altar. I wonder how people can have the face to clothe themselves so often in lies, and to walk about the world like so
many dishonored promissory notes.

*　　*　　*　　*　　*　　*

27th September.

This must assuredly be the paradise of idlers. I have seldom seen a place where the time passes so quickly, so pleas-
antly, and with so little effort, in the utter absence of anything
like an occupation. There are not very many people left now,
but he who is fortunate enough to possess a few friends among
them is petted and spoilt in a way likely to make the ordinary
life-militant a burden to him. People are ready to amuse
themselves, and above all anxious to amuse their friends, and
do not disdain to do it by simple unassuming methods. A
drive to Dives, relieved by a game of " quatre coins," and an
impromptu quadrille in a casual orchard by the wayside ; an ex-
pedition to drink milk at a farmhouse ; a journey to Honfleur
to gloat over the departure of that commerce which Trouville
is rapidly taking away from it—all these are, for some reason,
not by any means a bore, but the most delightful pastimes
possible. Or still better is it to drive to an outlying farmer's
for a whole day out. You take your dinner with you, or
rather the materials, for you are to cook it yourselves, and the
whole of the operation is one charming series of adventures
which make everybody laugh, although, or perhaps because,
there is nothing in them. Here is Madame la Vicomtesse beating up a " fromage à la crême" till her dainty arms ache, and

so carefully canting it to dry that it incontinently covers the floor of the dairy ; here is another lady chopping herbs, manipulating mushrooms, and trying all she knows to " faire revenir" the fowl which it is confidently hoped will turn out a fricassé.　Here again is the Comte tunefully cutting up everything he finds at hand into the fish, and here the Vicomte weeping ruefully over the strongest onion that ever man sliced. One volunteer is devoted to turning the leg of mutton which is browning on the spit before an immense wood-fire, and slowly absorbing the soul of the garlic cunningly introduced into it. Another is singeing his eye-brows over the " soupe à l'oignon," and vainly endeavoring to keep the beans from capsizing every two minutes into the ashes.　At last you are all burnt out, and basely leave the burden and heat of the cooking to the farmer's wife.　And now to dinner.　What fun to find the Comte declare that his own fish is uneatable !　What a triumph to discover that the gigot is the best ever roasted ; what ineffable delight to learn that although everybody has washed his hands in the fricassé, it is cooked and tender ; and what a crowning victory that the " fromage à la crême" (which has apparently been secretly wiped up from the dairy tiles) is delicious even to those who helped to make it !　You have earned your dinner, you enjoy it as never dinner was enjoyed, you eat it in a ceaseless fire of banter, and drive home again under a moon twice as big and twice as bright as nature, to wonder why it is that you never amused yourself before in your life.

*　　*　　*　　*　　*　　*

28th September.

We seem to spend half our lives in living and the other half in thinking of it.　While we live we do not think, nor when we do think do we life.　No man ever learns anything after thirty.　When once he has passed that age, if he should by chance meet aught that appears new to him, he at once puts it through a slight process of mental elaboration, and brings it down to the category of one of those things which he knew and had accepted already. If it were possible to get an accurate notion of the mind of any single individual, it would be found that in fact it consists of some eight or ten principles which he has accepted as rules in the great departments of life, and of one or two ideas which he has had himself, and which he would wish to accept if he dared. Once this stage reached, you may present to him the most extraordinary and novel phenomena, apparently the most opposed to his principles and his ideas, and he will yet find means to bring them by one method or another into his little circle. It is after all not so difficult as it appears. For things are admittedly not what they seem, and therefore any given phenomenon may be fairly brought down to its true proportions and significance other than such as it presents on the outside. Why, then, if my principles will make it intelligible upon a certain possible supposition, should I not adopt that supposition ? A man has committed suicide under circumstances which made his life apparently a most pleasant and successful one. Say that I have adopted the principle that there is no God and no law. Then I bring it all to this, that there must have been something which we do not know in his life which rendered it impossible to meet his engagements, and that therefore he had perfectly the right thus to declare himself bankrupt. But if now I believe that there is a law and no God, it becomes a question whether the law would allow him thus to repudiate his engagements. Or if I believe that there exist both God and law, I can but put the act down to ignorance or to insanity. In either event I arrive at a conclusion not upon the real merits of the case, but by referring its apparent merits to the principles I believe, and by adding thereto the belief that its real merits must be in consonance with one of my principles. But what is impossible to me is to admit for an instant that the affair has taken place outside my circle of belief. Thus it is that the man of the fewest beliefs has a task to perform with any given phenomenon by far the most difficult, because he has to reduce the most diverse and irregular acts down to the fewest heads. This shows us how it is that faith is really so blessed, and it should lead us to respect every kind of faith, and never to blaspheme even those which are apparently the most absurd. He who believes most can explain most, and do what we will, we never can escape from the necessity of explaining everything that happens.

*   *   *   *   *   *

I once knew a man (he was over fifty) capable of travelling alone with a pretty woman known to him without making love to her ; but I never yet knew a woman or a child who could remain quiet half an hour in a company where no notice was taken of them. I dined yesterday at a house whence a young lady departed in the worst of bad tempers, because the hostess monopolized the attentions of the men ; and I have just seen a baby of three years pour a shovelful of sand into his mother's coffee, because she would not leave her breakfast to look at his feats of equitation upon a stick. I believe this craving for attention to be the chief attraction that makes women and children so delightful. It is a kind of indirect flattery, as though they should say, " I only exist by virtue of the words you say to me, and the looks you cast upon me," and there has not yet been found a man able to resist such cogent reasoning. To do that one would have to regard women and children as creatures more or less reasonable, *not* invented for the sole purpose of flattering grown-up men.

*   *   *   *   *   *

SHOREHAM, 29th September.

Life is one series of disillusions. I haul out of Trouville basin, and choose a place which I have marked as a bed of beautiful soft mud, only to find myself when the tide goes down on top of a sunken boat ; I leave the pleasant shore and delightful memories with a fine westerly breeze, which develops into three parts of a gale of wind before I reach my port ; and now here is Sheba declining to eat porridge any more, and Bill, who wants to write to his mamma—as though the Billy Baby could not contain all his affections and thoughts ! It is enough to make one go to London and pay all one's quarter's bills.

CHAPTER XXII.

London, 3d October.

London is, I think, the only place in the world in which one can't endure to be alone. I suppose it is that in such a crowd as is always here one feels one's loneliness more than when there is nobody to look at it. Or maybe it is that there is something too exciting in the contact of other men and women to allow one to be content with that mere self-sufficient train of work and thought which in other places is so delicious. There is something feverish in the very air, something that whips one into a race for excitements of such kind as may be obtained easily. To read the newspapers, to receive and answer letters, to hear the gossip, and to see one's friends, become matters of necessity ; to read in the proper sense of the word, to think to any good purpose, or to dine alone, are matters of impossibility. And so it is that after a few days in town one becomes so surrounded by engagements, and so launched upon undertakings of a small kind, that it seems impossible one should ever get away again.

*   *   *   *   *   *

The man who, going to a town infested by thieves, and being recommended to carry a pistol, objected that the thieves would steal that too, was not so unwise in his generation, if we may judge by ours.

It is terrible to think how rare a courage is required to make any real effective use of the arms which nature has given to all of us. Rather than see with their eyes and reason with their intelligence, men will commit themselves body and soul to the first bold highwayman they meet. We hand over our religion to the priest, our liberties to the policeman, our knowledge to the philosopher, our public affairs to the politician, as though they were no business at all of ours, and think we have done well when we hand over to them our money besides, so as to make the race of usurpers and the desire for usurpation eternal. For truly speaking each man is bound to be priest, policeman, philosopher, and statesman for himself. The result of his declining and thinking to delegate these his most important functions, is that the modern highwayman no longer offers an alternative, but demands his money *and* his life—and receives both to do what he will with them.

*　　*　　*　　*　　*　　*

We English are a people of small niggling minds. We it is who invent potato-parers, lemon-squeezers, patent axles, and new coal-scuttles ; and so appreciate them that any man who can claim one such thing may make a fortune with it. But if it be merely a great idea that he has conceived, or a great principle that he would enforce, he had best hold his tongue, unless he is prepared to take to himself, and to enjoy as his reward, cursing, reviling, contempt, and poverty. There are indeed those who are equal to this, for it is one of the grand mistakes to suppose that there is no enjoyment in the evil things of this world, when a man is sustained by the knowledge that he is honest, or any enjoyment in the good things when that knowledge is absent. This is why those who have the good things are so anxious to remain in ignorance and inaction. They always fear they shall discover themselves to be impostors.

*　　*　　*　　*　　*　　*

An ingenious idea is that, for aught we know, we may be as surprised when we die as a man is when he awakes, to find that we have been dreaming till then, and have only then come back to realities. Of course it may be equally well said that for aught we know it may be precisely the reverse ; and this, indeed, is the common belief. I myself sometimes think that if this life plays anything like so potent and beneficial a part in the next as the next does in this, it hardly deserves all the hard things that are said of it. Now the idea I have quoted rests upon the assumption that we shall remember, that we shall know this life in the next ; whereas the whole influence of the next life upon this arises from the fact that we do *not* know it, and that we therefore fear it beyond measure. When we are all engaged in seeking knowledge, it seems humiliating enough to remember that we only respect, much less fear, that which we know not. As soon as we thoroughly understand anything in the universe, we incontinently despise it, and run away after something else. A man who can explain to himself *why* a woman loves him, who thinks he can see that it is for his intellect, for his looks, for his position, or for his money, cares nothing for it. But if only her love for him is inexplicable upon any reasonable grounds—if it appears to be in defiance of all laws and in contradiction of all possibility—then he will prize it and wear it as the brightest jewel of his life.

*　　*　　*　　*　　*　　*

It is the least of all things that a man should be honest ; and withal the rarest. For although we all know that none of our neighbors can deceive us, we all believe that we can deceive them into taking the semblance for the reality. And what is still more amusing is that each one of us believes that he alone of all men is entitled to be dishonest, that each claims to be paid in truth and to repay in falsehood. So that as far as any advantage to be gained is concerned, it comes at last precisely to the same thing as if all dealt in truth alone.

*　　*　　*　　*　　*　　*

CHAPTER XXIII.

PORTSLADE, Sunday, October 11.

I SHOULD like much to get at Bill's inner convictions on the subject of Dress and Society. He tried me once when bound for a ball at Cowes on a wet night by putting out my sea-boots well and duly greased. He believes that a white tie may be

worn unto seventy times seven, and he has sent me out to dine
and stay the night with nothing but a double-breasted gray
homespun, embroidered all over with pockets, for my only dress
waistcoat.　Now, this morning I warned him that some ladies
were coming to tea to-day.　On my arrival with them I found
knives, forks, and soup-plates ready laid, my last pot of apri-
cot jam open on the table, and five bottles of wine on the side-
locker.　Bill himself immediately appeared in the unwonted
glory of a paper-collar and a violet flannel shirt, while in order
the better to display it he had discarded his coat altogether.
His face was washed up to a point of shininess I have never
seen equalled, and as he appeared, bearing with elephantine
grace the teapot, he blushed like a girl at the sense of his own
magnificence.

I daresay now that if I were to tell Bill that there is any
higher or other standard of fine dresing than a paper-collar and
violet shirt-sleeves, he would suppose I was joking.　And of
this I am certain, that he would not think of believing me were
I to tell him that he looks far better in his blue jersey and
without any collar at all.

＊　　　＊　　　＊　　　＊　　　＊　　　＊

October 12.

There are, I think, three really good moments in life.　Two
of them may be left to the experience or the conjectures of
each ; the third certainly is that when, dog-tired, you throw
yourself down anyhow anywhere, and feel yourself passing into
that thick, black sleep that has no memory or tinge of the
outer life, and from which earthquakes would not wake you.
This is a moment one always seems to get on board ship, even
if one has *not* been on deck all the previous night.　Who shall
paint the intense luxury of turning into one's little bed and
jamming oneself up in a last struggle with the heavy eye-lids,
knowing that one will neither turn nor move, but will find oneself jammed up exactly in the same position to-morrow morning ?　Then with one plunge, all knowledge, all feeling, all

memory, all strife and trouble, all that is mean and low, and withal all that is great and high, are left behind—and one is bathed in grateful non-existence. Yet there are those who pretend that death is in itself horrible. Ah! if it were only like this sleep!

* * * * * *

19th October.

Two days ago I was invited to dinner "to meet an escaped convict," whom I found to be, so far as I can judge upon a short acquaintance, simply one of the noblest and finest men I have ever met—one of the few whom no money could tempt to betray a trust, and no fear force to desert a principle. He proved this in the sight of all men by his acts; for that he was condemned, and having now escaped he is at this moment being tracked by the police. When I saw him, poor who had had millions in his grasp, full of courage who had endured untold miseries, eager for the right who had suffered so many wrongs as to make a belief in it almost an impossibility, and when I thought of the sleek rogues, A, B, and C, who are protected by what is called the law in the possession of stolen moneys, and who with the produce of their thievings have been allowed to buy not only immunity, but position and honor, I felt sick at heart, and inclined to believe that all virtue must be lost in this world.

This morning I saw two small urchins condemned to prison for four days for playing cards, and a third sentenced to three days for playing at pitch and toss; and I thought of the Stock Exchange, of Tattersall's, and of the London club whist-tables. I also saw a woman who had been taken and put into jail for calling on her daughter and refusing to "move on" without seeing her. Also I saw a man who had been apprehended on a certain charge "remanded," or, in other words, sent back to prison on an entirely different charge which had never been preferred.

When one individual has seen such things as this in three

days, how many injustices must there not be in daily perpetration under the forms of law, and how natural must it not be that those who directly suffer from them should have a rankling feeling of discontent!

*　　　*　　　*　　　*　　　*

Nothing is more insecure than an unchallenged reputation. That which nobody questions always passes by a near transition into that which nobody cares for, and always finally ends in being that which nobody believes. If I had the misfortune to be a popular man or a pretty woman I would engage a select band of friends to go about and abuse me. Equally an unpopular man or an ugly woman can have no worse enemy than the friend who defends them from the common opinion. For in each case the opposition only brings out the strength of the strong side and shows it to be greater than was ever before suspected, or than ever would have been discovered had it not been challenged. It is the unfailing trick of conversation to modify and qualify whatever has been last said, the secret object being always not to deny the statement altogether, but to substitute for it the improved statement of the interlocutor. When you declare that A B has not the most perfect qualities, nor C D the most perfect features, in London, I cannot anyhow help replying that they nevertheless have remarkable qualities and features, and I end by talking myself into a greater belief in them than ever I had before. So also if you declare that E F is even a greater fool than he looks, I at once enter the lists to prove that he looks a greater fool than he is, which is so far something gained to him. Contradiction is now the soul of conversation, and " but " is the polite form in which it is expressed.

*　　　*　　　*　　　*　　　*　　　*

Just as we most of us circulate the best-looking of our photographs among our acquaintances, so we most of us desire rather to have a better reputation than we deserve than a worse. Yet manifestly this latter is far the most profitable. For in this case those who know us are surprised at every turn to find us better than we have been painted, and thence suppose that we must be even better than we are ; while in the other case they discover the exaggeration, and in mere indignation and resentment at the deception that they have undergone, strip us even of the good qualities we do possess. Now this also is to be remembered, that nobody has the reputation he really deserves, for to have that he would require to be really known, which none is, even to himself. Since, therefore, we must all be reputed either better or worse than we really are, it were wise to pray that we may be reputed worse rather than better. From the one there is redemption with those who know us, who, after all, are the only ones who for us exist ; from the latter there is no escape, but only a fearful looking for a justice and judgment to come.

$$* \quad * \quad * \quad * \quad * \quad *$$

Opinions, as they are called, seem to me to be just now the curse of the world. They are the Brummagem imitation of convictions, arrived at, or rather adopted, hap-hazard, mostly upon the merest hearsay, without knowledge and without reflection. Anybody may have an opinion upon anything, and everybody has one upon everything. It is so easy. You have only to skim a leading article, or to catch a phrase of conversation, and the thing is done. Upon the Regent's Park explosion, upon Count Arnim, upon the Carlists, the Pope, the prospects of a war in Europe, or what not, opinions are current throughout Europe ; and they have all been adopted in this way. Very different is the method by which a conviction, even the meanest and smallest of them, is reached. Hard labor to acquire information, much reflection, and that eternal struggle required to cull the one just, necessary, and inevitable conclusion are here indispensable ; and there are very few who will give so much trouble to anything unless it be to their own immediate money matters. Now how the man of convictions must despise and look down upon the man of opinions ! He has built himself painfully upon his own foundation : he knows that he is right, while the rest only know that they have rashly presumed to say that somebody else is right. But what is so irritating and wearing is, that the man of convictions is always called to be tried before the bar of the men of opinions ; which is as if the light should be judged by the darkness, or the seeing given over to the guidance of the blind. To have an opinion is to have a false imitation of a conviction ; but the worst falsehood of all is to present the opinion as though *it* were a conviction. Yet how few are ashamed to do this !

*   *   *   *   *   *

To me poetry—and by poetry I mean, of course, neither verse nor rhyme, which have indeed been terribly prostituted to base uses—is at once the most delightful and the most painful reading. To leave this lesser material earth and to launch forth borne upon the wings of the poet into the free, universal, unfettered ideal space is grateful beyond all things, especially grateful to those of us who have been soiled and bruised in the rough contact with material things. But I always feel equal sympathy and pity for the poet. I see him, having seized, perhaps created, an idea, grappling and wrestling with it, striving to hold it and to lay it down, placing it before all men, so that he shall say, "There, that is the whole of this my idea" —and always failing. He piles word upon word, illustration upon illustration, figure upon figure, and always falls short of the full expression of what is within him. Language fails, the sympathies of men fail, figures are poor and wretched, and the idea remains forever unrevealed save to those who can, with wings of their own, fly side by side with the poet, and reach with him at that he seeks to grasp. Yet none can grasp his idea as he grasps it ; and in the end the poet remains alone with that spark of divine fire which he has snatched from heaven, which he has sought to share with others, and which always at last falls back upon himself and inflames him, till at last it may even haply consume him.

CHAPTER XXIV.

At Sea, 7th November.

SAM is very like a dug-up Northman. He has hair like bristles, a beard like a yellow furze-bush, and hands like legs of mutton. He is a great lump of a man built on the Dutch model, with a good low floor, and he slouches about in a dog-ged, good-tempered way, which nothing could ever provoke into smartness. He wears a beautiful pair of ear-rings, and has been an oyster-dredger all his life. I was first introduced to him at Trouville, and now I have shipped him in place of Tom, who has fallen sick and gone home. We took the first watch to-night together, and have naturally soon made an ac-quaintance. I find Sam a man of much information, and excel-lently well-educated for his business, which is no small thing in these days of mere literary acquirements. His great ambition is to leave sailoring and get a place in some London warehouse. " Oysters is so scarce, they are, you can't make a living out of 'em." In his boat, which was just about the size of the Billy Baby, eighteen tons register, they were four men working on shares ; one share for each, and a share and a half for the owner of the boat and gear—" an independent gentleman, he is, that keeps a fish-shop in Billingsgate market." But then there are times when you can't go out for a month together, and he and his mates hadn't cleared above a pound a week each for a long time past. Yes, it would be a great thing if they could be allowed to sell their oysters in French ports. They will generally let you sell enough to get your food, but not always. He minds once at St. Vaast they wouldn't let them even do that, nor even let them lay down the oysters to keep them alive, so that they had to heave them overboard and lost them.

It is very improving to talk to Sam, and at the same time very disheartening. I believe I have as much natural ability as Sam, and as many natural advantages in every way ; and it seems very hard that my godfathers and godmothers should have precisely so educated me as to make a failure of me, while his have made of him a success. For all the real necessary purposes of life Sam is a thousand times my master, and it is only by virtue of a system of unreal and unnecessary conventions that I happen to be his. If we two found ourselves on a desert island, I should necessarily be his slave, and necessarily remain so, unless he would, like a fool, let me talk to him and protocolize him out of his natural superiority. For he can actually do much, while I at most can only think and say little. The work that he can do is essential in all times and places; that which I do is optional in all, and only even possible in a few. And what is worse for me is that he has really learned to do his work, while I am very far indeed from having learned to do mine. Every time he hauls his dredge he has done something to enrich his kind, while I who have fished all night am always obliged to confess at last that I have taken nothing.

* * * * * *

OFF CAPE ANTIFER, 8th November.

I came out of Shoreham yesterday bound for Dieppe, and hoped to make d'Ailly light about midnight. But the wind fell to a calm, and we were soon simply driving about at the mercy of these spring-tides. At four o'clock this morning, having been on deck all night so far and made nothing, I turned in for a nap, and it appears that a thick fog came on immediately after. Anyhow at half-past five I became aware of a far-off voice calling me, from thousands of miles away as it seems in sleep, and announcing " the land ;" whereupon turning out at once I found that the ship had been put about, and that we were so near the shore that, though it could not be seen, I could distinctly hear the waves breaking on it. In another few minutes I made out through the dense fog a light which, from its size and from the way in which I knew we must have drifted with the ebb, I reckoned could be no other than Fécamp, and no farther than a couple of miles off at most. We were therefore half-way between Dieppe and Havre, and as the flood-tide was now well-nigh half done, and what little wind there was was easterly, I put the helm up and squared away for Havre. It is now midday, the fog has lightened, but the wind is so poor that it is a mere toss-up whether we get in. I remember a friend of mine who lost his ship through leaving the deck for a sleep in the Channel, and he was very much blamed for it, by none more than by me. Possibly I, too, ought to have known better. But it is very hard to keep awake all night in a calm, easy as it is in a gale—which things are an allegory if ever there was one.

* * * * * *

HAVRE, 9th November.

Certainly one of the most amusing things in life is to get up at seven o'clock, after a whole night in, and go marketing with Bill. I think the charm of it lies in this, that one comes into direct contact at first-hand with the provisions and their producers. It is impossible to take any interest in a sole that has passed through a dozen dirty tradesmen's hands, and has finally found its way with a score of other soles to the slab of a fishmonger who has nothing in common with it. But it is very different if you can buy that sole of the fisherman who caught it. You seem to be brought nearer to the sole's own existence, and can understand his having left a wife and family to regret his loss. There is no satisfaction in buying the freshest of butter from a lank-haired, snub-nosed cheesemonger, or the finest of fruit from a Covent Garden Jew ; there is much in dealing with the very dairy-maid who has churned the butter, and can assure you that it was made yesterday ; much in getting with your pear the testimony to its worth of the peasant who has known it ever since it was a blossom. Then alone do you feel that you are face to face with a real natural product of the earth, whereas when you deal with the middle-man, or third or fourth hand, you can never divest yourself of the idea that what you are buying is not a natural product at all, but the result of a cunning manufacture.

Here in the market, filled from daylight with peasants bringing in their produce, one breathes the very air of dairies, or-
chards and gardens.   Pleasant, indeed, is it to walk through
the stalls, rich and glorious with all the kindly fruits of the
earth, spread out in their brilliant coloring as though to give
an earnest that the world is grateful and lovable if we only
knew it and would see it.   And then I always feel so much
elevated in my own estimation by the marketing itself.   The
science may, perhaps, be a difficult one ; but I find it easy
enough.   " Thirty-six sous a dozen for new-laid eggs !   Surely
that is very dear."—" Mais non, monsieur."—" Very well,
give them to me.   Pears three sous each !" (exactly the same
as I bought a week ago in Covent Garden for a shilling), " and
tomatoes one sou !   Why it is ruinous ; but give me them all
the same, and some potatoes and salad, and a pound of that
butter.   Now, Bill, will you not put the butter and eggs in
the same basket as the coke ? anybody would think you had
never heard the fable of the iron pot and the china pot."
Whereat Bill smiles as though I had made a good joke, and
takes a furtive bite at the green apple which he had dispend-
iously bought as a pleasant thing to eat the first thing in the
morning.   The amount of apples that boy survives is marvellous.

*　　*　　*　　*　　*　　*

It is fearful to think how a woman or a work takes hold of a
man if he will but look at them.   Considered in general they
are the greatest bores, the most uneducated nuisances.   To
make a fool of oneself for a woman, to give oneself up to a
work—be it the fairest woman that ever lived, or the greatest
work ever conceived—pah !   what nonsense !   Yet if you look
but out of the corner of your eye, but once, the merest glance,
at that one particular woman ; if you but throw the shuttle once
through that warp and begin to see the pattern growing ; if
you only touch lightly that work ; if once you set your hand
to that plough—there is no help for you—you must go on.
And the further you go the more you are identified with the

woman or the work ; until at last you are no longer at all yourself but her or it. I fear to look at any woman, or to begin
any work. If one could but be as the lilies that grow and take
no thought ! But once you enter the magic portals you leave
all hope behind. A pair of eyes, or a blue-book, are equally
fatal to your repose. Look for a moment, read for a page,
and you are lost, and given over henceforth to all the warring
forces that each man has within him. It is terrible to think
of it. But then who shall tell the fierce delight, the pangs of
painful pleasure, the stinging joys that he feels who has given
himself over to the woman or the work that has taken him cap-
tive ? Ah ! those moments when one grapples with the memory of her, with the pith of it ! when one rises exultingly feeling that one has taken a hold, and walks up and down in solitude, knowing that one has evolved out of one's nothingness
a feeling or an idea. I do not know which is the more delicious—to be certified that one has brought into existence a new
love, or to certify to oneself, while yet no other knows it, that
one has met a live idea. Yet so great is the thraldom of each,
that one is sometimes tempted to think it were better to vegetate like a cabbage than to live like a man.

    *   *   *   *   *   *

The rage for business will one day be recognized as one of the
most dangerous forms of modern folly. A big State governed
by a big Government means oppression at home and aggression
abroad ; a big city means immense vice and immense misery,
incapable from their very extent of being dealt with ; a big
corporation means enormous opportunities for jobbery ; a big
manufacture means scant work ; even a big house means
great waste and robbery, and great lack of service. Yet
we are all for bigness, as though it were in itself a good.
We applaud the " unification" of Germany, which is effected by killing many small states to make one big one ; we
plume ourselves over the exaggeration of London ; we take the
foreigner to see the bloated workshops of Birmingham and
Manchester, and show him the Grosvenor Place mansions as

the highest efforts of man in the way of habitations ; while we are even now engaged in the endeavor to substitute a big London vestry for the small ones that have hitherto existed. All this is a kind of lunacy. There may be a necessity for organization, and for taking away from each a part of his individuality to organize the whole ; but if so, it is a necessity to be deplored, not at all to be praised. And it is monstrous when, as is now the case in the centres of " civilization," it reaches the point of organizing a man out of his own existence. For a man's life is what he does in it, and the essential point of the big system is that by it he is taken in and done for down to his smallest details. On the original plan of little communities, he drew his own water from the spring that he knew, grew and knew his own produce, fattened his own pig, brewed his own beer, made his own bread, cleaned his own doorstep, defended himself against attack, and in general lived among and through his own works, thought his own thoughts, and made of himself a separate man from all others. On the big plan he is watered and market-gardened, butchered, brewed, baked, drained, and policed all under one with thousands ; lives among and through the works of others ; is thought for by able editors ; and is merely one unit in many columns of figures. The complaint I make against all this brigading into bigness is that it so belittles the man that it brings him at last to the condition of a mere pawn, having no individuality and no existence, except as an atom in a mass of other men to be organized, enregimented, and dealt with by pure wholesale. The foundation of it all is the notion that men are not worth regarding, or dealing with, unless you can get a large number. Yet the larger the body of men the less is each man in it, and we seem likely to go on increasing the brigades until we shall have brought down the individual to the point of nothingness.

CHAPTER XXV.

HAVRE, 17th November.

IT is a terrible reflection that no one of us completely understands what another says to him. Perhaps I generalize hastily, but so far as I, at any rate, am concerned I find that, in reading with any exactitude any author who really says anything, I am continually brought up all standing by the conviction that I have not seized through the words he employs the idea that was in his mind. Then ensues a painful struggle. I read again and again the passage, or it may be the one or two words which I have failed to interpret ; I wrestle with their sense ; and often at last I am compelled to admit that I really don't get any notion of the idea that they clothe ; and even if I do think I grasp it, it is merely as a possible notion which may or may not be the true one. That may be put down to my dulness, but then most of us *are* dull ; were it otherwise we should have little need of writers to instruct us ; and the hardship of it is this—that those who are most dull, and who therefore have the greatest need of the instruction, are precisely those who have the least chance of obtaining it. In truth it cannot be otherwise ; for each one of us, if we only knew it, gives his own special idea—the result of his thinking and living, or of the want of them—to each word he uses or meets ; so that we are in general all talking a different language each to each. Were it otherwise, universal wisdom would ensue in a few generations. As we are told, for men who " have all one language," " nothing will be restrained from them which they have imagined to do ;" but once our language confounded, we are and must be " scattered abroad upon the face of all the earth," incapable of giving or of receiving.support ; each fighting for his own hand and breaking his brother's head solely because he does not understand what he says. If only once we *could* get to understand each other we should be as the gods. But there is no danger of that ever occurring.

*　　　*　　　*　　　*　　　*　　　*

18th November.

When one has few friends it is cruelly hard to lose one of them, and I fear I have lost one of my very best. A bitter experience had taught me the necessity of exercising a little gentle constraint upon the female sex wherever there are attractions of any kind available beyond the dull everyday life ; and I had consequently carefully tied up the Princess of Sheba from the time we came into this port. Four days ago, however, she slipped her collar and ran ashore, and from that time to this I have not been able to obtain the slightest trace of her. I have been to the police, I have offered rewards, I have employed men to search, I have set the whole town of Havre upside down, I have had young ladies of every character and complexion brought to me—white, black, brindled, large, small, straight, and curly—but Sheba I have been utterly unable to find, and I begin to fear that she is lost to me forever, lured away probably by some unscrupulous *gandin* without respect for family ties, and perhaps taken clean off to Paris, where she will live in splendid vice, and forget, or maybe only remember to despise, her home and her friends.

It really is very hard to experience a misfortune like this when one knows that one has done nothing to deserve it. Now she is lost to me, I prize her far more than I had ever supposed possible. I remember her little ways and even her little faults with tenderness and regret—the clever stealthiness with which she would creep down into the cabin in bad weather, and the air of candid surprise she would take when I found her asleep in her wet coat on my best cushions. I recall that particular expression she knew how to put into her back at breakfast and dinner-time, the bashful yet decided protest she made when offered biscuit instead of meat, the wild races round the deck with which she would celebrate my arrival, the intrepid barking with which she would sometimes defend me from sleep and the ship from an imaginary enemy the night through. I think of her wistful brown eyes, of the way she would nestle up against my legs when I took a trick at the helm, and of the thousand little acts by which she revealed her character and almost persuaded me that we were five and not four souls on board. I think of all this and I am aware that I have really experienced a great misfortune not to be repaired. Poor Sheba! you will hardly find one who feels for you my affection. At least, I pray you may be happy.

* * * * * *

Diderot has remarked that whoever objects to the established order of things complains in effect of his own existence ; since he, such as he is, is but the product precisely of that particular order of things. In the same way a German has declared that " Man is what he eats." Both which propositions are true and false ; for just as any given man is the product of the established order of things *plus* his notion of them, so also a man is what he eats *plus* what he does—which greatly changes the matter. Indeed, we may go a step farther, and say that a man only exists in proportion as he contributes something from himself to the established order of things, and is something more than what he eats. Adam only began to fulfil his destiny when he gave names to all cattle, and to the fowls of the air, and to every beast of the field ; that is to say, when he invested the established order of things with notions of his own.

* * * * * *

There are many men who affect to despise the opinion of their fellows, but I have never yet found one who really did despise it. And this is natural ; for, say what we will, we all know (as, indeed, the most important and interesting things we know are precisely those we never do say) that it is mainly this opinion that makes us what we are. The great, the little, the virtuous, the vicious, the strong, the weak, are what they are by no other title than the consent of 'their neighbor, and their own belief founded on that consent. If all those members of mankind of whom I have any knowledge agree in declaring me to be great and virtuous, I have no choice but to take the appearances of greatness and virtue, even if I be the mean-

est and most vicious of men ; and by habit this grows upon me
until at last I am persuaded myself of my greatness and virtue.
So, equally, if you tell me I am a scoundrel—why, then, I am
a scoundrel, though I should be virtue in person.   And if, now,
one or two of you discover and say that I am nothing of the
kind, that is immaterial, and will remain of no effect at all
until you have converted some section of mankind to consent
generally to your discovery—and even then it is only of effect
in that section.   For all other sections I remain a scoundrel ;
when among them I must perforce confess myself a scoundrel,
and as such alone can I act.   We most of us know a great man
or two who is really but a miserable poor creature ; yet he is
not therefore dishonest, for he has been so often told that he is
great that he thoroughly believes it, and no one would be more
surprised than he if he were suddenly brought face to face with
the demonstration that he is an impostor.

*   *   *   *   *   *

The whole art of getting everything consists in producing
the belief that you will accept nothing.   No offer is ever honestly made in this life that does not come arm in arm with the
fear of refusal.   For those who make an offer make it with the
object of receiving, not of conferring, a favor.   If once you
let them know that the reverse is the case, you are lost for that
time.   If once it is suspected that you really want anything,
that is precisely the thing that you will never get.   I know a
man who has found means to make the woman he loves believe
that he thinks her a bore.   But he is very clever, and he will
have his reward.

*   *   *   *   *   *

HAVRE, 19th November.

For the whole of the last week there have been lying here
some five-and-twenty English fishing-boats, forced to run in for
shelter, and unable to face the constant gales that have been
blowing.   It is a piteous sight to see these poor fellows doing
down to the jetty every morning to " have a look at the

weather," and coming back, forced to decide that it is still
impossible to go to sea. They slouch about the town in their
long boots, looking in at the shop-windows in a melancholy
way, for they know that want of work for them means want of
food. One little boat left Shoreham eight days ago with only
a sovereign on board for the whole crew, and they have only
food for two days more, and no money to buy more when that
is gone. But they are kind and helpful, these rough men, and
of sturdy independence, too. For a friend of mine offered to
give them some money to help them out of their difficulty ;
but they refused it, saying that they thought they could get
along till the weather moderated, " and then you see, sir, we
borrow off each other." A touching revelation, it seems to
me, this of men who do not need to ask who is their neighbor.

*   *   *   *   *   *

Havre, 20th November.

The French have certainly the most ingenious contrivances
for wasting time of any people extant. I have had to pay two
and fourpence halfpenny for port and sanitary dues, and it has
taken Ned and me all day to do it between us. First I went
to the Custom House, where I was blandly requested to leave
my register and to go to the Bureau Sanitaire. The Bureau
Sanitaire I found tenanted by two functionaries playing
draughts, who politely interrupted their game to ask me my
names, Christian names, age, place of birth, what my cargo
was, and so forth ; all which they inscribed on a document
which they directed me to take back to the Custom House to
be *visé*. Having done this, I was instructed to go on to the
Mairie, at least a mile distant. At the Mairie it took me a good
half-hour to find the proper room, having discovered which I
had to wait till two questions relating to the *armée territoriale*,
and one relating to a *permission de mariage*, were disposed of
before my payment of one and fivepence halfpenny could be
received. Armed now with the solemn receipt of the French
Republic for that sum, I returned to the Custom House for the

third time, and after another hunt up and down wrong staircases and through wrong rooms, had the satisfaction of paying eleven-pence for port dues. Returning now to the first office, I was at last allowed to take again my papers, and therewith the per-mission to leave the port of Havre when I liked. To achieve this result I have had to walk, including staircases, a good four miles, and to hold no less than seven interviews. If, now, I had had to pay a louis, a lifetime would not, at the same rate, have sufficed for it.

*   *   *   *   *   *

CHAPTER XXVI.

LONDON, 8th December.

THERE is a kind of man who lives by making distinctions. He has no ideas of his own, but he lies in wait for the ideas of other men in order to dilute them with some trivial condition of circumstance. " Yes—but," is his ensign, and with that he commonly begins what he, and many besides, hold to be contributions to the stock of thought on any given subject. He is a man of half-tones and minor thirds, a whitewasher of cathedrals, an impertinent babbler to the gods, not compre-hending thunder. If to such an one you say, " The sun shines," he will straightway challenge you with the shade of a dunghill ; if you tell him of noble aspirations, he will tell you of bakers' bills ; if you pipe love, he dances lust ; if you sing spirit, he rejoices flesh ; if you question of the height, he an-swers from the depth. He is a critic of perspective and draw-ing, there where both have been sacrificed to conception. And the worst of him is that he has not the grace to be silent. He it is who has reduced God to dogma, and the Law to writing. He made the golden calf because he could see only with his eyes. And he still exists to weary the very soul out of the impatient. How long, how long ?

*　　*　　*　　*　　*　　*

The distinguishing characteristic of the modern Englishman is his extreme dislike to telling or hearing the truth, whenever the truth is of any importance. He will tell or listen to it " confidentially " and in secret ; indeed, then it is the only thing he really cares to hear or to tell ; but there is no trouble he will not take and no trick he will not play to avoid meeting or stating it to the dreaded third person, however proper and important it may be that the third person should know it. We all know about this wife and that minister ; but he who should tell the husband or the couutry what it so imports them above all to know, would be regarded as a treacherous dangerous person. And what is so irritating is that we yet profess to be greater lovers of truth than any other people on the face of the earth. How much better would it be if we were frankly to admit ourselves to be the greatest professors of lies !

*　　*　　*　　*　　*　　*

When I hear people talk of different styles and periods of art, of Cinque-cento, Renaissance, of the Barocco, the Greek, and the Italian, I am impatient. For it appears to me that the whole and the only interest lies in men, and the only thing worth considering is the life and character of the human beings who produced these different styles as shown in their works. To know them is the essential, and their fruits are only interesting because it is by their fruits that we do know them. Did they lead a spiritual or a merely material life ? Did they work toward a high ideal, forgetting and disregarding all else, or did they falsely betray—they the chosen exponents of it—all that is high and noble in the composition of our nature ? That is the point, and when once that is appreciated it disposes forever of any attempt to reproduce or to imitate any given style of art. For in order to produce the same fruits you must have the same men. You cannot build a Gothic cathedral by simply copying Gothic works; what is indispensable is to have the Gothic reverence and sense of awful mystery, the Gothic fidelity and laboriousness, and the Gothic religion and superstition. Neither can you do work like Palladio's nor like Michael Angelo's without living their life. You cannot be venal or even commercial in your ordinary life, and yet be pure and spiritual in your work. And since all artists are now venal and commercial it is absurd to expect from them work of any other kind, and doubly absurd to expect it in the shape of an imitation of the work of men who were not as they are.

*   *   *   *   *   *

Nobody seems now to see that the ideal, which (when we are true to ourselves) we are all working up to, must be taken not from among, but from above and outside of mankind. When the soldier-spirit burns within a man, he thinks it sufficient to be a Napoleon; if he is in philanthropic mood, he conceives that he may do as much as Howard; if a statesman, he may reach as high as Sully or Pitt; if an artist, as far as Michael Angelo; if a poet, he would emulate Dante or Shakespeare. Yet these men are themselves the proof that this is not enough. *They* reached at something higher than themselves; they knew of and sought better things than ever they did—for no man attains to his ideal. And to reach no higher than them, is to be content to fall below them. To make what has been done the limit of what may be done, is to accept a continued and increasing deterioration. To do well man must aim at the Best, and the Best has never yet been done in aught. Is not this also an argument, if any were needed, to prove the necessity for that mysterious presentment of the Best which we call God? Is not this also a sufficient reason why that Best should always be and remain mysterious and incapable of being touched, handled, and reasoned upon?

CHAPTER XXVII.

LONDON, 15th December.

AN irritating, terrible, despairing feature of life is the eternal round in which the individual and the mass give each other the lie as to the very fundamental nature of things. " I am everything," says the individual ; " there are grouped around me men, laws, conditions, incidents, past, present, and future, but they are all subordinate to me, who am in reality the one only important phenomenon that the Universe has produced." " You lie !" replies every creature and thing in a brutal chorus ; " you are nothing, you do not exist. You a centre ! You are not even in any way necessary, much less indispensable, and if you were not, none would know your place. When you fall overboard, as you must some day, the waters will close over you, and the ship will go on as before, without being aware that you who think yourself the captain have disappeared. What you are, that we have made you, and when you are no longer, we can as readily make another if we should want such a one. Prophet, Priest, King, nay, the very Divinity in person though you claim to be, we reck not of you, and can match you with one as good for our purpose whenever you may disappear." And the worst of it is that this is all true, and that it is nevertheless impossible for any one of us to believe it.

* * * * * *

This " vile body " of ours is indeed vile. It is the inevitable companion and traitor to all we do. There never was such an irritating machine as this, through which and by which alone we are condemned to work. It is like a lady's watch—always out of repair ; but far worse than a lady's watch, because nobody has the secret of repairing it. As these machines go, I believe mine to be a pretty good one. But at the best it is always coming in at critical moments with demands for rest and fuel, and interrupting thereby, or even quite upsetting, all the work one wishes to do with it. I can understand men breaking it out of sheer impatience. For if you force it, it will break *you*. Sully tells us how Henry IV. and his friends, after many days' fighting in the streets, were fain to lean up against the houses and thus rest, turn and turn about ; and I remember a Communard leader who told me that in Paris, during the last days of the fight, he was so utterly overcome by the want of sleep, that he cared not what might happen, and would even have regarded it as a happy deliverance to be set up against a wall and despatched. It is bad enough to have a soul, but really, when dispassionately regarded, it is much worse to have a body.

* * * * * *

Nothing seems to me to prove more lamentably the extinction of the race of real men, and the contemptuous indifference with which they are regarded, than the oft-repeated question, " Who is he ?" and the nature of the answer always expected to be made and always, in fact, made to it. Properly and naturally the only rational answer would be, that he is a man of such and such a kind and degree of intellect and moral quality, that he has done thus and thus and said this and this, and that his individuality and place in the world are so marked out. There is no relevant or important thing to be said out of this range. Yet nobody dreams of expecting or of giving such an answer to the question. The reply always avoids the man himself, and fastens itself exclusively on his purely accidental and incidental surroundings. He is the son of this man, who lives in that county, and has an estate near to that of the other man ; his sister married A B ; his mother was so much talked of with C D that people confuse his genealogy ; and he is very well or very ill off, as the case may be. This is, in effect, an admission that the man himself is of no importance whatever in the eyes of those who are professedly speaking of him ; or rather it is a general confession that there is no such creature as a man left remaining among us, so far as the world knows or cares to know. That there are, nevertheless, real men in existence—that is to say, men doing real work—is probable ; but then they are mainly, and often merely, themselves ; wherefore, there is no answer possible to the question who they are ; wherefore they are nobody—which is precisely what we delight to prove.

*　　*　　*　　*　　*　　*

The Billy Baby is at last laid up for the winter, dismantled of all her gear, with her mast painted, two coats of varnish on her deck, and Ned in charge till I can so far emancipate myself as to return to her—to my real home, where alone I feel as though I belonged more or less to myself. Ned writes me the most delicious letters, in which he mixes up the weather, the stores, the casualties at Shoreham, the desire he has to spend his first Christmas since fifteen years at home, and the breaking of two bottles of wine, in the most approved literary manner. Bill has returned to his mamma, and is probably now on his way to the Dogger Bank for a course of fishing. Tom has also gone on the same business, and without coming to see me in London, which he was afraid to do for fear of being run over in the streets. This delights me as being another proof that we only really fear that with which we are not acquainted. It would seem as absurd to him to be afraid in a gale at sea, as it does to many to be afraid in a press of traffic in the Strand— yet this latter ordeal proved too much for Tom. It is very necessary and proper that nobody should ever have returned from Death to give an account of it—for there are those who might laugh.

*　　*　　*　　*　　*　　*

I remember I once had a terrible interview which I certainly shall never forget ; yet when I now recall it, I am aware that into my share of it there entered no small amount of conscious acting, and that, indeed, I should have a difficult task were I to attempt to say where the real feeling ended and the acting began. Not that I overacted what I really felt—far from it ; but that I remember that I kept all the time a conscient watch over myself rather with the intention of underacting it. In short, I know now that half my appearance and words were an imposture. And this, I take it, is always true whenever a man is deeply moved ; were it otherwise he would go mad then and there. From this he is only, indeed, saved by that very intellectual and artistic criticism which he is making upon himself, and endeavoring to carry into force in the tone of his voice, the look of his eye, and down to the very trick and motion of foot and hand, whenever he is really moved in the presence of another. A man is never all real when he is before a second man, still less when he is before a woman. This comes not always or even often of dishonesty of purpose, but rather of the utter inadequacy of all language and all gesture to convey anything like a true impression of that confused storm which rages in him when the springs of the inner being are wrung, and the whole complex machinery is thrown into its original chaos. A man learns not to be himself all his life long ; he has painfully and by long effort clad himself in the garments prescribed for his particular condition ; how then shall he be not ashamed when he suddenly finds himself naked ?

CHAPTER XXVIII.

IF anybody ever thought of it at all, it would be painful and humiliating indeed to think how mean and petty is our daily life, and how completely occupied with microscopic trifling. Those of us, indeed, who affect to be superior, do occasionally put on, and flaunt about for a brief hour in, some uniform of belief or of principle—to lay it off again when the hour's masking is over. But our daily thought and converse are of things of rank detail. The Parson applies himself to candlestick and vestment, the Prince to court ceremony and precedence, the Statesman to a vote, the Woman to the fashions ; and, meantime, the law of God, the place of the Sovereign, the fate of the empire, and the art of dress are left unregarded and untouched. We are always working in our little bits of colored glass, without ever thinking of verifying the design of the mosaic. Thus have we become incapable of large principles or of sustained action. And withal we fancy that we have handed over all principles to the charge of men invented and paid for that purpose. As though they, who are our creatures, could be any different from us.

* * * * * *

There is an old lying platitude which declares that the idea, and the practical are two, and that of them the practical is the more excellent. Never was such a falsehood presented to the foolhardiness and indolence of mankind. Ideal and practical are one, and the practical only exists because and in so far as it is a realization of the ideal. What men would be, that, so far as in them lies, they are ; and conversely what they are, that they to a fuller scope would be. If now they are found striving above all to be loved and honored of their fellows, and yet to take no heed of those things which alone merit love and honor, then their ideal is that of supreme deception, the ideal of the gambler who would win even with cogged dice rather than not win at all. These are your practical men. Yet it were, perhaps, possible to conceive of another kind of man who should stand aside and, looking at the game, should reflect that he, having also those dice put into his hand, had thrown them down and had rejoiced rather to go forth a loser practically, but ideally so much the more a gainer. For, make up the accounts, and it will appear at last that of two who take each a step toward their point, he will remain uppermost whose point is above—though he have made infinitely less progress than he whose point is below.

* * * * * *

It is a fearful thing to be out of gear with the world, and he must be strongly persuaded he is right who can endure this. But how much more fearful for any to be in gear with it, and

yet not quite sure that he is right ! In the one case there is
only the doubt whether he is a martyr—in the other there is the
doubt whether he is not a swindler.

*   *   *   *   *   *

The meanness of this our generation is manifest in nothing
more than in the craving shown to be many together to indulge
in vice or corruption. It is bad enough that no man should be
any longer capable of virtue without companions ; but it is
worse that none should be capable of vice without abettors ; for
this involves the admission that the vice is known for what it
is ; that it would not be indulged unless there were too many
accomplices concerned to be punished. A man hesitates to be
a liar, a traitor, a thief, or a spoiler purely on his own account,
and taking all his own risks ; but he will readily lie as the
editor of a newspaper, betray his country in complicity with a
party, steal money as the financier of a company, or remove
his neighbor's landmark in the ranks of an army. Our virtues
are miserable enough, but there is something incredibly mean
and cowardly about our vices. Just as we fancy that if we get
a few hundred fools together, the result will be a body of wise
men, so we seem to think that when we follow a multitude to
do evil, the evil thereby becomes good. This is the theory of
the divine wisdom of majorities, in which all now believe, and
by which we are governed.

*   *   *   *   *   *

There is a very old but very foolish craze still in existence,
that men are all born to special uses ; whereas it would be
much more true to say that they are mostly educated to special
misuses. The notion is popular because it is pleasant, and en-
ables men to make the pretence of an excuse for their own idleness by representing it as an infliction of Providence. They
have not the talent necessary to do this, they lack the special
gifts required to do that, they will tell you, and give you to
understand that they are hardly used in that respect. One
especial instance of this is to be found in the popular notion of

public speaking and writing, which are freely alleged, and by many believed to be, distinct faculties given or withheld from on high ; and there are found orators and authors who support a belief which so magnifies their office. The simple truth, nevertheless, is that there is no mystery whatever in the assertion of conclusions, either vocally or on paper : the whole mystery lies in attaining to conclusions, which is by no means a gift reserved to a few, but the result of labor, open to all who will pay that price for it. The whole is done when the price is paid ; neither is there anything else at all worthy of being regarded. If you would see the real prophet, poet, statesman, artist, or orator—that is to say, one who in any of these characters has reached any conclusion—you will find him in the solitary man struggling and wrestling with his work, failing, falling, letting the oar fall from his grasp and coming to it again painfully, perhaps reluctantly, and always with distrust of his strength, the while there is none by to cheer and encourage him, no applause, no result even apparent, nor any present hope of a result. What he then can do in the silence and darkness, that he is ; and he is but a pale reflex and imitation of that when he stands forth only to show his work. Yet this, the least part and the merest incident of his business, is alone regarded and treated as though it were the whole. They turn with disgust from him while he is running the race ; and when he wins the prize they go about exclaiming that it is a gift.

CHAPTER XXIX.

Of all the feelings a man can experience, I should think the bitterest, the most humiliating, and the nearest of any to desperation, is that which takes him by the throat with soft gripping invisible yet resistless fingers, when he has had what is called a success in that particular department of life to which he has for the moment addressed himself. The wealth he has labored for is at last in his grasp, and all the pleasures and the powers it can command rise up to salute him ; the woman he has loved at last owns the spell, and falls into his arms ; the heaven-born principle he has discovered and revealed is at last accepted, and the universal crowd call him master ; the heathen are converted at last, and own him to be the true prophet : he has fought the fight and conquered. And then, even while the crown is being placed upon his head, then it is that he must fatally look in upon himself and know that he is a miserable impostor. Then in bitterness of soul he first realizes that the wealth is not truly his ; that he is not indeed the man whom that woman takes him to be and loves ; that the principle he has preached is not heaven-born or of his discovery ; that he is no revealer, no prophet, nothing of all he is taken for, and no true possessor of the rewards attributed to him. If a successful man could be found to speak the truth at such a moment, he would say, " Madam, or gentlemen, you are all fools and I am a swindler."

*　　　*　　　*　　　*　　　*　　　*

The pangs of despised love are so universal a theme with those who would move the feelings even of this our well-dressed and well-disciplined generation, that I am tempted to believe most men and women have that skeleton in one of their closets. I have indeed known—we all have—many instances of it, and I have observed that the despising of love commonly arises from the fact that the despised one has sought to mate unequally. We are all so unequal in every way when we arrive at the age for " falling in love," that it is a nice and difficult matter to find two persons who are exactly worth each other ; and this present difficulty is still further increased by the idea of what each feels capable of working out in the future ; besides which the whole is infinitely exaggerated and distorted by vanity, and by the small circle of opinion which each individual regards as the true measure of all things. Thus, without taking into consideration differences of rank and fortune—which, nevertheless, are to be considered—we find that when each reduces his or her moral, intellectual, and physical qualities to a common denominator, and adds them together, the sums total will be infinitely various. And now comes the history of the despised one, which is usually this—that A, having made the calculation for self and B, and seeing B to possess the superior capital, offers to go into partnership. B declines, and A remains one of the despised, and thenceforth fills the air with shrieks, as though B had done wrongfully to decline a bad bargain, and shamefully to look at it so far as to judge of its goodness or badness.

*   *   *   *   *   *

I once went to a theatre in Madrid to see a new piece played by actors and actresses none of whom I knew by sight. I had a playbill with the names of the actors and the names of the characters in the play ; but I found it absolutely impossible to match any one of the parts to any one of the players, the author having omitted that occasional mention of names which commonly affords the clue in such a case. So that to this day I don't know which character was the virtuous young man, which the foolish husband, or which the villain and arch-conspirator, neither have I any idea which of the actors severally played the parts.

I am always reminded of this when I reflect upon that perpetual comedy of politics which is played for our behoof. We all very readily see in it some virtue, more folly, and much villany. We know that there exist such people (for our playbill-newspaper tells us so) as Disraeli, a minister of state ; Lord Derby, a diplomat ; Gladstone, a banished noble (rival of Disraeli) ; Gortschakoff and Bismarck, friends of humanity and champions of the oppressed ; MacMahon, a soldier of fortune ; Pius IX., a sovereign pontiff ; besides bravoes, peasants, conspirators, and crowds, undistinguished. But which is which is more than any of us can make out. That man on the stage has just robbed the church. The fact is clear, for we have seen it. But is it Bismarck or Pius IX. who has so done ? Those others have hauled down a glorious banner and trampled upon it. Is Gladstone one of them, or is it Disraeli, or is it only the "Crowd"? Here, again, is a plan for murdering and plundering an unsuspecting female. Are those men Gortschakoff and Bismarck, or merely two "conspirators"? It is impossible to tell. Unless, indeed, one first knew the real off-the-stage Disraeli, Gladstone, Gortschakoff, and Bismarck : then it were easy to recognize them even through their paint and their comedy-dress. Or even if one knew but one only of them one might by a process of elimination get at the others as the piece went on. But we do not and cannot know ; those who do know will not tell ; and as each act of the comedy closes we lift up our hands in astonishment, and let them fall in despair at the pitiful things, done by we know not whom.

*   *   *   *   *   *

I believe our habit of interjectional conversation—the habit of flinging out a notion haphazard and leaving it there to take its chance—to be not merely the effect but also to a large extent the cause of our lamentable laxity of thought. The current notion of conversation is satisfied by an interchange of short sentences, just sufficient to carry a "view" or an "opinion ;" while it never enters anybody's head so much as to attempt an exhaustive statement leading to a reasonable conclusion, on any point. The reason of which is that scarcely any will take the trouble to collect the first elements required for a conclusion. Those who have taken that trouble cannot resolve the work into half a dozen words, if they would be intelligible. Perhaps a day will come when we shall see that the only excuse a man can have for saying anything is that he is able to say something—then, perhaps, we shall not be so impatient of giving him the time to say it.

*   *   *   *   *   *

Two doctrines always amuse me : that in order to be rich a man must save money, and that in order to be wise he must learn much. In reality the reverse is the truth. The measure of a man's wealth is not what he saves, but what he spends ; the rest, which is merely what he may spend some day, is not yet and possibly never may be his. So also the measure of his wisdom is not at all what he knows, but what he dares outside his knowledge. That which he has learned is not his nor any part of him, but only that which he conjectures, supposes, and believes beyond it. The essential part of Columbus was not the knowledge he got from Ptolemy, Marco Polo, and Sir John Mandeville, but his bold belief that by sailing into the west he should discover a great continent. But, then, Columbus is well known to have been mad.

CHAPTER XXX.

WHAT is it, then, that a man loves (as the word is) in a woman ? What is it that is so powerful as to make him give up all his approved beliefs, all his tried methods and principles, and deliver himself over to inconsequence and ridicule on a hint from that woman ? Assuredly it is not beauty, nor wit, nor wisdom, still less goodness or virtue of any kind ; for she may have none of these things, and be none the less powerful with him. What is it, then, that the man loves ?

Speaking diffidently, and as one who only knows what he has been told, I should say that what he loves is—himself. It is not that he is blind to the defects and deformities of that woman, still less that he believes them to be beauties, and has therefore argued himself reasonably, even if from false premises, into his " love " for her. Not at all. It is that that particular woman has found or chanced upon the kind of flattery he most loves ; that she has served it up to him in the most insinuating and unsuspected form ; and that he, as often as not unconsciously, has resolved to justify her, and to secure a constant repetition of that delicious testimony to himself which she is ready to afford. By a word, by a look, by a gesture, she has in the first instance conveyed to him that *she* has seen and acknowledged that particular great quality of his; this she has subsequently confirmed, and so long as she adheres to it the man is her slave. Now, women will readily continue to play upon that responsive chord, even after they have found out and laughed at the falsity of its note. For they, too, in love chiefly love themselves, and they get flattery for flattery. Yet, if one of them should tire of the comedy or should become aware that she can do better elsewhere with an equally small investment—and if at the same time the man fails to supply himself immediately with the one desire of his soul—then he breaks out into bitter lamentation on the falsity of women. Sometimes it *is* their falsity of which he complains; but as often as not it is of their return to truth, and the cessation of their ministration to his own false appetite.

* * * * * *

Palazzo Blanc-Bec, London, Tuesday, February 2.

I am going through a fearful experience and yet not an uninteresting one, for if one always finds something in the misfortunes of ones best friends that is not displeasing, one finds the same in one's own.

My experience is that I am trying to get into a new house, and so far signally failing. I had been months about it; I had conceived ideas and made plans for its fitting up and furnishing which, small as it is, were to make it the one only bachelor's house in London. I had made drawings in and out of perspective of all the novelties; I had met, and as I thought vanquished, the difficulties always incident to the new thing; I had settled that I would have no gas, no coal, and no paper in the house, and had contrived all my methods of lighting by wax, heating by wood, and hanging with stuffs. I had preached all this as a new religion to an eminent upholsterer—and now, when I come back from foreign parts expecting to find all ready, I discover myself to be in the most desolate and

melancholy desert ever seen since the time of Moses. I am
sitting in the midst of a hopeless mass of furniture, which
looks as if a shipwreck had just taken place of all my household gods, and am trying to smile. Of my two servants, one
(the man of course) has deserted me, and gone I know not
whither, and I only wonder I do not myself think it impossible
to sleep here in the fairy palace I had contrived for myself. I
am reminded of the rich man in the ancient writing who laid
up much store for himself only to learn that that night his
soul would be required of him.

*   *   *   *   *   *

Wednesday.

My male servant has definitely disinherited me. He met
Rosine this morning, and informed her that his self-respect and
regard for his health would not permit him to sleep in a recently
painted and white-washed room, and that he did not intend to
come back. Considering that he was lately a trooper of
Household Cavalry, and therefore presumably a soldier not
careful of small discomforts, I receive this as a compliment to
my own gigantic powers of endurance, who *have* just slept in
such a room. Also I have telegraphed for Ned to leave the
Billy Baby, and to come up and take me under his protection.
Him I know I can rely upon at any rate, and if I had but Bill
too I think I should feel quite easy. But this furniture is a
great cross to bear. There seems enough to furnish Bucking-
ham Palace in the middle of each room. All the fireplaces are
wrong, being in that stage of alteration when it is impossible to
burn coals in them any longer, and not yet possible to burn
wood. We can't find any of the candlesticks, a damp place
has declared itself in the dining-room, all the chimneys want
sweeping, and none of the locks, cocks, taps, bolts, or bars will
work.

*   *   *   *   *   *

Wednesday Evening.

Ned has arrived, and I am saved. The furniture and books
are all more hopeless than ever, in consequence of their having

been partially arranged, and the fireplaces are much in the same state ; but now I have two people who mean business and make the best of things. I have taken solemn possession of my palace by dining at home. It has been a matter of some contrivance. Ned went out and bought everything as the want occurred. Rosine turned out a perfect little repast, which justifies that reputation for a " *bonne cuisine bourgeois*" on which I took her, and I am once more happy in the midst of chaos. As for Ned, he is radiant with delight at being up in London town, and active and ready as ever, while he regards his room (the room which the household trooper rejected) as a dream almost too magnificent to be real.

*   *   *   *   *   *

I fancy that the importance given to such material surroundings as furniture, books, and " comforts" generally, is a pure invention as well as an innovation. Any man ought to be happy with a table, an inkstand, a pen, and a sheet of paper. It is not the things but the people about him that affect him in any important way. And those of old times were right who made it their object to have retainers rather than goods, and thus showed that they preferred troops of friends to heaps of furniture.

*   *   *   *   *   *

Rosine says that Ned is a marine monster, that he knows nothing, and can't even speak in pantomime, and that she doesn't know what to do with him. *I* shall go to bed.

CHAPTER XXXI.

An honest plagiarist is the most effectual work of God. He it is who having had the top rail broken by the original thinker makes the gap through which all the other sheep pass, and he is entitled to all the real credit for having adopted, assimilated, and made muscle out of the original idea, *because* it is not his own. To love one's own children is an easy virtue—being, indeed, only a kind of conceit ; but to adopt the children of others out of the gutter, and to set them on thrones till the elders blow trumpets before them—this is not so easy, and is by so much the more praiseworthy. And this also is to be remarked, that it is the plagiarist and not the original man who does the work ; it is not John the Baptist, who was right from the beginning, but Saul who first distinguished himself by stoning the prophets. For the plagiarist also adds something of his own to the original idea—no idea can pass through the human mind without having something added—little, perhaps, but often precisely that little which was required to stamp the original gold as current coin. There are not more than half a dozen original ideas conceived in a generation ; and since we cannot all be the first to conceive them, it were best we should most of us at the least adopt one, and provide it with food and raiment.

*　　*　　*　　*　　*　　*

There is only one science, properly to be so called, which is that of relativity. To know the part that a given man, thing, principle, virtue, or vice plays in the world is to know all that is to be known about that. And it is precisely what most men never do know. To hit upon the relatively important by chance is talent ; to choose it by conscious choice, and to reject for it the relatively unimportant, is ability ; to give to the important its due place, and yet to retain the power of treating the unimportant, is reserved for genius. I recognize genius in Napoleon (I mean, of course, that Napoleon who had the honor of being the uncle of his nephew) when I find him dealing fully with the subject of gaiters and harness.

*　　*　　*　　*　　*　　*

There is nothing, perhaps, which so clearly indicates and measures the great decline of those finer and higher feelings which men of race are supposed to possess (and which they should possess if they are not impostors) than this custom which has arisen of selling a noble or a gentle name for money. To do this is, besides being a flagrant breach of faith, a kind of social blasphemy, and a distinct act of social prostitution. Here is one who has inherited a great name, representing great traditions, and carrying with it equally great obligations. It is assumed by all men that he who bears that name cannot lie, or cheat, or descend to mean things ; that wherever it is found it is a tower of strength, and a sure guarantee of truth and honesty. Yet there is sometimes—nay, there is often—found a man, who, possessing such a name, makes no scruple of selling it to the first adventurer who will bid for it to ticket his wares withal. And if it be found that the wares are false, the gentleman who has given his name as their warranty thinks it enough to reply that he did not know it, as though the name itself were not a pledge given that he did know. A name of the so-called " influential" kind, whether made or inherited by its possessor, is a pledge of honesty and truth, and of the knowledge required to substantiate truth and honesty, which should only be given when it can be redeemed ; and he who gives it otherwise is the worst kind of social swindler, far worse than the dealer in any other kind of base coin.

*   *   *   *   *   *

I admire the foolhardy way in which men fall into love, as it is called. It is like the letting out of water. They begin with a mere idea of amusing themselves, and go on mostly with the same notion—till one day they wake up and find that there is a woman who can add ten years to their life whenever she chooses ; that for them the relative importance of things has been fundamentally changed, and that there is a certain little creature in the world whose moods and acts, whose fancies and follies have suddenly discovered themselves to be of greater consequence than all those weighty matters hitherto known to be such. They scarcely admit it to themselves, they will very hardly admit it to anybody else, and only with reluctance, perhaps, to the little creature herself ; but they know from their own incomprehensible acts that the whole of their plan is thrown out of perspective, and that any moment they may be deprived of their sleep, their digestion, and all their earthly happiness through a mere whim of a foolish woman. And the amusing part of it is that, when this happens, instead of taking warning from it never to fall into that trap again, they have but one object, which is to fasten it once more securely round their leg. It is lucky for us we are all such fools, or we should very soon get tired of ourselves, which at present is not a common failing.

CHAPTER XXXII.

TRULY God is good. And those who would know it have only to be out and about this beautiful country of ours early one of these winter mornings. I think there is nothing, for those who will but look at it and take it in, that more surely lifts up the heart in thanksgiving. Do look at it with me. Those warm, russet, velvety expanses of plough, so soft you could bury your nose in them as a child does in his mother's breast ; those green fields lying along the flanks of the hills, so delicately powdered with hoar-frost ; those rich brown hedgerows and trees, echelonned into the distance, and taking from the air each one its particular " value" of color ; that white road that curves over the shoulder of the declivity, and carries away with it the slowest imagination ; and over all that delicious soft gray sky, unlit by the sun, yet enriching all things with tender coloring ; do not they all turn heavenward their faces with an unceasing and ever-varying chorus of praise ? and can you and I refrain from joining in it ? Shall we not rather the more readily and certainly joinin it than we do in the garish summer, now that we see, as it were, the mere skeletons of things, and behold that they also are very good ? And shall

we not, when we come to think of that, be ashamed that there
are times when we pass by and see no beauty in them ?

*   *   *   *   *   *

It is a curious notion, that which all people seem to enter-
tain, that they are living at the end of the world.   It is often
said and written, in form direct and indirect, that we owe respect and reverence to the ages that have preceded us, which
are presented besides as affording the most useful examples for
our good guidance.   And rightly so.   But do we not also owe
much—nay much more—to the ages that are to follow ?   Do
we not at least owe as much to these as we have received
from those, in the way of example, and is not our responsibility to them on the whole much greater ?   From antiquity we
receive advantages, to posterity we owe duties.   For nothing
that we do is without its effect on the times to come.   All our
acts are imposed upon our successors with a resistless force ;
he who plants a tree endows them with its good or evil fruit ;
and those who doubt whether that fruit must necessarily be
eaten, have but to recall the numberless times and ways in
which they have been brought up, all standing, by a wall they
have found ready built, and which, do all they will, they cannot overturn.   True in physical, this is even more true in
moral concerns.   He who launches a false idea imposes on
men to come a false belief and false conduct ; and yet there
are many who will launch it, knowing it to be false, for the
mere sake of what they wrongly suppose to be their own immediate gain, and still more who will launch it without asking
whether it be true or false.   On such the curse of all generations must fall.

*   *   *   *   *   *

Most men, and women too, fail, I believe, to come into the
foremost rank among their fellows, not because it is so difficult
to win the first place as because it is so easy to win a second.
Seeing this early in the race, as all must see it who are in the
race at all, they run for the second, and only too late become

aware that they too were capable of winning the first. It is so inviting, when you have started and are pulling yourself together for a desperate struggle, to see a hand held out to you offering a crown of any kind, and a seat of honor of any dignity ; and the major part, looking to the length of the course, have not strength to resist the temptation, and so throw away their chance. Many a statesman, who might have won imperishable glory for himself and his country, has been lured away by an under-secretaryship or a party leadership of first or second order ; many a woman who might have been a pattern of true womanhood has been tempted by a " position" to become one of the common pattern.

* * * * * *

Formerly it was the man who did great things who was honored, now it is the man who talks great things ; as though talk were of any possible value whatever, except in so far as it indicates or provokes to action ; or as though the tree should be judged, not by its fruits, but by the noise of the wind that blows through it. Yet to talk well is held to be a great gift in itself, and men are chosen for no other reason than this to be the rulers of states and the arbiters of human destinies. That is, indeed, the essence of what is called parliamentary government—from which the Lord deliver us !

* * * * * *

To be above fortune and superior to care is, I believe, even still admitted to be the ideal state to which man should tend. Nevertheless, the only notion now current of reaching it is, that a man should increase those possessions which are the most exposed to fortune and the most fruitful sources of care. To gain money, respect, troops of acquaintance with hat in hand, is held to be the business of every creature ; and it is forgotten that exactly in proportion as he succeeds, so does he increase his vulnerability to the attacks from without. The distinction between him who has everything and him who has nothing is, that the former is everywhere vulnerable and the latter nowhere ; that the former cannot change but for the worse, and the latter only for the better. Is this, therefore, to say that we are to seek nothing ? By no means. But it is to say that we are to seek nothing that any can take away from us ; that we are to work for neither money, respect, nor any of the prizes exposed, but only for the true secret internal testimony of our own conscience that we have done well ; the which, as none can give it, so none can take it away. This is thoroughly old, and therefore entirely new.

CHAPTER XXXIII.

There are many things at which I always laugh heartily within myself, and at which, if I were the strong man armed, the prophet, or the martyr, I should laugh outright. One of these is the notion that England is a " free" country, when in reality we all well know, and most of us act upon the knowledge, that it is free only to such as hang upon the chariot wheels of the powers that be. It is free to anybody to do or to say anything that is already generally or partially admitted in good society ; it is free to him to say that Mr. Disraeli is wrong or right in his policy, that Mr. Whalley is a lunatic, Dr. Kenealy an obnoxious creature, and Mr. Mitchel a traitor ; but let him only say the entirely new thing, or in other words that which has not yet been received, and he will be stoned, as was Saint Stephen, and as all pioneers have been. There is, indeed, an exception to this, which is, that any, even the new thing, may be said, if only it be said ineffectually, in such a way and with such a voice that it cannot get into men's ears. In short, you may in England say what you like provided nobody listens to you, and do what you like provided nobody follows you. That is the measure of English freedom.

*   *   *   *   *   *

Another thing that amuses me is, to see that, in spite of Jeremy Bentham and other barefaced apostles of the principle so called of self-interest ill-understood, we do, all of us, to this day, expect and look to all men, other than ourselves, for acts dictated by quite other and opposite motives. We do expect our judges to be above bribes, the safe taking of which is absolutely dictated by self-interest ; we do expect our ministers to be patriotic rather than partisan ; we claim that even the tradesman shall be " honest," that is, shall be faithful to his word at the cost of profit. We claim that each of them shall, and we often go so far as to assume that they will, act upon this sentiment, this breath, this notion, that there is something more binding upon them than the desire to win as much as they can for themselves from the rest of mankind. And yet we each claim for ourselves that we alone may act quite unsentimentally and wholly selfishly. Is this not truly risible, if there were left in us any sense of humor—which, indeed, is but the sense of congruity ?

    *   *   *   *   *   *

It is strange enough that as soon as we come to be alone, we always admit ourselves to be much smaller people than such as we present ourselves to the world. This prince or that noble or statesman produces himself to the universe at large as though he were the inhabitant of splendid saloons, clothed in purple and fine linen, and faring sumptuously every day. But when the universe at large is not there, he is found living in a back parlor, clad in a second-hand shooting-coat, and dining off a chop cooked by the kitchenmaid, washed down by a pint of his third-class claret. Yet if there be anything in the appurtenances with which he furnishes himself for presentation in the face of the universe it, is surprising indeed he should himself alone abandon the enjoyment of them. I should expect to see him, most of all when alone, surrounded by those his attributes, if indeed they are his attributes. I should expect to find him living in the best drawing-room, with all the lights lit, dining with his score of lackeys and calling on his *cordon bleu*, and his butler, for their highest efforts. But then, perhaps, there is *not* anything in them, or perhaps they are *not* his proper attributes, but only an affectation reserved for the outsider.

*　　　*　　　*　　　*　　　*　　　*

"Messieurs de la Maison du Roi, assurez vos chapeaux ; nous avons l'honneur de charger."

Such was the formula with which the Household Cavalry of the Grand Monarch were hurled into battle ; and, ridiculous as it may seem to some, it indicated that the troopers thus addressed were gentlemen, fighting for what they called honor, which, whatever it may have been, was better than what we call "pay and advantages," or what other nations call conscription. If we knew it, perhaps, we should rather envy than affect to laugh at those who could be addressed as though they were taking the lives of their fellows for something to them intelligible ; for it is more than can be said of any soldiers during these last hundred years. To these no appeal is made—not even to their prejudices—neither is any reason presented to them. It is said by some leader of a faction, or mere chief of a conspiracy, "Thou shalt kill," and straightway each of them kills and holds himself innocent.

CHAPTER XXXIV.

It is not so much that nothing is what it professes to be, as that everything is the contrary of what it professes to be ; that paradox is received for truth, and truth treated as paradox. Take anything you please—say wisdom itself. What is wisdom ? Nought else but that which is approved as such by the general consent of mankind. Else it may be that madmen are wise, notwithstanding that mankind shuts them up and puts strait-waistcoats upon them. But now those who have been thus admitted to be wise have united in declaring that mankind in general are fools ; so that these wise ones themselves only hold their wisdom by the suffrage of fools, that is, by a title which is of no avail. Whence it follows, that wisdom, so called, is likely to be folly after all—which is true.

Or take " progress," that word which we all have in our mouth as representing something excellent. What is it ? What else than change, which is death as well as life ? So far as I can make out, it means coal, gas, railways, machinery, electric telegraphs, parliamentary government, universality of taxation, centralization—or, as it is called, unity of government. Well and good, if these were improvements, as is assumed ; but are they not exactly the reverse ? And are not those of us who think found coming back, whenever they can, and as a mere matter of profit, to the practice of the times before progress was ? Has it not by these been imagined that it is better to burn wood than coal ; to use oil than gas ; to ride than to steam ; to have the diverse and always human fruits of manual labor rather than the always similar and inhuman results of the machine ; to wait for handwriting, or even for speech, rather than be content with the telegram ; to have governors amenable to the State, rather than factionists responsible to a party ; to have the rich pay the taxes out of that they have, rather than the poor out of that they have not ; to multiply centres of power, rather than to diminish and unite them ? And if all this be true, is not progress rather a curse than a blessing ? As for me, I never see a gas-chandelier (so called), travel on a railway, recognize the product of a machine, receive a telegram, read the words of a parliamentarian, pay a tax, or submit to a hard and fast general statute, but I feel inclined to abuse the " progress" which has given us all these blessings.

*   *   *   *   *   *

It has been said that the object of a man's life should be to do all things well and one thing better than any other man.

Yet that seems to present the most lamentable and most humiliating notion possible of the ideal man. It amounts to this, that he is to exist for the gallery ; that he is to do all things so as to avoid their contempt, and one thing so as to excite their admiration. Whereas it seems to me, that whenever and so soon as a man at all regards the gallery he is lost, and has utterly renounced all his chance of separate existence, which is to say all his chances of any existence whatever. He himself, and not any other body, is his own judge, and unless he can bring himself before his own tribunal and establish that by its laws he has done all things well—nay, and all things better than anybody else—he is a failure and a mere imitation man. No doubt we all know that that is precisely what we are ; but that does not go to say that that is what we should all seek to be. God forbid !

*　　*　　*　　*　　*　　*

There are many who in these days believe, not only that the greater number of Englishmen are thieves, but that thieving is excusable, if not defensible, whenever a fair opportunity is given for it. The doctrine, indeed, is not put into that form —but into this, which, however, amounts to exactly the same thing : that it is criminal to expose people to the "temptation" to thieve, or in other words to afford them the opportunity ; and even scarcely less criminal not to make thieving impossible. All which amounts to this ; that the desire to steal is a natural and fair operation of natural instincts ; whence, if it be so, this follows also : that the desire to conserve "property" is an *un*natural instinct. And this indeed is so far believed that the Deputy Chairman of the Surrey Sessions has "concurred" in the "denunciation of the practice of tempting the poor by the exposure of articles," and declared it to be "a great temptation to expose goods in the manner constantly done." It may as well be said that it is a great temptation to a deputy chairman to talk arrant nonsense. Either the principle of property is respectable and ought to be respected, or it is damnable and a robbery, as Proudhon declared it. In the

former case exposure of it to attack furnishes no excuse for its
violation ; in the latter the most complete material defence of
it can furnish no argument for its maintenance.

CHAPTER XXXV.

Sitting in the stalls of a theatre the other night I observed
a lady next me lean forward and examine a shawl-cloak belonging to the lady in front of her.   Having glanced at it an instant she leaned back again, and turning to her companion, said,
with that look of scorn and disgust which the female face alone
can construct, " Paisley !" whereat they both smiled contemptuously.

Why, then, was this shawl less admirable for being Paisley
than it would have been had it been a true Kashmir ?   Mainly
because the one is machine and the other man-made.   The
results of the two methods of making are indeed very different, for the Paisley—spite of the " progress" it represents—
can never give the same rich yet soft blending of colors, or the
same interesting accidents of design.   Yet to those who look to
regularity in design and execution (as though that were of any
value apart from proportion) the Paisley product should appear the preferable.   It does not, however, so appear, even to
these ; and the only reason, if you come to look into it and to
find it, is, that the Paisley shawl brings you only mediately
into contact with the human being who made it, while the
Kashmir brings you into the contact immediately.   Turn it up
and you will see where the cunning needle has crossed and re-
crossed those delicate silken fibres ; you seem to assist at the
long, unwearied, loving labor that has been spent over it, to
follow the dusky travailer through the intricacies of the design,
and to sympathize even with those little failings to follow it out
which here and there you trace.   The Paisley machine makes

you a hundred thousand shawls of the same pattern, and all
alike ; the Kashmir embroiderer may make ten, and all unlike,
yet more like the original than the Paisley for having kept the
intention, if they have lost part of the form.   Who would, or
who, however " progressive," could, value the hundred thousandth part of the life of a machine as he would the tenth part
of the life of a man ?

*   *   *   *   *   *

I remember one who said that he loved men too well to care
for dogs.   No doubt this was a lunatic, for I always meet a score
of persons who care much for one dog, to one who cares anything for the whole of mankind. The tyranny of the dog, in fact,
is fearful.   The whole of one's life has to be regulated by its
requirements.   I have one consumed by two delusions : that a
looking-glass can be drunk like water, because she can see herself in it as she can in water, and that vehicles of all kinds are
capable of being immediately stopped by running after and
barking at their hind-wheels.   And whereas I believe that I
take her out in order to run after me, she believes that I take
her out in order to run after her.   Nevertheless, as she is the
only one of her sex I have ever been able to get to live with
me on any terms, and as she humors my weaknesses, I am devoted to her, and do run when she insists upon it.   I believe
the real reason why one prefers dogs to human beings is that
they have little sense of, and no memory for, injustice.

*   *   *   *   *   *

It was one of the ten wishes of Henry IV. of France to reduce all the religions of Europe to three only, the result of
which he believed would be that Europeans would be less
divided.   In this I believe him to have been thoroughly wrong,
as, indeed, every man must be who would rearrange the world
on notions derived from an earnest contemplation of his own
interests.   The form of religion is somewhat a matter of climate and temperament, and no form of it can gain a permanent hold that is not suitable to the locality and the people to

whom it is presented. The desirable thing, therefore, is, not that forms of religion should be diminished, but that they should be increased in number and variety ; until, if it be possible, every tongue and every nation may possess a sufficient number to cover the belief-capability of every individual in it. For what *is* essential is, that every man should thoroughly possess those beliefs that are called religious. And this, be it observed, does not touch true religion itself, of which the basis is always the same in whatever form or through whatever dogmas it is conveyed. It would be well if men were not driven to the last desperate resort of irreligion by finding no form of religion which they can receive—which will never be, until the professors recognize that form is of no moment. But then the professors live by the form.

*　　*　　*　　*　　*　　*

I saw a man to-day pass by a beggar with a contemptuous pitiless glance ; and I said to myself that, considering how many hard men and armor-cased with political economy there are in the world, the beggar's trade must be a poor one. When the hard man had gone a little way, he stopped, frowned, put his hand in his pocket, and drawing thence a sixpence went back and gave it to the beggar—upon which I saw that I was a fool. The thought of the hard man had clearly gone through several stages : first disgust, then toleration, then pity, and, finally, fellow-feeling must have moved him, all in half a dozen paces ; or perhaps it were more correct to say that he had felt none of these truly, and maybe least of all that on which he finally acted ; for if he had, he could not thus have successively abandoned each one for another, or so quickly have faced clean about. But it is enough to show that the final acts of men like him—which make up the history of the world—are not to be guessed at or predicted from aught they may profess, however honestly, at a given moment. What they say, they say not from any conviction, but out of a desire to say something, which is usually premature. And if you, being a fool, a fanatic, or a rogue, only go on hammering away at the

same appeal, ana remain accessible, as likely as not they will
come back to you and give you that you ask.

*   *   *   *   *   *

Reading an old black-letter chronicle, printed in 1580, I find
that in 1523 a Parliament assembled at the " Blacke Friers"
on the 15th of April, and that " after long debating the Commons granted two shillings of the pound of every man's goodes
and lands that were worth twentie pound, or might dispend
twentie pound by yeare, and so upward, and from forty shillings to twentie pound twelve pence of the pound, and under
forty shillings of every head sixteene years and upward, four
pence to be paid in two years." Now, as it appears from the
same record that beef was then a halfpenny per pound and
mutton three farthings, we may assume that money represented
something like thirty times what it does now. The state of
the matter, therefore, was this : that those who had an income
of £600 or upward paid an income-tax of ten per cent, while
they who had an income of £60 or upward paid but five per
cent, and those who had less than this paid but ten shillings
each, spread over two years. Yet if it were now proposed that
the rich man should be taxed in double proportion to the
moderately well-to-do and ten times as heavily as the poor, it
would be said to be a thing unwarranted by any example in the
world. Nevertheless all the subsidies that were of old granted
to English monarchs were calculated in this same way, so as to
levy a progressively higher percentage on the richer tax-pay-
ers. And in those times, too, the poor had their own property in the shape of Church lands, one third of the revenue
of which was theirs by law ; and also in the shape of six millions of acres of common land. Anybody, therefore, may see
how great a cause the poorer sort have to bless the Reforma-
tion, which deprived them of the monasteries ; the first Revolution, which endowed them with equal taxation ; and the
second Revolution, which provided them with a standing army
and a national debt.

CHAPTER XXXVI.

"By Jove, I am not covetous of gold, but if it be a sin to covet honor, I am the most offending soul alive." So said Hotspur, and it is a saying that might send a thrill of enthusiasm through the soul of a miser—if there be such a creature not in lunacy, which I doubt. It seems, indeed, so splendid, so godlike, to have none of the vulgar covetousness, but that other only which has always been held noble. Yet if they be looked at, there is little indeed to choose between them in their demerits. To covet honor is to covet not even the good opinion of men—which, God knows, is worth little enough—but only their good words, which do not always represent a good opinion, and are therefore worthless. It once meant to be quick in quarrel, to ride foremost in the fray, to protect ladies, and to be cited for these things between men for an ensample ; in these latter days it simply means to have your name often in the newspapers. This is not very hard to achieve for a man who will take the trouble ; moreover, when once the newspapers do begin there is no stopping them, and the name will go to the furthest ends of the globe six days a week regularly. But the facility with which this " honor" is gained, and the wideness of its reach, is more than equalled by its evanescence. There are those whose names filled columns of the journals ten years ago, and whom now nobody remembers or could remember. His is a very strong " honor" indeed that will live a generation. The names of the honorable men to be found, for instance, in the " Greville Memoirs" that are not absolutely new to this generation, may be counted on the fingers. Is it likely that their present successors will fare better ? Will anybody know fifty years hence who John Bright was, or Vernon Harcourt, or the fifteenth Earl of Derby ? Will anybody at that distance of time be ready to believe off-hand that Sir Stafford Northcote, Mr. Ward Hunt, Lord Hartington, and the Earl of Ripon ever swayed their country's destinies ? Judging from past experience, it seems highly improbable. So that, in spite of all teaching, they may yet be found wise who contemn glory, and prize above it that inner consciousness of having done their whole duty, which, while it never yet brought present honor, always brings present satisfaction.

*   *   *   *   *   *

He who would really do a work in this world must find a man and a woman. And these must belong to him, as he belongs to himself, and be felt to be as trustworthy (at least) as himself through fair weather or foul. The woman is of first necessity in order to dispose and get rid of women. Then, being free to put himself into his work, he must find the man who is fit to be his ally. Being alone, he is a visionary or a lunatic, but having gained his one man he has gained in him the whole of mankind. For it is thenceforth but a repetition of the same process that is required, and against two men standing wholly together nothing can avail. I speak only of such a one as has found something to do and means to do it. He who merely means to pass the time need possess neither man nor woman— not even himself.

*   *   *   *   *   *

The misfortune of the truly great is that they *are* great ; that is to say, that they have no appeal from themselves, and must therefore rely upon themselves alone. Just as a colonial governor can never dine out in his colony, so they can never submit themselves to judgment. For who is to judge the wise man of his wisdom ? Not the fools ; for that were absurd. But between two wise men, who in their wisdom disagree, who is to judge ? Again, not the fools ; for that were still more absurd, since the point of disagreement is too knotty even for the wise to decide. Who then ? None but the wise themselves. But this is despotism. It is. If you object to it, let us suppose that the fools shall judge. That is democracy. Then comes the question who are the wise ? To which you reply that the fools are the best judges, at any rate of that. Whereupon I thank you and go my ways.

*   *   *   *   *   *

It is not that the woman you love is different from all other women, but that all other women are different from her. Possibly they are better—that is nothing to the point, any more than it is that Velasquez could show you a better portrait than you will ever see in a mirror. For she shows you that you have already in your inner self as *the* portrait in which you delight, and all that does not answer to it is to you as though it did not exist. It may all be admirable ; yet not only can you by no means grasp the admiration of it, but you can only feel a generous toleration for those who, being ignorant of what you know, put those admirable qualities above those others with which you alone are acquainted. For it is the distinctive mark and proof that you love this woman, when you are convinced beyond all possibility of demonstration that you know her as none else does.

*   *   *   *   *   *

It is startling enough to remember that men can never appreciate anything in its own original self, that they will not even regard it until it has been translated to them, and that then all their admiration is reserved for the translation itself without its bringing them one whit nearer to an appreciation of the original. The thing, the man, the truth is nothing ; the comment and the commentator are everything. This beautiful world of ours would be unknown save for the poet ; the very human form would never have been regarded save for the artist ; the axiom does not exist till it is affirmed by the philosopher ; the notion is not with us till it is revealed by the prophet ; and once they have hardly done their copying work, we all fall to worshipping the copy and think no more of the original than we did before. Doubtless the poet, the artist, the philosopher, and the prophet are only recognized as such in so far as they appeal successfully to that sense of what they preach which has hitherto lain dormant and dull within us. Doubtless we only see the infinite beauty of that blade of grass when it is pointed out, because we had previously the power of seeing it without its being pointed out had we set to work. But it is precisely because he who shows it to us has done for us the work which we then know we ought to have done for ourselves, that we are grateful to him. So that it is not because the poet has brought us to see the poetry of the thing that we value him, but rather because he has rendered it unnecessary for us to seek its poetry in it, he having done this, as we think, for us, and done it sufficiently. Wherefore we look rather less to the thing than before, and are content with the poem which is, as we hold, its full translation. That is why we affect to love poetry and yet despise the world ; why we rejoice in art and yet are shocked at the human form ; why we honor the prophet and blaspheme the idea ; why we crown the philosopher and deny the truth. Otherwise each of us must seek to be poet, artist, philosopher, and prophet to himself—which would involve using the talents that God has given us—which is not to be thought of.

CHAPTER XXXVII.

RAILWAYS and newspapers are to me the chief horrors of what is called (and God knows why) a " state of civilization." It is not so much the railway or the newspaper, but the absolute and unavoidable necessity of travelling by the one and of reading the other that is so terrible. It is not that they ill fulfil their purpose, but that they have eaten up and destroyed all other methods of fulfilling it, and that they are the only means now extant of movement and information. The hardship of it is that there is no choice—that you cannot travel except by rail, or learn anything of what is being done in the world except from newspapers. Posting, riding, and even walking are extinct, except as feeders of the " lines ;" writing and conversation no longer have any existence, save as the preliminary stages of publication. And here comes the Nemesis, which is, that both railways and newspapers, having first destroyed all their rivals, have now at last destroyed the very objects of their own existence. They have made a complete end of travelling and of information, and have substituted for the former the transport of men as goods are transported, and for the latter rumor and the conflict of many lies. Sterne, when he made his sentimental journey to Paris, travelled ; the time he spent on the voyage was delightfully employed and thoroughly filled, and something was added by it to his life ; but a journey to Paris now merely represents so much time absolutely subtracted from life. We do it, indeed, in ten hours instead of five days, but that only means that we lose ten hours instead of gaining five days, which is a bad bargain. And so also with newspapers. There is more reading accessible, but less real information. Those who know, know that there is rarely a line in any newspaper that can safely be read merely as it is printed, so that the constant reader only attains to great confusion, and not to greater knowledge. All which is " progress."

    *   *   *   *   *   *

When Bacon published his " Organon," a smart man said of it that " it was a book which a fool could not and a wise man would not have written." There was, perhaps, more truth in the saying than would now be believed. I begin to think that Bacon is the real father of most of our troubles ; for indeed it was he who first invented and erected into a religion that " inductive" method of dealing with natural science which consists in fitting the theory to the facts. The result is that every theory appears to be and is accepted as being absolutely true, so long as all the known facts can be brought within it ; and that every man may have his own perfect theory according to his own knowledge or ignorance. Such a one has seen that the sun rises in the east and sets in the west ; for him, therefore, the theory is perfect that the sun moves round the earth. But such another one has learned another fact, and for him the theory is that the earth moves round the sun. Each will be and each, according to the Baconic method, is justified in being fully satisfied with this theory until he has acquired a new fact to disturb it, and to render a fresh one necessary. In truth, upon this plan no one could be certain that his theory is perfect, or, in other words, that his belief is true, unless he is previously certain that his knowledge is perfect ; but the essence of the system is that each *is* certain till the new fact proves him wrong. So that the result of this inductive method is to endow ignorance with the certainty that only rightfully belongs to knowledge. The elder Aristotelian method of fitting the facts to the theory had at least this advantage, that it enabled one to convict the theorist. A tailor who makes a coat to fit a man is a useful person, but a tailor who should make a coat that would fit all men would be a genius.

*   *   *   *   *   *

" Wise men learn from reason, fools from experience," is a saying which has often been repeated in various forms. But in reality there is nothing so difficult as to learn from experience—which is to say, to learn from the result of one series of event how to deal with another and a different series. For no two series, and, indeed, it may be said no two events, are ever wholly alike, so that no experience is every wholly applicable. And that being so, the original question still remains, *how far* it is applicable, which involves the reconsideration of the whole matter, which amounts to an exclusion of experience. If we only knew it, the simplest and shortest way through all the tangles of life were still to keep hold on the clue which has been given to us in such intelligence as we may possess. But that involves thought, and thought involves labor, being, indeed, the hardest kind of labor, which all of us seek most to avoid.

CHAPTER XXXVIII.

I HAVE a notion that we most of us wear our life the seamy side without. Whether it be in order to convince other people, or in order to persuade ourselves into the one only truly delicious belief that we are martyrs, we all seem to go about to say that we are worse off than we are. I declare I never yet met a man or woman who would admit that he or she was rich, happy, fortunate in love, lucky at play, or successful in the last new fashion. I have thirty thousand a year, but if you only knew the calls on me to keep up that estate ; I have youth, health, good looks, and no conscience, but Phillida flouts me, and the whole universe can't produce me a match for that bay ; the only woman I ever loved responds to my flame, but why on earth does she still go on flirting, God knows to what extent, with that or those others ? This outside edge backward is good, but look at my broken nose earned in achieving it ; the bonnet is pretty, but when I was in Paris I saw others which were really sweet, only I couldn't afford them. '' We are all miserable martyrs, let appearances say what they will ; we swear we are martyrs, and if you don't admire our courage in bearing up under it all, you have no heart.'' Nevertheless, perhaps some of us when we get alone, or lie concealed in that particular retreat of delectation which is known to us only, do sometimes think to ourselves, not how unhappy but how very happy we are. And then we go out into the world, and take up the old burden of woe—possibly for fear lest somebody should find out our treasure and come and steal it away

*   *   *   *   .*   *

Bacon once said that knowledge should neither be '' a couch whereon to recline a searching and restless spirit, nor a terrace for a wandering and variable mind to walk up and down, with a fair prospect, nor a tower of state for a proud mind to raise

itself upon, nor a fort or commanding ground for strife and
contention, nor a shop for profit or sale—but a rich storehouse
for the glory of the Creator and the relief of man's estate."
Which is to say that the business of each man is to sow
himself in order that the world at large may reap ; and this,
indeed, is true. If one should seek either knowledge or any
other thing for his own sole uses, his work were very slight,
and soon done, for the capacity for enjoyment of each is
limited ; but to fill the measure of the glory of the Creator,
which means the full development of the potentialities of the
creation and the relief of man's estate—which is the complete
material happiness of mankind—this is a work which will last
every man his life through. And if it be that it is worth while
to go into that vineyard at all, the whole faculties and force,
to the last ounce, of the laborer must be brought into and be
continued in action to the end. The couch, the terrace, the
tower, the fort, and the shop are not for him, but only an in-
cessant painful toil of gathering stores with one hand and dis-
tributing them with the other. He must look for no peace,
no delectation, no rest even, but a continual round of work.
And, as men are constituted, he is in the safest position who
has the most and the sharpest goads to work. So that, if I
were asked to provide a man with capital for his life, I should
provide him with poverty, debt, unrequited love, doubts, and
enemies. There are few who, when they are quit of these, do
anything worth doing, unless it be something for themselves—
which is not worth doing.

*   *   *   *   *   *

I never see the stars and the sky, which happens sometimes
even in London, but I think lovingly of the night-watches on
the Billy Baby, and wish I were at sea again. And the letters
I get from Ned only increase my impatience at walking about
these lanes of houses that hedge out God's world. I think,
of all the letters with which a relentless Post-office deluges me,
Ned's are the best. Here is one :

" Sir, i now Write to inform you that the vessel and things

are all right and that i am quite well and shall be glad when i get to sea again the weather has Been very Bad here this last fortnight. Sir i shall be much obliged if you will please to send me soom Money we shall want several Jobs done before we Go to sea a new topmast and some of our cooking pans Want New Bottoms in them i have got the standing rigging down and Repaired and up again and set up, and there was a man washed out of a boat here last week and i keep the things all well aired and most of the Bed Close are a shore getting washed so i must conclude."

This last phrase especially delights me, being always repeated, *so* I must conclude, as though that were a consequence of the bed-clothes being ashore and the man being washed out of the boat. How it all makes one long to be alone again with the sea and the sky and the books.

*   *   *   *   *   *

I am getting very sick of the widow and the orphan. Those stage properties have, it seems to me, been vastly overdone in the desire to win reprobation for the conventional villain. Many preachers have taken up their cause against the villain, who is represented as enticing them into financial schemes and bringing them to ruin through the confidence they place in him. Now, I am ashamed to confess that I don't believe either widows or orphans to be anything like such fools, or so confiding as they look. My conviction is that when they take their "little all" (I use the sacred phrase) out of the dull Three per Cents, and put it into the Snowy Mountain Mines (Salted), which promise them thirty per cent, they are well aware that they are going in for a gamble, which involves a risk proportionate to the chance of gain. And it is nonsensical to mark the misses and not the hits, to take no account of their winnings, and to represent them as victims whenever they lose. I have nothing, indeed, to say for the villain of the piece, and I am delighted when he is discovered and the most poetical justice is meted out to him. But what I claim is that the widow and the orphan, so far from being his victims, are his abettors, and, indeed, if the matter be thoroughly viewed, his accomplices. They, indeed, first invented him, for it is their craving for high interest which first put it into his mind to offer them great risks.

CHAPTER XXXIX.

IF there were wanting anything to convince an outside observer of the lunacy of Englishmen—which is, of course, to say of those who are commonly taken for their lungs and their impudence to represent Englishmen—it should be their methods of judging the policy of such foreign countries as have a policy. They know well that if they have to do with a tailor or a carpet manufacturer, with a workman or an artist, with a coal-owner or a parson, the only sure ground is that which is gained by a knowledge of his own self-interest (misunderstood), and they would and do laugh at the notion of religion, justice, sentiment, or chance being taken at all into account. Yet, when they come to consider the actions of Foreign Statesmen, they declare and seem to believe that sentiment, passion, and chance are the only, or at least the most, important influences at work. The marriage of a Prince and a Princess is sufficient to cancel all the policy that has been laboriously worked out for centuries. The proposal of a toast by a monarch is treated as though it were a pledge of peace to the monarch toasted ; even the dining of a company of shopmen volunteers is held to be a pregnant international event. Meantime the permanent officials carry on their traditions regardless of all ; certain sordid unavowed agents whose names are never printed, and who really do the work, continue to borrow their way to the desired end, and one day the world wakes to find that " family alliances," toasts, banquets, and the rest mean no more than treaties. Having learned this, the world continues to argue as though they did mean something.

*   *   *   *   *   *

What is the ideal man ? Nay, in what does the approach to the ideal man consist ? Are physical strength and beauty necessary ? Are the virtues necessary ? Is the development of faculties and of capabilities necessary ? And, if so, of what kind and in what degree are these to be ? Above all, of what kind ? For the notion of them differs in every clime, almost in every individual. The story of the painter, who exposed his ideal to the correction of the market-place, has been repeated over and over again any time since the world began, whenever any has dared the trial. Is there, then, no ideal man ? Yes, indeed, is there. It is enshrined in every man's breast, and is called God.

*   *   *   *   *   *

Probably no man—unless, perhaps, it be Sir William Vernon Harcourt—really believes in his own superior cleverness, but only in the inordinate folly of the rest of mankind. The best and wisest have confessed either directly or by implication the consciousness they have felt of being neither very wise nor very good ; but such men could but have seen that they were better and wiser than their fellows. Hence the disgust at the whole concern in which they have always ended. Perhaps it is still better to be a fool and not know it than to be a wiseacre and not be sure of it.

*   *   *   *   *   *

If it be the fact that some man has invented a means of toughening glass and porcelain so that they will not break, we are robbed of the greatest charm of the two most beautiful of all manufactured things. For the fragility of all that is beautiful is one of its chiefest delights. It addresses an irresistible appeal to you to enjoy it keenly *because* it cannot be enjoyed for long. Who would care for a violet that could retain its freshness and sweetness for a year ? The bloom of the peach is delicious and grateful, *because* a touch destroys it. The charm of it is in this, that it is a fresh creation come to us out of the unseen, it is irresistible *because* you must take it quickly or never. If unhappily we could put our peaches or violets by, and take them out again as fresh as ever, they would not be worth regarding—for the very sufficient reason that we could regard them whenever we pleased.

CHAPTER XL.

I KNOW a bootmaker who makes excellent boots; his great ambition is to cease to make them, to keep a shop, and to superintend workmen : I know a barber who, as soon as he was discovered to shave and cut hair well, declined to do so any longer, and took to selling scents and hair-brushes : I know the ideal butler and the ideal maid ; they have left the service they so thoroughly performed, and have taken a public-house together, where they are now in course of ruining themselves for the sake of a brewer. Yet all these people believe that they have " got on in life" as soon as they succeed in abandoning their proper business, and taking up one they don't understand. This notion is, indeed, so generally received that it is acted upon universally in these clever modern times of ours. We have elevated into a principle the practice of selecting people for one kind of work by testing them in another. A man is a great orator, therefore he is held to be a great statesman ; he is a successful partisan, therefore an admirable minister ; an able writer, therefore a good editor ; a good algebraist, therefore a good civil servant ; a winning advocate, therefore a good judge ; an arithmetician, therefore a soldier ; a theorist, therefore a practitioner. This might be well if the capacity for the work we want were not so often not merely not indicated, but actually excluded by the capacity for the work by which we judge. I have seen men compete at a greasy pole for the leg of mutton on its top, but I never heard the winner declared to be the best butcher. But then, it is true, this was a matter of no importance.

    *   *   *   *   *   *

Somebody has said, "There are more women in the world than one." Not so. There is either one woman only, or there are none. In the same way somebody has said there are more worlds than one. That may be, but if Mercury, Jupiter, Saturn, Neptune, and Uranus are really inhabited, it is by people of entirely different construction from ourselves. We can't inhabit them, that is certain, wherefore for us there is only this one world possible—only this or none at present, whatever there may be in the future when our resolved atoms may be brought together in different form. So with that woman. For as soon as you admitted her existence you thereby excluded all others, and saw them only " as trees walking." You can breathe her atmosphere, live with her seasons, grow in her storm and sunshine, and feed upon her fruits. To do as much with another you must be a different creature. You know no more how or why it is than how or why you came upon this planet ; all you know is that she and it are all alone for you, and that for you no others are possible—for the present.

*   *   *   *   *   *

I hate people who are open to conviction, no less than I detest those who never sulk : the former only prove that they do not reason, the latter that they do not feel. Yet one hears people constantly claim to their credit that when offended they are " very angry for a short time, and then it is all over ;" as though it were a merit either to take offence where there is none, or to dismiss it shortly where there is. When one's fellow is just there is nothing to forget or to remember, for so much is his duty ; but when he either goes beyond it and is generous, or falls below it and is unjust, neither the one nor the other can be, or should be, forgotten, nor can either fail of its effect upon those who appreciate what they mean ; for they throw the whole relations out of gear, and introduce into them a new element which must affect them to the end. It is the blessing and the curse of life that good actions and bad do not die, but bear their fruit to all time. You cut my father's

throat, or you rob me of a shilling, and I am not to forget it :
on the contrary, I am to hang and imprison you, without
anger. But you kill my trust in you—or, in other words, you
kill yourself in me—and you rob me of my one cherished
dream worth more than many shillings ; and then I am to cry
out on you with big words, and there an end.

*　　*　　*　　*　　*　　*

If you are perfect I will trust you ; but as I know you are
not perfect I can only trust you if you will lie to me. I have
not confidence in you, but I am willing to affect a confidence,
if you will ease my vanity by pretending thoroughly to deserve
it. But beware, above all, that you do not let me even suspect the truth. If once you admit to me that you have vio-
lated my confidence, or that you have been so much as sorely
tempted to violate it, if you are not ready to assure me that
you would go to the stake rather than do that, then farewell to
all confidence. What ? You say that the very fact that you
allow yourself not to be perfect, the very fact that you, unsolic-
ited and unforced, admit that you are not armed at all points,
should be to me the greater, as it is the only proof of your
sincerity and a guarantee that, so far as you can, you will redeem your trust. What ? You say that your confession of
fault is a proof of repentance and an earnest of amendment.
Why, you are talking old Christianity. *I* talk modern logic.
I tell you that your sincerity is nothing to me, that what I
want is to be able to regard you, and to say that you *look* as if
you were sincere. Be sure, then, that you lie to me. Be
sure you whiten the outside of the sepulchre—then will I swear
to all the world and myself that there are no dead men's bones
inside.

*　　*　　*　　*　　*　　*

Certainly the most tiresome of all inflictions is to hear one
of the modern lights hold forth against what they are pleased
to call " conventionalities." If you would believe them there
is to be no law, and no rule of outward conduct, the expression of that law ; but each creature is to exercise, perfect, and

carry into practice his own rule for every occasion that may arise, quite as it may suit that creature. There are to be no general principles, no general rules, but only a general invention of special rules. All which may be very well for the clever people who feel that they are not to be abashed by any combination. But then what are we fools to do? *We* can't argue everything down from Genesis to the Day of Judgment in the twinkling of an eye, and to us it is of great comfort and of great assistance to be able to appeal to certain rules as determined by the wisdom of our ancestors to be applicable to certain cases. I have been taught that I am not to eat peas with a knife, and that I am not to lie. It may be that a debate and a division in Parliament, which is the final test of all things, might prove that I am to eat this particular pea with that particular knife, or that I am to tell that especial lie. But meantime I have got to act, and how am I to do it unless I act under the rule that I know? Whenever I come across one who refuses the rule I look upon him with suspicion, for I know that one to be either a rebel or a genius.

*   *   *   *   *   *

My love and I quarrelled. She was wrong, and I forgave her and loved her the more for it. My love and I quarrelled again. She was right, and I forswore her and loved her no longer. But we quarrelled yet again. Both of us were wrong, and I forgave her again and loved her better than ever.

CHAPTER XLI.

THE truth. Yes, but which truth? Yours or mine? The truth in both of us is what we can manufacture out of our moral and intellectual machine when it works smoothly; but each machine must be used as it is—that is to say, as it has come to be with the mendings and patchings of a lifetime. There are parts of them that will work in like manner and produce like results ; but that is only because we have agreed beforehand upon all the pipes and cog-wheels. We both say that two and two make four, or fourteen as the case may be, but only by virtue of having agreed first upon the original notions, and then upon their subsequent treatment. But now take somewhat out of chaos—take the entirely new notion—and without agreement run it through any two machines, and you shall find it come out of each one monstrously unlike, both to its original self and to the product of the other.

*   *   *   *   *   *

No man does good work when his success is assured. It is when he is struggling with the world, when all men revile him and persecute him, when he is still utterly rejected, that he is strongest. Nay, it is then, too, that he is most confident, for his confidence then only springs from the faith that is in him, and is not made up of any external contributions. He goes to war then of his own cost, and then only is he sure to fight well. If he achieves success, the only way by which he can escape from its fatal influence is to work for generations beyond the present, and so retain the doubt whether it *is* achieved.

*   *   *   *   *   *

The *dénouement* of a play, so far from relieving me, only diverts me. It always amounts in effect to a renunciation of the play itself. Through four acts and the better part of a fifth you show by examples, extreme but still possible, that men and women are foolish, passionate, unreasoning beings—a fact which, indeed, commends itself to all who knew them, and upon which the whole interest of your play hangs. And then at the end you suddenly turn round and recant this as a heresy and a lie ; for you seek to show by your *dénouement* that they have been reasonable all through, or at least have been working unreasonably to a reasonable end. So that you have been laughing at us through those four acts and a fraction, and you do want us to believe that we shall gather grapes of thorns and figs of thistles. In reply to which we may fairly laugh at you for your folly, and despise you for your dishonesty. Poetic justice, indeed! Yes, in a poetic world, but not in this; yes, in the course of generations (for are not the sins of the fathers visited on the children?), but not now. There are many good plays, but in order to make them true or valuable as representations of this tangled ridiculous knot of life, which is never cut by any *dénouement*, they all want to lose their last act.

*   *   *   *   *   *

One of the phrases which most amuses me is that of the "power of the press." As though the mere fact of putting nonsense into print gave it any more power with reasonable people than it had before, or as though it were necessary to put it into print in order to get it into the heads of unreasonable people. The only power the press has is that of making silly persons believe that it has power, until they discover the contrary. This is, indeed, an operation which will take some of them a day or two, and during that day or two the press has their alliance—for what it is worth. But if, indeed, the press were honest—yes, if indeed.

*   *   *   *   *   *

Two things does this strange world respect—ignorance and weakness. They are called, indeed, by the names of purity and innocence; but in reality they are not these, neither are they like them. Indeed, the former exclude the latter. Purity implies the knowledge and rejection of impurity; innocence the possession and the forbearance of nocent power. But clothed in these names it is the easier for me to put a premium on the qualities which I really desire to find in those who come into my life. The man or woman who is neither ignorant nor weak may comprehend me, and my littleness—may perhaps conquer me and my pretensions. Thus shall I be reduced to nothing. Then let me find in them nothing but ignorance and weakness: and let me praise them for purity and innocence.

For this too, while it confirms them in their subjection, will add also to my renown with others.

*   *   *   *   *   *

Against stupidity the gods fight in vain. Yet, perhaps, if they were not gods but men, they might not vainly struggle even against this. For if at the moment it is hard to withstand the irritation which it is the privilege of stupidity to raise, by a single word opening a window into its own depths, yet when one comes to think of it there is something in it that appeals very powerfully to human nature. The wisest and ablest of men must, I should suppose, have a secret suspicion that they, too, are stupid in some matters ; and this, when they remember it, must make them look charitably on those who are stupid in others. Otherwise they would never have the patience to sit down and unravel so patiently the tangled skein of unreason, merely in order to demonstrate to others the conclusions which they have reached alone, and which others might therefore equally reach alone. It would be much shorter and more gratifying simply to break the heads of all the stupid people by a summary process. But then we should be badly off for what is called common sense, which is nothing else than stupidity highly developed.

*   *   *   *   *   *

It is amusing enough to see a man going about, as so many men do, declaring that he " wants something to do," and can't get it. The real meaning of that is that he means to do nothing. For in this world there is much labor and few laborers ; and those who really bear the burden have so much more than they can endure, that they are constantly on the look-out for men to whom they may delegate a part of their work. And they just as constantly find that of all things in the world it is the most difficult to discover anybody who will really take such a delegation, and conscientiously act in its spirit. When a man can readily be found honestly to groom my horse, to brush my clothes, or to clean my boots, then I shall believe that there are men ready and willing to undertake and to do honestly the work next above that in dignity, and consequently in difficulty. Until then I shall venture to think I understand how it is that one part of mankind complain that they can't get work done, the other part that they can't get work to do. It is that the former want men who will give themselves to the work, and the latter want the reward of the work to be given to them and yet not to give themselves to it. If we could only come to an agreement upon that it would solve most of the difficulties of this nether planet.

* * * * * *

I remember that what beat the National Guards in the siege of Paris was the marching and the carrying of knapsacks. They were both ready and willing to fight in battle ; but this dull, dreary plodding along roads like beasts of burden broke their constancy. Yet that is precisely the only valuable quality. Anybody will fight well in the excitement of battle—for, indeed, physical courage is the most vulgar of qualities—anybody will speak well to a listening senate. But to toil through the miry, unregarded ways that lead to the field ; to sit down in the closet and do work that shows as yet no fruit—this challenges a high spirit and a real faith hardly to be found.

CHAPTER XLII.

At the bottom of every man's mind there is the belief in the goodness of men. This alone explains how it is that we always feel surprise long before we arrive at indignation, when we become aware that any one has done to us an unjust or ungenerous act. We do all believe that men seek to observe the elementary laws ; which means that we do all believe in those elementary laws ; which means that we believe in those laws being embodied in any and every system of morality ; which means that any system is condemned that claims to be the only one embodying them.

*   *   *   *   *   *

Funny creatures, indeed, are those men and women with whom we have to deal.   They will say a thing—nay, they will swear it, invoking the worst penalty they have invented for falsehood in the shape of a *future* punishment—and straight-way they will go away and do the exact contrary thing, to their own stultification, falsification, and destruction though it be. They pretend to believe a something ; that is to say, they pre-tend to have given the whole of their faculties to its examina-tion, and to have reached a sure conclusion upon it—for this only is belief—and yet they are ready to be converted to a dia-metrically opposite belief at a moment's notice.   Nay, them-selves—their own dear selves—they present to you as though they were something more than mere grains of sand furnished with motive muscles, walking between heaven and earth. They have their dignity, forsooth, which you are not to offend.   And when it comes to the point you will find, such asses are they, that all this amounts to is that the offence is not to be inflicted in a particular manner or form ; that is to say, if you so manipulate it that they themselves do not understand you ; if you will but give them something on which they may fasten while all the world fastens on something else ; if you do but leave a loophole for their vanity to creep through, that will easily drag all that is behind after it.   But and if you leave *no* vent for this, the earth itself may not hold the explosion that ensues.   And what makes one so angry is that one knows that one is of them, and like them, and that one acts even as they do.   This is indeed better.

*   *   *   *   *   *

I don't wonder that every disgusted philosopher should always at last end in philology, for the confusion of tongues is as great as it was in Babel, and with this difference, that we

don't know, or pretend we don't know, the confusion. In
truth, nothing is ever understood as it is said. When I, A.
B., make an assertion, I can and do make it only according to
the limits of my capacity, and though it be the meanest and
merest of platitudes, yet it requires the whole of my nature, acted
upon by the whole of my life, to produce it in that precise
manner in which I have conceived and do present it. You, C.
D., may indeed repeat the same words with a form of assent,
but unless you were I, or I you, there is no possibility of your
accepting the assertion as I make it. The notions on which it
depends have a different history in each of us, the conclusion it
represents has been arrived at in a different manner and with a
differing degree of conviction in each, and it occupies a
different relative position among the aggregate of convictions
which make up the spiritual person in each of us. We all feel
this, even though we may deny it ; and the first thing we do
with any assertion is to make the endeavor to eliminate from
it the personality of him who makes it (that is to say, its very
essence), and to bring it down to such bare proportions as may
be clothed with *our* personality. Age is listened to under protest of senility, youth under protest of inexperience, the earnest
under protest of enthusiasm, the careless under protest of indifference. And so through the whole category, until we come
to this, that the only thing a man can receive is the echo of
himself, and even that the echo understands otherwise than he.

*　　*　　*　　*　　*　　*

The curse of novelty is that it devours itself and leaves us
still hungry. The new thing does indeed give me a moment
of pleasure, which is the moment before I have grasped it ;
once attained, it instantly becomes usual, natural, old, tiresome, disgusting. " More worlds to conquer" must he fatally
seek who has conquered this ; yes, and then a new universe.
To achieve success is only to reap disappointment in its worst
form. Why, then, the truly practical course would be to reach
at the impracticable. The impossible ideal that you set up
shall never be yours ; but you shall but the more certainly ap-

proach it, yes, and bring others toward it. You shall, indeed, achieve in this minor successes and reap minor disappointments as you make them good ; but your main stake is
safe ; and when the end comes you have not spent your fortune, but may leave it a legacy to the world at large. In fine
the greatest satisfaction is derived from seeking that you shall
never find, and sowing that you shall not reap. This is insane, but it is true.

*   *   *   *   *   *

"The bramble coveted the power which the vine, olive, and
fig-tree refused. The worst and basest of men are ambitious
of the highest places, which the best and wisest reject." So
says Algernon Sidney, and to this day it is true. But it is
only true because the men who covet the highest places do not
intend to fill them, but only to reap the rewards of them. The
burden he takes upon himself who assumes to instruct or lead
his fellows is so tremendous that, if he means to bear it, no reward of personal power or profit can be tempting. And, in
fact, the real instruction and leadership of men always has been
assumed by those who have derived neither honor nor profit
from it. But to the titular leadership both are attached, and
therefore is it that the worst and the basest seek them. It is
what is called the division of labor, that the soldier should fall
unregarded in the trench and the general march gloriously in
over his body.

*   *   *   *   *   *

Know yourself. Yes, but how? You can only judge
yourself *by* yourself—that is to say, you can only estimate
what you are by what you are. It is like telling a pair of
scales to weigh themselves. Yet the attempt to do it we all
make, and all find in it the greatest amusement, even if not a
great advantage. And it is the more amusing because it always takes this form—"If I were somebody else what should
I think of myself?" The answer, nevertheless, always does
depend upon what you are ; and the proof is that what you

thought of yourself, your aims, and your conduct in a given case a year ago is quite different from what you think of them now with reference to the same case.

CHAPTER XLIII.

THERE is no feeling, I think, so painful as this—that one is about to be ungrateful. You know that that man or woman has been good to you, and you see that you are about to do a thing, or a series of things, which must amount to asserting that you owe no thanks for the good, and are under no obligation to return it. You may make any excuse you like to yourself ; you may say that the chain by which you are thus bound galls you ; that you are worn out by it ; that after all, properly viewed, it is no chain at all. All this avails nothing, for you know better, and it is always with a secret pang that at last you go and do as other men do. For you, too, believe that you are not as other men are, and you cannot forgive yourself for so acting as they act, while you remember it. But, then, you can forget it, and since you alone know this secret history there is no harm done. For in all your confessions that which you will never confess is the act which you yourself blame.

*　　*　　*　　*　　*　　*

We know well that in this world nothing grows up as it is planted, and that the best laid schemes, if they involve anything more than the most simple and immediate object, do produce quite different results from those they were intended to bring about. Accident, we say, which is but another name for our own ignorance or carelessness. At any rate we might learn from the universal experience, that it is never to be expected that the present as we know it will come out in the future as we order it. If it does so come out, it is not because there has been no error in the calculation, but because the errors have compensated each other. We can't tell what to-morrow shall bring forth, and yet—which is my complaint—we all assume to act to-day as though we could. This we call foresight. To-day, indeed, is here, this moment is ours; whatever the rest my be. Suppose, now, we were to decide to live in it, and leave trying to live in the next until the next comes.

CHAPTER XLIV.

THERE is no murderer so ruthless and implacable as your able editor. He is the agent of all the swindles and all the hypocrisies, and he will emasculate, maim, destroy, and drag with his corkscrew pen the very soul out of all you shall write for him, who have given your whole soul and being to that writing. For his first notion is to serve the commercial devil who has taken possession of the swept and garnished house; he is a huckster who has set up a stall wherewith to make a profit. He calls himself prince, society, minister, pontiff, people, and he lives by the adulteration of your pure wares—which is competition. This, indeed, were little if you could edit yourself; but you cannot, and to the end of time you shall be called upon to hand over your offspring to be defaced, unless you will see it strangled at its birth. You have a message from God, and the Devil alone can publish it.

*   *   *   *   *   *

It is a fearful thing to think how soon one becomes accustomed to everything, even to things that appeared but a while ago the most monstrous, impossible, and unendurable. The loss of your fortune, of your beliefs, of your affections, each one of which now seems to you to be eternally bound up with the secret fibres of your very existence—this will not bring you to an end of yourself. Far from it. Each one of such capital losses amounts, after all, as you may see on every hand, to nothing more than the expenditure of a certain varying amount of time in recovering from it. Never fear but that you will recover. Yet a day or two, or a month, or a year or two, and these things shall be to you as though you had never known them. Which also is another of the Creator's mercies ; for it is a mercy that the value of the good we have should be so extravagantly enhanced in our appreciation while we possess it, and so extravagantly depreciated when we possess it no longer. As we go on losing one thing and gaining another we can always show a profit on our balance-sheet, since what we have, thus becomes of more value than what we have lost.

*   *   *   *   *   *

The most damnable of all the precepts of wordly wisdom is that which teaches us to accept the accomplished fact. History, from which we learn all we know of God and man, teaches, indeed, and in the abstract we will admit, that all good work that has ever been done in the world has been done in resistance and repudiation of the established fact. Yet now we are to believe, even to avow, that because a seed among the many planted has germinated, taken root, and come to flourish as a green bay-tree, we are not to meddle with it though it be the upas itself. Nevertheless, all schools of thinkers profess to accept this : those who would change equally with those who would retain. Thus is violence made lawful, might accepted for right, and the hazard of success brought to be the test of truth.

*   *   *   *   *   *

The most irritating people alive are what I call the money-changers. They have no wares of their own to sell, neither do they seek to buy the wares of others. But they set up a stall in the Temple, where they will give you for your piece of gold many pieces of silver, or *vice versâ*, and make a profit on the manipulation of the agio. At their best they are useless to whomsoever will deal with them, for they give but the same purchasing power back for that you offer, even if it be under a

different symbol ; and, in fact, they always sweat the symbol
and leave you poorer, though you may not know it. You
bring a fact or an idea to such a one ; he takes it and returns
it to you in small change. He produces no ideas of his own,
nor is he even a carrier of those that others have produced ;
for he deals only in words, which are the currency of spiritual
things. Rather than be plagued with such parasites, it were,
perhaps, better to leave words altogether, and sink to the level
of the stars, which have no speech nor language, though their
voice is heard among them.

* * * * * *

Is it pure nonsense to say that I can make the bramble an
orange-tree by the simple process of tying oranges to its
branches ? Will you presume to say that you will likewise
look at the leaves, that you will smell it, that you will take and
put it in your garden, and see whether next year also it will
give you a crop of like fruit ? Go to, you are talking against
Education, which is nothing else than this. Do you, then,
not know that the tree itself is nothing ; that to regard its
roots, twigs, leaves, and sap, and to estimate its vigor, or ask
what fruit it will bear when left to itself, is an impertinence ?
There are the oranges, and if you have what you declare to be
a real orange-tree, I will competitively count the oranges on
both, and prove that mine is the better of the two. You know
that we require simple methods in this world, and what can be
more simple than that ?

* * * * * *

Algernon Sidney says that no man can think that to be true
which he knows to be false. It would be more to the purpose
to say that no man can know that to be false which he thinks
to be true. For we so seldom know anything, and so commonly " think " everything—which means pretending to know
without knowing—that this is the state mainly to be considered. I think that the sun shines, or that ten thousand angels
can dance on the point of a needle. But now, if I want to

know whether this be so or not, I must leave thinking and treat the subject by a very different method of investigation, whereof the first condition is that I come to it with *no* previous bias. If I can succeed in seeing my angels dance on my needle, then I know the fact; if I go out at noonday and cannot see the sun shining, then I know either that he does not shine, or that I cannot know whether he does; and in both cases I arrive at my certain conclusion only by giving up my uncertain thinking. If you want to know you must not think, and if you will think you shall not know.

CHAPTER XLV.

WHY is it that we can never really and thoroughly despise any but of our own age, occupation, sex, standing, and acquaintance, and that we do really and thoroughly despise most of those? Can it be that it is because we know those alone at all thoroughly, and that this again is because they alone are sufficiently like unto ourselves to enable us to know them thoroughly? There may possibly be somewhat of this in the matter. A younger or an older than us, one of a different occupation or sex, of a higher or lower position, is equally beyond and outside our view. In estimating such a one we know that our estimate cannot be sure, and we make, for this, allowances of which we equally know that they cannot be of a surety just and no more; and we, therefore, necessarily halt and hesitate in adopting sure and decided conclusions as to their object. But give us one of ourselves, placed in the same position, and moved, as we know, by the same springs—then we will readily judge him or her with precision, for we fall back upon ourselves in case of doubt; and so we end for these in contempt, as for the others we end in confession of ignorance. It seems hard that we should be unable to find at last any other standard than ourselves, yet if it be humiliating it is also consoling : for if all mankind be to us nothing or as bad as ourselves, it is also nothing or as good as ourselves. Which also shows one of the advantages—to put it in a profit and loss way—of living up to a high ideal, that we thereby raise all of mankind that we can pretend to know up to the same ideal. And this is charity, so far as it can be carried out, to believe of others that they are as good as we may be, rather than to think them as bad as we can be.

*   *   *   *   *   *

What a fatal thing is this, that we seem to be absolutely incapable of appreciating anything in this world without at the same time wishing to destroy it ; nay, that this is the only way in which we can express our admiration. Cleopatra typified this correctly when she melted her most precious pearl in the acid and drank it, to her own discomfort. We signify that music has moved us by repeating it even upon the barrel-organ, that a scent has charmed us by dissipating it, that a flower has delighted us by plucking it to death and corruption, that an idea has found and swayed us by vulgarizing it even to a proverb, that a woman has appeared to us lovable by loving her. And in each and every case the pity of it is that nothing will satisfy us but the destruction of the very element in the thing which has captured us. To enjoy is to sink, burn, and destroy, we say, and without this no enjoyment. Nay we can go so far as to deny any excellence that we cannot thus annihilate and bring to an end. For we are, forsooth, practical, and will admit nothing out of which we can make no profit real or supposed. '' What care I how fair she be, so she be not fair for me,'' we say and repeat in every possible form. For me there *is* no pearl I may not dissolve, no scent I may not scatter, no music I cannot whistle, no flower I may not crush, no woman I may not love. This is a damnable notion, yet it is twisted into the very fibres of all human nature.

*   *   *   *   *   *

"The wearer knows where the shoe pinches." But if we were really reasonable creatures, why should everybody else not also know? I tell you that here is the place where the pinch is; I put my finger upon it. But yet you will not believe me. You will, indeed, receive what I assert if it agrees with the notion you have formed beforehand, but not otherwise; which is to say that you will believe yourself a little more if I corroborate you, but none the less if I do not or if I deny you. For the lame man a flight of stairs is a mountain, and you will never persuade him that it is not as high as the Etna, which you and Mr. Gladstone have ascended with infinite difficulty.

*   *   *   *   *   *

If I had a son I would train him to ride, to sail the seas, to fast, to think, to speak the truth, and to play tennis; to make love to women, and to love one. To use tact decently and to earn a livlihood I should hope he would learn by himself. And I trust that Providence will not deal so ill by me as to give me a son who will either reach perfection or fall below mediocrity in any one of these matters. For in the former case he would certainly either be stoned or made a peer by his outraged fellow-citizens, while in the latter he would earn my contempt; so that in either case I, his aged father, should be left without solace in my declining years. What frightens me is not so much the prospect of his being below the average in any one of the matters that I hold to be important, as the extreme facility there is for rising above it to that relative perfection which is so fatal. Take tennis, for instance. I have not been trying to play it for years without becoming aware that it requires obstinate labor, unflagging attention, full sympathy with your neighbor (who, as ever, is your adversary), and the power of instantly addressing all the powers of the mind to the sudden new thing—in fact, that it demands precisely the same qualities which go to make a great legislator, soldier, prophet, or street-preacher. Yet those who most excel in it are creatures of very ordinary ill-baked clay, and I

believe the greatest fool I know could in his own court give
me thirty and a bisque and beat me easily.   I could, perhaps,
give him equal odds with the same result in others of these
matters, and that would equally disconcert and exercise him,
for from the tennis point of view *I* am the greatest fool *he*
knows.   Which shows that it is easy for well-nigh anybody to
attain relative excellence in well-nigh everything, which, again,
must lead each of us who have not attained it in any, to be
thankful for these and all other mercies.

CHAPTER XLVI.

On Board the Billy Baby,
Fishergate, 11th June.

Ah ! this is real pleasure to be once more on the Billy
Baby, master of oneself and of all around one.   A little kingdom, indeed, which requires care lest one should knock one's
head or one's shins against its strait boundaries, one in which
a tall man or a fat man might find himself ill at ease—but all
my own, and therefore to me delightful beyond all others.
Merely to be here is a pleasure to me, and one which has this
inestimable and quite exceptional advantage, that I can enjoy it
now without having to wait till it has faded into the past, and
therefrom received that nameless charm attaching to all that
I shall never have or all that I have no longer.   We have
scrubbed our bottom, got a new storm-jib and topmast (the
late defunct being sprung, and therefore condemned), Ned
has grappled with the science of navigation during the winter so far as to learn to do a " day's work," and altogether
we are as handsome as paint and varnish can make us.
Bill, indeed, the faithful and perspiring Bill, has gone to
Iceland, and Tom is fishing somewhere in the North Sea,
which is a source of deep sorrow to me ; but we have shipped

two new hands to make up our ship's complement of four, and the only present trouble is that it has come on to blow three parts of a gale of wind from the westward, which, of course, is precisely the one point of the compass to which I wish to go. But then, how pleasant to hear the wind blustering and to know that one is in a safe snug place !

* * * * * *

12th June.

I have come to trouble already. Phil, my new butler, lady's-maid, valet, cook, and footman—(vice Bill, promoted to Iceland)—has been acting according to his lights. I brought down with me a supply of that especial coffee which is my only claim to distinction. It was newly-roasted, and I told him to grind as much as he wanted from time to time. Fancy, then, my horror at finding that he had spent the afternoon in grinding the whole of it, thereby violating one of the fundamental principles of coffee-making. Also, he has peeled the new potatoes, washed the keys of the piano, and destroyed my boots by putting them before the fire to dry till a cinder fell through their " uppers." Phil clearly has never set himself to consider the original principles of things. In addition to which, it is still blowing a gale of wind, and I can't get out.

* * * * * *

From all time men have professed to be philosophers without being scientific, to love knowledge without having it, to seek the final causes of things without paying heed to the things themselves, to reason on facts without possessing them ; and when Comte first laid it down as the essential principle of his new Positive Philosophy that no reality can be established by reason alone, he was nearly starved to death for his presumption. His system, indeed, demands so much hard work, even to comprehend it, that if once it were generally accepted we should have to admit the impossibility of there being more than a very few philosophers in the world, or at least the impossibility of our all being philosophers who are most of us very ignorant—which is revolting. Comte is consequently clearly wrong, and I only await a successful voyage by a captain who shall go to sea provided with much navigation and no seamanship, to conclude that he is an impertinent babbler.

*　*　*　*　*　*

The living prophet is always as sure to be stoned as the dead prophet is to be worshipped. Unless, indeed, like Galileo, he will solemnly recant his prophecy, and leave men to find out with time that his recantation was a lie which he knew to be a lie. So true is this, that whenever I see a man stoned I am always inclined to believe that he is a prophet without further evidence. Then comes the question : is it worth while to be stoned in this life, in order, if it be so, that one may look down from the next and find oneself libellously stuck up in the street as a statue and one's name vulgarized into every class-book ? Fontenelle thought not. "He that has his hand full of truths," said he, "should close it fast." Fontenelle was right in his generation. You may not say the new and true thing, but any man may say either the new thing that is not true or the true thing that is not new. Surely that is enough for glory.

*　*　*　*　*　*

The most hateful of all the Philistines who believe and would have us believe that the Promised Land is theirs and not ours, because forsooth they were born and live in it and have the present possession of its fruits, is your truly practical man. He blasphemes "vain theories" because they give no present practical results, not seeing and, indeed, not knowing that all present practical results have been reached by and through theories which appeared to be, when they were first conceived, equally unfruitful with those he denounces and despises. He would have laughed, even though he live by farming or on the rents of farmers, at Abel when he first conceived the theory that corn could be reproduced by putting a portion of it into the earth ; he will laugh to this day at Archimedes and Apollonius theorizing on conic sections, even though his merchandise or his life has been saved by an observation of longitude. He is an ass.

Yet this is not to say that the practical man has not his uses. On the contrary, he is very valuable, though otherwise than as he thinks—namely, in discovering the errors of the practice in which he believes, caused by divergence from the theory in which he does not believe. When the observation has been taken and worked out, showing exactly where the ship is and that she is running her true course, he shall be put in the chains with the lead or in the bows as a look-out, and shall discover that in spite of the perfection of the method of calculation she is running into land which, according to that calculation, should be leagues away. Having done this he will cry out upon the theory—still not seeing that it was the practice which was in fault.

CHAPTER XLVII.

On Board the Billy Baby,
Selsea Bill, 19th June.

It is a great luxury to love an ugly woman, because every time you see or hear of her ugliness you are reminded of that superior perception which to you alone of all men has been given of knowing that she is not ugly ; in fact, you love her as most men love a woman, because you think you know her better than others. But there is, perhaps, even a greater luxury than this—which is to love a woman you don't know, that is to say one whom you see but with whom you are not acquainted. For this also rests upon the notion that you do know her, that you have been able to divine her from that you have seen of her, and this, being apparently even more difficult than to divine one with whom you are acquainted, is also more flattering to you. It is not only in fairy tales that men

do this kind of thing. I, who write this, love desperately a
woman with whom I have never spoken, and who is not even
aware of my existence. Her face, not regularly beautiful, her
figure marked by what others would think striking defects,
her smile, her wealth of gesture, and the lighting up of her
eye, have been to me as arrow-headed inscriptions, which I
alone can read and in which I read all that which I would have
created for myself. I am warranted, therefore, in saying that
I love her. But God forbid I should ever know her, for I
might have to demolish all my card-castles, unlearn my arrow-
heads, and be forced, perhaps, to read in their place some very
ordinary inscriptions in very common characters on very perish-
able tablets. And I would not be robbed of my fairy-tale in
this world, which has so few.

*   *   *   *   *   *

COWES, 20th June.

"Great caution," say the sailing directions, "is requisite
not to be caught in the Looe by night, neither should a sailing
vessel attempt it with an adverse tide;" but to be a little "acquainted" is better than many sailing directions, and if you
can't get a fair tide and daylight too, you may perhaps manage
with the tide alone. After thrashing up to windward all day,
and feeling the strong spring flood beginning to make, I ran
into the Park, and there anchored just as it got dark, thinking
to stop a tide and go through with the first light with the last
half of the ebb. It was a beautiful night, with every appearance of fine weather, and I turned in till the morning should
come. But at one o'clock Ned called me with the news that
the wind had backed to W.S.W., with thick rain, and that it
"looked like dirt." So, indeed, it did, and, moreover, the
glass had fallen considerably. I thought, therefore, that I had
best get out of that and see if I couldn't blunder through the
darkness, which was as yet unredeemed. And now came the
Nemesis of a piece of carelessness of which, seduced by the
weather (alas! for the instability of women and weather), I

had been guilty in not getting a bearing of the Mixon, as I
might have done before dark ; the result of which was that I
had only the Owers Light, half obscured by the rain, to work
by. In the dilemma I stood boldly in toward the Mixon
under the protection of my lead, and by then I struck two
fathoms, made the beacon within a quarter of a mile. I then
gave her a cast off, and judging my distance, after a while,
having then, of course, lost the Mixon again and the light too,
made a couple of short boards, and went for the Pullar Buoy,
which I had the luck almost to run into before we saw it.
Thenceforth our business was, of course, easy enough, and we
were not long in finding ourselves at anchor here. Moral :
Always take every bearing you can get.

*　　*　　*　　*　　*　　*

I once knew one of the greatest heiresses in London who
used to sing with great feeling a ballad which turned entirely
upon the difficulty some Scotchman had (an especial Scotchman must he have been) in making a crown into a pound. This,
with other things, has led me to ask whether to have great
riches *is* after all the ideal state, even of those who are working the hardest for them or who possess them most completely
—nay, whether it is the ideal state of any man or woman.
And it seems to me that the negative is proved by this sole
fact, that the poetry—or, in other words, the sense of that
ideal—which we all have in us can find no food in riches, nor
even in that which riches can buy. The man of ten thousand
a year is no poetic hero, unless by ingenuity he be made poor
in spite of his ten thousands ; his houses, his furniture, his
horses, his purple and fine linen will none of them provoke a
song ; and if he wants one, he must go to such common and
inferior states of life as he will find among the creatures he
possesses in fee—to shepherds and sailors, 'to the afflicted, the
disappointed, the poor ; to all those whose lot has been cast in
those crooked, unhappy ways which he knows not unless by
hearsay. Yet to hear and to think he can comprehend the
poetry that fastens upon them is still even his highest enjoy-

ment. So that when we have worked all the day for money, ease, security, and troops of friends, the best we can get out of them is the ability to take refuge with poverty, hardship, danger, and solitude. This is human nature.

CHAPTER XLVIII.

The eternal history of this world is well told in the Neapolitan tale of the priest who went to dine with a fellow padre, as great a *bon vivant* as himself. The two ate and drank, till he who was invited scarcely felt able to walk back to his domicile. As he was waddling painfully along a beggar addressed him, saying, in piteous accents, " For the love of the Holy Virgin, give me something—I am dying of hunger !" " Dying of hunger !" exclaimed the overladen monk ; " dying of hunger ! Happy man ! I am bursting with having eaten too much. Thank God, and go thy ways."

Now, if the two monks had invited the beggar to dine with them, all three would have been better off. But there is still wanting the moralist or the legislator capable of persuading one man not to eat too much, in order that another may eat enough.

*   *   *   *   *   *

It is strange enough that while we are always doing what we can to conceal ourselves from our fellows, we are also always complaining that they do not know us. Yet all the time the real fact is that we are trying to cheat them into knowing the best part of us only, and that they, seeing through the deception, avert their eyes from the good we would present, and imagine with exaggeration the evil we would conceal. And if one would really be honest, he commonly can think of no other course than that of obtruding the evil and concealing the good —a kind of proceeding which is not without example, though indeed it is rare. But if any should be so ill-advised as to present himself as he is, and should give to the world that strange mixture of good and evil which each of us knows himself to be—if any should do this, he would be disbelieved as a liar, and also scouted as a hypocrite. No man, it would at once be said, was ever either so bad or so good as this. And so we all go on deceiving others, and at last ourselves, into the belief that we live in a world composed of creatures entirely different from those which really inhabit it. This is the result of that faculty of introspection which we are told alone distinguishes us from the brutes.

*   *   *   *   *   *

The man who said he could prove anything by figures only asserted that he and his fellows were a set of fools. And it is really irritating to see how many are utterly unaware of the difference between the precision of a statement and its certainty. A " circumstantial account," a " detailed statement," or a " complete exemplification," is held to be true in its nature, because it is circumstantial, detailed, or complete. Yet a precise statement may be as certainly false as a vague one may be certainly true. When I say " the moon is made of green cheese," that is thoroughly precise, but also thoroughly false, and when I say " all men must die," that is thoroughly unprecise but as thoroughly certain. And it follows that, statement for statement, the second is worth more than the first. But now if I say " the moon must die," that is both unprecise and uncertain, and therefore a purely idle assertion. Yet this is the character of ninety nine out of every hundred assertions that are made verbally and in print.

*   *   *   *   *   *

Just as anybody can get anything he wants except the one only thing he really does want, or do anything he pleases except the one only thing he really desires to do, so anybody can say anything except the one only thing he wishes to say. Put a man before the maid he courts, let him be sincere as the morning light, and then for the first time he shall hesitate, stammer, be cold and unimpressive, and leave her at last with the conviction, necessarily formed from his conduct, that he is a blunderer or a liar, or both. And yet if he *is* acting a part, how glibly and admirably it all runs ! I think no man was every deeply moved, and deeply anxious to communicate his emotion, but must have thought with humiliation, as I have done, of the *Gymnase*, where the right words adequate to the situation flow so surely and so truly—or rather, as it would seem from all experience, so untruly. It is a consolation to me to remember that I have seen one of the greatest of actors as much at fault as ever I was myself, when he was set to speak his own feelings in a simple matter. For in this also it is true, as in the rest, that we can act another man, but never ourselves.

CHAPTER XLIX.

It seems to me often that it is an immense impertinence to utter one's thoughts. For, after all, they are and can be only such thoughts as all men have, who only differ from the speaker and the writer in that they do *not* utter them. But then I console myself with this reflection, that the very utterance forces one to look one's thought in the face, to ascertain it more or less, and to make out to some extent what it really is. In fact, it is the having done this which alone gives a thought any proper existence. For although we all of us when we look up into our sky are dimly aware of great flights of them that come and go, passing for a moment and disappearing at once, there are but few who will take the trouble to lay snares for any one of them, to catch it, look at it, hear it sing for a moment, and then set it free again. And when a rare fowler comes and shows us his bird, that he has caught and caged so well that all men to all time may delight in it, a great part of our delight arises from the recognition of the fact that it is our bird also that we might have caught had we taken the same trouble.

*   *   *   *   *   *

They are admirable persons indeed who can chirrup all day and never tire of it, or ever have any uncomfortable suspicion that that is *not* a sufficient occupation and end of their existence. For, doubtless, the great object of life is to satisfy one's own self with it, and, this being so, they are the wisest who can effect it at the least expenditure of trouble. But how much are they to be envied who can not only satisfy themselves with their own chirruping, but also be satisfied with the chirruping of others!—who never feel the longing to hear other sounds than this, or even rather than this to hear no sound at all. " The grasshopper shall be a burden," said the preacher, but if you can arrive at such a blessed state as not to feel the weariness and weight of that burden, nothing need trouble you.

*   *   *   *   *   *

Well, now, why am I to obey your laws ? You will not say because you have courts and policemen, and, if need be, war and armies to enforce them ; for if force is your only sanction fraud will be my just defence : you cannot say because you have chosen to make those laws, knowing them best for us all, but especially for me ; for that is the very point at which we are fighting. No, at last you must say that it is because the laws I am to obey are the expression of the Law which is inscribed in the ineffaceable records of the universe itself, where all men may read it, and see that you have but declared and not made it. And if it be so I have no answer to you. But now if the Law of God and of Nature be found at variance with the laws, so called, by which you profess to declare it, I who reject them am no law-breaker, but only you who assert them.

CHAPTER L.

THIS instrument of language of which we are so proud has been the especial care of mankind since the world began. Pulled to pieces many times, and immediately reconstructed electrically out of the fragments ; added to, and thereby, as is thought, improved by every generation, and almost by every man who uses it ; modelled upon various patterns, yet always with the same object of making it a perfect vehicle for the transmission of every thought the human mind can conceive, it should be now, if ever it is to be, near to accomplishing that purpose. Yet with all its appliances, it is still very rarely capable of more than the presentation of those purely elementary ideas, the necessity of imparting which first gave it birth. Beyond this it is always vague and uncertain, and usually quite inoperative. " I love you—I hate you—yes—no—come—go," are nearly the limits of any common vocabulary, and he who goes beyond this does but launch a word-cloud which looks differently from every different man's position who views it, and which differs in fact with every breath of wind. Well, then, here is my dog, who, though a very imperfect linguist, understands these elementary assertions as well as any of us. For she pays attention, which most of us never do to our fellows, and I see that she reads the tones of my voice, to this extent, as plainly as any professor of English could read my words. Wherefore I say that in fact she understands what I say as well as the professor, since, try as I will, I can say no more to him than I can to her. For she, too, can and does measure very justly the degree of emphasis I put into each expression, and can and does judge therefrom how far I am sincere in it. For which, with other reasons, I judge that it matters less what we say than how we say it. And this brings me to my point, almost as tardily as Mr. Gladstone—which point is this, that of all the gifts Providence can bestow there is none anything like so valuable as a good speaking voice, that is to say a sympathetic voice. Power of conception, depth of learning, force and aptitude of expression, are nothing in comparison with the faculty of uttering words in such a way as that the sound of them is caressing to all ears. The sense of them matters nothing in comparison with this.

*   *   *   *   *   *

If you would know a man you must do business with him ; if you would know a woman you must make love to her. Thus alone can you discover the evil and the good that is in them, for thus alone do you meet them on the only ground to which they attach any importance. The worst part of the nature of each, now, is shown certainly and without the possibility of concealment, self now rises up in arms and asserts its supremacy over all else ; and if, in spite of all, you find a man who is generous in business or a woman who is faithful in love, set them as jewels in your heart of hearts, for they are rare indeed.

CHAPTER LI.

On Board the Billy Baby,
25th July.

That anarchical order of French ideas, such as " all opinions are free," " all tastes are in nature," and the rest, are to me utterly detestable. I so little admit all opinions that I deny that there can be so many as two. There may, indeed, be two or many degrees of knowledge, two or many degrees of attention ; but with due knowledge and due attention there can only be one conclusion. As for those who have not due knowledge of the matter or have not given due attention to it, they have no right to be heard at all upon it, and it is not true that they are entitled to their opinion. All they are entitled to is compassion and instruction. But then this condemns well-nigh all mankind to silence. Why, yes, of course, have you not yet discovered that that is their proper vocation ?

* * * * * *

The man who can pass a veterinary examination is king of all men. What does it matter to him that others have money, names, baubles without end, if they have not the sound body which he feels himself ? He would not change with one of them. He feels vigor and readiness in every part of him. There is nothing he would not undertake—few, if any, things in which he would not succeed ; he rejoices as a giant to run his race. With this kind of bounding exuberant health life is worth having with all its miseries, without it life is a burden with all its delights.

.* * * * * *

SOUTHAMPTON, July 26th.

These human companions of ours on the earth never look so intensely vulgar and abominable as when they put on their holiday attire. Here is this town, which is endurable enough, and which I have seen look more beautiful than Venice, in that delicious moment when the sun has just set, and has left to all things the so precious and so short a legacy of rich white light which brings all out in deep strong coloring—here it is decked with flags, hideous with blatant bands, peopled no longer with decent work-day people, respectable with evidence of labor, and smug citizens hurrying to effect a job, but with hideous attempts at fine feathers which would make the angels weep. And all this disfigurement takes place because, forsooth, the town and the people have determined to appear at their best, and have put on their finery to do honor to their regatta. Poor creatures, they are no worse in this than the rest of us. Like the rest of us they are utterly unaware, when it comes to the point, that all they have at all admirable about them is precisely that which they most seek to forget and to conceal. It takes a lifetime to learn not to be ridiculous, in anything beyond the earning one's bread by the sweat of the brow, and there are few indeed of whatever degree who are not at once ludicrous and odious when they set out with malice prepense to be splendid.

*   *   *   *   *   *

I thank God I have never acted purely upon reason but once, which once has endowed me with never-dying repentance ; neither have I many times attained to the height of laying down a principle and following it out consistently, for which, however, I do not thank God.   On the contrary, I am aware, when I look back over that waste of blunders and disappointments which one calls one's life, that I could not give a satisfying account of the motives for any one of my acts, to any creature not prepared to admit himself as great a fool as myself. The greatest efforts, of all those very little ones I have made, have had their origin in fancy, in sentiment, or even in mere perverseness ; my greatest failures have been undeserved, my greatest successes unmerited.   I find that neither my reason nor my convictions will ever explain my conduct, and I perforce conclude that they, therefore, have never suggested it. Yet I find, also, that I am quite ready, even with myself, to wrench reason and conviction to my conduct as though they had suggested it.   I wonder if many other men are as great impostors as I.

CHAPTER LII.

TROUVILLE, 28th July.

UNLESS one were a German, divided from them only by an imaginary line of frontier and a real gulf of mutual injuries, it would be impossible to resist these Frenchmen.   Having been on deck all last night, and fed all yesterday by Phil, I desired nothing else to-day than to have a little *dîner fin* and to turn in early, for such are the blessed limits of his aspirations who is tired and hungry.   The dinner, however, ordered at a famous restaurant, did not arrive at the hour fixed, nor an hour later, upon which I sat down in a shocking temper to more of Phil's barbarous gastronomy. I had half eaten this when there arrived a pert, active, sparrow-lie waiter, looking like Capoul in one of his most highly-curled parts, and bearing the *dîner fin*. He stepped on board, cast a pitying glance at the untutored heaps of plates and forks which constitute Phil's notion of a dinner-table, revolutionized it into order in the twinkling of an eye, praised the ship as being "*gentil,*" spread the dinner before my soured gaze, with a particular account of the excellence of each dish, finally persuaded me to eat it at this twelfth hour, and left me with the conviction that I was most unreasonable not to have waited his leisure.

*   *   *   *   *   *

At Sea, Sunday, August 1st.

"With lead and look-out no ship can be lost" is a sailorizing saw which means much more than it says. Especially I take it to mean that no science, however complete, and no methods of calculation, however perfect, can replace and obviate the necessity for constant appeal to the elementary, stupid information of the despised senses, and that these must be kept constantly on guard over all conclusions arrived at, by means more complicated than their own direct action. This is opposed to the notions now fashionable, which, nevertheless, do daily supply the proof that it is true. In navigation this is written so that they who run may read. When Magellan undertook to sail round the world, the navigators, we are told by the men of science who went with him, "content themselves with knowing the latitude, and are so proud that they will not hear speak of longitude," and even the latitude was calculated upon the very rough observations made with the astrolabe. In these days we have the nicest instruments and the most varied and complete means of ascertaining the ship's place on the chart, while the charts themselves are well-nigh as complete as it is possible to make them. And the result of it all is, that the very perfection of instruments and methods has become a new danger, for it induces and persuades the navigator to content himself with their results, and to neglect and despise, or even to disbelie ʔ, the evidence of his senses. Many a vessel has been lost through reliance on calculations, which would have been safe had she had nothing else to trust to than lead and look-out.

*   *   *   *   *   *

1st August.

Phil is really admirable. He will not, indeed, ever turn out the great *chef* that I made of Bill—I don't think he will ever achieve those four dishes which Bill learned to cook so well, because so conscientiously and carefully, in the course of six months—but he has strokes of genius which surprise one into admiration. When I first came down from town, laden with the spoils of Covent Garden, he came to me with a pine-apple, on which I had expended all my substance, and asked me, " *how* he was to cook this here thing." To-day he has done better, for I had confided to him an artichoke, which I love mainly because it seems to me so well to represent the history of all our desires and ambitions—that is to say, that it amuses you immensely as long as you are slowly pulling its leaves and getting a very little out of each, and only begins to bore you when you come to the heart, which is all eating and no picking. Well, Phil has simplified the matter by simply picking all the leaves himself and heaving them overboard, leaving me nothing but this realized asset of a heart !

CHAPTER LIII.

On Board the Billy Baby,

August 8.

The fearful and tremendous fact is that there are twenty-four hours in the day, which, after deducting the sweet eight of sleep, have to be filled up somehow. Who is there, not being one of those thrust into the groove of perpetual labor from their birth, who has not felt this? Who is there who has never—nay, who has not often—felt that he has been hardly treated by the Creator in not having left to him the power of absolutely suppressing a part of his existence? And yet in the face of this we dare to complain so loudly of the want of time. We venture even blasphemously to pretend that we lack the time to concern ourselves with the important affairs of our life, with the principles of religion, for example, or with the business of the State. And we comfort ourselves by saying that we will leave these matters to the experts, the very men of all others who are in them to be suspected, since they live only by professing and supporting the system that pays them.

In reality it is more nearly true that everybody has too much time than that he has too little. At any rate, there are none who have too little for their business in life. The trouble is that they will not apply it to *that* business, but go about painfully to waste it over trifling and superfluous business, or trifling and superfluous pleasures (for of these, too, some are necessary), and then complain that they have not enough left for what is requisite to be done.

*　　　*　　　*　　　*　　　*　　　*

Not only is there time enough, but there is virtue and intellect enough in the world to make it as well worth living in as the Creator has by his works declared it to be. And however foolish we may be, we are all wise enough to know that it is important to give to virtue and to intellect their proper place, which is to say the principal place, in the conduct of human affairs. Yet it would seem as though all effort from generation to generation had been directed to doing exactly the reverse. The vulgar herd of men are only capable of playing about, of wondering at all things, and of believing and doing as they are told. A few only there are who can content themselves with none of these things, and who are thus marked out as having been sent into the world on more important errands. You take the vulgar herd and call one king, another prince, priest, lawgiver, subject, vassal, what not, which changes not their nature, and is only your way of lying in the face of Heaven by declaring that one of them, taken indiscriminately, is afore or after other. And the few to whom the highest title and the office of right belong, find both usurped, and themselves relegated mostly to the hewing of wood and the drawing of water. It is not that the blind lead the blind, but that the blind lead the seeing, and push him into the very ditch which he alone could discover.

*   *   *   *   *   *

At Sea, August 9.

Those who see the Creator in his works cannot fail to love him. And they who know why they love the sea know that it is because here they do see him—because they find themselves without their shoes in the holy of holies. In the tempest, when the rack scours the sky, as it did last night, thick and black, when the wind howls, when lightnings jag down a vivid light on the dark waters, and the waves come up and look in at you over your rail as you plunge and dive into them—then you feel that you are in the hands of Omnipotence, and that the most you can do is to take or to guess at the Omnipotent decrees, and to act upon them and by them. Or when, as to-day, the calm succeeds, the clouds lie lazily about the blue in white and gray fleeces, when the sun shines and the waters lilt to the gentle measure of a soft breeze, that you drink in through your nostrils as though it were immortality—who can fail to feel in these the Majesty, the Might, and the Beneficence of the Almighty?

CHAPTER LIV.

In Port, 14th August.

It is a pregnant fact that no man has yet been found to challenge the perfection of the material world, or of any part of its furniture. Never has it been so much as conceived that any one of the created things and beings we see around us is not thoroughly adapted to its immediate uses. This has been felt by all men in all ages, and in every stage of knowledge, as completely as it now is or, so far as we may judge from analogy, which is all we have to judge by, ever will be felt. It was believed of the solar system, when the Ptolemaic hypothesis of the sun moving round the earth was received ; it is believed now that Copernicus has re-established the more ancient eastern system of astronomy. It was believed of the human body before and after Harvey had established the circulation of the blood ; of all animals before Buffon, Cuvier, or Darwin. It is to be accepted, therefore, as an eternal truth—for that belief is certainly entitled to be so considered which no increase of knowledge can affect ; and this is, perhaps, the only belief which no increase of knowledge ever has affected. Surely, then, here at last is an impregnable standpoint ; surely here is the one proof that has never failed of the Omnipotence, the Beneficence, and the Majesty of the Almighty ; surely this is the one great rebuke to those who have presumed to say that there is no Almighty.

*　　*　　*　　*　　*　　*

To give attention to things is to give all we can, and what is remarkable is, that while the first and the last result of attention to the works of God is always admiration, so the result, first or last, of attention to the works of man is always dissatisfaction. We feel that the former are perfect and satisfactory, even if we do not know it ; we feel equally that the latter are imperfect and unsatisfactory, if only we did know it. Whence arises the spirit of criticism. And whence, also, it arises that every man will as little question the works of God as he readily will those of man. For we each of us believe that we possess in ourselves all-sufficient canons of judgment. Even the very little feel capable of criticising the very great ; for to say that they are great is to criticise them. And the amusing part of it is, that he is the greatest of men whose work is most completely accepted by the littlest. So that universal popularity amounts to nothing more than a certificate of excellence from those who are least competent, according to ordinary notions, to give it.

* * * * * *

Descartes, in his discourse upon reason and truth, informs us that as soon as he was old enough to be quit of his schoolmasters he " entirely quitted the study of letters, and resolving to seek no other science than that which I could find in myself or in the great book of the world, I employed the rest of my youth in travelling, in seeing courts and armies, in frequenting people of diverse humors and conditions, and in so reflecting everywhere on the things I saw, as myself to draw more profit from them—for it seemed to me that I should find much more truth in the reasoning that each one makes touching the affairs which interest him, and of which the event will shortly after punish him if he has judged them ill, than in that which a man of letters makes in his study touching speculations which produce no effect, and which are of no consequence to him unless it be that he will satisfy his vanity in proportion as they are far from common sense, and in proportion to the cleverness and artifice he has employed to make them appear probable." This is doubtless the right way to proceed ; but then in order to do that we must each consider the tenement that has been given to us for our habitation in this world, and ourselves make the furniture appropriate to it. Whereas it is so much simpler to live in the furnished lodgings that men of letters have provided for us.

* * * * * *

The way the great sixteenth century sculptor, Torrigiani, died was this. He had made in Spain a statue of the Virgin ; the pious persons who had ordered it of him sought to pay him for it much less than he held the work to be worth, whereupon at last Torrigiani, being a sensitive and impatient man, took his mallet and broke the statue to pieces. This was declared to be an act of impious sacrilege, and Torrigiani was put into the prison of the Inquisition and condemned to be burned for it, from which he only saved himself by starving himself to death.

Is not this the very typical history of what is sometimes known as impiety, blasphemy, and the like ? By man's hand, and out of man's imagination, a something is made which is intended to represent, and which maybe does more or less represent, the Almighty. And then it is declared that to deface or to injure that creation is to defame and to insult the uncreated original that has been sought in it. The artificer takes the wood—of one part he makes a god and worships it, and of the other a fire wherein to burn all those who will not worship with him.

*   *   *   *   *   *

Benvenuto Cellini's father had conceived the ambition of making him the first flute-player in the world, and to the day of his death was wont tenderly to reproach his son with having neglected that divine vocation in order to become an artist in the working of metals. And if this is noteworthy, no less noteworthy is Benvenuto's own desire, shown in his delightful memoirs, to present himself as a roystering gallant and soldier, rather than as the artist he was. When the Constable Bourbon besieged Rome, Benvenuto obtained the command of a few pieces of artillery in St. Angelo, where the Pope had taken refuge, and he tells of the good shots he made with far more detail and pride than he shows for any of his immortal works. But this is to be forgiven for the good story he tells of the tiara and jewels. When the castle was supposed to be in imminent danger of being taken, the Pope sent for Benvenuto, who, by his orders, broke up the triple crown and all the apostolic jewels, melted down the gold, and sewed the precious stones in pieces of stuff on the Holy Father's back ! Is not this a charming and suggestive story ?

CHAPTER LV.

At Sea, 17th August.

There come, perhaps, to all of us those moments of profound disappointment and depression when all energy seems to
fail, when all enjoyments disgust, and all tastes turn to bitter in
the mouth. This does not commonly arise from the apparent
nature of circumstances ; on the contrary, when these seem
most desperate and hopeless, then it is that a man will feel the
most spirit rise within him, then that his courage will be
greatest and the work he does be the hardest. It is rather
when all things appear to go smoothly, when his desires seem
satisfied and his prospects fair, that this handwriting appears
on the wall declaring that there is no delight in anything that
he knows. And then he feels that desire to pluck himself up
by the roots from all that he does know and to seek that he
does not, which always seems to promise consolation, and
which, indeed, always brings consolation. This being so, we
are, perhaps, less unfortunate than we think in knowing little,
since that in itself assures us that the field open to us is by so
much the greater ; for if there were any who had tried everything and knew everything in the world, the only resource for
him on such an occasion were to go out of it.

*   *   *   *   *   *

He who would really go to war, and not merely make a
noise with his weapons, always does do it at his own cost.
Bayard lost his own life, Galileo his own liberty, Palissy
burnt his own furniture to fire his ware, Cellini melted his own
plate to found his Theseus, and not one of them was ever
repaid by the enjoyment of ease, wealth, or glory for the vic-
tories which they won, and by which others have profited.
There is no chance but this—either to fight in the van with
certain loss of tranquillity and probable loss of life and honor ;
or else to do sutler's work in the rear of the army, and when

the battle is over to come forth by night and plunder the dead. The latter trade brings a reward which all can appreciate ; but he who would enter upon the former must be very sure of his mission, very sure of his methods, and very sufficiently satisfied with the sole testimony of his own conscience that he has done well ; for he will get no other.

* * * * * *

It is a common saying—and like most common sayings, a false one—that tastes differ, as though taste were of many kinds, or as though it consisted in aught else than the power of recognizing excellence. What really differs is the extent to which each possesses this power, which varies with the knowledge acquired, the attention given, and the opportunities possessed. Yet those who have fulfilled none of the conditions, assume equally with those who have fulfilled all to have a taste —whence it is made to seem as though excellence varied in proportion to the power of detecting it. We should all have loved Helen of Troy had we but known her, seen her, and lived with her as Paris did ; and if we love another it is that our knowledge, attention, and opportunities have not extended beyond that other. " A poor thing, but mine own," we might all say ; instead of which we all do say, " a rich thing, because mine own," and declare that we have selected by taste that which has been forced upon us by necessity. This is one of the consolations of ignorance.

* * * * * *

Is it not strange that with all the work that has been done since the world began, it is precisely those truths which it most imports us to know that are still farthest from being demonstrated ? The demonstration that two and two make four, that the whole is greater than the part, nay, that the square of the hypothenuse of a right-angled triangle is equal to the sum of the squares of the other two sides—this is perfect ; no human creature who has been taken through the steps that lead to the demonstration ever could doubt or ever has doubted it.

But the nature and the attributes of the Almighty, the nature of good and evil, the immortality of the soul, these are matters which are still as problems to mankind, and which have received demonstrations, nay, which still receive them, as various as the tongues and the climates of the earth. This may show us that it is not only the right, but also the duty of each to approach these tremendous subjects for himself ; not, indeed, lightly or without aim, but honestly and laboriously, so that he may at last have something more to say for his belief than that he has received it from a chance nurse, a chance priest, or, worst of all, from a chance atheist.

*   *   *   *   *   *

That a man should love his friend and hate his enemy is a rule far less easy to act upon than it seems. It is, indeed, more difficult to hate than to love ; for if there are few who deserve at our hands more than endurance, there are still fewer who deserve more than contempt. We all are ready to return good for good, and evil for evil ; we do it, rather as a matter of debtor and creditor account, than from love in the one case or from hatred in the other. And even as a question of account this is also true, since if there are few who can confer true benefits there are fewer who can inflict real injury. The mere disposition and intention to inflict it, however they may by acts be made manifest, can of themselves only excite pity and laughter—not hatred. I am sure that I must have esteemed a man much, and I am not sure but that I must have loved him much, in order to hate him a little.

CHAPTER LVI.

Off Nieuport, 25th August.

With fine weather and the right amount of wind to enable you to go nicely, " trade with the tide," it is hard to resist the temptation of playing about with the fish, and I have just

got a haul of my trawl over these Flemish Banks, which are a
famous place for it. The mere notion of it enlivened the
whole of my immense ship's company, and we regard ourselves
as spoiled children of Fortune now that we have realized our
take. For it consists of two bucketfuls of soles, ray ('' virgins,'' Phil calls them, '' because,'' he says, '' they are little
thorn-backs'') '' monkeys,'' crabs, and star-fish. There is all
the fun of gambling in it, with this advantage, that you stand
to lose nothing ; unless, indeed, it be your tide in, as I fear
we shall do. And the delight of circumventing '' them artful
beggars,'' the fish, is greater even than the pleasure of eating
them fresh out of the water, which, however, is not small.
The amusing part of it is that the more you catch the more
useless they are to you ; so that unless you have caught but
few indeed, you always have to throw the major part overboard. Which, in fact, is the history of all acquisitions by
land or by sea.

*　　*　　*　　*　　*　　*

BRUGES, 27th August.

Probably nine out of ten of any given persons would say off-
hand that Bruges is a very interesting city, and it is in all like-
lihood that the tenth would believe it. Yet in truth it is a
most poverty-stricken assemblage of ghost-like houses without
inhabitants, without life, and, what is most cruel of all, without architecture—even Flemish architecture, which is not asking much, heaven knows. The Cathedral is a kind of brick
skeleton which may or may not have been intended for a stone
covering ; the *Hôtel de Ville* is of that pretentious Gothic which
has made so many modern victims, and the only truly interesting features are a few houses which the Spaniards have left as
their legacy of glory here, just as the Moors left theirs in Spain,
to be the principal ornaments of those who are no longer under
their rule. The famous belfry, a fourteenth-century monument
though it be, is not at all beautiful in itself, and is stuck in the
midst of a mass of low builidngs like a beacon in a sand-bank.
The redeeming part of it is its intention as a rallying-point for

free citizens, sufficiently indicated by the bell and the two
balconies. To bring the populace together and to make
speeches to them, have been from all times the methods of
popular government, and Bruges long lived in the belief that
popular government was the perfection of all things. Now it
lives upon the past, and the remnant that remains of its inhabitants pass their days in regretting the time when Damene was
a port and Bruges a great city, and in aping the fashions of
Paris. It is a sorry place. Also it is full of mosquitoes.

*　　*　　*　　*　　*　　*

There are here a Nativity by Holbein, a *Mater Dolorosa* by
Themling, and a Martyrdom by Meinling, in all of which pictures I believe, for they have all the character of the Flemish
school so far as I know it ; there is also a Virgin and Child
attributed to Michael Angelo, in which statuary I do not believe, since it has not the character of Michael Angelo's work
so far as I know it. Yet the verger who showed it assured me
it was his. So that I claim to prefer my judgment, founded on
my knowledge of Michael's undoubted works, to his tradition.
If this is allowable for the works attributed to man, is it allowable for the works attributed to God ? I had also to ask myself this question, because another verger showed me pictures
of the miracles of St. Ursula and the eleven thousand virgins,
which miracle he assured me was historical and undoubted. Yet
I could not bring myself to believe either in that. In fact, I
fear I am not master of my belief, that I am the slave of the
evidence presented to me and weighed by my judgment, which
means that I am to decide upon imperfect information by fallible reason. Doubtless the vergers are best off who believe
in their Michael Angelo and St. Ursula, without weighing evidence, because they have been told to do so. This reminds
me of one of Diderot's *Pensées philosophiques :* "Lost in an
immense forest during the night, I have but one little light by
which to conduct myself. Then comes a man who says, ' My
friend, blow out your taper in order the better to find your
way.' That man is a theologian."

*　　*　　*　　*　　*　　*

When I think of all the books I have read and of all the speeches I have listened to, even the best of them, it seems to me as though successful utterance in either form were in proportion to the boldness and insolence of the author. It seems as though the most famous had but put down recklessly the first trivialities that passed through their head, only taking care *not* to omit that which was most trivial. There is, indeed, the use of the tools to be learned ; but that is learned in using them, and as soon as you have acquired a sufficient vocabulary to express your idle fancies, and sufficient immodesty to dare it, you are a great author or a great speaker.

* * * * * *

A certain man would never have but one shirt at a time, because he had but one body at a time on which to put it. From which it follows that at certain intervals he had no shirt at all, unless, indeed, the one he had was everlasting, which is inadmissible. And thus it is that we are reduced to the desire to possess the superfluities of life, not because we care for the superfluous, but because we desire to make sure of always having the necessary.

* * * * * *

OSTEND, 28th August.

" Now, Phil," said I, " *that* is the right way to deal with a cucumber. You saw me cover the slices with salt and set the plate up on a slant, and now you see, as I told you, that all that water has run from it." Phil says, " Yes, sir ;" but Phil has an infinitude of different ways of uttering those two words, which make up pretty well the whole of his conversation with me, and on this occasion he did not bring them out with that enthusiasm appropriate to indicate that a new and great light had broken in upon his soul. This grieved me ; for if there is one only thing in the world that I do understand it is cookery in all its branches ; and I have observed that Philip has shown great flippancy in receiving my revelations on this —in fact I strongly suspect a conspiracy in the forecastle to

treat the whole matter with unbelieving derision. I remember
teaching Phil the immortal omelette, and suddenly seeing him
go head first into the frying-pan under strong suspicions of a
Parthian shove from Ned, who was going on deck, and whom
I believe I there heard chuckling in concert with George. I
may be wrong, but when I heard Phil say, " Yes, sir," in a
hesitating, half-convinced way, I felt wounded. It was clear
he did not believe as he should. " Do you see?" I said,
severely looking at him. Phil has a way of half grinning occasionally, and here he half grinned, and repeated his " Yes,
sir," with an even more unsatisfactory intonation. " Well,
but don't you see the water ?" I asked, angrily. " Oh, yes,
sir," he replied, readily, with an accent of the most profound
conviction. " Well, then—" but here I suddenly saw that
I was embarking in a disquisition on the nature and properties
of cucumber, and on the effect of getting rid of this water
from it ; so I simply added, " All right," and left Phil to
digest the brutal fact that when you put salt on cucumber
water results, without, I feel sure, having conveyed any persuasion into his mind that the cucumber is better afterward
than it was before.

*   *   *   *   *   *

I have been half through the town to find a washerwoman
who would undertake to wash the ship's linen in two days, and
had almost resolved to go to sea dirty, when I was directed to
a little street at the end of unknown turnings. I turned and
turned till I came to it ; and walking into the first house, according to my instructions, I found myself face to face with an
old harridan, who, as usual, spoke nothing but the most ac-
cursed of the Flemish tongues. But now, as I was trying to
come to terms with her by the help of German and pantomime,
there stepped into the passage the most splendid creature that
ever wore brown eyes for the injury of man. With hair
deftly plaited on the top of her head, crowning a face the very
Fornarina's own, with bare arms, and the free port and carriage of a goddess, and above all with a smile that never ceased

but only played in diverse accents over her features, she suddenly made me forget my washing, my departure, and Phil, who stood behind me with the bundle over his shoulder, altogether. "Yes," she said, "she would do it." "And would she be careful really to starch the shirts?" "Yes, of course." Here, for the twentieth time, she showed a glistening row of pearly teeth. "And she would be sure to have them ready?" "Quite sure." "And—yes—that was all. Ah!—and, let us see—let us see—to-day was Wednesday?" "Yes, Wednesday," she re-echoed abstractedly, rolling her sleeve a little further up, so that a dimpled elbow came into sight. "Wednesday—yes—well, then, on"—but at this point she gave another roll, raising her hand to the ceiling to do it the more easily, and again showing those teeth. Of course I had to wait till she had done this, and then I added, "Well, then, on Friday. Now, Phil, what are you waiting for?"

There is occasionally an unnatural and untoward smartness about Phil which is intensely irritating. If ever I lie in my berth till half-past seven, then it is and then alone that he has my coffee ready by seven; and when I turned out this morning the first thing I saw was a gigantic basket full of the clean linen. But who was to tell whether he had got it all, or whether he had paid the bill, or whether—clearly it was necessary I should myself go and see to all this. Go, therefore, I did, and I don't know why, but so it was that, when I saw my *belle Ostendaise* again, I had a kind of jump just the same in nature, if not in degree, as one might feel at suddenly coming across the Sacharissa of one's most constant devotions. She smiled—and then I smiled. Then I asked in the most innocent way if the linen were ready. At this she smiled again, and put her thumb and finger—a wonderful taper thumb and finger for a washerwoman—on the edge of her sleeve, whereat I stood abashed and engrossed. "Why, then, did not Monsieur know that his man had been to fetch it?" Monsieur, with eyes still fixed upon that sleeve, evasively answered,

" Vraiment !" as though this were quite new to him ; but feeling unequal to keeping up, suddenly remarked that there were very many people at Ostend—as though that naturally followed or explained something—and thereupon went away.

*   *   *   *   *   *

OSTEND, 30th August.

I feel extremely small. I have navigated so long without pilots, without tugs, without any of the appliances which are usually held to be necessary, that I have got to believe in the Billy Baby, in her captain (for Billy Baby purposes), and in her crew, as in a religion. I have become, in short, convinced that she can do anything " off her own bat" (as they say, I believe, in cricket); and now I have got a " facer" (as they say, I believe, in pugilism), and am humbled. Nevertheless, I so far hold on to my belief in the Billy Baby religion as to be still convinced that if I had been in any less lucky ship I should have gone to pieces ; in fact, I did think we should go to pieces, and the excitement of it was great.

It was all the fault of an abominable Norwegian brig, whose papers were not in order, and who kept us for three mortal hours in the lock before we could get out. The wind was strong from N.W. all but right into the harbor, and the spring tide (to-day is the new moon) was setting right across the harbor to the eastward at thirty thousand miles an hour at a moderate computation. I knew well the danger of getting borne down on to the eastern jetty with wind and tide, but my faith was strong, and I declined all help, and started. We were nearing the entrance when I saw that between the wind and the tide she wouldn't fetch out. I put her about ; but the heavy sea knocked her out of time—she declined to stay—and in a moment we were into the east jetty, jammed against it with the whole force of wind and tide, 'and thumping in a way which was perfectly awful. Down sail was the only thing to do, and then to get a line if possible to the west jetty. But the sea was very heavy—would she hold together till then, or smash up ? Our boat was on deck, unluckily, but after a time

I saw one coming down the port, and hailed him. Meantime she kept thumping against the jetty in a way it seemed impossible she could stand, and I expected every instant to see something or everything go. This lasted for some five mortal minutes, but at last the boat got down to us, took a line, and in about two years, as it seemed, we heard the welcome sound " haul in." Haul in we did, ran the foresail up, got her round, and sailed ignominiously into the harbor again—for it was useless to try to get out. And now I have been ascertaining my damages, which, considering all things, are very small. My gaff is broken, three bolts and a plank or two, including the covering plank, sprung, cat-head broken off, and some paint gone, is about the sum of everything. We have come off cheaply enough, and but for the humiliation I should not care. But I really thought the time had come to sing my little hymn, and even Ned, who believes in her as much as I do, avows that he doesn't know how it was she didn't go to pieces. Well, I shall start again at low water, and repair damages when I get to England. I am only consoled by the fact that exactly the same thing has happened this morning to two other vessels, a Ramsgate smack and an Ostend fisherman, and that it was all the fault of the Norwegian brig, which prevented me from going out as I intended at half-flood over the slack of the stream.

CHAPTER LVII.

At Sea, 8th September.

It is a terrible thing to think how continually this problem, " What shall I do with my life ?" presents itself. For the man whose whole efforts can barely suffice to procure bread, the problem is indeed simple ; he has to get his bread somehow, and there is an end of it. For the man who is in, and has at his command, one calling just sufficient to procure bread, it is no problem at all ; all he knows is how to make dolls' eyes, and he has no choice but to go on making dolls' eyes for bare existence. But go a stage higher ; go only to the designer of dolls, and you will find a man harassed by this problem, from the moment that it is time till the moment it is no longer time to solve it.

And what is still more terrible is that, so soon as you attempt to grapple with this first essential, and as often as you attempt it, you find yourself driven still further back to this other question—"Shall I be honest?" Shall I do what I know, and say what is in me, to the end they point to, or shall I do and say other things to my own ends ? I have my hand full of truths ; shall I open it and overwhelm myself together with the rest ; or shall I close it, and use it, the more heavily weighted for them, fist-like, to hustle my way through this crowd ? Can I, the centre and pivot of the world to myself, trail the pike and do soldier's, ay, or it may be sutler's duty ? —shall I not break through and lead the army, or at the least a brigade ? When you have settled this your life is won or lost.

*   *   *   *   *   *

It is the curse of man to make the monster that devours him. And the worst of all is that monster Want, to feed and gorge which till he dies, beyond all resurrection, of mere satiety, seems to be held the only proper purpose of life. When he first comes to you he is but little in stature, soon satisfied and easily pleased, a true friend and a charming companion, pointing out the uses of things, full of suggestion, serving you like a lackey for the smallest of rewards. And then you foolishly have thought to increase his value by increasing his stature. With strange inventions and unholy charms you have, as you proceeded on your journey, succeeded in blowing him out to the dimensions of a giant, standing with feet wide asunder as the poles, and head in the clouds of heaven. You have made him immense, terrible, tremendous, untiring, insatiable, that he may serve you the better ; and lo ! he is your master. You may not stir but as he directs ; you may not speak or think but

as he orders ; there is no more any God, any glorious sky and
earth, any light of the sun and moon for you but as he wills ;
things are and are not, as he pleases ; and you—you who made
him what he is from what he was—you are condemned to ramp
and grovel among garbage to the end of your days, to fill a
bottomless maw and satisfy the insatiable.

*   *   *   *   *   *

The one true satisfaction that a man can take of his life is to
feel that he is doing some fruitful thing with it, that he, too,
like all those that he holds to be the ignobler works of God, is
giving back to the earth what he has taken from it.   He who
can convince himself of this—that he is truly engaged in work
which will better the world while he lives, knows then that he
is about his duty ; he who is persuaded that his work will live
and bear fruit after he is gone, has already achieved immortality.   The applause and acceptation of men, and all that goes
to make up honor and fame, are only of value in so far as they
begin or confirm this conviction.   But, now, if the conviction
be not there—if, instead of this, there be doubt, or perhaps a
strong suspicion of the contrary sort—if the martyr has gone
to the stake for gods of which he does not know that they *are*
gods, then fame, honor, and to be seen of men is no salve, but
only a torture the more.

*   *   *   *   *   *

I know a few men—alas ! not many—of whom I am sure
that they are honest, nor do I see any reason why I should not
continue to be sure of it.   But I know, also, some of whom I
am convinced that they are rogues without faith or law ; and
when I come to think of these I am compelled to admit that of
them, at least, I dare not be sure.   Do we not each of us remember how small—how infinitesimally small—a part even of
our acts—much less of our motives—is known to any who
would judge us ; do we not remember how great a wrong has
been done to us by judgments passed glibly on this imperfect
knowledge ? and shall we not hesitate before we also judge

others ? But, above all, shall we not entirely cease to care how others judge us ? But I speak as a fool, assuming that what we want is a true judgment—not a false character.

The foregoing observation is what is called commonplace. That is the point of it ; since that shows that all men feel its truth. For the most fearful of all things is to see the most common convictions most commonly denied in practice.

Columbus did not discover America, for he took it to be Asia ; neither did Magellan first sail round the world, for he was killed at the Philippines when the circuit was barely half completed. Galileo did not believe that the earth moved round the sun, for he solemnly recanted that heresy. But they went into the unknown, and adventured themselves over the edge of the world, and there is, therefore, nothing to abate from their fame. For to measure the value of work and the credit due for it by the results achieved, is as foolish as to measure the morality of facts by their accomplishment. Yet these are the only methods of measurement admitted, even by those who affect to revere Columbus, Magellan, and Galileo.

CHAPTER LVIII.

In Port, 15th September.

I once heard a man wrangling with a cabman over sixpence. "It isn't the amount, you know, but the Principle," he explained to me, with which I agreed. Some time after the same man confided to me the negotiations respecting his marriage settlements, as to which a great fight was being waged over a certain sum of ten thousand pounds. He said nothing of principle then, and treated the matter as deriving its importance solely from the largeness of the amount at stake. From which I was forced to conclude that there was in his estimation a point somewhere between sixpence and ten thousand pounds, at which Principle may cease to operate and be disregarded, and Amount be alone taken into consideration ; which further led me to reflect that all men, with the fewest possible exceptions, do also recognize that point.   The point itself varies with the wants, real or invented, of the individual ; but when once that point is passed, whoever can offer to him the satisfaction of his want is his master, who may dispose of him, of his Principle, and his virtue together.   The cabman, we will say, at sixpence gives up Principle for Amount ; he is salable therefore at sixpence.   The gentleman, we will say, gives it up not under ten thousand pounds ; he is salable, therefore, at ten thousand.   And between the two there must be many who are salable at ten pounds, at fifty, at a hundred, or a thousand. So that Walpole would not be wrong even in this age of virtue. Only of the two I should far less condemn the cabman who sold his Principle for sixpenny worth of necessaries, than the gentleman who sold his for ten thousand pounds' worth of superfluities.

*   *   *   *   *   *

That the end does not justify the means we all are or profess to be agreed ; but what is strange is that nobody has ever questioned or ever does question whether the means justify the end. The received code is that you may not do an unlawful thing because it tends to compass a lawful end, but that you may do a lawful thing even though it tends to compass an unlawful end.   You shall not lie and save innocent blood, but you shall speak the truth and spill it.   You shall not murder, steal, or betray your country ; but you shall truly and honestly serve a murderer, a thief, or a traitor, without crime, and shall be harmless in bringing about his wicked ends, because your means have not been wicked.   You may know the ends to be wicked, but you are not to know it, being concerned only with the means that *you* employ.   You may not do evil that good may come, but you may and shall do good that evil may come. You have nothing to do with the end, forsooth, and are bound not to look at it.   You are a wheel in a fixed place, and all you have to do is to turn without eccentricity on your axis. Cowardly and degrading notion which prescribes the honest service of roguery and the faithful following of treachery! What kind of answer, too, will it be when one day the answer is called for, to say that we never inquired as to the end, and thought ourselves secure in the fair appearance of the means?

*   *   *   *   *   *

I consider all the self-made men I know, and I conclude that all the great fortunes, which is to say as times go all the great successes, of our days, have been made either by superiority in the mean swindling by which money is transferred in a generation too cowardly for open violence—or else by the more honest method of hitting upon a very small modification in some article of universal necessity. One millionnaire represents an improved axle-tree, another a new stitch in a sewing-machine, a third a novel mixture of lubricating grease, and I have at this moment a man in my eye who has been offered thirty thousand pounds for a mere notion of bolting together railway rails. The men who first invented axle-trees, sewing-machines, lubrication, and rails, were miserable failures as compared with these, their latter-day parasites—and so it is that while all the great untried original ideas are still going a-begging, and only get at last received by chance, all the small supplementary contemptible ideas that fasten upon them when once they are received, are madly scrambled for and bring certain reward.

Thus it is that with our minds bent on small objects we are become a small people with the small ideas that pay, looking with distrust and contempt on the larger that only wear, their originator. It is not that the age of heroism is past. There are still heroic things—alas! how many—to be done; and still heroic men—alas! how few—to do them. And he must be the greater hero who attempts them, seeing that he must sow his life, his repose, his very soul, spirit, and reputation, and leave to others who shall pass casually by, to pluck with careless hand all the fruit of the tree he has planted.

Yet not all, for he has his own knowledge of the worth of his own work. If he can be content with this he must, it is true, be a hero indeed ; but if he be less than content with it he is no hero at all.

CHAPTER LIX.

In Port, 25th September.

It is a pitiable thing to think that, with the exception of the fishermen, and a few of us favored ones who have been fishermen ourselves, there is scarcely a creature in those sea-girt islands of ours who knows the proper taste of fish. The dead bodies of fish kept for days or weeks, or even for months, in ice-cellars they know indeed ; but these are not fish. They are like to one another, except in shape and sauce, and no more like to the fish cooked fresh out of the water than mummy is like to man. If those who look at *menus* and go away believing, on the faith of them, that they have eaten turbot, brill, sole, mullet, or what not, were to get one haul of a trawl, or a trammel, or even of a " dabbing" line (most delicious of all fish is the dab, and therefore, I suppose, least known), and were to eat of their take, they would never again look at an ice-preserved fish. This icing is another of our delightful devices by which we improve out of everything its natural salt and taste, and make all things insipid and alike ; which reminds me that all the inventions I know of for improving upon the original simplicity of things, acts, and beliefs do commonly end in suppressing their original, like wicked children that eat their father. The taking of notes to aid memory kills memory ; the study of other men's thoughts to provoke our own thought makes an end of thinking ; theology destroys religion ; legislation destroys the Law ; many inventions have left man less upright than God made him. And now there is not one but feels the yearning to go back to the time when inventions were not, and mankind ate their fish either not at all or fresh out of the water.

*   *   *   *   *   *

"No man can bathe twice in the same river," is an axiom accepted by all who will think of it, and upon this it has been remarked that no man can even bathe *once* in the same river, for before he has bathed even that once, the water in which he began has run away. Just so no man can be twice the same self—no, nor perhaps once. Most of us are conscious that by efflux of time their personality has changed—that all that constitutes it, whether corporeal or mental, has undergone alteration, and that they are no longer what they were. They know also that this alteration has not taken place suddenly or by jumps, but so gradually as to be imperceptible to themselves except by comparisons made at considerable intervals. A personality they have, but, like the river, it is always running away, and its place being filled by another. I who write this am not the same precisely as the I who wrote the last sentence of this paragraph, nor as the I who will write the next. The intermediate I is, indeed, the son of the first and the father of the third, yet not the same. And now I ask myself which one of my many selves it is which will live, eternally or temporarily, when the long succession of them is closed? There are one or two, perhaps three of them, which I should repudiate with indignation, there are many of which I have a mean opinion, and there are a few which I admire. If I could only pick and choose! But no, this principle of averages will come in, and I shall live forever or for a day, in the spheres or in one man's mind, as my average self—which is the only one of all my selves that I have never known. It is bitter to think that when I am gone I should not recognize what remains of me if I were ever able to get a glimpse of it.

*   *   *   *   *   *

Mr. Holloway ought to be Prime Minister of England. I never go anywhere at home or abroad, but I see his name; I never take a newspaper, English or foreign, but I read the praises of his pills—and what is best of all, I am not obliged to take them, and never mean to. But, since we estimate the worth of men, and especially of ministers, by the extent to which their names have been advertised, why not frankly accept the situation, and call upon Mr. Holloway to save his country? His name is a household word where Gladstone and Disraeli have never been heard of ; his might and majesty and the cures he has made are written in every newspaper in the world. If this does not make a claim, what does? And then, as I say, you are not obliged to take *his* pills.

CHAPTER LX.

At Sea, 16th October.

It is humiliating to find what elementary difficulties crop up for the first time when you actually try to do anything—a thing which, so long as you only talked of it, seemed the simplest in all the world. Here am I who have set my heart on an Irish stew. I have got the recipe to make it—"Two pounds and a half of chops" (how am I to eat two pounds and a half of chops?), "eight potatoes" (that seems a small allowance for so many chops), "and four small onions ; stew for two hours, and serve hot," which last direction assumes us all to be mad enough to serve it cold. Well, I have had Phil up on the quarter-deck, and read all this to him, when he asks me "When he's to put them onions in ?" "When ! why with all the rest of course—at least I suppose so." "But all the goodness of 'em 'll boil away." Of course I couldn't admit this, and held him to putting everything in together. But suppose, now, that all the goodness *does* boil away! It will be very hard on me, for, in fact, it is precisely those onions that give the thing its flavor. I wonder when you ought to put them in,

This Phil is a perfect revolutionist in a ship, with his questions. I don't believe it matters a bit.

*   *   *   *   *   *

I have often marvelled how it is that this blessed and bountiful Solitude, consoling mistress of men and mother of all great things as she is, should be so maligned. For even her worst enemies court her whenever they are moved into action. No man cares to have a company about him when he is very joyful or very sorrowful, very much in love, very full of hate, very determined, or even very drunk. If, therefore, he shuns solitude as a rule, it is that, as a rule, he lives a pale colorless life, so devoid of occupation that he must needs look upon many faces in order to fill the void, and cause him to forget that there is a void. But what is amusing is the notion, that for one unoccupied and objectless man to look upon another is in itself an object and an occupation. This reminds me of those Chinese boxes fitted exactly one inside the other. You open them all to the last, and in that you find—nothing.

*   *   *   *   *   *

' Every one for himself and God for us all." Very fine, no doubt, is this modern gospel, made, like the razors, to sell, to a generation which believes in self-interest well understood— which is to say understood as self-interest. But now if that topmast goes, or that standing rigging betrays me, as this stanchion has done which has come away in my hand with a heavy lurch of the ship, will the shipwright be guiltless who supplied them ? Of course he will, you reply ; for I ought not to have trusted him or anybody, and ought to have examined, tried, and tested all sticks and ropes before I paid for them. I thank you.

*   *   *   *   *   *

OFF SHOREHAM, 17th October.

Judging from what I have read even of the most favored heroes, I should suppose that to wait for the woman one adores must be trying ; but I doubt it is quite as trying to be laid to at nightfall off your port, as I now am, with a heavy sea, the wind dead on the shore, and blowing harder every minute, and no chance of getting in under five hours at least. There has been every appearance of what sailors call " dirt"—last night an immense " burr" or ring round the moon, this morning another round the sun, and a strong southerly wind all day. It is a question whether we hadn't better go to sea again, for if the bad weather which is coming comes too soon, we shall have what Ned calls a job of it, since I am forced to admit secretly to myself that the Billy Baby would *not* claw off a lee-shore at this distance.

In this situation I remark, for the thousandth time, the tremendous consolation there is in the uncertainty of life and our ignorance of the future. The troubles one foresees from any distance are never those that happen, the misfortunes one fears are never those that overtake one. Your human providence is always at fault. You provide for being run over by this omnibus, and you get drowned at sea ; you fear you will not live through that gale, and a tile falls on your head ; you mourn over the infidelity of your lady love, and the misery that overtakes you is that you marry a vixen. And as the worst part of all trouble is the apprehension of it, it *is* a comfort to remember that those of which we have had the most lively apprehension are precisely those we have escaped. Wherefore I opine that we shall get in all right, and I shall turn in and make up by a nap for being up all last night.

CHAPTER LXI.

At Sea, 24th October.

Ah, yes ! There is comfort and consolation in this dear cherished Mother Nature in all her moods, and, I often think, more of it in those of her moods from which men avert their faces than in the rest. Look with me, look at this sea, kissed into passion by the strong breath of the gale. Look at that angry red streak of sky that announces the long-wished-for day. Look at the torn rift that scours overhead, and the dark masses of squall-cloud lying on either hand, racing over the water and the coast, with their burden of rain and wind. Look at those waves which no man of the millions who have tried it has ever yet described, or given a notion of their infinite play, their infinite change, and power, and color ; look at them with me, tired with a night's watching, anxious about the ship, full of work changing and reefing sails—look at them all and say if you can resist their beauty, or not see that in them is the very face and voice of the Eternal. Praise to Him who has given us these glimpses of majesty which alone make us to know our own nothingness, and which ever remind us that it is all very good, and that we have only to go and look upon it to know that. How dull, foolish, and flat are the things that man has made out of such rags as he has stolen from the elements, in the presence of the elements themselves ; how antique, moth-eaten, and rusted all his inventions when you take the very best of them, and think of them now in the presence of this eternal beauty, force and youth, which are always at our doors, and which we all love, and all are affected by, though we do pretend to despise it as an old dust heap. Yes, indeed, it is good for us to be here.

*   *   *   *   *   *

It is very humiliating, this love of little children, when one comes to think of it. For if we find our fellows are more lovable in the child than in the man, it must mean that we know them to be essentially and innately unlovable, and only to be really worthy of affection before their essential and innate qualities have had time to become developed. A good fruit is best when it is ripe ; but mankind, we conclude, are best when they are unripe. The very qualities that charm in the child in their immaturity, are precisely those that disgust in the grown man in their maturity. A little selfishness, a little gluttony, a little ungenerosity, artlessly and shamelessly shown by the child, appear to us not only innocent, but charming ; yet those same qualities when developed render our fellows odious to us, and all the more odious when covered with hypocrisy.   It pleases to see the child ape the worse parts of the man ; it revolts to see the man ape the better part of the child.   Possibly we misjudge both.

*   *   *   *   *   *

Can a man pray who does not believe ?   Certainly he can, and certainly in time of imminent need, if at no other, he will. For he, too, does believe in something, if not in that very thing you put before him ; and he will pray to that in your formula, while all the time he is praying through that to the thing in which he believes.   The world presses upon him, unknown and uncomprehended powers compass him about, and if in his anxious yearning he finds aught near at hand claiming to be a symbol of the Power in whose hand he feels himself to be—ay, even though it be the rudest and most manifest fetich —he will pray to the fetich rather than not pray at all, and if for no other reason, yet for this—that he does not know but that there *may* be something in it.

*   *   *   *   *   *

In Port, 26th October.

I have sometimes idly enough wondered whether there is really anything pleasurable in being addressed as Sir Tom, Sir Dick, My Lord, Your Grace, and so forth.   Because that is all the advantage a man really gets out of being one whom his Sovereign, in the name of his country, has delighted to honor.   All the rest—the sitting above the salt, the best cut of the joint, the arm-chair, the off-side of the carriage, and the going down to dinner first or second, instead of second or third —are advantages that come to every man on occasion, and are not especial to the honored one ; the one only advantage that is specially and exclusively his, is his being called out of the common.   Well, now, *is* there anything in it ?   I always be-

lieved there was not—for it is a mere notion, or more properly the mere notion of a notion, signifying nothing but a
belief taken on trust and mostly unfounded, testifying to nothing but a falsehood, exhaling in breath, leaving nothing but a
melodious twang which Sir Tom and My Lord know well must
be a discord to any who has an ear for music.

So I have always said to myself ; yet I am converted from
to-day so far as this, that I am come near to understanding
how it is that the twang is melodious to its beneficiary, if to
nobody else.   For here, at a large French watering-place, I
have come shamefacedly into the largest hotel, a kind of town
in itself, and have found myself absolutely its one sole occu-
pant besides the proprietor and the waiters.   I have been accustomed to see two hundred people dine at its *table d'hôte*,
and when I asked the hour of dinner to-day I was requested to
fix it myself.   For *I* am now the *table d'hôte*, and, amused as
I am at myself, I can't quite forbear a sense as of promotion at
this distinction.   It titillates me gently and caresses me to be
asked, " A quelle heure, Monsieur, voudra-t-il la table d'hôte ?"
and I verily believe that if the same prostration before me of
the whole physical, spiritual, and culinary resources of the
place were habitually repeated, I should in time come to
believe that I had done something to deserve it beyond being
the only guest.   What surprises me now, therefore, is that
I have known melodiously twanged men who have *not* believed
this of themselves.

*   *   *   *   *   *

" Go where you will, you will never find the equal of what
happens every day in this world." So said a French émigré,
and so to this day he might say.   Now of all things that do
happen in this world, the affectation, which I find is still
common, of belief in the reasoning faculties, and of readiness
to s. mit things in general to their decision and to abide by
their mandate—this is the most unmatched ; and I venture to
believe that, when we do go elsewhere, we shall find in no
sphere or planet, or any one of these countless worlds I see

above me, anything like it. You and I know very well that we judge nothing by reason, but everything by the sympathies, the antipathies, the prejudices perhaps, which that series of chance events called our education has brought into activity within us. A matter as to which we care nothing, and which is therefore of self-confessed unimportance, we may indeed hand over contemptuously to reason. That two and two make four, that the two angles of a triangle are greater than the third, that the angle of incidence is equal to the angle of reflection, that the earth revolves on its axis—all this we will submit to abstract investigation and decision ; for we care nothing which way it is decided. But whether this man is honest whom we have learned to hate, or that woman true whom we have learned to love—these are questions which reason shall not touch, and which shall be decided at any rate as we wish ; in other words, which have already been decided for us. In despite of which, we will go on declaring that we are reasoning and reasonable animals, whereas in truth we are unreasonable, passionate, sentimental creatures, and nothing more. For which let God be praised who has made us such, and man be condemned who, even in this. the world's senility, has never discovered that such we are.

CHAPTER LXII.

On Board the Billy Baby,
At Sea, November 20.

There is this great advantage in cruising about during the winter, that you never want for wind ; but there is the question whether this is not counterbalanced by your having sometimes too much of it. It seems hard to leave one of these tidal ports, where you are out-of-doors at once and can't run back, with a rising glass and a fine fresh northerly breeze, only to find yourself reduced within a couple of hours to taking down every reef in your mainsail, and balancing yourself with a mere spitfire jib. Of course there is great delight in the feeling that you are in a nice comfortable ship, instead of being on some cold bleak hill ashore, in a railway-carriage, or in the street of some town full of insecure chimney-pots ; but then at sea you always have the notion of something worse coming than you have yet had. I am short-handed, too, having lost one man of my crew, which amounts to forty per cent. on a full complement of two and a half. Phil has capsized the Irish stew once and the coffee twice, and his final results are so gritty and uncertain that I suspect he must have mopped them both up together, instead of separately, to put them back into the saucepan. But then you can't have everything all at once.

*   *   *   *   *   *

Sunday, November 21.

I thought we never should get that anchor this morning—and also with Ned that it did " blow uncommon hard," and I have, besides, a mean opinion of myself for shirking the Looe. But you may prove to yourself as much as you like—on the chart—as I proved to myself last night, that you have only to run down to a line of bearing of your one light and then haul your wind to be safe ; you may demonstrate this most clearly ; and yet you may not face a channel half a mile wide on a pitch dark night with such a breeze blowing as there was then and still is. In such circumstances one says " of course if it were necessary I'd try it," but, then, what is to be the measure of the necessity ? Ought it to be necessary that the enemy were bound for your port, and you sent to give warning ; or should it not be sufficient that you want to see your Sweetheart six hours earlier ?

*   *   *   *   *   *

SOUTHAMPTON, Tuesday, November 23.

I remember, when I got that handsome ninety miles' tow in a dead calm this summer, being ungrateful enough to remark

how absolutely useless any and every steamer must be as a
school of seamanship.   There was the monster steaming straight
ahead, and I hanging on to her, both relieved absolutely from
any necessity whatever for paying that constant, unceasing,
vigilant attention to the wind and the weather which makes the
good sailor.   No need for vigilance in this respect, no need
for foresight, no need for shifts and devices, no need for readiness of resource—the whole science of seamanship, as I felt,
had disappeared, and in its place there was nothing left but a
stoker and a steersman.   Mind there was none, and no necessity for it beyond this ; for although in the original contrivance
of the steam machinery there had been a mind, this had been
left ashore, and here at sea there remained of it nothing but
the rote-knowledge of the formula of stop-cocks, stoke-holes,
and oil-cans.   The charm of the thing was gone, one might as
well be ashore, and I vowed that I would never be towed again.

And I have seen now, within a very few hours, two striking
proofs that steam is the end of seamanship.   Yesterday afternoon I passed a large screw collier most inexcusably run ashore
on Calshot Spit, close to the castle, where she had no earthly
business to get, with Calshot Light to guide her, either by day
or by night ; and this morning I had the delight of seeing a
huge German Lloyd's steamer coming down from Southampton
also run plump ashore opposite Netley.   The point is, that
there was no kind of excuse to be conceived for either one of
these two blunders, and that they were both precisely the sort
of blunders which could not occur to any man with a proper
seaman's training.   I am only sorry that they have both got
off apparently without much damage.   But if such things are
done when there is not any excuse, what must be done every
day when there is ?

CHAPTER LXIII.

On Board the Billy Baby,
29th November.

I KNEW a man who had found the two only pearls of price —a true friend, and a good brave woman. To the woman he plighted his troth, to his friend he wrote to ask for a blessing : and then he saw what it was to have such an one. For the friend wrote him thus—a letter which should be printed in letters of gold, and given for a fortune to every hesitating pair in England :

" Yes, God bless you, and guard, and guide, and prosper you—a form of prayer which I have never offered up to God but for my own wife ; and if the girl you have chosen is in the future but one half the joy and pride that mine has been to me, you will have drawn the great prize in the lottery of life —a prize to which no other prizes are to be compared. My heart would have broken but for the most beautiful and sustaining love of my wife. I should go out into the highways and byways and preach marriage to all men, in simple honesty and good-will toward my fellow-creatures, knowing what marriage has been to me. Heaven only knows what would have become of me but for a tenderness which has never tired, a devotion which has never failed me, and which has had in it something surely divine.

" So I say with all my heart ' God bless you ! ' again and again ; and be of good courage. You will not want much money if you have much love. It is the right and duty of a man to support his wife, and it is better for both of them that he should be in every respect the head and mainstay of the family. There is nothing to fear in poverty when a man's heart is whole and his affections satisfied. I was for a short time, as you know, very poor, and nothing has ever impressed me more forcibly than the fact that poverty, when it came so close, had no terrors for me. Moreover, the possibilities of

life are infinite, and no man of enterprise, intelligence, and
character need be poor.   You and your wife will never be poor,
and the only counsel I would give you, the outcome of years
and experience, is ' Cultivate your affections and till your
hearts.'   There is no harvest so bounteous as that of love.
Let no shadows come between you, no sulks, no misunder-
standings, and no unkind words.   Accustom yourselves (using
a sort of resolute mental force when required, and it will be required) to look upon each other as perfection.   You are sure
to have something, perhaps much, to forgive each other as
time rolls on.   Well, forgive—forgive freely—and with that
sweet eager grace which forgives beforehand, and which offers
assurance and warranty of all future forgiveness.   If your be-
trothed is very young be careful not to scare away her trust.
Encourage her to tell you everything ; be father, mother,
sister, husband to her.   Approve her in all things, that she
may conceal nothing, and lead her very gently away, without
reproof, from anything which may displease or grieve you.

" And above all things, I would say, make her the companion of your thoughts.   Associate her both with your business
and with your pleasures.   Let her have no idle, listless days,
no lonely evenings.   Let her see that you are just and fair in
all your dealings with her, so that when she compares other
men with you she may feel that you are rather a hero than a
man.   Teach her to dress in her best and bravest for you, and
make her glad with your admiration, so that all her life long
she shall hear no such music as her husband's praise.   On your
part also dress better than ever you did in your life.   Marriage
should not be the grave of Hope, but Hope's garden.

" Once more, God bless you !"

*   *   *   *   *   *

November 30.

It is a consoling thought which should alone, and of itself,
redeem this much-maligned scheme of creation from all the evil
that is so hastily spoken of it, that we owe all our misery to

ourselves and all our happiness to others. If I do my duty and act up to my warrant as fully as I can read it, even if that be not very fully, no man can truly take away by peace of mind. He may sadden me for a time, but my sadness is for him not for myself, and bears with it its own sure antidote. Say he betrays and deserts me, deeply injures me, ruins me, kills me. *I* know, and I alone, whether he does any of these things justly ; if so, I know then that I am the cause of all ; if not, it will be, as in all ages to all men it has been, a sufficient con-olation to know that I suffer unjustly, that I am punished without cause—and then I cannot be truly miserable.

And now, just as there is something—and not a small thing either, for I know it—of pleasure in the worst earthly misery, so there seems to be something of poison in the best earthly happiness. You have struck the sweet note, it answers to the touch, and now even while your ears drink in the full, round, beautiful sound, you are aware of that after-twang which is as a vibration of pain. There shall be a man who is drunk with happiness—with happiness of the purest and most unalloyed kind—and that man as he walks through the streets shall be moved with tears to see all those men and women going about their avocations, and to know that they cannot be as happy as he.

CHAPTER LXIV.

On Board the Billy Baby,
20th December.

Say what you will, it is a fine thing to be married, were it only that it always seems to bring with it the lesson, even in the merest and most trifling of the congratulations, ay, and of the presents it brings, that the world is far kinder than in its usual aspects it seems. My friend, who is in this case, has received another letter from *his* friend, and it is so true, so wise, and so touching, that I give it here ; let those laugh at it who can, it is a dower any bride might be proud of.

"December 3, 1875.

" My Dear Friend :

" I also do not read your letters unmoved. It brings my own youth and hopes back again to see you so young and so brave. And what you say is right about the fulness of happiness which a true-hearted girl brings with her as a dower from heaven. Never suffer yourself or her to forget that there is nothing really worth having in this world but love—for love is joy, and neither money nor the gains of ambition have the taste of pleasure in them. Money makes all but very high-hearted folk intolerably impudent ; ambitious dreams realized make men either proud or sad—bumptious if they are selfish, sad if they sought for power as a means of doing good, and find themselves as impotent as before when they have got but the shadow of it, which is all that can be had in this world.

" Therefore, cling firmly all your life long to the home affections. There will be always peace at your own hearth if you seek it honestly. There is no peace elsewhere ; and it seems to me as though a man should go forth to his daily labor as to a task which he must do, and return home to cast up his accounts with God at night. There, when the flowers cluster round his open window, and the pet bird sings in summer-time, or when the curtains are drawn, and the sea-coal burns in the familiar fireplace on winter evenings, while the disinherited and the miserable wander homeless through the dark cold without, he may thank the Giver of all good for exceptional grace and mercy with a very humble spirit, and ask his wife to help him while they search if they have not soothed some human anguish, dried some tear, and made some one happier or better since last they lay down to rest. If they have, their slumbers will be very light, for they will sleep beneath the smile of God,

" And now let me say to you that if you will take me for a
guide in life while I remain here, there is nothing which I
would more earnestly commend to you than the daily practice
of prayer.   Never go to your work or return from it, never sit
down to your table or rise from it, without a brief appeal or
thanksgiving to heaven.   You will find that piety will thus
become a habit to you, and that the practice of reading the
lessons for the day every morning will give a nobler key-note
to your mind.   It will put your thoughts in harmony with
those of all wise and good men, and with all worthy womanhood.   It will be of infinite comfort to you in those times of
trial when all of us must pay tribute to our mortality.   It will
give you fortitude in adversity, and secure you in prosperity.

" When you remember this counsel, dear boy, as I trust you
will do, even should you reject it for a time, think of it, not as
the advice of a pedant or a churchman, but as the innermost
thought which a world-worn old diplomatist expressed to a
friend whom he loved, and in whose welfare and career he took
a very tender and true interest.

" Some fifteen years ago I was very intimate with the late
Baron Prokesch-Osten, then Austrian Internuncio at Constan-
tinople.   He was one of the best and wisest men I have every
known, and he was then seventy-five years old.   I remember
he once said to me, ' There is nothing true but Christianity,
and every really able man I have ever known has arrived sooner
or later at this conclusion.'   Bear it, therefore, steadily in
mind, and recollect that it comes to you from two generations
of diplomatists, who both agreed with the priests.''

*   *   *   *   *   *

In craft of my size it is a usual thing, when you have let go
the anchor, for all hands to go ashore and get drunk, leaving
the vessel to look after herself.   Nevertheless, I have been
taught in the course of my nautical education that the anchor-
watch is of great importance, and that not only should there
always be a hand on deck to tend her when she swings, and,
if necessary, to hoist a bit of sail that she may cast the right

way, but that there are many possible events to be provided for even in the best anchorages—such as another vessel running into you—which require constant attention for their avoidance. Yet it is hard to get this into one's head, and, anchored here as we are in the most quiet and peaceable of rivers preparatory to laying up, it seems impossible to suppose but that all we have to do now is to go ashore and amuse ourselves, retaining only the memory of our cruises for fireside yarns.

At any rate here, for the present, is an end of Flotsam and Jetsam. It has been often foolish, no doubt, sometimes presumptuous, and betimes flat and dull. Perhaps, nevertheless, it may have interested some as being the true reflection of the derelict thoughts of a man small enough himself, but brought betimes into contact with great things, and feeling somewhat the greatness of them, and feeling also, and at the same time, the constraining influence of the little things of his daily life. They are not very unlike that man, and so may be like many another, which, if it be so, will give them a value to that other as though he himself had kept such a disjointed, often mistaken, and always to be corrected, dead reckoning of his course. I myself cannot look back to them without a certain feeling of tenderness and affection, much as a painter might look upon an ill-daubed, unfinished portrait of part of himself by himself, nor without the same kind of regret both that the original was not better, and that the portrait was not better painted. Yet I think that, if ever a man had a chance of seeing what he himself is like, it is when he is living by himself in this kind of way, or in some way like it; and that, if at all, it would be by keeping a record of such idle thoughts as are here put down, as and when they are provoked by his reflections, his work, and his communion with Nature, and that better part of man which is found in books. Doubtless, these thoughts are not sufficient for a life, yet they have an interest if they are unforced honest thoughts; and possibly figments of the brain even such as these, floating and drifting at mercy as they have done, may haply be picked up and help some mariner to piece out and patch up his ship.

Once more I hear the ripple of the water against the bows of the little ship that has carried me so well, and been my one only true home for so many months ; once more I have that feeling that the world is before me to go where I will, and no man to say me nay ; once more I look around my narrow limits and rejoice in them as those of my own kingdom.   In a few days she will be dismantled, stripped, her white wings gone, her crew dispersed, and the whole economy and principle of the thing changed.   It is as a kind of death ; yet, as the natural, proper, and desirable death, which is a passage from a good world and a happy life to a better and a happier.

CHAPTER LXV.

On Board the Lively Sally,
Cowes, 2d December, 1881.

You may say what you like, but there is no abode for rest, occupation, sport, variety, and interest like a good stout ship. When I think of people staying in country houses to shoot poultry, and of other people living in town and going to plays and fancying that they are making the best of their lives—I can only wonder that they should content themselves with such things, when they might be comfortably installed in a fifty-ton cutter bound for a pleasant winter's cruise.   Houses, no doubt, are to some extent necessary evils.   There are women, children, parsons, politicians, and other weak vessels to be provided for ; there are spare-sails, spars, blocks, and gear that have to be kept in store ; and of course there are nautical almanacs and other things which can conveniently be attended to ashore.   But what is so odd is that even in this country, which

calls itself maritime, there are people who fancy that a house
is the best place to live in, and that a ship is merely a
contrivance for making occasional journeys in fine weather !
Of course the only thing to be done for such people is
either to elect them Members of Parliament or to pray for
them.

Meantime here we are all ready for a start across the Bay.
The water is filled ; there are potatoes and cunningly-preserved
meats and three live ducks on board ; there is a splendid
moon, which must by no means be wasted, at a time when the
night lasts for sixteen hours out of the twenty-four—and as a
matter almost of course the wind hangs in the one quarter that
won't do for us.   One would imagine that after blowing from
the S.W. for a month on end, it would show some signs of
change—but so far nothing will move it.   Every day we flatter
ourselves we detect hopeful signs of its going round to the
westward, and so up to N. or N.E.   It ought to do so, for
during the last three days the barometer has been steadily rising ; yet it is still nailed fast in the old quarter, and every
harbor on the south coast is full of wind-bound vessels, bound,
like ourselves, down Channel.   There are a score here from
the biggest to the littlest, and you may see the crews loafing
about ashore in that aimless way which marks the sailor who
is hung up by the weather.   Then the Yankees have promised
us another hurricane between to-day and the day after to-morrow !   Will it come ?   I doubt it ; but certainly the weather
is wild and far from encouraging.   In sheer desperation we recall experiences of how, when the wind backs too much and
gets beyond S., it sometimes tumbles, as it were, over the
edge, and gets into the finer quarter in spite of itself.   We
cheerfully reflect that it can't blow forever, and that unless
there is an extraordinary stock of spare wind somewhere we
must soon get to the end of it.   Finally Dick, the mate, who
is of a somewhat despondent turn, remarked to-day that he
thought, he did, that there " must be an easterly wind just at
the back of this here ;" and, in short, we have pretty well hoped

ourselves into a conviction that there will be a change to-morrow.

The smart triflers who so admire Cowes during the fine fort-night of the year, would hardly know it in winter. All that hoisting and hauling down of bunting, ringing of bells, and pulling ashore in four-oared gigs, which is supposed to repre-sent the whole art of navigation and seamanship, is entirely absent. In the roads there lie no dapper yachts, but only a few disconsolate *chassemarees*, a Norwegian bark with her bul-warks and boats carried away, and her royals and top-gallant sails hanging in ribbons from the yards. The yacht skipper, elegantly bound in brass, no longer is seen on the shore, and the Squadron Club-house is a scene of desolation, presided over by William and a strong body of painters and other British workmen. In the streets you meet a few uncouth men inartis-tically clad in sea-boots and mufflers, who have come ashore from the wind-bound vessels in the roads ; beyond that the place is deserted, and might be Falmouth or any other real sea-port for all its appearance.

The Lively Sally is the very picture of what a fifty-ton cutter should be. She is what would be called a thoroughly " whole-some" vessel. In form, and in the smallness of her mast and spars, she would remind you of a North Sea smack, and, as to sea-going qualities, she would drown three quarters of the yachts and five eighths of the big steamers afloat. She is put together like a light-ship for strength, and she is found as very few vessels are, everything being about as big and as strong again as is usually the case with the fine-weather yacht. Her crew are not yachtsmen—they are sailors, which is quite another thing—and she is kept with the utmost jealousy and perfection.

As for me, I am only a passenger on board. The effect of this position is to make one feel that the vessel may do any-thing and go anywhere, since one is not responsible. This is a pleasant sensation, but I have not yet quite arrived at the stage of being on board ship without feeling ready to turn out and be on deck at a moment's notice.

3d December.

The wind has taken up from the S.E.; but there is scarce any of it ; so we give it another day.

4th December.

Now we really *are* off.

Monday, 5th December.

Not a bit of it. We are not off at all, but still here. Being only a passenger I am of course impatient ; but still I can understand and sympathize with the skipper. I know well the effort required to come to a decision in the face of unpromising signs, and the temptation to hold on till they look better. Here we have the captain of the port with assurances that the wind is S.W. outside, and doleful accounts of vessels that have just come in ; Dick saying he don't like the looks of it, he don't ; the bread not on board and he bakers not yet out of bed ; the barometer a shade on the fall ; that Yankee prediction ; the wind sensibly getting back to the south even in here —and now there's a good hour of the ebb tide gone—oh, hang it, we'll hang on for another day and see what the morning brings. We shall be *quite* ready then, and can go out at once. So that's off one's mind. After all you must be *somewhere*, and better here than thrashing about outside and making no progress. We'll see if we can't get that stove to draw a bit, and make ourselves comfortable.

What one really wants in order to start with confidence is a number of conditions, all together. 1. The wind must be in any quarter but the S.W. 2. But it must not be W., because you have got to go down channel. 3. Nor S., because that breeds " dirt." 4. Nor S. E., because you never knew that come to any good. 5. In fact, it must be N. or N.E. 6. And it must have got into that quarter through W. or N.W. 7. And the barometer must be high. 8. But not too high. 9. It must be rising. 10. But not too fast. 11. The sky must not be thick. 12. And yet the sun must not be glaring, for that is a bad sign. 13. The Yankees must not have predicted anything. 14. And then, if we go on too long with fine weather, there will be another breeze due. 15. Dick must be satisfied with the look of things—which never happened yet. 16. Bills of health, bread, meat, water, and the rest must all be on board. 17. Then there's the moon ; you must have that, these long nights. 18. But by the time you get the weather and Dick and the provisions into order, there is no moon left.

In short, there are so many conditions, that if one insists on having them all favorable in the middle of winter, one runs great risk of never getting away at all. But we shall get some of them. and chance the rest, I suppose.

CHAPTER LXVI.

On Board the Lively Sally,
At Sea, Sunday, 11th December, 1881.

" Well, there's one thing, we *kin* go out if so be as you like."

This was Dick's not very encouraging way of summing up the situation when, last Tuesday, the Skipper had hardened his heart and got under way with the wind still in the S.W., and when we had got as far as Yarmouth. It certainly looked dirty, and the collation of various opinions, including mine, for putting our nose out, ended in our bearing up, running back to Cowes, and anchoring once more in the roads. I am bound to testify that the event fully justified the Skipper, for in the evening it blew a whole gale from S.W.

The odd thing about it all is, that while things have been so bad the barometer has been high and steady. In fact, as Dick says, " the weather fare to beat the glasses." Last night, however, there came a fog, and the wind began at length to blow from the northward. Therewith the glass fell, but this morning the wind stood and freshened, and driving snow seemed to promise a real beginning of winter. So at half-past ten we set our snug trysail and squaresail and got under way ; this time for a real start. The snow whitened the uplands of the Isle of Wight, and made everything so thick that we could barely see a mile. Sea-boots and oil-skins and thick woollens underneath notwithstanding, one felt—as indeed one always does at sea—shrivelled up to nothing, and as though one had nothing on that nothing. By half-past one we were abreast of the Needles, and, carrying a fine slashing breeze with us, we made Portland lights at half-past five, and by half-past one this morning were four miles off the Start, whence we took our departure, bade good-by to the land, and set the course W.S.W.

As I have said, I am upon this occasion not in command, but only a passenger ; yet I am expected to work my passage, and it is my business to keep the reckoning. To-day I have worked it up to noon with the result that there is only half a mile difference between my latitude by observation and by dead-reckoning. The wind is steady at about N.N.E., and as the weather looks fine the Skipper, on my representation, has indulged in the dangerous extravagance of a single-reefed mainsail, which is against his principles, for he maintains, and with good reason, that it is not sound cutter-sailing to run under a mainsail in the winter time in this part of the world.

Monday, 12th December.

Our reckoning to-day puts us sixty-five miles west of Ushant. This is a good berth off in all conscience, and in these days of steam, when it is the fashion to go from point to point and to make all the lights, it may seem that we are too far to the westward. If it were a mistake it would be one on the right side, for I need not tell the inhabitants of a maritime country that it is not the sea, but the land, that is dangerous to the navigator. It is, however, no mistake at all, but a wise precaution. You can't get too far to the westward when crossing the Bay in a sailing vessel, for you then have everything under command. And especially is it well to be far outside Ushant and Finisterre, for about those points there is almost always bad, thick weather.

We are now fairly at sea. The big Atlantic billows are rolling in from the westward, and the little ship rides up and down their sides, now perched on the summit, and now low down far below view of the horizon. Our deck is limited, for there are the two boats carried on it, and then there are the three white ducks who pass their time in pecking at each other and quacking over their mess of barley-meal. One hour would be very like another, were it not for hauling in the log, marking the movements of the barometer, and, above all, watching the sky for signs of the weather. What a book it is! How rich, how changing! If I could describe our sunrise of this morning you would think it worth while to come here on the mere chance of seeing such another. The gray twilight, the ruddier dawn, the gold and purple-edged masses of cloud on the horizon, and the tinier cloudlets overhead shepherded by the N.W. wind into long droves, the fresh crispness of the air, the saltness of it, the purity of it, the sense of freedom and ease! Ah! yes, there is that about the sea which no land can ever give.

AT SEA, Wednesday, 14th December.

The wind has got round into the old quarter of S.W.; the glass is falling; it is thick of rain, and the sea is getting up. We have therefore taken in the mainsail, and got snug again under the trysail and third jib. The sun has not shown himself, and so we have no observation to-day, but the dead-reckoning puts us about two thirds across the Bay, and well out. The little ship is too much on the jump to permit of any triumphs of cookery being achieved, and our dinner has been a scratch affair of cold beef and sardines, washed down by a bottle of champagne. But we have killed one of the white ducks, and when we get finer weather we will eat him.

Thursday, 15th December.

No sun again to-day, and therefore no observation. The weather is of that disagreeable kind one always finds about capes like Finisterre, which just out into the sea ; but in the night the wind veered to N.N.E., and it is now steady, though slight, at N.E., with constant squalls, and an overcast and threatening sky.

Friday, 16th December.

To-day we have had a bit of a dusting. In the night the wind backed to the dirty old quarter, S.W. There was one of those big rings round the moon that always promise bad weather, and the sun rose very red and threatening. We had put ourselves—by dead-reckoning, for we have had no sun at noon since Tuesday—a good seventy miles to the west of Cape Finisterre ; but at half-past nine this morning we made land, which can only be the high mountain inside of that cape, distant, as far as we can judge, no more than thirty miles. This puts us no less than forty miles to the eastward of our dead-reckoning. It is no doubt to be accounted for by the inset into the Bay of Biscay, which, when it exists, runs at the rate of a mile an hour. But, as it does not always exist, one never knows whether to allow for it or not. Here is seen the wisdom of keeping well to the westward. Had we steered a course with the view of making Finisterre and passing close to it, steamer-wise, we should be by this time, not off Finisterre, but off Corunna or Cape Ortegal, forty miles to leeward !

About twelve o'clock I was on the rail, lashed to a davit, and vainly endeavoring at once to keep my sextant dry and to catch the sun between the clouds and the horizon, between the big waves that rose up and kept washing it out. The wind had freshened constderably, and was blowing three parts of a gale. The sea had got up too, a school of porpoises were playing about our bows, and the two white ducks were huddled up in a corner of the hen-coop. It was no easy matter to stand on the wet and slippery deck as the litle ship put her nose into the seas. The sky seemed to have come down on to the top of the

mast, and had that dull, leaden, greasy look which usually por-
tends a real good hustler. With our topmast housed, trysail,
small foresail, and third jib, we should have been snug enough ;
but, as the weather still got worse, we hove to at one o'clock,
took the bonnet off the foresail, set the fourth jib, and made
sail again on the starboard tack. She was pretty lively at it,
everything fetched way in the cabins, the crockery began making a concert in the pantry, and, when one was below, the only
thing was to sit down to leeward on the cabin floor, consult the
chart, and hope for better weather. This has gone on all day,
but things have got no worse, and now, at 6 P.M., the wind
has veered to N.W., and moderated a bit, which I attribute to
our having sailed on the starboard tack out of one of those
Yankee " disturbances."

Saturday, 17th December.

Quite a fine day again, though there is still a good deal of
sea running. But the wind stands at N.W., and as there is a
sun, I have at last got observations both for latitude and
longitude, after an interval of four days without either. To-
day, too, we have eaten the duck, and on the whole things
look quite prosperous.

Sunday, 18th December.

Another fine day with a nice breeze from the W., and also a
bit of the sun amiable enough to show himself at noon. At
two o'clock we made land, bearing S.E. by S., opined by
Dick to be the Burlings, but evidently, as an inspection from
the mast-head showed, the mountains of Cintra over the Rock
of Lisbon. At dark this was put beyond question by our making the Rock of Lisbon light. But here comes another aggra-
vating element of uncertainty ; for on timing the revolutions
of the light, I find it revolves in two minutes and a half,
instead of revolving—as according to the sailing directions and
the latest light-book it should—in one minute and three quarters. Hereupon has ensued that anxious reasoning out of bearings and courses and possible insets, by which one strives to
arrive at a conclusion—the result of which is that we have de-

cided that there must either have been a change made in the light and not published, or else that the machinery has got wrong or wants oiling, and has thus become irregular in its intervals—which is not by any means a rare occurrence with Portuguese lights. But, by taking two bearings and the distance run between them, I put our distance from the light at no more than twenty miles, which again places us ten miles further to the eastward than our reckoning made us. Oh, these insets !

Monday, 19th December.

A nice westerly wind and a smooth sea tempt us again to set our mainsail, which brings us at noon within sight of that fine landmark, Monchiqua ; and now at five o'clock we are off Cape St. Vincent, and going the, for us, marvellous rate of five knots. The air is warm and genial, the sea is like a mill-pond, and below one is hardly aware that the vessel is under way, so smoothly does she run. The P. and O. steamer that left Gravesend last Wednesday passed us off Cape St. Vincent, a day later. I doubt we shall find she had a breeze to the northward of us last Friday.

Tuesday, 20th December.

So far as the sun goes, we might as well have been in England, for during the eleven days we have now been out we have only had him properly out at all four times, and during these last three days we have never seen him at all. As, however, we have now got a new departure from Cape St. Vincent, we care but little about him. And, though the sky is so overcast, the weather is marvellously fine, and warm as an English June.

Wednesday, 21st December, 10.15 A.M.

We made Cape Spartel light at one o'clock this morning and Cape Trafalgar soon after ; and, having duly shown our ensign to the Spanish fort at Tarifa Point—the failure to do which the proud Spaniard occasionally rewards with a round shot—we are now running into Gibraltar bay, and smartening up to go ashore.

For the depth of winter the voyage has been a very fine one,
of exactly eleven days, and I don't know how one could spend
eleven days better.   I look forward with something like horror
to the renewal of letters and newspapers, from which we have
been delivered during this time.   It is *such* a rest to be without those triumphs of civilization.

CHAPTER LXVII.

On Board the Lively Sally,
Gibraltar, 24th Dec. 1881.

Whenever I get abroad I find it impossible not to feel proud
of my countrymen.   They may seem commonplace and vulgar
enough in England ; but put them down among foreigners in
a foreign country, and upon my word they look like lords of
the human race.   Here at Gibraltar one is especially struck
by this.   The narrow and tortuous streets are filled with dirty
little shrimps of Spaniards got up to represent Parisian dandies,
lemon-colored Italians, coarse-fibred Germans, swarthy Portuguese, stalwart Maltese, and turbaned and dignified Moors ;
but among them all the fair-haired, blue-eyed Englishman
walks with the lordly air of a man among women and children.
Charley from Aldershot, at whom we shoot forth gibes when
he appears in the Park, looks here so clean, so well-groomed,
so well-dressed, as he saunters grandly with his bull-terrier at
his heels, that one feels inclined to embrace him and ask oneself to dine at his mess that very evening.   Even Tommy Atkins
is transfigured, and the smartest and dandiest little Spaniard
ever got up to kill, looks a wretched being beside Tommy,
wrestling in his shirt-sleeves and overalls with the construction
of a shanty or the laying out of Lord Napier's last new garden.
The very seamen, ashore from the colliers, bearded and sea-
booted as they are, have an air of quiet dignity about them as

compared with the men of the other countries that are so liber-
ally represented here.   I fancy that, if a man came down to
Gibraltar from the moon, wanting a score of men he could trust
not to lie to him or to desert him in an emergency, he would
stand in the street here and pick out twenty Englishmen.
Indeed, the Moors—who may be almost considered as inhabitants of another planet—do unhesitatingly prefer the English
to all other people.   Perhaps, however, that may be because
we buy their cattle and eggs.

The people of Gibraltar are, I am told, far from prosperous
just now.   They want, it is said, two things—rain, and a revolution in Spain.   The want of rain shows itself very plainly,
for everything on the rock is dry and dusty.   The revolution
in Spain, on the other hand, is required for the sake of trade.
Gibraltar, being a free port, is a great depot for all the goods
that are wanted by the Spaniards, and that are prevented from
reaching them by the heavy and, indeed, prohibitory duties
imposed by the Spanish Government.   There is in all times a
certain amount—though now less than formerly there was—of
smuggling which tempers in some degree the tariff to the
shorn Spaniard ; but when a proper good *pronunciamiento*
takes place, then comes the great opportunity of the Rock
scorpion.   The *carabineros* and custom-house officers, who
guard the frontier of Spain, being on such occasions doubtful
which side is going to win, prudently hold aloof, and give
themselves a severe holiday till the question is settled as to
which side is to be the Rebellion and which the Government.
For several days, therefore, the frontier is not guarded at all,
and the beneficent laws of Free Trade have full play.   Then is
seen a great crowd of carts, wagons, calesas, men, women, and
children, hurrying and jostling through the narrow gate of
Gibraltar, with the goods that the Spaniard buys.   In a short
time all the stores that have accumulated on the Rock are run
into Spain, the profits are great, and the Gibraltar people rub
their hands over well-filled pockets, till a period of quiet brings
again the *carabinero* and the *guarda costa* into action.   It is

not merely the carpets of Mr. Bright and the screws of Mr. Chamberlain that are thus provided for the Spaniard, but many other products of our favored isle ; and at the last Spanish Revolution, in the midst of the surging, fighting, blaspheming crowd that was pressing through the gate, was seen a well-known Presbyterian parson who, with the wisdom of the serpent, was taking advantage of the providential period of anarchy to run his stock of Bibles into Spain. The Society for Promoting Contraband Knowledge could hardly improve upon that.

The remarkable fact about Gibraltar is, that the most fervent advocates of the English occupation of the Rock are the Spaniards themselves. They would not for anything see it pass again under the dominion of their own Government. And the reason is simlpe enough. Gibraltar is the one point of security and stability in the Spanish peninsula. It is at once the safe and the refuge of the whole south of Spain. The Spaniards bank there because they know that, once under the English guns, their cash is safe, which it is very far from being wherever there is a Spanish official. And when the periodical storm of revolution and throat-cutting breaks, they bear up and run for the Rock as one man, knowing as they do that they may there count upon the hospitality and protection of the English. Half the notable public men of Spain have been our guests here at one time or another, and whatever they may say in the Cortes to please the people of the north of Spain, who are too far from the Rock to fly to it or to smuggle from it, they would be in truth very much alarmed if they foresaw any serious probability of the shutting up of so precious a bolt-hole. But they know that there neither is nor can be any serious probability of such a catastrophe ; and, therefore, they readily earn a little cheap popularity by advocating, in rolling and sonorous Castilian periods, that expulsion of the English and resumption by Spain of the Rock which they are well assured will never be effected.

The same thing is true of the smuggling, over which so much virtuous indignation has recently been expended. It is not

the English who smuggle, but the Spaniards themselves ; and
neither English nor Spaniards could do it at all were it not
for the connivance of the Spanish guards and custom-house
officers.   Nobody who wishes to run a cargo thinks of braving
or even of giving the slip to the custom-house guards—for it is
so very easy to buy them.   It is all a matter of business.   You
pay so much for the beach for so many hours, and during that
time nobody will hear or see anything of what you may do at
the place agreed upon.   But there is more than this.   So corrupt are the custom-house officials that they positively will not
let you pay the regular duties of the tariff.   If you insist—as
an Englishman at a certain port of the south of Spain has recently insisted—upon doing so, they simply " Boycott" you,
place every impediment in your way, and render it practically
impossible for you to carry on your trade.   But pay half, or a
quarter, of the duties, and give the officials a share of the sum
saved, and the impediments all disappear as by magic.   In addition to this, you must be prepared on each voyage to bring
little parcels of cheese, butter, and cutlery for the subordinates, and then you will find everything run as smoothly as possible.   These are facts for which, if necessary, I could give
names, dates, and places ; and as long as such things are, it is
more than ridiculous for anybody to suppose that the Spaniards have any grievance in such smuggling as still takes place.
It is their business—as it is the business of the French and our
other neighbors—to protect their own revenue, and if they
would either reform their tariff or pay their officers a salary
that would hold body and soul together, there would be no
difficulty whatever in doing it.   But to ask, as some, not
Spaniards but Englishmen, do, that England should make regulations for English territory in order to protect Spain from
the consequences of her own corruption, is absurd.

   If the possession of Gibraltar by the English is recognized as
a blessing to the Spaniards, it requires but little to make it recognized as a blessing to the world at large.   Hitherto there has
been, and even now there is, too great a disposition to treat it

simply and solely as a fortress, and to withhold rather than to grant those facilities which might make it what by its position it should be, one of the great trading centres of the world. For instance, it is a fact, though to some it will seem scarcely credible, that there is at this moment no such thing as a dry-dock at Gibraltar, and, indeed, no means of repairing and re-fitting vessels that come in crippled by bad weather. Any number of such vessels do come into the bay, both from the Mediterranean and from the Atlantic, in the course of the year ; but there is no means of doing anything for them, beyond, perhaps, providing a spar, and for any serious repairs they must go, either to Malta or to Cadiz. Yet there is, in the Camber by the New Mole, an excellent site for a graving dock, and if it were made it would be a priceless boon, not merely to the trading vessels of all nations, but also to our own men-of-war, and it would be an addition of great weight to the reasons why the retention of Gibraltar by the English is a benefit to all mankind. Again, the New Mole is not yet finished, and, what is worse, is that the works by which it was to be completed are entirely suspended, and present a dismal array of deserted der-ricks and loose stones. Meantime an enormous expense is being incurred in getting out two hundred-ton guns from Eng-land, and a further expense of several thousands of pounds will have to be incurred in getting them into position. This may be necessary—I don't say it is not—but the Graving Dock and the completion of the New Mole are at least equally neces-sary, and, as a matter of policy, are even more pressing.

CHAPTER LXVIII.

TANGIER, MOROCCO, 28th December, 1881.

OUR fussy, fevered, worrying Western civilization is doubt-less a necessary blessing ; and that incapacity for enjoying, or even possessing, anything which results from our always being

in a hurry to get at something else, is, I suppose, one of its
greatest advantages.   Yet when one gets a breath of the ragged, poor, patient, unprogressing East, one cannot but feel
that there is a charm and a repose about it which railways,
telegraphs, cheap newspapers, and Party government can never
afford.   Look at this little Tangier.   It is a mere collection of
low white houses lying on the Barbary coast in the Straits of
Gibraltar, and not above thirty miles distant from the Rock.
You may come here from thence in something under four hours
by the Hercules tug ; and when you land you find that you
have left Wapping and Woolwich for a new world.   The Sultan of Morocco is not precisely what would be called a highly
civilized or progressive Sovereign, and though the soil is rich
and fertile his people are very poor.   But on every hand there
is an air of dignity, of calm, and even of content, such as you
would look for in vain among the cities of the West.   The
streets are steep, dirty, ill-paved with the most knobbly stones,
and go crookedly round endless corners ; the shops are holes
in the wall of the size of dog-kennels—but the men are mar-
vels of quiet dignity and grace.   Most of them are ragged, all
of them are poor, but in spite of all there is something grand
about all of them.   It is, I suppose, partly due to the turban
and the flowing white or brown *jeelab* in which they drape
themselves with so much dignity ; but it must be much more
due to their views of life, to their sobriety and simplicity, and
to the fact that, like all Mussulmans, they believe in their religion.   It is noteworthy that they are almost all—except, of
course, the black-fezzed Jews—clean in their persons, however
ragged in their dress.   In Europe we wear clean coats over
dirty bodies ; in the East they possess clean bodies under dirty
coats.   Many of them are extremely handsome, with their fine
eyes and blue, shaven heads ; and it is a fact that among these
people a European clad in the hat and breeches of the West
looks a shameful and vulgar object.

Three days ago there was held here the Moorish market or
fair, which made the hillside outside the town a most animated

spectacle. Scores of camels from the interior, laden with dates, grain, leather, and country produce, stood or knelt about the ground. Near the gate squatted a number of white-clad-women, each holding her *haïk* or robe with one hand over her mouth to complete the covering of the head, and bargaining with some other for the half a dozen eggs and the fowl that constituted her whole stock in trade, and that she had brought perhaps ten or fifteen miles to sell. Further on, the banging of drums and the shrill sounds of the reed-pipe announced a band of *Aïssouas*, round whom was formed an admiring circle. In the centre a half-naked snake-charmer danced and shouted wildly, invoking with an unceasing iteration his patron saint. After a time, stooping down to what looked like a bundle of rags, he made passes over it with some dirty charms that hung round his neck, and putting in his hand, drew forth by the tail a snake at least a couple of yards long. After apostrophizing and exciting the reptile, which showed a disagreeable desire to wriggle toward my side of the circle, he put forth his tongue and allowed the snake to bite it, a feat which both man and snake seemed equally to enjoy. Then he cut himself with a knife, after which he began his dancing again, and as I passed at dusk I found him still at it, with apparently unabated energy.

A desire to see something of the judicial system of Morocco made me pay a visit, first to a gentleman who sat in a hole in the wall, and who I was informed was the Jewish judge, or, as I understand, a kind of police magistrate. The judge was at that moment engaged in disposing of some case ; but when he saw me, he summarily convicted the defendant, and addressed himself to saluting my unworthy self. I was much flattered at such a mark of attention, and was wondering why it was never paid to me in my own country, when the judge produced a silver charm in the shape of a hand and tried to sell it to me at five times its value. On this I fled to the Moorish tribunal at the gate of the town. This was held in a small room some ten feet square, on the floor of which sat the Deputy-Governor of the town—a grave and dignified man in the conical red fez of the country. By the side of the room squatted two of his friends, and just inside the doorway, which was open, and around which clustered the " public," were two suitors. The suitors were both talking together, in an excited manner and with much gesticulation ; occasionally one of the public volunteered a remark ; then the friends began to take an interest in the matter, and also began to speak ; and finally the grave judge, having vainly motioned first to one and then to the other to keep silent, gave his decision in the midst of a general row. At a later hour, as I passed this way again and looked through the open door, I found the court asleep on the bench, while suitors and soldiers outside were patiently awaiting the end of his siesta. The prison is hard by, and contains some three hundred miserable objects clanking about in fetters, a large proportion of whom neither know, nor ever will know, why they have been shut up.

Among other things that the helpless stranger must allow himself to be shown here is one of the Moorish *cafés*. They represent the whole of the dissipation and public amusements of the place, which are of a very simple-minded character. The *café* is a room with a dado and flooring of matting. From the low roof hang a score of cages of singing birds ; in one corner stands the coffee-maker with his charcoal fire and his little pots ; and round the walls, on the floor, are seated the customers. Some are smoking the *keef* or chopped hemp, which is in favor here ; others are drinking coffee or green tea ; and soon some of them produce tambourines and various stringed instruments, which might be either mandolines, guitars, or banjos, and begin an amateur concert to an accompaniment of hand-clapping. Therewith soon arises singing, usually of the amatory kind ; and I am bound to say that the tunes seemed to me extremely pretty, most of them reminding one somewhat of Italian church music. The rank and fashion of Tangier go on for hours in this manner, always grave, always sober, and apparently always satisfied.

One other entertainment I have had of a private character.

This was a dance of Moorish women, organized for my especial benefit, and as to which so much secrecy was enjoined, that I felt it necessary to ask whether the dance was one which a young lady might allow her mamma to see. Being reassured as to this, I accompanied my native friend to a Moorish house in the evening. Here, in a small upper room, we found five musicians squatted on the floor, and with them three women in rich Moorish dresses with uncovered faces. Two of the women were very handsome ; and of these two, one, who I was told was but fourteen, had, I think, the most beautiful dark-brown gazelle-like eyes, the most magnificent black hair, the best complexion, with a mantling red in the cheek, and the prettiest and most expressive features I have ever seen in a brunette. This girl was dressed in a long loose garment, with a sash round her hips, and a silk handkerchief tied round her head, and when she stood up to dance I saw that her feet, which peeped out from under the long dress, were naked. She seemed to have none of the gravity of the East ; on the contrary, when she had recovered the fright which the presence of a Nazarene seemed at first to cause in her, she was full of laughter and as playful as a kitten. She mocked the grave musicians, imitating their gestures and caricaturing their notes ; she caught up and repeated the words of their singing, and generally demeaned herself like what she seemed to be—a beautiful spoiled child. Then she arose to dance, and I thought I had never seen anything so lithe and so graceful. The dance was of the simplest kind. It consisted mainly in movements of the hips, accompanied by small steps in the few square feet of vacant space, while in her hands she took the two ends of a silk handkerchief which she now twisted round and round and held before her face, and now suffered to fall lower. There was nothing in it all, but the grace and the charm of it were marvellous. After a time she sank down exhausted close to me, and taking my hand placed it on her heart, which I felt was beating quickly. Then she laughed at what appeared to be a rebuke addressed to her by one of the other women, and relapsed into her little tricks. After this much tea was drunk by everybody, and the other women danced in like manner. There seemed no reason why it should ever end, and when I retired the ball was still going on.

Eastern as Tangier is, something is being done to civilize it. There are here nothing less than four thirty-ton Armstrong guns, and there is a Mr. M'Hugh, formerly in the English army, but now a Morocco Colonel, who has already mounted two of these guns, and is now hard at work getting the other two into position. There are troops, too, who are drilled every day—with English words of command, by the way—and there is generally an aspect of much determination not to submit without a struggle to any enterprise of the hated Spaniard, who is generally suspected of taking a much livelier interest in the place than he has any business to do. The English, on the other hand, are looked upon by the Moors as their natural protectors. For an Englishman they will do anything, and Sir John Hay, our Minister here, is quite the king of the place; which, indeed, he well deserves to be, for, in the midst of temptations to which most of the other foreign representatives succumb, he has always kept the English name pure and unsullied, and has sought only to be a friend to the much-worried and much-plundered Sultan of Morocco.

One word only remains to be said about Tangier. It is that there is here one of the best hotels anywhere to be found, and far superior to anything I know either at Gibraltar or even in London. It is very clean, the *cuisine* is quite excellent, and the charges are very moderate—ten shillings a day for board and lodging and everything except wine. This hotel is kept by M. Bruzeaud, a Frenchman, who was formerly messman to an English regiment.

CHAPTER LXIX.

On Board the Lively Sally,
At Sea, off Malaga, New Year's Day, 1882.

Having rejoiced over two yachts which have come into Gibraltar crippled (one of them twenty days from Cowes with her bulwarks washed away), while we have not carried away a rope-yarn ; having dined with Charley from Aldershot, filled up with water, and laid in a sack of new potatoes and some fresh meat, we got under way yesterday, bound for Algiers. We started with a little air from the westward ; but it is needless to say that we were hardly clear of Europe Point before it first fell calm and then began to blow from E.N.E., which is as nearly dead on end as a Mediterranean wind can manage. We have, therefore, done but little good, and this evening as I write, there is a big ring round the moon, the wind is singing a lively little tune among the rigging, and the little vessel is beginning to jump in a way which makes us foresee that we shall come badly off for dinner.

At Sea, off Cape Sacratif, 2d January.

Just as I thought. A strong wind and a nasty sea have forced us to take in all the flying kites with which we started, and having taken down two reefs in the mainsail, we have been thrashing to windward along the Spanish coast all day, without making anything to the good worth talking about. And now things look worse instead of better, and we have stripped once more to the storm-trysail, and are trying to persuade ourselves that we are altering the bearing of the light.

Off Cape Sacratif, 3d January.

We have had a shocking bad night. The wind increased to three parts of a gale, and we had at last to heave her to. The breeze now begins, however, to show signs of abating, and both wind and sea seem to be rapidly going down.

Off Cape de Gata, 4th January.

Yesterday afternoon we had four hours quite calm as regards the wind, though there was a pretty good swell still running. Then a breeze sprang up from the S.W., and we set our studding-sail and ran past Cape Sabinal nicely. But at four o'clock this morning we got a heavy thunderstorm with torrents of rain (what a ridiculous sea this is !), then we had a succession of squalls with the wind " fannying" about anyhow—and now at four o'clock we have got it hard again from the old quarter, N.E., freshening too rapidly, and looking like mischief with a heavy sea.

At Sea, between Europe and Africa, 5th January.

We were thumped about pretty handsomely all night, and my bones begin to feel quite sore. I wish I could find out some way to keep the clothes on me in the night ; to prevent myself from taking headers into the bulkhead ; and to bring myself up on one side or the other of my berth as it rolls me over incessantly from port to starboard and from starboard to port. When this kind of thing goes on, you get rolled out of the soundest sleep before long, and then the only thing is either to go on deck and " see how it looks"—which is somehow a satisfaction, however bad it *does* look—or else to lie and listen to the howling of the wind, the creaking of the ship's timbers, and the wash of the water outside, varied occasionally by that heavy thud and rush which tell you that she has taken a little green water on board and is getting rid of it through the scuppers.

Squalls all day—the only diversion to the wind, which still sticks right ahead. It is a horrid wind, a Black Levanter, full of strength and bad weather. They tell me it is what is called in these parts the " Majorca Carpenter," a name it well deserves, from the number and importance of the jobs it brings to the trade. This evening, however, we have managed to get hold of Cape Ivi light on the African side—but it is very slow and very hard work, and it strikes me that we are having rather a dusting over this passage.

Off Cape Tenez, Africa, Friday, 6th January.

We are still jamming along under our trysail, and this morning just before sunrise we managed to make Cape Tenez light. The wind is still very hard, the sea heavy, and the weather most gloomy and depressing. I have now been well-nigh a month at sea, and *I have never seen the sun since I left England.* This is a fact which I note for the benefit of those who leave their native shores in the belief that by going a thousand miles nearer to the equator they will be sure of sunshine and warmth. I have forgotten what sunshine is like. Cowes is the last place at which I saw such a phenomenon, and the eccentric luminary has been playing hide-and-seek with me ever since, as though he were determined I should never get an altitude on or off the meridian again. The whole sky is covered to-day, as usual, with gray clouds, and every now and then there comes a squall which knocks up a sea, pours down torrents of rain, and makes the wind fly about till you don't know what course to steer next.

Then as to warmth. Afric's burning shore is a mere missionary's delusion. It is wretchedly cold and chilly, and but for the persuasion that I am looking at Algeria I should say that I was off Orford Ness in a November breeze. It is true the thermometer is at 60°—but there is a rawness and dampness about the air very real and sensible—which, indeed, must be so, for under it Dick has disclosed a revival of spirits which nothing could produce but a palpable reminder of Suffolk.

As a sea the Mediterranean is a mere swindle. It is, indeed, not a sea at all, but a miserable puddle with nothing of the salt and savor that make the breath of our northern seas so invigorating. Withal, in its angry moods it is vicious and nasty, yet always mean and pretty—a very woman among waters. The sea never seems to run whole and handsome as it does outside, with great swinging billows ; it is cross, and short, and jumpy, and very vicious. I think quite the worst and most dangerous sea I ever saw was one I met with off Cires Point, when coming from Tangier to Gibraltar in the teeth of a whole gale from the eastward. It was so steep, so deep, so hollow, and so cliff-like, that it seemed impossible any vessel could rise to it ; and the ship I was in—a fine steamer of 700 tons—took it in green over the bows. To-day we have been turning to windward against a strong north-easter, but the sea there is with it is out of all proportion to the wind, and, as the good little ship plunges down the steep and dives into it, she has hardly time to shake her bowsprit clear of one wave before the next is upon her. Yet she is not being forced ; for we are under a storm trysail, a mere spitfire fourth jib, and a trifle of foresail with the bonnet off.

ALGIERS, Saturday, 7th January.

At last. We made Cape Caxine light at midnight, and this morning early we got abreast of our port, in which we are now happily moored, after thrashing about with head winds and seas. and taking seven days to do our four hundred odd miles.

CHAPTER LXX.

ON BOARD THE LIVELY SALLY,
ALGIERS, 10th January, 1882.

" KNOW ye not that my people are a nation of brigands, and that I am their chief ?"

Such was the explanation and defence of his own position, addressed by the late Dey of Algiers to the English Consul who remonstrated with him against the practices of the Algerine rovers—practices which consisted in a free appropriation of other people's property, and a still freer delivery of other people's persons into slavery. The same answer may be, and practically is, made by Monsieur Gambetta and his fellows in reply to any observations addressed to them with regard either to Tunis or to Algiers. This answer is, it is true, often ac-

companied by assertions that the progress of civilization has
been much helped, and the material condition of Algiers much
improved, by the French occupation.   But it is hard, indeed,
to see any great signs of this.   Dirt and oppression seem to
reign supreme throughout the city.   You walk ankle-deep in
mud, and from the most poverty-stricken Arab in rags to the
most consequential official in gold lace, all the inhabitants appear to be struck with an abiding grief.   One reason of this is,
as I am informed, that the English have, with one accord,
abstained this year from coming to Algiers.   They are under
the entirely erroneous impression that the insurrection which is
smouldering in the remote provinces of the colony might affect their precious persons ; and they are, perhaps, somewhat
moved also by the knowledge which former writers have impressed upon them, that Algiers boasts quite the worst hotels
in Europe, combined with some of the highest charges and
worst cooking to be found in any quarter of the globe.   At
any rate the English have not come ; and as the French colo-
nist, who has been banished for State purposes from his beloved
Paris, casts his eyes and his thoughts eastward toward Tunis,
or southward and westward toward the insurgent tribe on the
borders of Morocco, he curses the day when he quitted the
boulevard, and indulges in prophecies of the speedy downfall
of Monsieur Gambetta's Government.

What strikes one in the first aspect of Algiers, is that it is
one large attempt to reproduce the Rue de Rivoli.   The same
arcades, the same heavily-built houses, the same shops, and
the same cafés, full of the same people, are found here ; and
if the scene is somewhat diversified by ragged, coffee-colored,
bare-footed Arabs, this seems rather an accidental and tempo-
rary feature than an abiding characteristic of the place.   All
day long the troops fire guns and play upon drums and trumpets in distressing efforts to remind the natives that they are
there as masters.   The natives, indeed, are not at all inclined
to dispute the fact, though they certainly lament it.   Up one
of the by-streets in the Arab quarter lives a friend of mine—

an Arab barber—and, finding I was English, he has imparted to me his sorrows. He was here as a lad in the good old times of the Dey, when everybody was rich and well-to-do, and when you could buy two fowls for a shilling. Now, he says, all is changed, and as he shaves his compatriots, turning the patient's head from side to side as he clears off every vestige of hair, not merely from the crown of the head, but all over the face, with the sole exception of the eye-brows and the mustachio, he details his griefs. "Oil is dear, bread is dear; everybody is poor—even the French are poor; the only people who are rich are the Jews. Even the razors are not what they were when I was young. They used to cut beautifully—now they won't cut at all. But God is great, and, perhaps, things will mend."

As far as climate is concerned, there ought not to be much to mind in this country. But withal the melancholy fact remains, that for those who are not too consumptive to think of anything else but their health, Algiers is a dreary place. Beyond the cafés, where the Frenchmen spend every day a happy two or three hours in drinking three halfpennyworth of absinthe, there are no amusements whatever. The only entertainments I have been able to devise for myself are two. One is having my hair cut, and the other is going to the native Turkish bath, where I have found shampooers so skilful and scientific as made me blush for those brother professionals of theirs in England, who rub one over as though they were polishing plate. I have tried a third amusement—that of going ashore and walking about the streets in the endeavor to buy something—but I do declare that there is nothing here to be bought that is worth taking away, unless it be at prices too fabulous for belief. I find indications that in former times the country produced fine stuffs and rich embroideries, but at the present time they manufacture nothing but the most barbaric trumpery.

It is not particularly warm and not at all sunny; and on the whole, if any of my compatriots wish to see what Algiers is like, I should advise them to go to Paris, and stay there.

INDEX.

THE STANDARD LIBRARY.

WHAT REPRESENTATIVE CLERGYMEN SAY OF IT.

Chas. H. Hall, D.D., Holy Trinity Episcopal Church, Brooklyn, says :

" Great book monopolies, like huge railroad syndicates, are now the monarchical relics against which the benevolence and radicalism of the age, from different standpoints, are bound to wage war. Each source will have its own motives and arguments, but each will resolve to conquer in the long run. At one end of the scale we have the Life of Dickens offered for $800, that some one wealthy man may enjoy the comfort of his proud privilege of wealth in having what no other mortal possesses ; at the other, we find the volume offered at 10 or 20 cents, which any newsboy or thoughtful laborer uses in common with thousands. In the great strife for the greatest good of the largest number, put me down as on the side of the last. I enclose my subscription order for a year."

Rev. Chas. W. Cushing, D.D., First M. E. Church, Rochester, N. Y., says :

"One of the most pernicious sources of evil among our young people is the books they read. When I can get a young man interested in *substantial books*, I have great hope of him. For this reason I have been deeply interested in your effort to make *good* books as cheap as *bad* ones. I mentioned the matter from my pulpit. As a result I at once got fifty-four subscribers for the full set, and more to come."

J. O. Peck, D.D., First M. E. Church, Brooklyn, N. Y., says:

" Your effort is commendable. You ought to have the co-operation of all good men. It is a moral, heroic, and humane enterprise."

Pres. Mark Hopkins, D.D., of Williams College, says :

"The attempt of Messrs. Funk and Wagnalls to place good literature within reach of the masses is worthy of all commendation and encouragement. If the plan can be successfully carried out, it will be a great boon to the country."

Geo. C. Lorrimer, D.D., Baptist Church, Chicago, says :

" I sincerely hope your endeavors to circulate a wholesome and elevating class of books will prove successful. Certainly, clergymen, and Christians generally, cannot afford that it should fail. In proof of my personal interest in your endeavors, I subscribe for a year."

J. P. Newman, D.D., New York, says :

"I have had faith from the beginning in the mission of Messrs. Funk & Wagnalls. It required great faith on their part, and their success is in proof that all things are possible to him that believeth. They have done for the public what long was needed, but what other publishers did not venture to do."

Henry J. Van Dyke, D.D., Presbyterian Church, Brooklyn, N. Y., says :

" Good books are great blessings. They drive out darkness by letting in light. Your plan ought not to fail for lack of support. Put my name on the list of subscribers."

T. W. Chambers, D.D., Collegiate Reformed Church, New York, says:

"The plan seems to me both praiseworthy and feasible. I trust it will meet with speedy and abundant success."

Sylvester F. Scovel, D.D., First Presbyterian Church, Pittsburgh, Pa., says:

"Your plans deserve a place in the category of moral reforms. The foes they meet, the width of the battle-ground they can be expanded to cover, the manifold incidental blessings they may convey to thousands of households, the national and international currents of thought they may set in motion, entitle them beyond all question to prompt and efficient aid from clergymen and the whole Christian Church."

Ezra Abbot, D.D., LL.D., of Harvard College, says:

"I heartily approve of your project. I shall be glad to receive and commend the volumes to buyers. I send you my subscription."

Thos. Armitage, D.D., Fifth Avenue Baptist Church, New York, says:

"Your plan is grand and philanthropic. I wish you success, and ask you to put me down for one set, *with the assurance* that I will aid you by every kind word which opportunity suggests."

William M. Taylor, D.D., Broadway Tabernacle, New York, says:

"The success of the plan depends very much on the character of the books selected ; but if you are wise in that particular, as I have no doubt, you will be benefactors to many struggling readers in whose experience a new book is one of the rarest treats. I am glad to see, too, that you are making arrangements with the English publishers, so that in conferring a boon upon readers here you will not be doing injustice to authors across the sea."

James Eells, D.D., Lane Theological Seminary, Cincinnati, O., says:

"From the reputation of your house I am ready to believe that you will publish only worthy books. I heartily wish you success."

E. J. Wolf, D.D., of the Lutheran Seminary, Gettysburg, Pa., says:

"A more laudable project I can hardly conceive of. Vicious literature has long had the advantage in that it was put within easy reach of the masses. The poverty of many who fain would use the very best books has often distressed me. I feel in my heart that the noble enterprise of your house is deserving of the most liberal encouragement."

Bishop Samuel Fallows, Reformed Episcopalian Church, Chicago, says:

"Your plan for supplying the masses with the best reading at such a nominal price cannot be too highly commended."

J. L. Burrows, D.D., Baptist Church, Norfolk, Va., says:

"Every endeavor to supersede poison by food for the people deserves encouragement."

Rev. W. F. Crafts, Lee Avenue Congregationalist Church, Brooklyn, says:

"In the West they displace the worthless prairie grass by sowing blue grass. The soil is too rich to be inactive. It will have a right or wrong activity. So about the love of reading in the young. It is prime soil and will bear tall wire grass if we do not give it blue grass. It will have bad reading, if the good, equally cheap and attractive, is not provided."

CLOTH-BOUND
STANDARD LIBRARY, 1883 SERIES.
Edition de Luxe.

Each volume of the Library is strongly and luxuriously bound in cloth as issued, bevelled edges, gold stamp on side and back, extra paper, good margins.

PRICES:

25 cent Numbers, in Cloth.............. ....$1.00.
15 cent Numbers, in Cloth... .... .75 cents.
26 Numbers, in Cloth, payable half now, and half July 2, $16.00.

Subscribers for the paper-bound may transfer their subscriptions for the cloth-bound by paying the difference.

P.S.—The paper used in the volumes succeeding the "Life of Cromwell" will be much superior.

———•••———

Analytical Bible Concordance, Revised Edition.

Analytical Concordance to the Bible on an entirely new plan. Containing every word in Alphabetical Order, arranged under its Hebrew or Greek original, with the Literal Meaning of Each, and its Pronunciation. Exhibiting about 311,000 References, marking 30,000 various readings in the New Testament. With the latest information on Biblical Geography and Antiquities. Designed for the simplest reader of the English Bible. By ROBERT YOUNG, LL.D., author of "A New Literal Translation of the Hebrew and Greek Scriptures," etc., etc. *Fourth Revised, Authorized Edition.* Printed on heavy paper. One large volume, 4to, cloth, $2·50; sheep, $4.00; Fr. im. morocco, $4.65.

Spurgeon says: "Cruden's is child's play compared with this gigantic work."

John Hall, D.D., New York, says: "It is worthy of the lifetime of labor he has spent upon it."

This is the *Fourth Revised Edition,* containing 2,000 CORRECTIONS not to be found in the American Reprint. It is the only correct edition. It is invaluable to the reader of either the old or the new version of the Bible.

Analytical Biblical Treasury.

By ROBERT YOUNG, LL.D., author of Analytical Concordance, etc. 4to, cloth, $2.00.

CONTENTS: (1) Analytical Survey of all the books, (2) Of all the facts, (3) Of all the idioms of the Bible. (4) Bible Themes, Questions, Canonicity, Rationalism, etc., together with maps and plans of Bible lands and places. (5) A complete Hebrew and English Lexicon to the Old Testament. (6) Idiomatic use of the Hebrew and Greek Tenses. (7) A complete Greek and English Lexicon to the New Testament.

———————————

☞ *The above works will be sent by mail, postage paid, on receipt of the price.*

Bertram's Homiletic Encyclopædia.

A Homiletic Encyclopædia of Illustrations in Theology and Morals,
A Handbook of Practical Divinity, and a Commentary on Holy
Scripture. Selected and arranged by Rev. R. A. BERTRAM, com-
piler of "A Dictionary of Poetical Illustrations," etc. Royal
8vo, cloth, 892 pp., $2.50; sheep, $3.50; half morocco, $4.50.

The London Record.—"Its illustrations cast daylight upon more than 4,000
texts of Scripture. A treasury of practical religion."
C. H. Spurgeon.— . . . "A very valuable compilation—a golden treasury—
an important addition to a minister's library."
The London Literary World "No book of illustrations . . . that, for
fullness, freshness, and, above all, suggestiveness, is worthy to be compared with
the work."
Edinburgh Review.—"Nothing can be more serviceable to students."

Biblical Notes and Queries.

By ROBERT YOUNG, LL.D., author of the Analytical Concordance
to the Bible. Royal 8vo, cloth, 400 pp., $1.75.
This book is made up of Biblical Notes and Queries regarding
Biblical Criticism and Interpretation, Ecclesiastical History, Antiqui-
ties, Biography and Bibliography, Ancient and Modern Versions,
Progress in Theological Science, Reviews, etc. It answers thousands
of questions constantly presented to the minds of clergymen and
Sunday-school teachers.

Christian Sociology.

By J. H. W. STUCKENBERG, D.D., Professor in the Theological Department of Wittenberg College. A new and highly commended
book. 12mo, cloth, 382 pp., $1.00.

Commentary on Mark.

A Critical, Exegetical and Homiletical Treatment of the S. S.
Lessons for 1882 for the use of Teachers, Pastors and Parents.
New, Vigorous, Practical. By Rev. D C. HUGHES, Editor of the
International Sunday-School Lesson Department of THE HOMI-
LETIC MONTHLY. 8vo, cloth, $1.50.

Companion to the Rev. Version of the New Testament.

Explaining the Reason for the changes made on the Authorized
Version. By ALEX. ROBERTS, D.D., member of the English Revision Committee, with supplement by a member of the American
Committee. Also a full Textual Index. *Authorized Edition.* 8vo,
paper, 117 pp., 25 cents; 16mo, cloth, 213 pp., 75 cents.

Complete Preacher.

The Complete Preacher. A Sermonic Magazine. Containing nearly
one hundred sermons in full, by many of the greatest preachers
in this and other countries in the various denominations. 3 vols.,
8vo, cloth. Each $1.50, or, per set, $4.00.

The above works will be sent by mail, postage paid, on receipt of the price.

Conant's History of English Bible Translation.

Revised and Brought down to the Present Time by THOMAS J. CONANT, D. D., member of the Old Testament Revision Committee, and Translator for the American Bible Union Edition of the Scriptures. This History was originally written by Mrs. H. C. Conant, the late wife of Dr. T. J. Conant. It is a complete history of Bible Revision from the Wickliffe Bible down to the Revised Version. 2 vols., paper, 284 pp. (Standard Series, octavo, Nos. 65 and 66), 50 cents; 1 vol., 8vo, cloth, $.100.

Cyclopædia of Quotations.

With full Concordance and Other Indexes. By J. K. HOYT and ANNA L. WARD. Contains 17,000 Quotations, classified under subjects; nearly 2,000 selections from the Latin poets and orators; many Latin, French, German and Spanish proverbs. with 50,000 lines of Concordance, making at once available every quotation. Prices, Royal 8vo, over 900 pages, heavy paper, in cloth binding, $5.00; in sheep, $6.50; in full morocco, $10.00.

Hon. F. T. Frelinghuysen, Secretary of State: "Am much pleased with the 'Cyclopædia of Quotations.'"

Henry Ward Beecher: "Good all the way through, especially the proverbs of all nations."

Henry W. Longfellow: "Can hardly fail to be a very successful and favorite volume."

Wendell Phillips: "Its variety and fullness and the completeness of its index give it rare value to the scholar."

George W. Childs: "Inclosed find $20.00 for four copies. It is unique among books of quotations."

Abram S. Hewitt: "The completeness of its indices is simply astonishing. . . . Leaves nothing to be desired."

Ex-Speaker Randall: "I send check for copy. It is the best book of quotations which I have seen."

George W. Curtis: "A handsome volume and a most serviceable companion."

Oliver Wendell Holmes: "A massive and teeming volume. It lies near my open dictionaries."

Boston Post: "Indispensable as Worcester and Webster. Must long remain the standard among its kind."

N. Y. Herald: "By long odds the best book of quotations in existence."

Boston Traveler: "Exhaustive and satisfactory. It is immeasurably the best book of quotations."

N. Y. Times: "Its Index alone would place it before all other books of quotations."

Eastern Proverbs and Emblems.

Illustrated Old Truths—selected from over 1,000 volumes, some very rare, and to be consulted only in libraries in India, Russia and other parts of the Continent, or in the British Museum. All are classified under subjects, enabling teachers and preachers to fix in the school, the pulpit, or the press, great spiritual truths by means of emblems and illustrations drawn from the depths of the popular mind. This book is the opening of a rich storehouse of emblems and proverbs. By Rev. A. LONG, member of the Bengal Asiatic Society. 8vo, 280 pages. Price, cloth, $1.00.

☞ *The above works will be sent by mail, postage paid, on receipt of the price.*

Fulton's Replies.

Punishment of Sin Eternal. Three sermons in reply to Beecher, Farrar and Ingersoll. By JUSTIN D. FULTON, D.D. 8vo, paper, 10 cents.

Gilead: An Allegory.

Gilead; or, The Vision of All Souls' Hospital. An Allegory. By Rev. J. HYATT SMITH, Congressman from New York. *Revised edition.* 12mo, cloth, 350 pp., $1.00.

Godet's Commentary on Luke.

A Commentary on the Gospel of St. Luke. By F. GODET, Doctor and Professor of Theology, Neufchatel. Translated from the Second French Edition. With Preface and Notes by John Hall, D.D. New edition, printed on heavy paper. 2 vols., paper, 584 pp. (Standard Series, octavo, Nos. 51 and 52), $2.00; 1 vol., 8vo, cloth, $2.50.

Gospel of Mark.

From the Teachers' Edition of the Revised New Testament, with Harmony of the Gospels, List of Lessons, Maps, etc. Paper, 15 cents; cloth, 50 cents.

Half-Dime Hymn Book.

Standard Hymns. With Biographical Notes of their Authors. Compiled by Rev. EDWARD P. THWING. 32mo, paper, 96 pp. Each, 6 cents; in lots of fifty or more, 5 cents.

Hand-Book of Illustrations.

The Preacher's Cabinet. A Hand-Book of Illustrations. By Rev. EDWARD P. THWING, author of "Drill-Book in Vocal Culture," "Outdoor Life in Europe," etc. *Fourth edition.* 2 vols. 12mo, paper, 144 pp., 50 cents.

Home Altar.

The Home Altar: An Appeal in Behalf of Family Worship. With Prayers and Hymns for Family Use. By Rev. CHARLES F. DEEMS, LL.D., pastor of the Church of the Strangers. *Third edition.* 12mo, cloth, 281 pp., 75 cents.

The above works will be sent by mail, postage paid, on receipt of the price.

The Homilist.

By David Thomas, D.D., author of "The Practical Philosopher," "The Philosophy of Happiness," etc., etc. Vol. XII. Editor's Series (complete in itself). 12mo, cloth, 368 pp., printed on tinted paper, $1.25.

How to Pay Church Debts.

How to Pay Church Debts, and How to Keep Churches out of Debt. By Rev. Sylvanus Stall. 12mo, cloth, 280 pp., $1.50.

Murphy's Commentary.

A Critical and Exegetical Commentary on the Book of Exodus. With a New Translation. By James G. Murphy, D.D. New edition, unabridged. With Preface and Notes by John Hall, D.D. 2 vols., 8vo, paper, 233 pp., $1.00; 1 vol., cloth, $1.50.

"Thus far nothing has appeared for half a century on the Pentateuch so valuable as the present volume (on Exodus) His style is lucid, animated, and often eloquent. His pages afford golden suggestions and key-thoughts. . . . . Some of the laws of interpretation are stated with so fresh and natural a clearness and force that they will permanently stand."—*Methodist Quarterly.*

"As a critical, analytical, candid, and sensible view of the Sacred Word, this work stands among the first."—*Congregational Quarterly.*

Pastor's Record.

The Pastor's Record for Study, Work, Appointments and Choir for one year. Prepared by Rev. W. T. Wylie. 12mo, paper 50 cents; cloth, 75 cents; leather, $1.00.

Popery.

Popery the Foe of the Church and the Republic. By Rev. Joseph S. Van Dyke, author of "Through the Prison to the Throne," etc. 8vo, cloth, 304 pp., $1.00.

Teachers' Edition of the Revised New Testament.

With New Index and Concordance, Harmony of the Gospels, Maps, Parallel Passages in full, and many other Indispensable Helps. All most carefully prepared. For Full Particulars of this Invaluable Work send for Prospectus. Price in cloth $1.50. Other prices from $2.50 to $10.00. (See, on another page, what eminent clergymen and others say of this work.)

The above works will be sent by mail, postage paid, on receipt of the price

These Sayings of Mine.

"These Sayings of Mine." Sermons on Seven Chapters of the First Gospel. By JOSEPH PARKER, D.D. With an introduction by Dr. Deems. 8vo, cloth, 320 pp., $1.50.

Through the Prison to the Throne.

Through the Prison to the Throne. Illustrations of Life from the Biography of Joseph. By Rev. JOSEPH S. VAN DYKE, author of "Popery the Foe of the Church and of the Republic." 16mo, cloth, 254 pp., $1.00.

The Treasury of David.

By Rev. CHARLES H. SPURGEON. 8vo, cloth. Price per volume, $2.00.

Spurgeon's Authorization.—"Messrs. I. K. Funk & Co. have entered into an arrangement with me to reprint THE TREASURY OF DAVID in the United States. I have every confidence in them that they will issue it correctly and worthily. It has been the great literary work of my life, and I trust it will be as kindly received in America as in England. I wish for Messrs. Funk success in a venture which must involve a great risk and much outlay.

"Dec. 8, 1881.   C. H. SPURGEON."

Complete in 7 volumes. First 6 volumes now complete.

Philip Schaff, D.D., the Eminent Commentator and the President of the American Bible Revision Committee, says: "The most important and practical work of the age on the Psalter is 'The Treasury of David,' by Charles H. Spurgeon. It is full of the force and genius of this celebrated preacher, and rich in selections from the entire range of literature."

William M. Taylor, D.D., New York, says: "In the exposition of the heart 'The Treasury of David' is *sui generis* rich in experience and pre-eminently devotional. The exposition is always fresh. To the preacher it is especially suggestive."

John Hall, D.D., New York, says: "There are two questions that must interest every expositor of the Divine Word. What does a particular passage mean, and to what use is it to be applied in public teaching? In the department of the latter Mr. Spurgeon's great work on the Psalms is without an equal. Eminently practical in his own teaching, he has collected in these volumes the best thoughts of the best minds on the Psalter, and especially of that great body loosely grouped together as the Puritan divines. I am heartily glad that by arrangements satisfactory to all concerned the Messrs. Funk & Co. are about to bring this great work within the reach of ministers everywhere, as the English edition is necessarily expensive. I wish the highest success to the enterprise."

Van Doren's Commentary.

A Suggestive Commentary on Luke, with Critical and Homiletical Notes. By W. H. VAN DOREN, D.D. Edited by Prof. James Kernahan, London. 4 vols., paper, 1104 pp. (Standard Series, octavo, Nos. 54-57), $3.00; 2 vols., 8vo, cloth, $3.75.

The above works will be sent by mail, postage paid, on receipt of the price.

MISCELLANEOUS WORKS.

Bulwer's Novels.

Leila; or, The Siege of Granada; and, The Coming Race; or, The New Utopia. By EDWARD BULWER, Lord Lytton. 12mo, leatherette, 284 pp., 50 cents; cloth, 75 cents.

Carlyle's Sartor Resartus.

Sartor Resartus; the Life and Opinions of Herr Teufelsdrockh. By THOMAS CARLYLE. Paper, 176 pp. (Standard Series, octavo, No. 60), 25 cents; 8vo, cloth, 60 cents.

Communism.

Communism Not the Best Remedy. A pamphlet for the times, containing the following three great discourses in full: "Social Inequalities and Social Wrongs," by J. H. Rylance, D.D.; "How a Rich Man may become Very Poor, and a Poor Man Very Rich," by Theodor Christlieb, D.D.; "Vanities and Verities," by Rev. C. H. Spurgeon. 8vo, paper, 10 cents.

Dickens' Christmas Books.

A Christmas Carol, The Chimes, The Cricket on the Hearth, The Battle of Life, The Haunted Man. By CHARLES DICKENS. 2 vols., paper, 270 pp. (Standard Series, octavo, Nos. 48 and 49), 50 cents; 1 vol., 8vo, cloth, 75 cents.

Disraeli's Lothair.

Lothair. By Rt. Hon. B. DISRAELI, Earl of Beaconsfield. 2 vols., paper, 256 pp. (Standard Series, octavo, Nos. 61 and 62), 50 cents; 1 vol., 8vo, cloth, $1.00.

Drill Book in Vocal Culture.

Drill-Book in Vocal Culture and Gesture. By Rev. Prof. EDWARD P. THWING. Sixth edition. 12mo, manilla, 115 pp., 25 cents.

Five Remarkable Discourses.

"The Voice of God in Us," by R. S. STORRS, D.D.; "Jesus as a Poet," by THOMAS ARMITAGE, D.D. "Protestantism a Failure"— two lectures delivered by F. C. EWER; "The Signs of the Times— Is Christianity Failing?" by HENRY WARD BEECHER. 8vo, paper, 66 pp., 15 cents.

The above works will be sent by mail, postage paid, on receipt of the price.

Guizot's Life of Calvin.

John Calvin. By M. GUIZOT, Member of the Institute of France. 4to, paper (Standard Series, No. 47), 15 cents; cloth, 12mo, 160 pp., 50 cents.

How to Enjoy Life.

Clergyman's and Students' Health; or Physical and Mental Hygiene, the True Way to Enjoy Life. By WILLIAM MASON CORNELL, M.D., LL.D., Fellow of the Massachusetts Medical Society, Permanent Member of the American Medical Association. Fifth Edition. 12mo, cloth, 360 pp., $1.00.

In Memoriam—Wm. Cullen Bryant.

A Funeral Oration. By HENRY W. BELLOWS, D.D. 8vo, paper, 10 cents.

Knight's History of England.

The Popular History of England. A History of Society and Government from the Earliest Period to our own Times. By CHARLES KNIGHT. Tables of Contents, Index, Appendix, Notes and Letter-press unabridged. 8 vols., 4to, paper, 1370 pp. (Standard Series, Nos. 12-19), $2.80; 2 vols., 4to, cloth, $3.75; sheep, 1 vol., $4.00; 2 vols., $5.00; 1 vol., Fr. im. morocco, $4.50 ; 2 vols., $5.50.

This is the most complete, and in every way the most desirable History of England ever written. The former price of this History was $18.00 to $25.00.

Lord Brougham says: "Nothing has ever appeared superior, if anything has been published equal, to the account of the state of commerce, government and society, at different periods."

Noah Porter, D.D., LL.D., says: "The best history of England, for the general reader, is Knight's *Popular History.* For a single history which may serve for constant use and reference in the library, or for frequent reading, it is to be preferred to every other."

"The very thing required by the popular taste of the day."—*Edinburgh Review.*

"The best history extant, not only for, but also of, the people."—*All the Year Round.*

"This work is the very best history of England that we possess."—*London Standard.*

The above works will be sent by mail, postage paid, on receipt of the price.